# PRAISE FOR
## DRAGONS OF THE GREAT WYVES

"Wow, talk about nailing the dismount!!!! The interplay between characters, the emotions, the depth of plot, and still giving me the McCaffrey vibe I caught in the first book, this was a perfect 5 star, which I don't think I've ever said before." – *Amber Simmons, NetGalley*

"i had a FANTASTIC time. ride or die for mary bennet I'd punch a foul crawler in the face for her. and then it would kill me but at least i would die for a good cause" – Miriam Brookler, author of *Rainfall*

"Verant marries the pageantry of Jane Austen with fantasy in a remarkably compelling fashion. If you've loved the reimagined Austen world from the first two books, then this one amps up everything that was already great." – *Adam Aguilar, Goodreads*

"Unputdownable Gritty and Grand Gaslamp Fantasy. The Jane Austen-Napoleonic War period paired with a world of magic and dragons and strong, capable women heroes. Romance, dragons, intrigue, and war make up this grand phenom trilogy. Pulse-pounding to the finish." – *Sophia Rose*

"I've now read *Miss Bennet's Dragon* three times. And *Emma's Dragon* twice. And for me they get better with each read. This is the final book in the trilogy and it's fabulous. Love, passion, betrayal, greed, war... the list goes on." – *Deborah Thornton, NetGalley*

"A fantastic and gloriously satisfying read. I adore this series and the world that Verant has crafted. And of course... there are the dragons. Little and squishy, to vast and imperious, they are each beautifully drawn and utterly fascinating. *Great Wyves* is a fantastic conclusion to a story that is beautiful, mythic, intense, and intimate by turns." – *Kate Pennington,* author of *A Rose by Another Name*

"Finally! A very satisfying wrap-up to the story begun in *Miss Bennet's Dragon*, this time weaving together the stories of Elizabeth Bennet, Mary Bennet, Emma Woodhouse, and (of course) dragons." – *Jill, Goodreads*

"Intricately woven between three books with a deft hand and culminating in a visceral and emotional end. Miss Mary Bennet: Scholarly, musically inclined, and deeply passionate. She comes into her own in this final book, and her development is intricate and brilliant. I highly recommend this whole saga. It will be one that I re-read again." – *Carole in Canada, NetGalley*

"Excellent conclusion to a fantastic trilogy. It's an absolute page turner. The merging of fantasy and history is beautifully done. All the characters have powerful journeys and it's easy to get swept up in their lives as they face new dangers, work together, and form friendships and relationships. I'm a fan of Jane Austen's stories and I highly recommend this book and the trilogy if you love to read books that merge fantasy with Jane Austen's world." – *Jen H, Amazon*

"Verant's final book in the series is another great work of literature. I just love his prose and the continuation of the notable Austen characters. The story is exciting, the characters are familiar and well-drawn, the conclusion dramatic but thought-provoking. Like an Austen book, this isn't so much to be read as to be savored." – *A Kindle reader*

"This is a brilliant conclusion to this series and I heartily recommend that you read all three." – *Gill Murgatroyd, My JAFF Obsession*

"One hell of an opera! The story ends in a breathtaking finale where such lovely images like 'the perfect chord whispered by melted drops falling in a snowy glen' transpire, transporting us to emotional heights that stir our emotions to the breaking point." – *Quantum, Goodreads*

"One of the things that's really notable about the series is that all the main characters - Emma, Lizzy, and Mary - have their own arcs and character quirks, and at different times each of them becomes my favorite. There's plenty of romance, social commentary, battle and excitement, and a beautiful ending. I highly recommend." – *wrenling, Goodreads*

# DRAGONS
## of the
## Great Wyves

FIRE AND SONG

JANE AUSTEN FANTASY - BOOK 3

M. VERANT

ACERBIC

First edition: November 2025
Acerbic Press www.acerbicpress.com

ISBNs: 978-1-7366629-8-4 (paperback), 978-1-7366629-7-7 (ebook), 979-8271751202 (hardcover)

Publisher's Cataloging-in-Publication Data

Names: Verant, M., author.
Title: Dragons of the great wyves : fire and song / M. Verant.
Description: California: Acerbic Press, 2025. | Series: Jane Austen Fantasy, bk. 3.
Identifiers: ISBN 9781736662984 (paperback) | ISBN 9781736662977 (ebook) | ISBN 9798271751202 (hardcover)
Subjects: GSAFD: Fantasy fiction. | BISAC: FICTION / Fantasy / Historical. | FICTION / Fantasy / Romance. | FICTION / Adaptations & Pastiche.
Classification: LCC PS3622.E731 D73 2025 | DDC 813/.6–dc23

# BREEDS OF DRACA

*Bound breeds, from greatest to least social prestige:*

**Wyvern**: A winged, two-legged draca. Near the size of an English foxhound (60-75 lb).
**Firedrake** (drake): A winged, two-legged draca the size of a large goose or eagle (16-18 lb).
**Lindworm**: A draca with a heavy build like a bulldog or badger (20-25 lb).
**Tykeworm** (tyke): A draca the size of a Yorkshire terrier (5-7 lb). Does not throw fire. Unusually affectionate with their bound wyfe.
**Roseworm**: A draca the size of a rabbit. Distinguished by red or rose scales on its belly.
**Broccworm**: A tunneling draca with powerful front legs. Rather like a small badger.
**Ferretworm**: A tunneling draca, long and thin like a ferret.
**Tunnelworm**: A nocturnal, palm-sized draca that burrows and prefers to be underground.

*Unbound breeds:*

**Song draca**: Robin-sized. Scaled muzzles and heads; feathered wings and swallow-like tails.
**Needledrac**: The size of a dragonfly. Two-legged and clawed like a miniature firedrake.

# CAST OF CHARACTERS

*Bennets, Bingleys, and acquaintances:*
**Mrs. Elizabeth Darcy** (Lizzy): The second-eldest Bennet sister.
**Miss Mary Bennet**: The middle Bennet sister.
**Mrs. Jane Bingley**: The eldest Bennet sister. Married to Charles Bingley.
**Miss Kitty Bennet**: The next-to-youngest Bennet sister.
**Mrs. Lydia Wickham**: The youngest Bennet sister, deceased.
**Mrs. Bennet**: Mother of the Bennet sisters. Mr. Bennet is deceased.
**Mrs. Bruichladdich**: A Scottish laundry maid.

*Darcys and acquaintances:*
**Mr. Fitzwilliam Darcy** (Fitz): Lizzy's husband.
**Miss Georgiana Darcy**: Mr. Darcy's sister.
**Mrs. Reynolds**: The Darcys' housekeeper.
**Lucy**: Lizzy's lady's maid.
**Nessy**: A young student, healed by Miss Woodhouse.
**Mr. Digweed**: Headman of the Pemberley Briton clans.
**Thomas Digweed**: Mr. Digweed's teenage son.
**Lady Catherine de Bourgh**: Mr. Darcy's aunt and mistress of Rosings Park.
**Mrs. Charlotte Collins**: née Lucas. Married to Mr. Collins, clergyman of Rosings Park.
**Mr. Rabb**: The Pemberley gamekeeper, deceased.

*Woodhouses, Knightleys, and acquaintances:*
**Miss Emma Woodhouse:** Mistress of Hartfield estate.
**Miss Harriet Smith:** Emma's half sister.
**Mr. George Knightley**: A gentleman musician.
**Isabella and John**: Emma's sister and her husband.
**Mr. Elton and Mrs. Augusta Elton**: Vicar of Highbury and his wyfe.
**Miss Bates**: A spinster in her mid-forties.
**Mr. Weston and Mrs. Anne Weston**: née Taylor. Anne was Emma's childhood nanny.

**Mr. and Mrs. Otway**: Friends of Emma. They have a teenage daughter, Caroline.
**Mrs. Prince**: Harriet's mother.

*London, Scotland, etc.:*
**Dr. James Barry**: A doctor and surgeon.
**la Demoiselle des Parfums**: A member of the French court.
**Lord Wellington**: Leader of England's armies in the Peninsular war.
**Dr. Davenport**: A physician teaching medicine to Mary Bennet.
**Mr. Tinsdale**: A member of Parliament and a traitor.
**Mistress MacLeod and Mr. MacLeod**: Headwoman of Helmsdale and her husband.
**Lieutenant Colonel John Fremantle**: Aide-de-camp to Lord Wellingon.
**Miss Rees**: Mary's friend and a member of the Marys; died at the London ball.
**Miss Rebecca Spoon**: Another friend and member of the Marys.
**Napoleon Bonaparte**: Napoleon I, Emperor of the French.

*Draca:*
**Yuánchi** / 元气 : The scarlet dragon bound to Lizzy.
**Fènnù** / 愤怒 : The black dragon.
**Hé Shēng** / 和声

# PERFUME

## MARY

The broken glass from the bookshop windows had been swept away. The few jutting shards left in the sills glistened like teeth. Inside, rows of neatly labeled bookshelves stood empty behind a sign that read: *CLOSED DUE TO WAR.*

"They moved," I said. It was only a shop, but every vacant shelf was a hole in my heart. I had come here since I was a child. "The books were not ransacked. They are just gone."

"I am sorry, Mary." Georgiana slipped her arm through mine and rested her temple on my shoulder—a lover's touch discreet enough for public display.

We had visited nine London bookshops in the last few days. Six were closed. The other three had no scholarly works on draca, only children's fables or hastily printed melodramas where handsome colonels drew their sabers to challenge dragons.

Real dragons had fought in London's skies. A shadow of this roofline was burned onto the street; the flash from Yuánchi's fire had scorched the cobblestones. A half mile away, Westminster Palace lay in ruins, frozen by Fènnù's black breath. Challenging a dragon with a saber was as far-fetched as any children's fable, entertaining only if one had not beheld their power.

But sabers killed soldiers well enough. The Sussex front was twenty miles south of us. Wounded and dead arrived regularly.

"Shall we try another shop?" Georgiana asked. Her words were supportive. Her tone, somewhat less.

"You think I am foolish," I said.

"I did not say that. We both want Lizzy back."

An image of Pemberley lake filled my mind's eye: a winter memory, gray waves and frosted shore. My sister and her scarlet dragon had battled Fènnù there and fallen, grievously wounded, into the water. Vanished and lost, but alive. Trapped in the strange, water-bound sleep of draca, which lasted for decades or centuries—a sleep I sought to interrupt.

"I need knowledge to save Lizzy," I said. That sounded stubborn, so I mocked myself: "How hard can it be? I only seek to raise a dragon."

Georgiana turned me from the broken window. Her irises were steady sapphire rings behind her long lashes. "Yuánchi and Lizzy fell together. They will rise together. What if all this was meant to be?"

Trust. Have faith. That frustrated me. Patience did not breach barriers. Georgiana, one of the three legendary great wyves, had fantastic power in the realm of draca—not to mention growing up wrapped in wealth. She inhabited a world that bent to her wishes. My world was stacks of dusty books.

But even a bookworm could miss a sister, and Lizzy's absence was an endless pang. Stubbornness felt good. "I will not sit and wait. I do not care if this is beyond me."

"I did not say *that*, either!" Georgiana protested. "Your sister raised a dragon, and you share her blood. I am advising patience because you *could* succeed. We must respect what nature intends."

She was sincere, yet... "Why did you not argue while I dragged you around London yesterday?"

"I am practicing a speech to my brother," she admitted. "At least you want to understand. *He* is a bold Darcy. He only argues when I say we should wait." She scowled, thinking. "My brother is why we can find no references. He emptied these bookshops of draca lore years ago..."

And then his books were stolen.

Her scowl became thoughtful. "What about the museum?"

"That is an idea." They would not release documents, but they had an overeager scholar of Tudor queens and dragons. I added, "Thank you."

Georgiana smiled triumphantly. Her dress was amber sarsenet silk, square-shouldered with brass buttons; the wartime fashions had mimicked military uniforms. She rose on her toes and whispered in my ear, "*I am a bold Darcy*," which left me heated and flustered.

Our driver called in his thick northern accent, "Miss Bennet. We should not linger." He was seated atop our battered hackney coach, purchased second-hand four days ago. The coach was a disguise, chosen to be less conspicuous than one from Chathford House, the Darcys' London home. The driver was a constable, an unlikely friendship I formed when we argued nose-to-nose during a sweltering street protest last August. Impressively burly, he satisfied Mr. Darcy's insistence on security. London was dangerous, particularly for Darcys and Bennets.

I turned to go, but Georgiana caught my elbow.

A black-clad young woman was hurrying across the street. She arrived breathless and passed me a folded page. "Mary! Another crawler sting. They called for you."

THE FRONT OF ST. George's Hospital, groomed and pretty, faced the park. The alley behind it was for workers, and our coach followed that to stop by the wooden outbuildings: stables, stores, and the privy vats, thankfully covered until night collection. An entire yard was hung with wet cloth steaming in the morning air. Hospital laundry was a Sisyphean chore.

Between the cobblestones, bright blades of grass had sprung. Yellow dandelions stuffed every untrod corner. London, freed from the dragon Fènnù's unnatural, punishing winter, reveled in spring.

Georgiana watched from the open coach door. "Shall I come in with you?"

"No. Rebecca will meet me. Stay with the coach. I am less likely to be noticed alone."

The constable was snooping down the alley. I called to him, "Can you wait at Hyde Park Corner? I will come there when I am done."

"Aye, Miss Bennet," he answered, clambering back into the driver's seat. "You be careful. Those Britain Awake thugs are all about."

The coach rolled away. I hurried toward the hospital, wrinkling my nose at a strange fragrance like sweet, rotted citrus, then I was stymied by the laundry lines. I ducked under one, clean drops splashing my neck, and spotted a hand waving above the linen. A woman's voice called, "Mary!"

I followed an aisle framed by washed towels and sheets to the rear entrance.

Miss Rebecca Spoon waited for me. Another musician, she had survived abduction by the Blackcoats—Lizzy and I rescued her near death from a stinking cellar—and then overcame the deadly addiction caused by her captors' drugs. She celebrated by publishing *Inviolata*, a defiant clavichord composition.

Rebecca's black clothes, styled to mimic mine, were lost in the shadow. A gray-haired woman in a nurse's blue uniform stood with her. The nurse squinted at me, curious.

"Are you sure it is a crawler sting?" I asked.

The nurse said, "There's no question, ma'am."

"The third woman this week," Rebecca added. "They are lucky you are in London."

"They were not all lucky," I said. The second woman I had saved. The first I reached too late.

The nurse opened the door, but I said, "Wait a moment," and whistled a few notes from my first composition, a fantasia titled "Not One Word From Her." That had become our summoning tune.

An iridescent blue, robin-sized form winged overhead, flicked a turn that skimmed the hospital's bricks, then soared to a perfect landing on my shoulder. He was a song draca, the first I met, dazzling me in a London park with his peacock-bright feathers and gem-scaled muzzle. He was my devoted companion, and his claws, hooked and razor-edged, dug into the leather pad I had sewn beneath my dress shoulder—literally to save my skin.

The nurse's eyes popped when she saw the draca land. She curtsied, almost kneeling. "Great Wyfe."

"Not here," Rebecca hissed. "The Great Wyfe must not be recognized." The nurse straightened hurriedly.

I glared at Rebecca; I had told her many times I was no great wyfe. She shrugged, unrepentant. Our network of women in the city—who copied my black clothes and called themselves "Marys"—revered the legends of great wyves. They did not know that actual great wyves lived: Georgiana, Emma Woodhouse, and my lost sister, Lizzy.

Inside, we descended a narrow, whitewashed corridor to the less used basement. The sour putrescence of illness tinged the air, but it was fainter than the healthy scents of soap and boiled cotton. A wooden door in need of paint led into an examination room. Rebecca stayed outside to watch the corridor. I entered with the nurse.

A woman of thirty and some years lay limp on the table in street-worn, rumpled clothes. Her eyes were closed, her complexion sallow and beaded with perspiration, her breath labored.

A well-dressed man was taking her pulse, his eyes on his pocket watch.

Surprised, I stopped. No doctor had been present for my other visits. The Marys received their clandestine summons from the nurses, or even from washerwomen when the poorest women, prostitutes or beggars, were denied a nurse's visit.

"The doctor asked for you, ma'am," the nurse explained.

He may have asked, but he was as surprised as I. His gaze fixed on the shimmering draca perched on my shoulder. The draca cheeped and whistled another bar of the fantasia.

"I am Miss Bennet," I said. An introduction was required, and I preferred a name to grandiose titles.

"Doctor James Barry," he replied, and bowed. He was smooth-cheeked and slight-shouldered, his voice contralto. Young. An apprentice physician, perhaps; St. George's was a teaching hospital. "This woman was found delirious on the hospital steps. Stung, I estimate an hour ago."

He drew the woman's skirt aside. Her left ankle had punctures from a foul crawler's sting. The twin pricks were separated by the width of my little finger, so it was the small variety. Red streaks climbed her calf, inflamed and grossly swollen.

I lifted my gloved hand to my shoulder. The little draca hopped onto my palm, and I held him near the sting. His muzzle darted close, and he gave a chittering growl, his needle obsidian-black teeth bared. Not good. I gave him a light toss, and he fluttered to perch on a cabinet at a safe distance.

"Are you a surgeon?" I asked the gaping doctor while I drew off my gloves.

He started, then patted a leather medical bag on the table. "I was certified at Edinburgh. But I have heard the nurses talk about you. I hoped you could save the leg."

"We can, but I need your help to administer a tincture." I drew a corked bottle from my reticule. "Venom remains in the wound. We must drain it and infuse this, then give an oral dose as well."

He took a scalpel from his bag, and it was done in a minute, a curt partnership of "Cut here," "Squeeze," then "Steady her" when the pain penetrated the woman's delirium. The doctor had a confident hand, unhesitating but careful, better than the heedless butchery of some surgeons.

I applied the tincture and bandage, then measured the oral dose. The doctor administered it in trickles, stroking the woman's throat to encourage swallowing.

"What is this tincture?" he asked.

"The common name is draca essence. It is brewed from a flower pollinated by draca. It grows only in the north."

"These crawler attacks are becoming frequent. The hospital should have a supply."

"I have sent for a shipment to distribute. It is overdue."

He nodded; shortages were routine since the war. Then he reached for the bloody cloth that had mopped the wound.

I caught his hand before he touched it. "Have the nurse burn it. A man can be killed by a fraction of the venom tolerated by a woman. You should wash your hands with soap and hot water."

He drew back, though he seemed unalarmed. "Thank you, Miss Bennet." I turned to go, the draca flapping to my shoulder, and he added softly, "Great Wyfe."

REBECCA AND I EXITED THROUGH A WORKERS' door and entered the laundry maze.

"Three stings in as many days," she said. "I like spring weather, but if it wakes those vermin..." Her voice petered out, and she looked back at me.

I had stopped. The song draca was purring a woodwind whistle into my ear. The tone rose and fell, an eerie siren, and a strange sense within me resonated in counterpoint. Hairs tingled on the nape of my neck.

Most of the laundry yard was obscured. Ropes as heavy as ship's rigging were laden with boiled bandages and dripping smocks. A breeze labored among the wet fabrics, revealing glimpses when the swaying gaps aligned.

"Miss Darcy is at Hyde Park Corner," I whispered. "Hurry there and ask her to send the coach and driver." Rebecca's gaze was concerned, but she nodded and rushed away. Strange times had taught us to honor strange requests.

When she was gone, I called loudly, "Who is here?"

A young woman's voice answered. "I sought a meeting, Mademoiselle Bennet." Her accent was French, Parisian, and, as best my ear could judge, aristocratic.

Napoleon's invasion of southern England had halted travel between London and France. A few French remained, dislocated or emigrated, but they strove to Anglicize their speech. This woman spoke with the careless amusement of a baroness indulging foreign consonants.

I separated a pair of tangled wet towels and stepped an aisle closer. "You know my name, *madame*. Will you share yours?"

"Perhaps. If I approve of you."

I dodged below a row of flapping bandages as she stepped into the same aisle. A few yards separated us. She wore an English dress, bonnet, and spencer of slate gray, all expensively edged with lace, but she had tied a white silk fichu around her neck in the French fashion. With her flamboyant accent, it was a poor disguise, if disguise was her intent.

She studied me as well, her head tilting.

The song draca's claws pricked through the shoulder pad of my dress, and his purring growl deepened to a thrum that vibrated my jawbone. With a silent swoop, a second song draca alighted on the laundry line to my right.

"So, it is true," the Frenchwoman said, inspecting the draca. "*Les présages*"—she made a pretty moue while hunting for the English word—"the harbingers follow you." Her gaze traced my dress. "Black clothes. You mourn your sister?"

Lizzy and Yuánchi were entombed countless fathoms deep. After they fell, two dismal months had passed before Emma sensed Lizzy's survival—sensed Lizzy's unbroken binding to Yuánchi. But our family hid that revelation. To the world, Elizabeth Darcy was dead.

"My family is no concern of yours," I said. Was this a spy sent to discover the fate of England's scarlet dragon?

"Your family is Bennet. You are a Bennet. Bennets are important." She tapped a slim finger to her lips. "Our glorious Emperor, Napoleon, has divorced Marie Louise, the Austrian pretender. He will choose a French Empress. One who proves she can bind a great draca."

I had heard nothing of Napoleon divorcing, although he had done so before, but a different question came to mind. "Bind? There are no draca in France." There had been none for centuries, one of the mysteries of draca.

She dismissed that with a pitying glance, then smiled. "I met one of your sisters. Ly-di-a." She stretched her mouth, mocking the English vowels. "Then, I was only *une demoiselle du palais*, a lady-in-waiting, and Lydia was powerful.

Now, I am changed. And you..." She pointed her index finger at each draca—one, two—then at me, three. "*Vous êtes formidable.*"

"Why are you in England?"

Outside the laundry yard, a clop of hooves and clatter of wheels drew up. The coach had come.

She spoke swiftly. "I seek something old and valuable. You are a Bennet. You know where it hides."

Did she mean the dagger? That was lost with Lizzy. I tried to list other possibilities, but my mind felt fuzzy. Sticky, as if honey-laden. "There is no purpose to riddles. Of what do you speak?"

"The great flute made from dragon claw. The flute is of music, and you"—her finger stabbed at me—"you compose music."

*Fang, scale, and claw. Then death, they saw.* Those were the three fabled items of the great wyves. The fang was the dagger Gramr, sunk in Pemberley lake. The scale was mounted in an amulet; the last historical reference to that was centuries ago.

About the claw I knew nothing. I had not even known it was a flute. "You are mad if you think I will discuss this with you."

"*Non.* Not mad. You search London for books. Were books taken from you?"

My heart leaped into my throat. I swallowed to force my voice flat. "Lydia stole books from the Pemberley library."

"*Oui.* Have you a need for these? You seek the great song."

The Darcy library of draca lore had been unequalled in all Britain. Regaining that knowledge might save my sister. But...

"What is the great song?" I asked.

She pursed her lips. "If you ask that, you know nothing."

I forced a shake of my head. "I do not have the flute."

From the alley, the constable's voice rose. "Is that you, Miss Bennet?"

The Frenchwoman heard. She cocked an eyebrow. "A Bennet can find the flute. It is a relic of the third dragon. Of music. So, I come to greet you and make this offer. Find the flute—or learn where it is—and I shall return your books." As if in punctuation, her finger brushed her lips again.

Some part of my brain had been fiddling with a puzzle, and now a piece slid into place. "You poisoned those women to draw me here."

"Oh! You are clever." Her eyes widened in a mockery of concern. "Will this one live?"

8

Until now, distrust had made me wary. Anger severed that restraint. I strode forward, uncomfortably close. I was taller, so she lifted her chin to meet my gaze, her smile deepening.

It was her eyes that I studied. Lydia, my dead, traitorous, and little-mourned sister could command foul crawlers by consuming their venom. But this woman's pupils were normal—tiny dots in the morning light. She was not dosed with crawler venom.

The ridges of her cheekbones glittered as if dusted with sugar crystals. Her lips glistened with an oily sheen.

"Will she live?" the woman repeated.

"The first did not," I said. "This one will."

"*Bien joué.*" She tapped a finger to her bonnet in playful respect. "You earn your name, Great Wyfe. My name is also earned. I am *la Demoiselle des Parfums.*"

Lady of Perfumes. She spoke it as a title. I became aware of the bloom of scent around her, musk heavy and citrus-sweet. Insidious and potent.

"A constable is here," I said. "You will be arrested for murder."

Her laugh was scornful and very French. "You think a *man* frightens the Emperor's lover?"

A soft scrabble like tapping pins passed my feet. I looked down and saw an armored, segmented worm the length of my hand vanish toward the alley, dozens of legs flicking.

I lurched back and shouted, "Stay away! She has crawlers!"

The scent of crawler venom, bitter almond and sour orange, flooded the air, burning my nostrils. The tiny draca on my shoulder screeched and tumbled. I reached for him, a fumbled reflex that half-broke his fall before he struck the stones, wings taut and convulsing. The other song draca landed a few feet away with a pathetic thud, twitching.

Distantly, I heard, "*Au revoir.*" Our aisle of flapping cloth was deserted. I yanked a sheet off the line. The next aisle was empty as well.

I knelt and gathered the song draca. They twitched in my hands, small handfuls but dense, not fragile like holding a bird. I could feel the bumps of scales on their throats and the racing hearts in their chests.

I shouldered through sodden rows of cloth. A two-inch, segmented shape skittered by. The gleaming olive-brown head of another crawler squirmed up between the stones. I ducked under more cloth and reached the alley.

The constable was perched on the coach step and swearing, his ruddy complexion pale. At least ten crawlers the length of a lady's finger scuttled over the cobblestones. At the alley's edge, the verdant strip of grass and weeds had putrefied to a black, rotted smear.

"Did a woman in gray run past you?" I asked.

"A woman?" He grabbed the doorframe and leaned dangerously, peering both ways down the alley. "Not that I saw."

Georgiana ducked out the door, beneath his arm, and jumped lightly to the ground. A startled crawler reared its paired stingers. Carefully, she crushed its head under her bootheel, then she rushed to the song draca I held. "What happened to them?"

"Stunned by venom scent."

She caught my fingers in hers, cradling the draca between us, and sang a wordless tune. I felt the power of the great wyfe of song rise, shining like the spring sun, and the draca stirred and shuddered. Softly, she sang, "Be calm, little ones," and they flapped and scrambled to perch on my wrists, flight feathers fluffing in annoyance.

The draca hopped from my wrists to the ground. The new arrival, a female, cocked her head like a robin hunting a worm, then ran to a small crawler. I feared she would eat it—surely that would be deadly—but instead she breathed a thin streak of blue fire from her jeweled muzzle, crisping the writhing crawler to a crackling mess. The two draca began chasing about, burning the crawlers, their nearly invisible flame flaring crimson where it seared moss and lichen from the stones.

"I wish they did that earlier," I said.

"You smelled venom?" Georgiana asked. Behind her, a burned crawler shell popped like a roasted chestnut.

I nodded. "I do not know how. Small crawlers do not spray. They only sting. The Frenchwoman must have spread it."

Her brows lifted. "What Frenchwoman?"

"A woman from the French court. She said Napoleon has divorced. He plans to remarry and bind."

"Bind? That cannot be good. He will marry in the occupied south?"

That explanation had not occurred to me. Why were my thoughts so muddled? "The Frenchwoman is a perfumer. She has a court title, *la Demoiselle des Parfums*. Her scent..." I tried to recall it, but unlike words and images, I had no gift for scent memory. "Sweet and dark, like buckwheat honey..."

Georgiana's eyebrows climbed higher. "You *smelled* her?"

"She was very close. It may have been on her lips."

"Her lips!" Georgiana straightened.

I touched her shoulder and felt slender muscles as tense as wire. "Be patient with me. My mind is recovering from... an intoxication. A chemical effect. It is fading."

"I see," Georgiana said testily, but she relaxed.

"The Frenchwoman is Napoleon's intimate. His lover. She aspires to be his Empress. She wants me to help her find one of the great items, a flute made from dragon claw."

Georgiana gave an incredulous laugh. "And I thought Darcys were bold."

"She offered a bribe. The books that Lydia stole. She said they would explain 'the great song.' Do you know what that is?"

"I have never heard that phrase. You should ask Fitz. But draca live in song. Their names, their thoughts... it is all music. Their song is around us, even now."

I was reviewing my meeting. "The perfumer possesses an unrivaled library of draca knowledge, and yet she thinks I can find something she cannot. Because I am a Bennet."

"*My* Bennet," Georgiana said firmly. "I dislike this perfumed lady who offers bribes."

"We are wasting time searching for books," I decided.

Georgiana clutched a hand to her breast and gasped, "You *are* poisoned!"

"No—" I began, then realized it was a joke. "I have been searching for books because... because that is what I do. But scholarly histories do not matter. This Frenchwoman thinks I can find the flute because I am a Bennet. You said it too, in another way: I share blood with Lizzy." Georgiana was serious, listening, and as my mind cleared, a memory clicked. "I *have* heard of 'the great song.' If I can save Lizzy, it will be because the secret lies with my family."

## 2

# A VISIT HOME

## MARY

Longbourn's lanes were paved with a local white gravel suffused with tiny, ancient shells. The distinctive crunch beneath our wheels plucked strings in my memory. As a child, I had dashed across these stones to hide, first playing games with my sisters, then later to read in solitary shade when the press of people became too great.

The hollyhocks were my secret place. They were constantly overgrown, filling the crumbling remnant of an old stone-fenced paddock. Their leaves felt like feathers. Thinking back, it must not have been very secret—Mamma would come retrieve me if I forgot about dinner.

The flower gardens looked small after so much time at Pemberley. The vegetable gardens were larger. Longbourn was a practical estate, not a wealthy one.

"I feel at home, yet also like a visitor," I said as the coach swayed to a stop. Unnamable emotions jostled in my chest.

"While you are being wistful," Georgiana said, "I am fretting about your mother."

I pulled my attention from the spring foliage of our elm trees. "Why fret? You intimidate Mamma."

"I do not want to *intimidate* her. Mary, I have not seen her since the ball in London. We have not seen her, together, since then. What do we say about *us*?"

Irreconcilable rules collided in my brain: the imperative of truth; the prejudices and naivete of my mother's generation; her reliable, if disorganized, love. After futile seconds, I gave a despairing laugh. "When we performed for the Prince Regent, I knew immediately what to say. But I have not the most remote idea what to say to Mamma."

Georgiana sighed, but she smiled. "I suppose we shall improvise."

I RANG THE DOORBELL. Whoever came would be a happy surprise: our housekeeper, or Kitty if she were in a frivolous mood and answered herself, or one of the maids.

Instead, the door was tugged open by a small boy, nine at most. He set his nose in the air and said officiously, "Good morning."

"Good morning," I said. "Who might you be?"

"I am the butler," he piped. He lowered his nose to see me better, gave a surprised, shy smile, and ran down the hall.

We followed, peering into familiar but empty rooms, until we reached the parlor where Mamma was sound asleep in a chair, an embroidery hoop askew on her knee.

She woke with a start. "Mary! How those children wear me out. I only closed my eyes... Oh, Miss Darcy!" She stood hurriedly, straightening her skirt as they exchanged curtsies. Mamma said, "Are you not pretty with those shiny buttons," and Georgiana complimented her partially embroidered coif. Then silence fell.

"Have we hired a four-foot-tall butler?" I asked.

"That is the schoolchildren playing their games. Lizzy sent the London children to Jane's, which is very sensible. Country living is much better for children. Although I think Lizzy was more worried about dragons. They quite destroyed the city. I suppose you know about that?"

I had been walking to Chathford House when Fènnù and Yuánchi fought above London. The sky blazed, and I stopped in the street, face lifted to a skyscape of divine wrath. Coal-dark plumes rolled to the horizon like black thunderbolts, stroke-by-stroke occluding the afternoon blue. Unbearable sun-bright flares ripped in opposition, each an eruption of streaming gold. The thunder shattered windows. Rained broken birds. Then the dragons took their battle to the streets, and buildings toppled.

"You know I was there," I said. "Only part of the city was destroyed."

Mamma clucked and patted my arm. "Well, you are safe here, just like the children, and I am glad for both. Jane and Charles hold the school classes at Netherfield, and it is a fine manor, but the children do not all fit, so the littlest ones are here. It makes us very busy. I told Harriet we must have the teachers back, but she goes on about the war. Still, there is the wyvern." I did not understand that last part, but I forgot it when Mamma asked, "Is there news of dear, sleeping Lizzy?"

We had simplified Lizzy's situation for Mamma, not hiding the bizarre aspects of it—those could hardly be concealed—but conveying confidence that she would return soon.

"There is no news yet," I said. "I devote all my energy to finding a way to wake her."

"As does my brother," Georgiana added.

That, I knew, was an understatement.

Mamma nodded, her age-thinned eyelids crinkled with concern. Her gaze narrowed as she examined my clothes, which were very London in style.

"I am afraid this must be a short visit," I said. "We are on our way to Pemberley, but I wished to fetch a book."

As if addressing the air, Georgiana observed, "I *knew* it would be a book."

This was firmer footing for Mamma as well. "Nose buried again," she scolded me. "How many times have I told you that a lady's accomplishments must be in moderation?"

"It is lucky that Mary looks charming with her nose in a book," Georgiana said with a brilliant smile.

Mamma blinked. "Is it in fashion?"

"Oh, it *is!*" Georgiana assured her and took her arm. "Shall you and I visit the schoolchildren until she is done?"

Papa's library was how I had left it after visiting to deliver Jane's daughter. The Longbourn business ledgers filled most of one shelf. 1786 through 1810 were labeled in Papa's hand. 1811 and 1812 were labeled by Lizzy; secretly, she had managed our estate when Papa's health failed.

Longbourn belonged to Jane and Charles now, but this year's ledger, 1813, was labeled by me. I flicked it open and saw only my spikey numerals, the digits' columns exactly aligned. I had caught up the bookkeeping while Jane recuperated, but Jane and Charles had added nothing since. The optimistic explanation was that they consolidated both their estates' accounts through Netherfield's records. More likely, they paid any bill they received if it came with a smile.

For no sound reason, I opened the 1812 ledger. Lizzy's neat numerals and annotations awaited. Accurate. Prettier than mine. The image turned watery, so I closed the cover, then squeezed my eyes tight until my feelings settled.

Why would a member of Napoleon's court think a Bennet could find the mysterious flute?

The *Loch bairn* journal, the reason for my visit, was shelved beside the ledgers. For generations, its title had been misread as "Longbourn," even causing the misnaming of our estate. It recorded the history of the Bennet family, and it was old. The first entries preceded the Tudor era.

I drew it out, the aged leather soft and rough as velvet. Faded embossing showed a wyvern clutching an empty chest. Lizzy had solved that riddle. Gentry ladies, titled "wyfe" even before they wedded, had the right to bind draca on their marriage night. But marriage gold, the wedding offering collected by the Church to ensure a binding, was meaningless. Draca bound for love, not gold—to experience the human emotions they never felt.

Or did draca experience emotions, but fail to understand them? That would be like my life, buffeted by feelings that others named with a wink or a shrug while in my breast they burned like unwatchable suns, or inscrutable gods even, overwhelming and enigmatic. Save for a few I had come to recognize. The heat of love. The collapsing hollow of grief.

I riffled the pages. I had committed them to memory, but it had been many months, and even my recollection faded. Some of the oldest pages were not intelligible, and in my mind's eye those were a blur—precise recall without comprehension was difficult.

The Frenchwoman said the third great item was an artifact of music.

I knew less about the third item than the other two. I had held the dagger in my own hand; it was one of Fènnù's ten-inch serrated teeth fitted with a leather-wrapped hilt decorated with a gold medallion. And through Fènnù's memories, I had glimpsed an ancient wyfe holding the amulet, a splash of scarlet on a golden chain—a scarlet scale from Yuánchi, whose Chinese name meant vitality and life.

If the flute was made from dragon claw, logically the claw came from a third dragon—the dragon of song. And the flute was for the wyfe of song, Georgiana.

I turned a page, and my finger alighted on the passage I had recalled:

*For the Great Song, I knowe the three relicks, edged, chayned, and hollow. The Queene holds the edged and chayned, but not the thryd, the hollow relick of Musike bathed in tears of betrayal.*

Before, that had seemed mere stylistic rambling. Tudor authors enjoyed that; the Loch bairn journal, ostensibly our family history, was no exception. But three relics could be the three great items. The dagger was edged, and the amulet, poetically, might be called chained. A flute, the relic of music, would be hollow.

The reference to a queen, at least, was clear from the dates: Queen Mary the first, the great wyfe who gave golden touch pieces as blessings with her healings, sent her knights to steal the dagger Gramr, and eventually acquired the amulet as well.

I had no intention of giving the flute to the French. But if it related to our family, it might help Lizzy, or perhaps it led to the "great song" which might. And all three items mattered. They were made to heal the dragons' broken song. Heal the growing blight that Georgiana saw in her visions.

The Frenchwoman had said a Bennet could find the flute. The peculiarity of that struck me at last, and, foolishly, I found my gaze wandering Papa's shelves. But draca claws were a distinctive, lustrous black. There was nothing made of dragon claw at Longbourn. There was not even a flute. As a child, I had poked through every cabinet and crevice a hundred times.

I tucked the Loch bairn journal under my arm. The French had stolen books before, so the journal would be safer at Pemberley. I added the three slim volumes Papa had published as a young man. I had read them as a child; I read every book in the house. They were social and political theory, not history, but they were by a Bennet. Finally, I tucked in one more book, simply a keepsake.

A happy ruckus of children's voices drifted through the open window, so I went out the back door into a bedlam of young laughter. A dozen children between five and ten were playing around a shining gold creature as tall as my waist—Jane's wyvern, sitting stoic as a sphinx while a little girl petted her tail.

Georgiana and Mamma were seated at our garden table with a pot of tea. Georgiana met me with a smile and dancing eyes. "Your mother has been describing the local gentlemen to me. The single ones, that is."

"Mamma!" I scolded her.

"Why ever not?" Mamma said, offended. "Hertfordshire gentlemen are suitable for any class of society. After all, if Mr. Darcy can marry Lizzy—" She faltered and took a sip of tea.

Unannounced, my sister Jane appeared around the corner of the house. She wore robin's egg blue and had her new daughter, Jemma, in her arms. Jane gave a happy cry, then freed one finger to point at her wyvern. "I knew someone was visiting! I feel her moods sometimes, and she is so excited. Has Lizzy..."

I shook my head. "Not yet."

Quieted, Jane took a seat. "We must be patient. It is just that Jemma is growing so fast. Lizzy has not even met her."

Jane bounced her baby girl a few times, then passed her to me. I took her happily. Jemma gawked up, fascinated, her plump fists wandering.

This cheered up Jane. "Look! She adores her Aunt Mary. Of course, you are the first face she saw." I had delivered Jane's baby at Netherfield after a four-hour labor so routine I finished Anna Barbauld's *Eighteen Hundred and Eleven* between contractions.

"She was too young to remember me," I said, "but she enjoys my spectacles." I grinned at her lively blue eyes. Her blonde hair had puffed into fine curls, and she had gained two healthy pounds. Already, she was the image of her mother. She likely slept through every night just to be considerate.

I offered her to Georgiana, who shook her head and sat on her hands for good measure. "Not me!" Everyone laughed, and she said, "No babies, thank you. Mary has mastered them sufficiently for us both."

Instead, I passed little Jemma to Mamma. Mamma promptly began extolling the joys of motherhood to Georgiana. "Just wait until you marry! You will have little feet running all about."

"I shall not hold my breath," Georgiana said, slipping me an amused glance.

Impulsively, I said, "Georgiana and I are residing together. At Pemberley. But we have discussed taking a house."

"That is a clever plan," Jane said. "You must do it."

Mamma was puzzled. "Unmarried ladies taking a house? That is for spinsters. You are not even twenty." She eyed our clothes. "A house in town?"

That was an excellent question. One Georgiana and I had never discussed. Suddenly panicked, I looked at Georgiana.

She ventured, "I always imagined the country..."

"I also..." I said.

"...but your medical practice must require a city?"

"Only for study. Once that is done, London would not feel..."

"Exactly! The music and socialization are wonderful, but if one stays too long—"

"—it is exhausting," I finished, and Georgiana smiled in radiant relief.

"Well, a Darcy can afford all manner of houses," Mamma observed. "Just be certain to choose a town with a regiment, or you shall have no officers."

Having survived one improvisation, I sidestepped that one. "Is Kitty in Meryton?" She was likely shopping for officers herself.

"She is helping Harriet at Netherfield," Jane said. "Most of the teachers went home after the invasion. They were frightened, but that left poor Harriet teaching herself hoarse. Kitty is trying, but I am not sure she is very good. She reads them *novels*."

"Your wyvern seems helpful," Georgiana noted.

The children had formed a spinning circle around the draca. The scene was very Jane-like, children playing with a creature that a troop of armed soldiers would fear to approach.

"The children adore her, and she does like to keep watch," Jane answered. Softly, she added, "The poor thing was very affected by what happened at the ball. Spending time with the children helps her mend. She has become attached to them, and to baby Jemma."

Unwanted, that horrible moment filled my eyes. It had been five months since the London ball where Jane's wyvern killed my friend Miss Rees. The wyvern had been compelled to attack—the madness of Fènnù reached through Lizzy and seized her mind—but those very claws had torn my friend from my outstretched hands.

Images of that memory, as vivid as life, overcame the idyllic garden scene and turned it into a spectacle of terror. The muscles rippling beneath those adamantine scales seemed tensed for violence. The four-inch claws cutting Longbourn's turf were poised to strike.

As my heart pounded, the wyvern's muzzle swung to me. Her faceted eyes sparkled in the sun, and a river of calm washed away my fear. The memory retreated.

An ethereal voice chimed in my head:

*hear me, wyfe*

Wonder filled me. When I was with Lizzy, Yuánchi had spoken to me this way, his dragon thoughts thunder in my mind. Afterward, I decided that Lizzy's extraordinary skills fostered that connection.

But Lizzy was not here. Jane and Georgiana were chatting. Neither seemed aware of anything unusual.

The wyvern's voice chimed again, aged and wise:

*the wyfe of song shines. you shine. you are paired*

"I love her," I said. Mamma was laughing at the others' conversation. Nobody heard me.

The wyvern rose. Delicately, she sidestepped the playing children, her wingtips flicking for balance. She took three swift, avian strides to stand by Jane.

*you have seen visions from the past. wyverns, too, hold the lore. but look forward, shining wyfe, and see: i will never fail your sister again*

Jane, delighted by her wyvern's arrival, dangled her enchanted baby a few inches from the gleaming, fanged muzzle. The baby cooed, as fascinated by golden scales as by my spectacles. The wyvern stood regally, watching the garden around us, and I knew Jane and her daughter would be defended to the death.

# 3

# THE SHRINE

## MARY

Five hours out of Longbourn, our coachman, a military rifleman discharged after losing an eye, rapped on the front panel and called down, "Trouble."

I pushed my head out the side window. Two farm carts had blocked the road. Four men lounged beside them wearing long, belted black coats, their cheeks shaven and hair cropped.

"Blackcoats!" I shouted up. We had been warned of raids.

The driver cursed and snapped the reins. The horses surged sideways, cranking the coach a quarter turn and into the fields, wheels bouncing over the rails of a fallen fence. That seemed reckless—we could have broken an axel—until I saw the second group of Blackcoats running up behind us, muskets in hand.

A gunshot rang out, and the horses leaped to a gallop. The coach banged and rocked, hammering across furrows of sprouting wheat. I leaned farther to see the men chasing us, and the doorframe cracked the side of my head, knocking me half out the window.

Dazed, it took a moment to understand why I did not fall. Georgiana had caught my flailing arm in her stretched hand, her other grasping the far door white-knuckled. She hauled me back through the open window. We fell in a tangled mess, then held on—to each other, to the seat frame, to the door handle.

The horses veered parallel to the furrows of wheat, and the motion changed to seasick swaying. A bullet passed, its whine dropping a perversely perfect octave, then a gun bellowed over our heads, the footman's blunderbuss.

The coach banged again, almost knocking us airborne, then the wheels were rushing on gravel as the horses found their stride on clear road. "We're past, ladies," the driver shouted. "We're safe. They're not mounted."

"Keep your head inside next time," Georgiana whispered.

LATE THE NEXT AFTERNOON, our coach rolled into the valley below Pemberley House. The four-horse team was tired, having drawn us since morning, but the clop of their hooves quickened. They were Pemberley horses, stabled in Derby on our trip out and eager for home.

I was eager as well. Pemberley was safe.

Usually the valley was quiet, but today a crowd was gathered beside the lake. Carts and horses lined the road. Two massive, industrial wagons had been wheeled near the shore, and fifty feet onto the water, a strange, square barge floated, topped with heavy lumber trusses and busy men.

Georgiana called to stop the coach, and we made our way through the crowd. Most were Britons from the Pemberley hills. Welcoming "Miss Darcys" and "Miss Bennets" trailed us.

Mrs. Reynolds, the Pemberley housekeeper, was at the front. She met Georgiana with a concerned frown and said, "This is unnatural madness, to be sure!"

"Where is my brother?" Georgiana asked, puzzled.

Mrs. Reynolds pointed outward. And downward. A stream of bubbles was bursting beside the barge.

"Mr. Darcy is underwater," answered a white-haired, stooped gentleman, seventy years old if he was a day but beaming with boyish pride. He rolled on in a Scot's brogue. "James Rennie, machinery maker, at your service. Mr. Darcy is testing my improvements to the diving bell." At our stunned expressions, he added, "He is quite safe."

On the barge, a man waved a pair of small flags. Mr. Rennie squinted and translated, "The bell is at five fathoms. Mr. Darcy has 'pulled twice' through the signal rope. That means 'all is well,' and he wishes to descend to seven fathoms."

Georgiana's arms folded into a knot. "Is that deep?"

"Five fathoms is thirty feet. Well within design capabilities. See the force pump?" Mr. Rennie pointed to the barge where four men strained to turn a huge, horizontal crank. They looked like oxen turning a mill. "That drives air into the bell. In the laboratory, I have measured two atmospheres of pressure, sufficient for ten fathoms. But five fathoms is enough for today."

Mr. Rennie made a chop motion with his hand. An assistant picked up a pair of flags and signaled back. On the barge, ropes were lashed. Different cranks turned. A dripping hawser wound onto a shaft.

"Was he on the bottom?" I asked. That was hard to conceive.

Mr. Rennie's buoyant confidence sank a notch. "The barge is anchored in fifteen fathoms. At the lake's center, our sounding line did not reach bottom. It is a hundred fathom line, so the lake exceeds six hundred feet." His mood bobbed back up. "However, Mr. Darcy is extremely... that is, he has offered to fund development."

Six hundred feet. Could Lizzy be so far? Emma had sensed that Lizzy and Yuánchi remained bound, proof that Lizzy had survived her plunge into the lake. Anything more was conjecture.

My mind filled with myths of Amphitrite hiding in the depths, pursued by her Poseidon.

A massive metal bell, open at the base and big enough to conceal a man, rose ponderously into view. A wooden boom swung the bell over the barge, and two crewmembers helped a tall man crawl from the bottom while lake water sheeted down. They wrapped a blanket over his sopping black tailcoat and dripping neckcloth. I snorted. That could only be Mr. Darcy. His hat was likely in the lake.

Mr. Rennie was bouncing on his toes with delight. He was exactly the sort that Lizzy adored, a gentleman inventor remaking the world without a thought for the damage to humanity or nature. I imagined her peppering him with questions, and I muttered, "Lizzy would love this."

"Tell my brother I am returned," Georgiana announced icily. She was angry —at my words, or at Mr. Darcy. She strode off, her steps scattering pebbles, not toward the coach but along the water. I went after her, puzzling.

A hundred yards from the crowd, we reached Lizzy's memorial, a life-sized, granite statue. Gentle waves sloshed a few feet shy of the base.

I thought I understood Georgiana's anger now, but my explanation stumbled. "I meant how Lizzy admires inventions. She loves bolts and hoses..."

Georgiana pointed at the statue, sculpted as if Lizzy were stepping from the lake. "This is what I have seen. *This* is how she returns. What Fitz is doing... it is all wrong."

I caught her outstretched wrist, and we faced each other, her eyes bright, the lakeshore breeze flattening the brim of her bonnet.

"You have *seen* her?" I said. When Georgiana played or sang, her power—occasionally—provided visions. Once, she tried to show me one and failed. Many times, she tried to describe them and frustrated us both.

With Emma, naturally, she had shared one effortlessly.

"I have not seen *her*, exactly," Georgiana admitted, "but I have seen her melody return. Mary, you must know what Fitz is doing is wrong. Lizzy was ill, and Yuánchi was terribly wounded. Blinded. Their rest—their sleep together—is a gift, not a vault to be pried open. It must not be interrupted. It is how they *heal*."

Lizzy had been worse than ill. She was in the last throes of meningeal consumption, a ruthless killer. When she and Yuánchi vanished into the lake, she had, at best, a day left. If Lizzy had survived five months since then, it was a miracle—but that was nonsensical. Lizzy was submerged. Five minutes was a miracle.

"You tell me this now?" I heard the burr of accusation in my tone. "You know I am trying to raise her, too."

"But you have not *done* anything!" Georgiana cried. I dropped her wrist—I recoiled—and she lifted her hands in frustration. "I do not mean it like that! It is just... you will think before you act. Fitz does not." Her cheeks flushed in the breeze. "Yuánchi will rise as all draca rise, summoned by love and need. Not by ropes and hooks. *He* must choose when they are ready. He will bring her to us."

She was beautiful in her certainty, and she had gifts I did not comprehend. But she did not understand. "He may sleep a hundred years. A thousand. The last wakings of dragons are lost in myth."

"Then... then we shall not be here to greet her when she returns." Georgiana's voice caught but cleared with a singer's hard-won control. "I am not despairing. Or saying we cannot help. But this has happened for a purpose."

My shoulders were shivering. To disagree with Georgiana was to plunge a knife into my own heart. And I believed her. Every word. But knifed or not, my heart could not agree.

"I miss my sister, not her dragon," I said. "Lizzy has been gone five months. Soon it will be a year, then it will be ten. Her life is in our world, and it is passing her by. I will not let her return abandoned and alone. Yuánchi may rise when he wills, but my sister has a will, too, and it is a will of iron. Whether I need a flute or a song, if I can reach her—if I so much as make her stir in her sleep—*she* will choose whether to rise."

The breeze pressed Georgiana's clothes to her slender body. For once, she looked unsure. She was so much more poised than me, her gifts so remarkable, I sometimes forgot I was the older of us. She would turn eighteen next month.

She stepped to me and slipped her arm through mine. Deliberately, she turned us to face the memorial.

The base of Lizzy's monument had always held mementoes and remembrances. Bunches of field flowers. Notes from the household and the Britons in the hills...

Now, it was a shrine. Flowers tumbled in drifts two feet thick. Burned candles rested in wax puddles. Bark chips held offerings: an edge of bread, a sliver of cheese, a spoonful of grain. More unsettling yet were the rusted knives sunk among the blooms. And atop it all, several feet long and woven of sharp holly and hawthorn, a woman's figure slept, violent with spikes and thorns.

"She may choose to rise," Georgiana said. "I do not think she should."

# 4

# PEMBERLEY PROTECTED

## MARY

We sent the coach ahead and walked to Pemberley House, the swish of our skirts and the leg-straining slope welcome after sitting so long. The garden stream, swollen with spring rain, gushed and sprayed beside the road, tumbling down the slope to feed midnight-blue depths.

At one of the garden promontories overlooking the lake, Georgiana stopped and squeezed my fingers. "You know I will do anything to recover Lizzy."

"I know." From here, I saw the barge as Georgiana must see it—an angular, technological intrusion. "You were right. Ropes and hooks are foolish."

She gave me a swift kiss. Then, tired, she continued toward the house. I stayed, submerged in one of Pemberley's wilder, more formless gardens.

Rowan wreaths, symbols of the druids, hung in the trees. Today was the twenty-ninth of April. Tomorrow, Pemberley's Britons would celebrate Beltane eve. Druidic beliefs were widespread in these hills, older and stronger than any English or Roman church.

Almost a year ago, on last Beltane eve, Lizzy and Mr. Darcy married in the old Briton ceremony. Their impending anniversary and the transformation of Lizzy's memorial merged in my thoughts, a pair of linked symbols. I do not believe supernatural machinery ordains the future, but the Britons' rituals were derived from the druid calendar and rooted in the natural world. The Britons understood mysteries of draca unknown by any modern naturalist. Their veneration of Lizzy's statue, even if I did not share their faith, was charged with meaning.

"Do you sense the spring?" I whispered to the lake. A breeze gusted like breath. The distant waves lapped a drowsy pulse.

A pair of people had exited the house. Now they arrived: Emma, elegantly dressed in canary yellows, and, unexpectedly, Lord Wellington. Neither was my favorite person, although Emma, at least, was loyal to the Darcys. Lord Wellington's presence simply made me suspicious.

I greeted him by pointing accusingly to the lake. "Is this a Council project? Are you dredging up Lizzy and her dragon for your war?" I was tired, and I could not imagine why else he would be so far from the fighting.

He smiled politely. "I advised Darcy against it. And no, the War Council has not decided to drag the lake for Mrs. Darcy. The government—and I—thought she was dead. That was an unusual misstep for you, Miss Bennet."

I shuffled, frustrated with myself.

Emma said quietly, "You did not reveal anything. Mr. Darcy told him yesterday."

Told him what? That Lizzy lived, but not that Emma had sensed her survival—Mr. Darcy was too protective of Emma for that.

Lord Wellington's gaze shifted to the lake. He stood with feet apart and hands clasped behind his back, a commander's pose, as if lurking portraitists might sketch him on the sly. Perhaps they did.

"I am glad he told me," he said. "It explains his moods in these last months. Mourning, then giddy relief, then a slip to despair." He nodded to the barge. "That is the onset of desperation. Despair is passive. Desperate men are courageous fools."

I expected respectful silence after such a weighty pronouncement, but after the barest pause, Emma asked me, "Has Mr. Knightley returned to London?" There was a quiver in her voice. Emma was capable of artful concealment, but on this topic, her guard failed.

"He was not yet in London," I said, "but he has left the occupied south. When I last heard, he was in Surrey."

"Oh," Emma said and blushed as if a gentleman's presence in one's home county was profoundly intimate.

I rubbed my stiffening shoulder, remembering our trip. "I am glad he is returning. Travel is perilous, even north of London. Our road from Hertford-shire was blocked by Blackcoats. We had to gallop across a field to escape."

Lord Wellington scowled at the south as if he could see the miscreants from our lofty perch. "Rabble," he pronounced.

"Rabble with a purpose, even if the purpose is vile," I replied. "They cry their slogan of Britain Awake. Whole neighborhoods of London support their propaganda: that Napoleon will cast down the effete aristocracy in a new Reign of Terror; that slavery is a God-granted boon; that supreme male authority will be restored by the Napoleonic Code. It is like hatred was stewing and needed only the thinnest flame of rhetoric to boil."

Lord Wellington studied me. Perhaps he thought I was a hypocrite; the conservative newspapers that praised his military policies also accused me of leading mobs, if a dozen women blocking traffic to demand a political voice was a mob. But he said only, "Gather yourself. When Darcy dries off, he will wish to speak with you. You will want your wits about you for that."

I WALKED the corridors to our bedroom, a salon-like space on the third floor with a view of the eastern hills. Properly, it was Georgiana's room, but Lucy, the endlessly energetic lady's maid, met me and chattered while we unpacked my things into the armoire Georgiana and I shared. Perhaps it was our room after all.

The bed was untouched. Georgiana's fatigue had been more musical than physical; she had been away from her instruments for days. Soft clavichord notes sounded from the adjacent parlor. She had chosen Elizabethan music rich in thirds and sixths, a Dowland composition for lute. Her clavichord matched it well, having a luteish timbre, and the keyboard action let her ornament with vibrato, a technique far beyond my skill.

Soon she would move to the grand pianoforte and storm through page after page, playing for three hours, or five, or ten.

"I gather my sister is returned," Mr. Darcy observed dryly, and in dry clothes, from outside our open door. He had been listening.

I had not seen him for a week, and without Georgiana, I was unsure how to greet him. I settled for a curtsy and "Mr. Darcy."

His bow was informal, at least by household standards. "Are you recovered from your trip?" I said yes, and he continued, "Would you join me for a discussion? Lord Wellington will attend as well."

This was the predicted, or threatened, conversation. Should I be apprehensive? "Without Georgiana?"

"I prefer that. We can speak more directly without her." That was unnerving, but then he smiled, tired and friendly, and I was even less certain what to expect.

We walked to his study in the west wing of the house, tromping yet more halls and stairs. I pondered what his purpose might be and forgot to invent a social topic, but he was silent as well.

His study was a gentleman's space, filled with heavy oak furnishings and thick cut-glass decanters brimming with ancient ports and whiskies. Fortunately, Mr. Darcy abhorred smoking, so there was no tinge of tobacco. Engineering drawings were pinned on one wall, cranks and pulleys and metal bells. I spun them in my mind to match aspects of the barge and its diving bell.

Lord Wellington was present and gravely formal, and my puzzlement grew. It seemed unlikely this was an intervention to save Georgiana's honor, or her soul, or whatever punishment the Church threatened when their rules were flouted. Georgiana was very open with her brother, and Mr. Darcy had embraced us both after our barely disguised declaration before the royal court.

Re-sorting my list of possible topics, I took the proffered seat at a small table with three leather-upholstered chairs.

"Do you wish to speak about *la Demoiselle des Parfums*?" I asked. That would explain Lord Wellington's attendance.

Mr. Darcy looked puzzled. Not that. I struck it off my list.

"The perfumer!" Lord Wellington exclaimed. "How did you hear about her?"

I switched my attention to him. "I met her in London."

"Good God. And you survived?"

"She did not attack me. How do you know about her?"

"At the southern front, she killed half a company with her foul crawlers. Afterward, the men whispered wild stories of *la parfumeuse*. I would have discounted them, but they were too like my encounter with Lydia Bennet, may God rest her soul—or keep it at least. I have no desire to meet her again in this life."

I wondered if I should conceal the bribe I was offered; Lord Wellington had run roughshod over our family's secrets before. But the social rules of dissembling baffled me—what was a half-truth? what was a lie?—so I recounted my encounter with *la Demoiselle des Parfums* word for word.

Mr. Darcy's jaw knotted when I mentioned Lydia and Wickham's theft from Pemberley. When I finished, I asked him, "What do you know of the great song?"

"It is mentioned in the stolen volumes, but the descriptions were vague and mystical. I made no effort to unravel them. There may have been others. Some volumes awaited translation. Old High German, Anglo-Saxon..."

"I think the great song relates to the flute, and it affects the world of draca."

Lord Wellington had an expression of intense interest. "Will you accept the perfumer's offer?"

That surprised me. "Will I find the flute, an item of unknown but tremendous power, and deliver it to a murderous Frenchwoman in exchange for books?"

"Not for books," he said. "To save your sister." His gaze was steady, and I wondered how much he guessed of my thoughts—of my desire to reach out to Lizzy.

"I will not." He looked unconvinced, so I explained. "Lizzy would be furious with me. Also, I have no idea how to find the flute."

Mr. Darcy had listened to our exchange with such perfect politeness that I suspected impatience. I still had no idea why he brought me here, so I said to him, "You did not wish to discuss *la parfumeuse.*"

"No," Mr. Darcy confirmed. "My topic is a family matter. If we are ready to proceed?" Lord Wellington nodded, and Mr. Darcy added, "Arthur is present as a witness."

I had never heard Lord Wellington addressed by his first name. Uneasy, I said, "A witness to what?"

Mr. Darcy squared his shoulders, his habit when gathering his thoughts. "Elizabeth and I had seven married months together. There was, of course, no child. Now, she has been lost for five. I devote my life to her recovery, but I am all too aware of the unpredictable hand of fate. So, I wish to secure Georgiana's future and the future of our family."

"What has that to do with me?"

A smile cracked his stern aspect. "You are part of our family. Georgiana is adamant about that, and I approve of her choice. However, English law does not recognize your commitment. I cannot correct that moral failure, but I can remedy a practical risk." He stretched out a long arm to a thick sheaf of papers on his desk. The top page was elaborately titled and embossed. "These are trusts and wills. Unfortunately, they are complex. For this, English law is an impediment, not a friend. These grant you and Georgiana equal standing."

"You wish to share her fortune with me?" I said, not actually believing it. Georgiana had thirty thousand pounds set aside for her marriage. Massive wealth. Not something I desired or deserved.

Mr. Darcy flicked his fingers dismissively. "That, too. The important change is that you and Georgiana are joint heiresses to Pemberley." When I stared blankly, he continued, "The implications may differ from what you expect. When I inherited, I enfranchised Pemberley's worked lands. The Britons administer their hills. The towns and farmland are cooperatives, for which we provide administration—mediation, mostly—but receive no income. However, that leaves the manor and grounds, which are substantial, and the investments and holdings in Great Britain and abroad. Those comfortably exceed the old estate income. The shipping company alone—" He paused, recognizing my stunned state. "I am merely preparing a contingency. If both I and Elizabeth..." That sentence jammed. He swallowed and started again. "In the event that I die or am lost before Elizabeth returns, this protects you, and Georgiana, and Pemberley. I would not ask it otherwise. I know Pemberley is a large undertaking—"

"*Large?*" I choked out. "It is one of England's great estates!"

From the sidelines, Lord Wellington chuckled. "Miss Bennet, your expression is remarkable."

"I have no idea what I am expressing. I just do not wish to... possess land." I had marched more than once protesting the tyranny of England's landholders. "Property should be held for the common good."

"Pemberley's land is, now," Mr. Darcy pointed out. "But your ancestral home, Longbourn, is entailed. It belongs to Charles and will be inherited by his and Jane's son, or if they do not have one, some cousin you do not even know. Pemberley has no such entailment, and if Georgiana could marry legally, I would protect her with a marriage settlement. But a single woman holding Pemberley will face claims from a host of obscure relations, all argued by corrupt lawyers citing archaic laws. I have discussed this with Georgiana, and we agree: If I am gone, Pemberly should be secured for her and for the person she loves. But Georgiana has no interest in managing an estate—"

"Neither do I!" I interrupted.

"You managed Longbourn after Elizabeth married. But what *matters* is that you fight for your rights." He gave a curt laugh. "My own aunt covets Pemberley, and she knows too well the fragility of a woman's property. She would cajole and bully until Georgiana was sleeping under her pianoforte in a rented salon. If not her, it will be some remote, grasping cousin. But neither would intimidate you. In that, you are like Elizabeth."

He stopped, for which I was grateful. My mind was at sea, frustrated by the familiar evils of inheritance and inequity and patriarchy, but also, strangely, my heart was warmed. Welcomed.

That sensation turned to alarm when Mr. Darcy took my hand. "Mary, amid darkness, it strengthens me to know my sister is protected. To know that Pemberley is defended. I trust you."

That was too much. I freed my hand. Surely holding hands was not normal business practice. And he called me Mary! Was I supposed to call him Fitzwilliam?

In that silence, he said, "You love Georgiana."

The warmth returned to my heart. "I do."

"Then protect her for me. This is no more than the rights you would have if the law were just."

I could think of no counterargument. I nodded.

Mr. Darcy inked a pen and signed the document. He passed it to Lord Wellington, who signed as well.

Now I had thought of fifty arguments. "This is beyond me. I will not sign these."

Thoughtfully, Mr. Darcy leaned back in his chair. "If you wish, I will tear up the documents. But Pemberley is not beyond you. You would wield her resources to great effect—for you, and for Georgiana. For whatever cause you feel is just."

That was the seduction of property and power: accept it to protect those you love. Tearing down the aristocracy would be awkward if I were one of them. But I had stared poverty in the face when we were about to lose Longbourn, and, for better or from cowardice, I was a pragmatic moralist. Better to live and do good than perish on principle.

"I would protect Georgiana," I said. "You and I would not agree on much else."

"You might be surprised." He stacked the papers.

"Should I not sign?"

He smiled wryly. "A woman's signature would be ruled invalid by a court. You see what I mean about English law?"

# 5

# REACQUAINTANCE

## EMMA

"Miss Woodhouse?" Lucy asked.

I looked up from hovering my gloved fingers over the stone bench's mossy armrest. Lucy curtsied. "Mr. Darcy regrets that he will be unable to attend today."

That was expected, with Mary and Georgiana returned. I thanked her, and she hurried back to the house, shoulders square with duty to her absent mistress.

I did not regret the solitude. Pemberley's north garden was alive with cheeps and bobbing branches. It was a relaxing setting, chosen by Mr. Darcy for our... I thought of them as lessons, but he preferred to give our meetings businesslike names. "Our discussions." "Our joint endeavor."

Well, today's lesson was just me, now. An independent endeavor of Miss Woodhouse.

I settled myself on the bench, drew off my long gloves, and lay them on the seat beside me. That was too easy, so I scrunched them into a crumpled stack of satin bumps and folds.

Mr. Darcy's mother had kept a journal describing how she confronted her compulsive habits. She found that constant practice weakened their grip on her mind. Mr. Darcy was very much in favor of practice.

Mr. Darcy also droned on about patience and the hazards of testing myself.

Fortunately, he was occupied. So, I poked the scrunched cloth with my finger-nail, adding ugly kinks and rumples.

Images of illness did not fill my mind. Trickles of miasma did not fill the shadows.

I liked practicing. It was active, a project to reclaim my life. Last night, secretly, I had dumped half my wardrobe in a mess on the bed and watched it while the house creaked and cooled, the candle melted to a stub, and owls hooted in the night.

Practice was healthy. The other projects that had consumed my life were not. Perfecting my clothes, perfecting Hartfield's decor, perfecting Harriet's life —those were dangerous because, no matter how carefully I performed my rituals, flaws crept in. Then, when illness or injury struck, my flawed rituals became the cause. Fear and compulsion falsely coupled in my mind, dragging me in rutted circles.

The frustrating part was that, in quiet moments like this, the notion that an unfastened button caused illness was obvious nonsense. So, how did the cycle begin? Mr. Darcy insisted that *how* and *why* were irrelevant, a distraction, but I wanted to know. I wanted to blame something. I had drowned in this night-mare for years.

A test, then. An investigation by the Woodhouse independent endeavor. When had my habits turned to compulsion?

Even when I was little, Papa had obsessed about sickness, perhaps because of my mother's premature death. But I did not remember my mother, so that did not affect me, and I had no obsessive symptoms as a child. My first hints of fixation started when I was a young woman—the same age they had afflicted Lady Anne Darcy and, according to Mr. Darcy's research, Queen Mary.

Mr. Darcy thought fixation was preordained, an ironic yoke for any great wyfe of healing. That seemed too simple to me.

The sun had moved while I thought. Deep in the folded shadows of my creased gloves, silver glistened. That would be the satin shining. It began to puddle, transparent and threatening...

Hastily, I shook out the gloves and pulled them on, fastening the pearl button on each inner wrist with trembling fingers.

Perhaps Mr. Darcy was right. How and why did not matter. But as tests went, that had been no disaster. Particularly considering I had not touched Mr. Darcy for nine days. The last strength I borrowed, that scarlet surge of Yuánchi's binding I absorbed through him, had faded and vanished days ago.

I could survive without Mr. Darcy. Survive without Pemberley.

I could go home.

The thought of the simple routines of Hartfield caught hold of me, a giddy tug under my breastbone.

Nessy was hiking up the path from the lake, her growing limbs coltish, her school dress the color of bluebells. She saw me and waved, then ran through the gardens, her book bag flopping as she rounded hedges and flower beds.

She arrived happy and puffing. "Aunt Emma!"

"You are back early," I said, smiling. Her health was a gift from Lady Anne Darcy. Or from the ghost of her wyvern.

Nessy announced in one excited breath, "The school has too many children! They canceled my afternoon lessons! Will you do some magic for me?"

Very properly, I said, "I cannot imagine what you mean." Nessy crossed her arms and scowled, so I made a show of relenting. "You must not tell anyone."

"I never tell! Besides, everyone knows you can."

"It is not magic. Not really," I said, looking around the garden until I spotted a pair of black eyes gleaming beneath a hedge. I lowered my gloved fingertips by the lawn and smiled invitingly, and a roseworm emerged and scurried over, stopping slightly short of my hand. She wriggled with skittish curiosity. Like all roseworms, she was rabbit-sized and very quick, with finely wrought scales like a sheet of beads.

"Have it do a trick!" Nessy demanded.

"She," I corrected. "Draca do not do tricks. But I have seen her chase squirrels..." I put my hands on my knees, leaned close, and said with huge enthusiasm, "Go get the squirrel!" The roseworm cocked her head, mystified, and I laughed. "When I was a child, we had a dog that would search every bush if I said that. I suppose a draca has no way to learn the word."

Nessy gave me the long-suffering look that children reserve for simpleminded grownups. "Use *magic*!"

Could I? I sensed the roseworm's binding—that was my talent. Her binding matched the delicate pink of her belly scales. It wound around her rather than leading to a wyfe; she was feral, not bound. But other than sensing bindings and generally intriguing draca, my great wyfe status provided no special affinity. I could not command them like Lizzy or do whatever Georgiana did—calming them or communing with them. She described it as musical collaboration.

I peered into the draca's eyes and tried to... touch her binding or... do something a great wyfe would do. And something did happen. My sense of her binding brightened and sharpened.

Then it was overshadowed by another presence, huge and old. I looked up.

The inky silhouette of a dragon cruised above us, level with the lowest clouds. Fènnù. When Lizzy was first lost in the lake, Fènnù came every day, skimming the waves and searching for her wyfe of war. But in the last few weeks, her visits had become irregular and remote.

Today, she passed high over Pemberley House, then stroked her great wings to pass higher yet over the lake. She banked and vanished into the cotton tufts and skeins decorating the eastern sky.

As if angry, another force shuddered—the force always present here, quiescent and massive. Lizzy and Yuánchi's binding rippled in scarlet sheets of immense power. If anything, it had strengthened in the last month. It suffused all of Pemberley. But it was different today, streaked with black. The yearning attraction I felt for it, the pull of the wyfe of healing to her fated dragon, Yuánchi, had also diminished. Was that good or bad?

Nessy sighed impatiently. I had forgotten my assignment.

Perhaps a direct approach would work. I caught the roseworm's gaze and said firmly, "Pay attention." She took a step closer.

In my mind, I pictured a squirrel lounging on the lawn. The draca's little rose-tone legs tensed. That was promising.

I tried imagining the visceral hatred our little terrier puppy had harbored for squirrels. They were scruffy interlopers. Fluffy invaders hiding in every tree—

The roseworm tore off, running crazily around the garden, circling the shrubs and snapping at the air. She looked very silly, and Nessy clapped her hands in delight.

The roseworm skidded to a stop at a particularly suspicious hazel bush. She crept closer, each little foot placed with such drama that Nessy laughed. Then the draca's little chest swelled, and hissing blue flame shot out, burning a round, six-inch hole clear through the bush.

She sat back on her haunches, pleased. The bush, fortunately, was plump and green, and the flames subsided to steam and smoke. It looked like a charred attempt at hedge sculpture.

Nessy's eyes were saucers.

"This can be our secret," I said, gathering my things. "Shall we see if the kitchen has any tea?"

THE KITCHEN WAS BUSTLING with dinner preparation, and no tea was made, but Nessy was the sole child in this sprawling palace and very spoiled, so a kettle was put on and a plate of biscuits provided. While Nessy nibbled, the cook told me her expansive plans for dinner. That made me think of Serle, our Hartfield cook, and I felt another pang of homesickness.

Should I leave Pemberley?

For a time, I had feared that Mr. Darcy's moods endangered him. But I disagreed with Lord Wellington's claim that Mr. Darcy was desperate. I thought he had become healthier. Determined.

Then there was the war, but the French and American invaders were well short of Surrey. Besides, I refused to abandon my home due to vague threats. All England might fall. What would we do then, scurry north and freeze in Scotland?

A more practical problem was my lack of funds for the trip. My letters to Hartfield were unanswered—southern mail was disrupted—and my despicable brother-in-law, John, refused any letter I sent to London. But it was false pride to call funds a barrier. Mr. Darcy would provide a coach and driver if I asked.

While Nessy chose a third biscuit, I smoothed the fit of my gloves and wondered why I was reluctant to leave. Perhaps I feared loneliness. Harriet was teaching at Netherfield, the Bingleys' home. She did reply to my letters, but her notes were short. She might even be angry because of my... well-meant missteps.

I heard Mrs. Reynolds approach in the corridor. She was speaking formally, likely with a member of the family, so I kissed Nessy on her forehead and went to see.

Mr. Knightley, whom I had thought a hundred miles away, stood conversing with her.

His back was to me, the taper of his tailored coat pronounced from shoulders to waist. His hair, tied back in his old-fashioned style, had grown a half-inch; the corkscrews spilled down his brown neck and past his collar. Even without that, I would have recognized the set of his body, so similar to how he stood when he played his violin, shoulders square but canted a little as if he were leaning into an intense note.

Recollections rattled my mind. When he last set out to the occupied south, I had cried in my room, afraid of a horrid outcome. Before, he had asked me: What if a proper life were offered to you? I had not answered, which of course was an answer: No. A Black gentleman had enough barriers in society without a wyfe who feared crumpled gloves.

Mrs. Reynolds spotted me over Mr. Knightley's shoulder. She apologized to him—some urgency in the pantry—then said "Miss Woodhouse" to me before curtsying and hastening down the corridor.

Mr. Knightley turned.

I said, "Good afternoon." The noisy kitchen behind me had fallen perfectly silent. I recalled I should add, "Mr. Knightley."

"You look remarkable," he said. "Wonderful."

It took a few seconds to believe he said that. I dragged a huge breath into my lungs to fend off a blush. "You wish to be informal, I see."

"Honest, not informal. If you prefer, I can pronounce your dress handsome, but my patience for social understatement has faded in the past weeks."

"Was the south so dangerous?"

He shrugged.

My heart was bounding in my chest like a silly girl's, which I was *not*. I hunted for a calming topic. "Did you call at Hartfield? I fancied you did. I could all but see you beside the fireplace." I did picture him then, lounging in one of the deep chairs, relaxed in his high-collared shirt and patterned waistcoat, his coat... missing for some reason. That was less calming than I expected.

Mr. Knightley, though, stiffened. "I was unable to visit Highbury."

I felt foolish. "Naturally. It was hardly a social trip."

"You have a brother," he said.

Even my newly vivid imagination could not guess why he brought that up. "Brother-in-law. John."

"I did inquire, you see... Your family is well known in Surrey."

"Of course," I said, because it was.

That made him laugh, but he turned serious. "I was just asking Mrs. Reynolds where to find you. I brought news from the south, and Lord Wellington has asked that we gather. He requested you by name."

# 6

## WYVES AND WAR

### EMMA

While I pondered why Lord Wellington would ask for me, Mr. Knightley and I ascended to a room I had never seen. It was on the top floor and very high-ceilinged; the attic had been opened to expose the building's roof, and much of that had been replaced with hinged copper panels that could open wide. Below, a huge black-iron telescope rested on a wheeled platform, the tube eight feet long and ten inches across.

Remarkable as that was, nobody else paid it the slightest attention. Mr. Darcy, Lord Wellington, Georgiana, and Mary were waiting, and the ladies had not seen Mr. Knightley since his return. Georgiana hugged him, and Mary squeezed his hands for a long moment.

We gathered at a round table whose surface charted the sky. The constellations were drawn, and the sun, moon, and planets were inlaid with shining mother of pearl, their paths shown as engraved curves annotated with degrees and dates. Nebulae and stars were inset beads of different colors. Beautiful as it was, it had some scientific purpose, but I knew no more than that. Stargazing was a gentleman's pastime, popular since the great comet passed two years ago.

A canvas bag rested in the table's center, wrapping something long and narrow.

We took our seats. The setting felt deliberately equal—six people at a circular table—but everyone's eyes were on Lord Wellington.

He worked his tanned hands together, eyeing the canvas bag, then he laid his palms flat on the tabletop. "I came to Pemberley for advice about strange events on the southern front. Mr. Darcy is an authority on matters of draca, and Miss Darcy"—he nodded to Georgiana—"has aided the military by assisting injured draca and wyves. I did not plan to involve others." His gaze touched me on that last word. "But the situation has changed."

Surprising me, he gestured to Mr. Knightley, seated to my left.

"I just returned from the occupied south," Mr. Knightley said. "I went as deep as Brighton, almost the coast. We helped fourteen people escape, three of them children. I suppose those details are not relevant. But when we crossed the line of battle to return, we learned of a new terror."

He pulled the canvas bag to him and, carefully, drew out a foot-long, scythe-shaped horn. Or was it a shell? Shiny olive-green, it had a pointed tip and irregular bumps on the inside edge. It looked like half a lobster's claw, but sharper and much longer.

He placed it in the center of the table. Georgiana gasped. Mr. Darcy drew back with an expression of revulsion. They recognized it.

Mary picked it up, using two hands once she felt the weight. She turned it, examining the underside, and her nose wrinkled. "There is an odor. Very faint. Not the ocean... it is like crawler venom."

"It is a foul crawler's pincer," Mr. Knightley said. "A huge one."

Mary hastily pushed it back onto the table, where it rocked and clacked. I recognized it now and shivered. Crawlers had a pair of these pincers on their heads, although for the crawlers I had seen, they were the size of grains of rice. This was unimaginable. To think it had been crawling around Brighton...

Mr. Darcy said coldly, "Lydia Bennet summoned such monsters. They are unnatural. Afterward, we uncovered Wickham's projects in the forest. He was farming crawlers. Breeding them to enormous size."

"The French have them now," Mr. Knightley said. "We collected that pincer while crossing the aftermath of a terrible battle. Many soldiers died to kill that monster, and the enemy has more. And always, there is a woman to control them." He added, "The battle was at Horley."

"Horley!" I exclaimed. "But that is in Surrey." Everyone turned to me, everyone except Mr. Knightley. He seemed to avoid my eyes.

Lord Wellington prodded the pincer with a finger, testing its weight. "I came to Pemberley to discuss rumors of a Frenchwoman the soldiers call the perfumer. Miss Bennet has discovered her court title, *la Demoiselle des Parfums.*

She is the mistress of Bonaparte, and she controls foul crawlers. One person like that is bad enough, but it seems the enemy has many. The threat has multiplied"—he tapped the huge pincer, making it wobble—"and grown."

Abruptly, Georgiana stood. She walked to the telescope and stood, silent, her back to us.

Lord Wellington leaned closer. "Miss Darcy had a frightening encounter with Lydia and these terrible creatures—"

"It is the blight," Georgiana said without turning. She sounded angry, not frightened. "It is spreading."

Lord Wellington's compassion became puzzlement. He looked around the table.

"Georgiana has seen visions of a blight," I said. "A darkness in the east that corrupts life." In her music room, she had shared that monstrous illusion, vivid and frightening.

For a stretched moment, Lord Wellington's attention fixed on me. He had asked that I attend. Did he suspect I was the third great wyfe?

Mr. Darcy noticed our interaction, and he frowned, doubtless dusting off his lecture on why I must keep that secret. I could have recited that backwards, but even forwards, his last rendition had seemed quaintly old fashioned in a country where women commanded dragons.

Lord Wellington resumed, "Miss Bennet also reports that the French seek a flute made of dragon claw, one of the artifacts associated with the three great wyves. The artifact we found, the dagger, is immensely powerful. When our enemy stole it, they used it to raise the black dragon and sent her to destroy England's navy, palaces, and Parliament. The dagger is lost in Pemberley lake, but I must assume the others are equally potent, and that Bonaparte seeks them all." His gaze swept the table. "I asked you here because I know you have kept secrets about these matters. I do not question your motives, but ignorance is a weakness I can no longer afford. What do you know of the other two items?"

I could not answer his question, but hiding my identity felt uncomfortably like dishonesty.

Mary, in her quick factual manner, did answer. "Queen Mary sought all three items. After her marriage to King Philip, her agents smuggled several tons of Spanish silver into Guangzhou. Soon after, an amulet described as 'a scarlet Chinese jewel' arrived at court. The amulet is jade, hung on a gold chain, and holds a scale from Yuánchi. The last reference to the amulet was in 1557, when it was sent"—Mary's stream of words hitched, then resumed—"to Surrey to be examined."

Even she was protecting me. I knew what she had excluded. The queen had sent the amulet to "the Witch of Woodhouse," my paternal ancestor, centuries past. Mary had asked me about the amulet months ago, but I knew nothing of it, and there was nothing like it in Papa's things after his death.

"Surrey," Lord Wellington repeated. "The recent French attacks appeared to be probes preparing for assault on Surrey, but I doubted that explanation. The better strategy would be for them to seize the rest of Kent, blockade the Thames, and starve London. Now, though, I understand. They seek the amulet." He folded his arms, studying Mary. "What of the flute?"

"I told you of my meeting." Mary met his gaze unflinchingly, but it seemed an oddly terse answer for her.

Lord Wellington apparently agreed. "Miss Bennet, I know we have clashed. If that has fostered your distrust, I am sorry, but for me, it only proves that you are your sister's equal. Mrs. Elizabeth Darcy is a great wyfe. Miss Georgiana Darcy is the second. And you... draca alight on your shoulder. In London, a clandestine network of women even call you 'Great Wyfe'..."

Mary laughed bitterly. That was all.

Lord Wellington drew breath, but my frustration at this dance, or my pride, or perhaps the prospect of war entering Surrey made me interrupt. "There is no need to badger her. It is not Mary. I am the third great wyfe."

Lord Wellington turned to me, surprised. Well, a little surprised. Not a lot. Mr. Darcy, however, was staring at me as if I had lost my mind.

Whatever their reactions, ending the secrecy felt good. Healthy. Keeping secrets had not done me any favors. And it was not like I was shouting the news in a town square.

That led neatly to my next announcement. "So," I continued, "I shall go to Surrey and find the amulet."

"Surrey!" Mr. Knightley burst out beside me. "Bands of Blackcoats roam through Surrey. The French army is massing on the border. One does not simply walk into Surrey!"

I gave him a pleasant smile. "Certainly not. I thought I would take the barouche and four. That will make a grand entrance!"

"A grand entrance," he repeated, stunned.

Gentlemen were so thickheaded. "I am joking. It is two hundred miles. A barouche is completely impractical. What if it rains?" His eyebrows rose farther, so I put my hand on his. "Listen. What could be more natural than a lady returning home? It raises no suspicion. I know everybody, so I can make inquiries. It is sensible."

Unexpectedly, Mary supported me. "Emma is right. In Fènnù's memories, the great wyfe of healing wielded the amulet. Emma senses Yuánchi. She is the amulet's intended owner. She may find it where no one else could."

"There!" I said. "It is settled. In any case, it is time I returned to Hartfield."

"This is wrong," Georgiana exclaimed, turning from the telescope. "We must stop the blight. It is driven by the broken song, and it is growing stronger. The great wyves must stay together. That is the only way to heal the song."

"You were just in London," I pointed out. "When I find the amulet, I will bring it back, and we will all be together again."

Mr. Knightley placed his hand atop mine. I realized I had held his this whole time.

"I will go with you," he said.

"Thank you," I said. "That is very welcome."

I had hoped he would offer. His depiction of Surrey concerned me, and it certainly ruled out bringing a housemaid as companion. But traveling with a single gentleman had its own complications. I could ask Harriet to join us, but I thought she would refuse. My half sister had been distant since discovering I knew about Papa's scheme to conceal her true parentage.

People stood, and the formality broke into odds and ends of conversation. Lord Wellington and Mr. Darcy launched a discussion of iron-barred carriages with Mr. Knightley. Those had been fashionable a year ago when ladies fanned themselves in wide-eyed consternation at the thought of feral draca. Now there were real risks on the road.

Mary said to me, a little grudgingly, "You are brave."

"I am going home," I said.

Mary nodded. She seemed to understand that.

I stepped closer and whispered, "Do you know more of the flute?"

"Nothing that would aid the army," she said flatly.

She excused herself and went to Georgiana. They spoke softly, their fore-heads almost touching, then Mary left without a backward glance. She often left gatherings suddenly. I was not sure if it was a statement or an oversight.

Mr. Knightley drew me aside. And farther aside.

"Yes?" I said when we were jammed by the farthest window.

"I made a serious error. I must tell you unpleasant news. If this changes your mind about the trip, I will explain to the others."

Was the war worse than he said? "You had better tell me."

"I misled you about Hartfield. I did call, but I was not received, merely dismissed on the doorstep in a desultory manner." I opened my mouth in dismay, but he waved that aside. "My dismissal was by your brother-in-law, John."

John. I could imagine it. Easily. I could practically hear his self-satisfied sneer.

When I did not speak, Mr. Knightley said, "He has declared himself master of Hartfield."

"I understood you."

I was an idiot not to have realized. My letters to my housekeeper, unanswered. My letters to his London residence, requesting my living allowance, returned unopened. Was my fortune lost, too? As good as gone, certainly. He might dole out enough to appease my sister's feeble appeals but never enough to provide me with resources. What little power I had to counter him came from holding Hartfield.

"What will you do?" Mr. Knightley asked.

"Go to Surrey and claim my home," I said. "Thank you for trying to spare my feelings. Please do not do that again. A woman alone cannot afford to be fragile." Mr. Knightley looked distressed, so I said, "I am not angry. Just... not again. Excuse me, I must speak with Georgiana."

She stood alone beside the black and brass of the telescope. I approached her. "I am sorry my departure upsets you."

"It is not you. Not really. It is... this disagreement on how to help Lizzy. And the news of soldiers dying. We say that so casually, but I know soldiers who died. They were all so noble and so young." She meshed her fingers, stretching the way keyboardists did, her gaze on the windows and the darkening north sky. The evening star had emerged. "I will stay here for a while. I wish to observe marvels that make our world's trials seem small." She knelt and released a bronze brake on the telescope's platform, then spun the handle on a complex clockwork. The telescope, slowly, lifted toward the sky.

I rejoined the gentlemen, but the three of them had moved on to bluff, masculine opinions about risks and routes.

Instead, I looked at the crawler pincer. It had repulsed everyone, a corruption of nature.

I drew off my glove and touched it. The surface was cool and smooth. It was inanimate, but before, it had lived. So I waited, stilling myself the way I had when touching Nessy to sense her disease.

A feeling formed. I expected to be overwhelmed by abomination, but instead of revulsion, I felt... pity. Like I had touched someone desperately ill who needed to be saved.

# 7

## DEPARTURE

### EMMA

The sun climbed above the hills, and I said my farewells outside Pemberley's tall front entrance.

A coach waited, not iron barred but solidly built of heavy oak. It looked almost nautical, with narrow windows and brass locks on the doors. I suppose iron bars were little use against Blackcoats with muskets.

Mr. Knightley was overseeing the loading. He had brought two mid-sized leather cases. I had two travel chests, a large carrying case, and two hatboxes, and that was after ruthless sorting. The rest would wait at Pemberley to be shipped later, or, if I found the amulet soon, I could collect it when I returned.

Mr. Darcy assessed our piled baggage with a careful eye, then went into the house and returned with a polished wooden box, narrow and long. He opened it to show Mr. Knightley a gun of burnished walnut and steel.

"A Baker rifle," Mr. Darcy said. "I do not hunt with it—I found it unsportingly accurate—but your circumstances are different." He pointed to a folded paper tucked by the powder horn and gleaming lead bullets. "Loading instructions. It is more involved than a musket. You have pistols?" Mr. Knightley nodded.

Mr. Darcy turned to me. His attire was always perfect, but there were signs of extra care this morning—an involved fold for his neck cloth, and coattails so crisp I suspected he had not sat on them once.

"You have been very kind," I said. For Mr. Darcy, that was sufficient. More would be maudlin.

He accepted that with a slight bow. "I owe you thanks as well. You brightened Pemberley through a dark time." He spoke with extreme seriousness, and I remembered when Lizzy fell and I pleaded with him to turn back from the lake's depths, both of us deep in the freezing water.

He assessed me, rather like how he examined our baggage, and I wondered if I would be offered a gun. Instead, he passed me a hand-sized notebook bound in mauve cloth—his mother's journal where she had noted her experiments in managing her condition.

I pressed it back into his hand. "That belongs with you. Besides, I have read it twice. If I wish to fall asleep, I shall ask Mr. Knightley to recite the dangers of Surrey. I have heard that twice, too."

"Take this, then," Mr. Darcy said. From the notebook, he removed a plaited red lanyard that marked the page. "This was significant to my mother. A symbol of her marriage and binding. Perhaps it will be a talisman."

Georgiana shooed him aside so she could embrace me. She whispered, "I will sing of you."

Mary simply studied me, her spectacles shining amid her hanging brown locks. She folded her arms and said, "Be careful."

Lucy curtsied. I laughed and pulled her in for a hug, then held her at a distance to admire her. "You are growing into a young lady. Will you come visit me in Surrey?"

That was a silly invitation amid a war, but Lucy only said, "Yes, madam. Once Mrs. Darcy can spare me."

"That will be wonderful," I said with a smile.

Nessy was brave, but her eyes filled, so I hugged her too. "We will see each other before long. Think of all your new friends at school."

She stuck out her bottom lip. "They do not have magic."

Then it was goodbye to the servants and staff, and questions about what box could be balanced atop what other. The driver and footman climbed to their seats, and Mr. Knightley presented his hand by the open door. "Miss Woodhouse."

When I departed Hartfield for London, the darkness inside the coach had frozen me until Harriet gently helped me forward.

Now, I placed my gloved fingers in Mr. Knightley's and stepped easily into the carriage, beginning our three-day, two-hundred-mile trek to find the amulet and win back my life.

FIFTY FEET DOWN THE ROAD, Mr. Knightley asked, "May we make a stop? A family we helped escape Sussex is near Lambton. I would like to look in before leaving."

I agreed, of course, so we passed through Lambton and followed a road into the uncleared forest that covered much of Pemberley's land. We arrived at a wattle-and-daub house, the house a little ill kept, the garden a disaster. A man was inexpertly mowing the overgrown weeds with a scythe, his hat, coat, and waistcoat removed.

Mr. Knightley greeted him, then introduced us while his young daughter watched solemnly a few steps behind.

"I'm sorry to be in such a state," the man said, wiping a handkerchief over his sweaty brow. He was brown skinned, like many who had fled the south. "Carpentry's my trade." He put his hands on his hips, breathing hard and surveying the half-cut weeds. "I am developing a healthy respect for farmers, I can tell you that."

"Are you going to sow it?" I asked. In places, the mown weeds were six inches tall. They would grow back in a week. "You will need to plow it, too."

"I just thought to tidy it. Not right to have a house look shaggy. We'll be gone afore it matters much."

Mr. Knightley waved gallantly to the expanse of Pemberley. "Mr. Darcy was able to provide several unused homes. We placed four families that escaped the south. I have written letters to businesses in Sheffield inquiring about employment for the men."

"You just scattered families through Pemberley?" I exclaimed. Mr. Knightley nodded, suddenly wary. Rightfully so. "Well, that is no good. What if they are here for a time? We must get them settled." I smiled at the daughter, who was listening with an overly mature, intent focus. "Have you attended the school yet?"

Caught off guard, she bobbed a crooked curtsy. "No, ma'am."

"It is just in Lambton. You can walk there easily. My friend Nessy attends, and she is about your age. She adores her lessons." Well, she adored her friends at least, even if she was pleased when a class was unexpectedly canceled.

"Tell Momma about it," the girl said. She took my hand and led me toward the side of the house.

I glimpsed the men's surprised reactions. Her father half-reached to stop his daughter, and concern creased Mr. Knightley's face. Was the mother ill? Old fears slipped into my thoughts, scratching away at my careful exercises and practice. I clenched my free hand to suppress a reflexive check of my collar.

The corner of the house was a few quick steps. We rounded it and startled a thin woman with braided hair. She seemed to have been hiding. She gasped, "Madam," and curtsied amid the knee-high ragwort, bowing her head.

"Please do not," I protested. "I am only another guest of Pemberley. I was telling your daughter about the school..."

She straightened, and I saw the burn on her face. It was recent and partly healed, a pink streak as if a hot poker had been laid on her temple and eyebrow. She saw me notice—I was too slow to shift my gaze—and her hand covered it with an awkward, over-practiced gesture.

Her husband rushed past me and wrapped an arm around her waist, half hiding her against his side.

"Did that happen in the south?" I asked, as simply as I could. It would be worse to pretend I had not seen.

"The slavers had us for a time," the husband said, his voice shaking with anger. That smoothed as he told his wife tenderly, "You are as beautiful as ever."

The child piped up, "It's true, Momma."

The woman was handsome, with huge dark eyes and a sculpted face, although too thin. Food must have been scarce during their flight.

An impulse took me, and I removed my glove and offered my hand. After a moment, she stepped away from her husband and took it, her touch long-fingered and smooth.

Her injury seared my awareness, an echo of the original hurt, worse because it had been violent. That faded, muted by her partial healing. My sense of her health deepened, and I saw how the shiny skin would smooth and darken in the months ahead.

"Burns are slow to heal," I said, "but it is not deep. I am sure it will fade. Your family is right. It does not diminish your beauty." I smiled. Hesitantly, she smiled back. "These hills have good people. Do not hide yourself. They will welcome you."

Through our touch, another sensation grew. Her husband, watching anxiously, filled her with warmth. Their love was a shining thing, and from the forest around us, I felt an answering stir, the tawny brown attention of an intrigued observer.

"Have you seen draca in these woods?" I asked.

"Yes, ma'am," she said, brightening. "A handsome broccworm comes and goes. A proud thing."

That was the draca I sensed, unbound, his binding latent and loose. I imagined his binding reaching to this woman and then, almost like I had tugged it, the end stretched to graze her shining love.

I leaned close and whispered in her ear, "Hold your husband close tonight, and see what happens in the morning."

We departed. As we passed back through Lambton, I had the driver stop so I could speak with the mother of another girl who attended the school. When I climbed back in, I told Mr. Knightley, "She will visit them and explain about the school."

"That is kind of them," he said. He crossed his arms thoughtfully. "And of you."

"They left so much behind. Letters to businesses are well and good, but they lost their home. I do not see why they cannot stay in Pemberley. Carpenters are always needed." I watched the few streets of Lambton pass. "They would be better here than in a big city like Sheffield. Here, everyone is a friend. Appearances are forgotten. A city is filled with strangers. You cannot imagine what it is like for a woman to be harmed that way. We are so judged by our faces." Mr. Knightley did not answer, his complexion as brown as the oak panels, and I realized I had blundered. "Of course, you do know what that is like."

"I understood your point." He watched me with peculiar attention. I wondered if I would get another lecture about projects. Instead, he asked, "Did you try to heal her?"

I looked at the trees passing the window. "Mr. Darcy is wrong about me and healing. I have the most useless gift. I feel what is wrong with people, but I cannot help. It was Lady Anne's gift that healed Nessy. I have no skill like that."

"That must frustrate you."

"If I could imagine doing it, or even how it would happen, I would be frustrated. But I cannot. It feels as unimaginable to me as it would be to you. It is not frustrating. Just... disheartening."

A little sad, I looked through the things I had brought to pass the time of our travel. The red lanyard from Lady Anne's journal was loose in my reticule, so I tied it to the drawstring so it would not be lost.

"That couple will bind, though," I said. "To the handsome broccworm. She will like that."

## 8

# ÆFENSANG

## MARY

From somewhere in the crowded village square, I heard Lucy's cheerful call. "Come see, Miss Bennet!"

At breakfast, Pemberley House had been abuzz for Beltane eve, but the true celebrations were in the hills, so for an afternoon walk I set out to one of the larger Briton villages. It was even busier than Pemberley: vegetables stacked for paring, meats set to roast, and ladies and children preparing decorations, which was where I spotted Lucy waving.

"I am making a Green Woman," Lucy said as I sat beside her. The table was covered with flowers and twigs. Lucy folded a scrap of linen to protect her fingers, then tucked tufts of spikey holly into a vaguely feminine, hawthorn-branch form. "The Green Woman listens to our wishes—especially at Beltane! —so she will tell Mrs. Darcy that we are thinking of her."

Satisfied with the holly, she wrapped a piece of ribbon around a few twigs, avoiding the thorns, wicked things an inch long. She tugged it tight, pricked her knuckle, and muttered a curse as raw as any urchin in a London gutter. Her guilty gaze sprang to me.

"I attend women in childbirth," I told her. "They would shock a Navy quartermaster."

Lucy nodded seriously. She was fourteen, or a year more, her woman's figure filling in. Girls her age hung on any scrap of knowledge about marriage, love, and childbirth, and she had no mother to give her an organized explanation. Perhaps we should take a stroll and talk.

I asked, "How will the Green Woman know it is for my sister?"

"She will know," Lucy said. "Mrs. Darcy likes pretty things. I weave in woodbine, which is what they call honeysuckle here, and I add cowslip, because Eostre likes yellow—that is why egg yolks are yellow—but Mrs. Darcy has a dragon, so mostly it will be *this*."

She held up a stalk of draca breath, the row of blooms blue and mauve, deep-belled and fragrant. Stewed for hours, this became draca essence, the treatment for crawler venom.

I touched a petal. "I thought the blooms were difficult to gather?"

Lucy rolled her eyes and pulled up her sleeve to show a row of scabbed pricks. "Needledrac scratches. Watch, you'll see. The needledrac find the flowers, even after they're cut. I got scratched when I helped gather for the next batch of essence. But we had more flowers than we could boil down, so I took the extra."

Mr. Digweed, the headman for Pemberley's Britons, strolled to us, a lad at his side. The boy was fit and tan, about fifteen, old enough to wear a gentleman's coat and trousers. I invited them to sit, and Mr. Digweed introduced his son Thomas.

Thomas bowed to me politely, then his eyes sank to his toes while he murmured, "Good afternoon, Lucy." Lucy mouthed a wordless "Good afternoon," color rising in her cheeks.

Mr. Digweed settled on the opposite bench and smoothed his formidable mustache. "Will you attend the celebration this eve?"

He was a straightforward person, so I answered honestly. "Georgiana has tried to persuade me, but I do not enjoy dances."

"It is a day of feast and community. We would be honored if you joined. Dancing is not required." He swept his arm toward the festive clearing. "Beltane has many names around the world, but in all of them, it celebrates the nurturing Earth rounding her celestial path and lifting her face to the sun. It is a blessing for love and fecundity." His gaze found the golden musical note necklace I wore, a twin to Georgiana's. "Beltane eve is a time of commitment. Our ways are not restricted by the Church. We have had pairs of women or men handfast."

"You and Miss Darcy could handfast," Lucy suggested, as if that were a perfectly normal thing to say. Lizzy's lady's maid was growing into a proper pagan at Pemberley. It was a touching suggestion, though. Lizzy had handfasted Mr. Darcy, so in Lucy's opinion, the ceremony was perfection.

Did Georgiana wish to handfast? I felt our commitment was sealed by our performance for the prince, but she grew up among the Britons' culture. Might she be hesitant to ask? I sought a hint from memory, and a flood of recalled glances and spoken asides filled me, the emotions from those moments a torrent. How could I be so in love, so committed and trusting, yet still be tossed asea by such a question?

I listened to the pound of my heart and found the sensation joyful. But I could not resolve this when Georgiana was miles away. Could I hint when I next saw her?

"Are *you* going to dance?" I asked Lucy.

She blushed scarlet and bent her nose to her project, stuffing in draca breath at a prodigious rate. "If... if someone asks me."

Matching color climbed the lad's cheeks. It appeared that young romance beckoned. I should take Lucy for that walk soon.

An insect buzzed to the table, hovered, then darted lightning-swift among the piled draca breath blooms.

"Needledrac," Lucy announced. She held her hands well away while it explored the flowers on her project. Then it rose to hover a few inches in front of my spectacles, so near my eyes crossed and I felt the wind of its blurred wings.

We inspected each other. Its dragonfly-like body was nacreous lapis and jade, two-legged, not an insect at all. After several seconds, it flew away.

Mr. Digweed straightened the flowers. "After your letter about the attacks in London, we boiled a large batch of essence. Very large. Every cook pot was overflowing. The hospitals should have their shipment by now." I nodded my thanks, and he continued, "The rise of crawlers is not only in London. We have not had attacks here, but crawlers have been sighted more often, and they are larger. You know that Miss Darcy has seen visions of a blight. Could it be a blight of crawlers?"

"Her visions are difficult to interpret." The blight reminded me of *la Demoiselle des Parfums*. She had crawlers, and after we met, a patch of spring growth had putrefied to black ooze.

Mr. Digweed's wizened gaze studied me. He lifted a finger in front of his eyes, mimicking the hovering needledrac. "You have your sister's blood, Miss

Bennet. Draca attend you. Your paramour is a great wyfe, but you have your own strength. I have known Miss Darcy since she was born. She is dear as a daughter to me, and unimaginably gifted. Her strength flows with the ease of her song. You, I think, are her complement. If she is melody, you are form. Structure and analysis. And, a Bennet."

Ironically, I found I was analyzing his words. My compositions were founded in form, but I did not think of that as a complement to melody. Rather, form embraced melody.

Music aside, Bennets were certainly popular. Both the French court and Pemberley's Britons were aficionados. I would be flattered if it had implied more than admiration for my famous sisters.

Lucy had finished adding flowers. Gingerly, she stood her Green Woman upright. The figure was exuberant with spring blossoms, although the juxtaposition of delicate petals and spikes was odd.

"I want to take it to Mrs. Darcy," Lucy said. "To her memorial."

"I will go with you," I said as Thomas burst out, "May I accompany you?" Lucy looked back and forth, flummoxed by the pair of offers.

Mr. Digweed said, "Perhaps Miss Bennet would accompany you both."

IT WAS AN EASY DOWNHILL WALK, about half an hour. Lucy and Thomas were clearly good friends, talking happily on a dozen topics, but occasionally falling into shy silences. When the three of us emerged from the forest shadow onto the stony shore of the lake, the weather hinted at summer. Hazy clouds scuttled across the blue, and the lake breeze was warmed by the late afternoon sun. The barge was moored half ashore, temporarily abandoned while Georgiana and her brother argued about it.

Lizzy's memorial, or shrine, had grown. The Britons removed the wilted bouquets and old offerings of food, but they left the icons of the Green Woman. Their piled forms now spread six feet wide at the base and rose past the waist of Lizzy's statue. The tangle of their brown branches was mixed with green-and-red holly, colorful even when dry. Some figures had vibrant paper skirts and bonnets, or ribbons.

An incongruous image clicked into my mind: a woodcut of Jeanne d'Arc atop a pyre awaiting her burning for witchcraft. But Lizzy, even carved, looked joyfully alive, the opposite of the insipid skyward longing that artists inflicted on martyred saints.

Lucy nestled her creation atop the heap beside other recent additions. A flint and several candles had been left near the base. She knelt and kindled tinder, then lit one of the candles, shielded inside a glass jar.

She rejoined Thomas and me, and he said, "You made a nice one."

"Thank you," Lucy said. She took a formal breath and addressed the statue. "Mrs. Darcy, if you would like to come back, I have a fresh dress all laid out, just as you like. I even sorted your bowl of bolts, though I have not learned to make one myself. I will, I promise."

That was so heartfelt, it should have filled me with loss, but Lizzy's lifelike image and the sparkling lake banished that. Instead, I felt a surge of sisterly closeness. A surety that my doubts about her welfare were foolish.

"Men are here," Thomas said, looking behind us.

Three men were strolling toward us from the trees, peering at us and at Lizzy's shrine. They were dusty from the knees down, travelers on foot. Despite an odd uniformity to their clothes, they were not well-dressed; their coats were stained, unbuttoned and flapping. They carried nothing, except the leading man held something wrapped in his palm.

Although they were all carefully shaven, their hair was raggedly cropped. Their coats were black with wide, hanging leather belts.

Blackcoats. My first reaction was frustration that their evil had reached this far north. Then came alarm.

The men spread out, a few feet between each. Our London protests had taught me about thugs and bullies. Shouting men who bunched together were nuisances. Men who quietly spaced themselves were dangerous.

Lucy and Thomas had never seen a Blackcoat. Their expressions were wary but polite.

"You are not welcome here," I told the leader. "These lands are patrolled. You would be wise to leave."

Lucy's polite smile vanished. Thomas took a half-step in front of her.

"That was rude," the man said. He waved his clenched fist toward Lizzy's shrine, and I saw a glimmer of metal—he held a short chunk of thick brass rod. "What's the statue, then? That you?"

"The statue is no business of yours," I said. "I am not being rude. I am warning you. Briton tribes control these hills, and they will know your dress.

But if you turn around and follow the road out of Pemberley, they will let you pass."

One could not travel through Derbyshire without hearing the name "Pemberley." The two men behind exchanged an uneasy glance.

The leader scoffed. "Big names mean big money." He gave Lucy a false smile. "How about you, sweet thing? Who's this fancy lady?"

He reached for her with his free hand. Thomas batted down the outstretched fingers, but the man's other fist was already swinging in a vicious, brass-weighted arc. It struck Thomas's temple, knocking his head a quarter turn. He fell bonelessly on the rocky shore.

Lucy screamed a piercing, young cry, her hands at her mouth.

I started to go to him, but a pair of arms caught me from behind, wrapping my waist and my chest, yanking me off my feet. The memory of another violent day flashed through my mind's eye: Lizzy summoning the Longbourn firedrake to save us from a mad dog. I tried to whistle the summoning tones, even though a tiny song draca was no lethal drake, but the grubby hand on my chest shifted to grab my mouth and cheeks, stifling sound. Blocking my nose. Blocking my breath. Panicked, I clawed until I was thrown to the ground. A boot landed between my shoulder blades, driving me prone, my cheek jamming into the pebbles, trapped but finally able to draw a sliver of air.

Lucy had dodged behind the shrine, but the other men chased her and dragged her back crying. They pushed her down beside me.

Thomas lay a few yards away, his face toward me. Pages of medical reference burst into my mind. Pterional fracture. Occipital fracture or rupture. But there was no bleeding from his nose or ear. His chest rose and fell. Concussed, hopefully no worse.

The leader shouted, "You're a pair of troublemakers. The Code says we don't got to take that. Fancy girls is good for one thing—"

He recited a man's usual threats, nothing I had not heard a dozen times at protests, but exposing Lucy to that vileness turned my shock to anger. Then, a fear rose: What if I had a role to play in rescuing Lizzy, but I died here first?

I strained for thin breaths. Lizzy's statue watched, the powerful sister, impassive in stone. Whistling for birds felt childish, and it was impossible anyway, my lips distorted by rocks. As my head spun with anoxia, I stretched my arm to my sister and dreamed I sang my summoning song, but not alone. An unseen chorus joined me in unfathomably complex harmony.

Reality replaced that fantasy. Behind the statue, a stream of hot smoke streaked upward. Flames began to lick. When Lucy ran behind the shrine, she pushed her candle into that mass. She acted while I did nothing, but now I could help. I forced out a shout, drawing threats but keeping the men's attention.

The dry leaves caught like paper. Twigs flared and crackled. Lucy's Green Woman filled with fire, the draca breath thumping into flame as if oil-soaked, the thorns orange-silhouetted knives. The whole pile roared up, and the men howled in alarm. It would be a short-lived bonfire—parts were already caving into ash—but the flames crowned Lizzy's head and higher, a metaphorical pyre turned literal, staining her granite figure sooty black.

Huge clouds of smoke billowed. We were in the center of Pemberley, in plain view of the distant house, and this was a blazing beacon. Two of the men stomped frantically on the fire's fringe. The leader shouted ill-thought orders, his bootheel jarring my spine with each utterance.

A wave surged up the stony beach, swishing frigid lake water past my nose. I snorted and coughed. Steam boiled from the base of the fire. The water trickled away like freezing fingers on the front of my dress.

A large splash sounded. The man's boot lifted. He cursed. My lungs filled properly, and I raised my head.

A gigantic fish, ten feet long, was thrashing itself ashore, its mouth gasping in the air, its body distended and thick as a barrel. The tail flapped madly, flinging the whole length aloft to slap the stones, beaching itself in flailing froth. When two thirds were ashore, it stilled, fins trembling and gills gaping, the flesh scaleless and translucent as a tadpole.

"What the devil," the leader said. I levered myself up. Lucy stared, her mouth open, interrupted mid-sob.

The fish shuddered. A black spike jabbed out the belly. It ripped toward the head, rasping like tearing cloth and gutting the fish from within. Organs spilled out, and a noxious, briny odor spread, redolent of cloves and heated copper. A bleached white foot appeared, then a woman's naked figure was expelled in a rush of viscous liquid. The fish collapsed like an emptied chrysalis.

The woman curled fetus-like and coughed a vomitous spray. Her shoulders, paper-white where they were not buried by her mass of soaked, dark hair, convulsed as she bent in two, choking. Finally, she subsided to hoarse gasps. She pushed erect and took a swaying step from the shallows.

I scrambled to my feet. My rational mind shouted it was Lizzy, but my heart did not recognize my sister. The pallor of her skin was not so strange; some newborns were that pale. But her hair had grown impossibly, a foot longer, or two feet, a wild, drenched cascade that tangled front and back, sticking in dark ringlets that reached her hips. Her body had shed fat like a starved beggar, thinning her breasts, but her limbs were wrapped in feminine muscle, the hard-won strength of a charwoman or washerwoman who hauled and scrubbed fourteen hours a day, or the strength they would have if they dined at the rich table of their lords.

From the slack fingers of her right hand, the black dagger Gramr dangled, dripping, the serrations on its blade gleaming. Before, she had not been able to touch the dagger. It had overwhelmed her with visions and violence.

One of the Blackcoats whispered a prayer. Their leader seemed stupefied. Unsteadily, I walked around him. I intended to embrace my sister, but my nerve failed at the last, undermined by her pose. Lizzy could not have stood casually, naked among strange men.

Her head was lowered, her eyes veiled by a curtain of curls coated with syrupy beads. She was still short, at least.

"Lizzy," I said.

She dragged her wet hair aside with her left hand. I saw my sister's dark eyes, and at last my heart believed. I hugged her tight. She was warm despite rising from the cold lake. She did not resist my touch, but there was no reciprocation. No recognition. I stepped back, and her gaze met mine, unperturbed, distant, and foreign.

When I last saw her, her eyesight had entered the final deterioration of her illness. Her pupils had been unresponsive, her tracking unsteady. Those symptoms were gone. I lifted my hands to palpate the sides of her neck. Her lymph, which had been a mass of hard tubercles, was soft and healthy.

Miraculous as that was, it seemed proper. Her body radiated preternatural health. A self-satisfied voice within me thought: See? There was no need to wait.

She had one blemish: a jagged blush on her cheek, like a birthmark. I brushed my thumb over it. The skin was as soft and smooth as a child's.

Gently, she moved my hand away.

"Lizzy." I tasted tears on that word. "I am Mary. Your sister."

"I heard you call," she said absently. The first syllables were a croak; her voice was harsh from disuse. More clearly, she resumed, "I have many sisters." Her tone implied far more than our family's quite respectable count of five.

Her gaze left me, ticked once on each staring man, once more on Thomas sprawled on the ground, then ended on Lucy, crouched holding Thomas's hand, her cheeks wet. It was a tableau of violence and threat. One by one, her slack fingers wrapped the dagger in a firm grip.

"Mrs. Darcy?" Lucy said uncertainly.

"Who?" This time, her voice was an uncertain whisper.

The leader of the Blackcoats broke from his stupor. He shook himself, frowned at his frightened friends, then spat and blustered forward, shoving me aside to gawk at Lizzy. "Fish got your clothes?" He barked a false guffaw. "Guess I'll call you Jonah."

Despite his foulness, I shouted a warning, "Do not touch her!" but he grabbed a handful of her sopping hair, lifting it to expose a slim breast.

She drove the dagger into the underside of his jaw, so hard it sank to the hilt, a blow that pierced tongue, shattered hard palate, and sliced brain. His limbs locked in seizure. She pulled the dagger loose, and he fell at her feet.

Horror knocked me back a step. It doubled when she gave the dagger a nonchalant flick, spraying red drops that left the impermeable black blade pristine.

Her gaze turned to the other two men.

"Sweet Mother of God," one of them whispered. He backed a step, then they both broke and ran down the shore.

Lizzy watched them go, then raised her empty hand high, a fist in the sky. Unseen power hammered my senses, squeezing my lungs and purging my breath. For the first time, I sensed what Georgiana and Emma had described: the incredible command of the wyfe of war.

The ground stirred fitfully, trembled, then slammed sideways. I staggered. The forests swayed. Tumbling rocks fell down the slopes, spinning trails of gray dust.

The water's edge shrank like an undersea god drew breath. A rumble climbed my ankles and spine, blurring my vision. For a pent moment it stilled, then the lake's center surged and exploded as a huge, winged form broke free. Yuánchi, the scarlet dragon, had risen. His wings snapped wide, launching water that lit a rainbow, and he twirled in a joyous climbing spiral before soaring in an effortless glide toward Lizzy.

His landing was an awkward mess. One clawed foot smacked the ground too soon. He half spun, hopping and flapping to regain his balance.

His scarlet hide had transformed. He was unlike any draca I had seen, mottled in wide streaks, half his old color, half ebony black. As black as the blade of Gramr. As black as the black dragon, Fènnù, fated steed of the wyfe of war. His wings were healed—the rips mended, the broken bones sound—but when he bent his head to Lizzy, his muzzle hunted aimlessly. The horrible wounds on his face had closed, but his glorious eyes had not regrown. There were depressions where they had been, covered with weeping black scales, and my vindication from seeing Lizzy's health slunk away.

Lizzy caressed his muzzle. "I am sorry."

With an airy whoosh, a cream-colored firedrake flashed past me. She flew a wide oval around Yuánchi, then landed at Lizzy's feet. A second, matched female landed beside her. The two draca examined each other, their necks craning with curiosity.

Lizzy stroked each drake's chisel head and swan neck. "Be his eyes," she said, and the firedrakes flew off in the direction the two Blackcoats had run.

She walked toward Yuánchi's shoulder.

"Lizzy!" I cried. "You cannot *leave*."

She looked back. "Why did you wake me, if not for this?"

Of my hundred churning thoughts, I said the most childish. "You do not hurt people."

Lizzy laughed—her old, delighted laughter, as if I had made a clever joke.

I ran to her. "Will you not come to Pemberley? To... to see everyone. To *dress*." When she shook her head, social rules latched hold of me, and I said firmly, "You cannot leave unclothed." Thomas had recovered enough to groan and touch his head, so I called to Lucy, "Can you help me?"

Lucy settled Thomas, then crept over and undid the back fastenings of my dress. I pulled it over my head, leaving me in petticoats, and dropped the wet cloth on Lizzy. She stood patiently while Lucy, falling into routine, fastened the dress. It hung a little loose and far too long. The black, an especially dark dye I preferred, was stark against her ivory skin. She pulled her mass of hair free of the collar and let it slap down the back, soaking the cloth darker still.

"It must be hemmed," Lucy said in a tremulous voice. "You will trip, otherwise." Wordlessly, Lizzy reversed the dagger and held it out. Lucy swallowed, took it, and cut six inches off the bottom, the blade slicing soundlessly. She returned it, having held an artifact coveted by Napoleon himself, and hurried back to Thomas.

The sound of galloping hooves was nearing. Horses burst from a hunting trail. Mr. Darcy led several Briton men, all armed with sword or gun. Relief filled me, then apprehension; Lizzy was so changed.

Mr. Darcy reined to a hard stop and leaped down. He swayed and grabbed the saddle with whitened fingers. His other hand reached out as if to touch a phantasm. "Love."

"What?" Lizzy said uneasily.

I actually laughed. It was the first time she had sounded like herself.

Mr. Darcy stepped forward. Lizzy stepped back. She raised the dagger, vertical like a fencer's salute—a barrier, not a threat.

"I am your husband," he said.

She eyed him. "Do you greet everyone with 'Love' and 'I am your husband'?"

He gave an amazed smile. "Only you."

"I can have no husband." Her lips compressed. "Certainly not one so prettily dressed."

His features furrowed, then twisted, then ended in an odd, disbelieving grin. "You have one, like it or not."

"I do not," Lizzy said. His grin vanished as she walked to Yuánchi. The dragon crouched, pressing his neck and wing to the earth. She stepped onto the knurl of his wing joint, walked easily up the heavy leading bone to his shoulder, then leaped to straddle the base of his neck. The dragon stood, lifting her a dozen feet over our heads.

"Elizabeth!" Mr. Darcy shouted as the great wings spanned the sky, then booming gusts scoured us with blinding sand and spray.

When I lowered my arm from my eyes, the dragon was passing the far end of the lake. The two cream-colored firedrakes circled a point in the forest, about as far as the two men could have run. Yuánchi reached them, a brilliant golden spark kindled, and I looked away as blinding radiance from his fire saturated the valley, dazzling my eyes and heating my skin. A second later, thunder slammed. It echoed round the lake, roaring and grumbling. That swath of forest was a raging, sun-bright inferno.

Yuánchi rose again, Lizzy visible on his back as they swung eastward. I could see the cream-colored Vs of the firedrakes' wings, flying ahead, one on each side.

Mr. Darcy was gripping his stamping horse's bridle in one hand while he stroked the animal with the other, softly talking it down. When it settled, blowing uneasily, he mounted. He watched Yuánchi vanish over the hilltops, then turned his horse left and right, studying the shores of the lake. Choosing a path.

"You cannot chase a dragon on horseback!" I cried.

"I assure you I can," he replied.

"Lizzy is not herself. She killed three men!"

"She did not kill me." His smile was terrible and joyous. "My wyfe is alive, Mary. Care for my sister. Care for Pemberley."

He galloped away.

# 9

# FITZWILLIAM DARCY

## DARCY

Four days ago, Elizabeth rose. When her gaze met mine, it rocked both our souls. Whatever denials she uttered afterward, whatever foolishness a listening stranger might conclude, I had seen the truth. My wyfe knew me.

I twitched the reins, guiding Escalus onto a cart path that led to a farmhouse. His gray head wandered longingly as we passed a shady patch of grass. Four days of travel, even carefully paced, had tired him.

Riding in pursuit had been impulsive, but travel imposed discipline. The outline of a plan had formed as I rounded the lake, and the long miles since had honed it like the relentless questioning of a Socratic tutor.

Hunting a woman on a dragon was futile. Instead, I hunted for bait.

The long miles had led here, the southern tip of Derbyshire. The local farmland was divided in twenty-acre parcels abutting a long, wild forest. Each parcel was planted with a single crop: wheat, oats, peas. Commercial production, not subsistence, and chosen for the wartime market.

Not perfectly chosen, though. I would have rotated those crops with clover and turnips. Wars start with a blow, but they last for years. Forage and fallow would matter. Still, this was clearly a managed estate... although the gentleman's name escaped me. I blinked to steady my own wandering thoughts. I was tired, too.

I dismounted outside the farmhouse and stretched, spine grating, hamstrings unlocking with pinprick stabs. I dropped Escalus's reins a few paces from a stone-rimmed well and signed *Halt*. That earned me a butt on the shoulder. I stroked his muzzle and whispered, "Patience." His ears flicked.

The farmer emerged from the house, a stocky, half-bald fellow, arms crossed but in thought, not defiance.

I acknowledged him. "How do you do?"

"You tell me, sir." He unfolded his arms and rubbed dusty, muscled hands against his coarse wool trousers. "Good enough, I should think."

My appearance was little better than his. At dawn, I had rinsed my clothes in a brook and hung them to dry. That left them marginally fresher but, even after half an hour, damp. They dried while I rode, but they were comically wrinkled. That should not matter, but a lifetime of perfect dress was hard to dismiss. At Pemberley, I would have told my valet to throw them in the nearest fire.

Still, they were a gentleman's attire, and the farmer bowed.

I nodded. "I wonder if I could water my horse?" Escalus edged one hoof longingly toward the well.

The farmer shrugged. "Surely."

I drew a pail. Escalus gulped noisily, and I began unhitching his saddle.

The farmer strolled over. "Fine mount you got there. Big, to be sure. Eighteen hands?"

"Yes."

"He's a little over run."

"We have had a long road."

I draped the saddle over the fence. The farmer's gaze noted the pistol and sword. He studied me, a sturdy finger rubbing his chin, neither afraid nor dismissive. A sensible man. Sensibly cautious.

"Have you any oats?" I asked. Oats were the best feed for energy. He returned with a ten-pound sack, and I gave him two shillings, a fair price with pence to spare. That earned a pleased grunt. Did he not expect a gentleman to pay his debts?

I poured a third of the bag onto a patch of grass. Escalus dug in, and I began rubbing his back with the small towel that had wrapped the hoof pick and game snares. I wished I had a curry comb.

Impulsive trips are poorly equipped. On the second day, I bought a blanket and razor from a passing trader, but my quarry was too elusive to risk detours for proper supplies.

"Good to see a gentleman who cares for his horse," the farmer observed.

"He has carried me for five years. It seems fair."

"I'll do his withers," he offered. I passed him the towel, and he rubbed them down, leaning to massage the muscle. Escalus cast him a curious glance, then relaxed, bobbing his head in approval.

"You know horses," I said, working my shoulders and looking over the farm. Any distraction was welcome to quell the tension of being stopped and far behind Elizabeth.

The field was tall with pea plants, but their color looked off.

"My father was a groom." The farmer passed the towel back and patted Escalus's shoulder. "He's in fine condition."

I wiped down Escalus's flanks, then draped the sweaty towel beside the saddle. "Have you heard reports of Blackcoats?"

"Those raiders, you mean? Troublemakers, to be sure." He pointed to the forest. "Rumor is they're heading south. What's left of them. If you follow the road a few more miles, you'll hear fresher stories than mine."

"What do you mean, what's left?"

"The angel caught two of their crews already. The rest are hiding." His laugh cracked the air. "Folks say angel, but you tell me. Forest burned away to rock, smooth as glass. Always at night, and there's nary a tooth nor a buckle left behind. I figure it's devil, not angel. Not that those raiders don't have it coming." He grinned, enjoying his story, not knowing I had heard a half-dozen variants already. "You tell me. The devil barters for souls, then sends his she-devil to claim them. She drags them down. Hellfire spills up." His grin widened. "I saw it."

Hope replaced fatigue, but with a bitter edge. Every day in the saddle, I relived the idiotic words I spoke to Elizabeth by the lake. Why had I not listened and tried to comprehend the miracle I was witnessing?

My shoulders had tensed. I forced them loose and level. I had chased stories of the angel into Notts and back but never heard a firsthand account.

"You *saw* the angel?" I asked gruffly.

"Nah. Saw the hellfire. Three nights ago. Far away, past those hills, which was fine with me. Clouds lit up like gold fire. Night sky black as soot above them. Strangest thing."

Three nights. But this was the closest I had come. "Are the remaining Black-coats in that direction?"

He drummed his fingers on his trousers. "You tell me. But if you're asking advice, I'd go the other way. The worst of them is what's left. One man can't challenge twenty. That sword'll be no help. Men like that, they'll shoot you at fifty yards for your hat."

The house door opened, and the man's wife came out. The rigor of etiquette was a relief. I bowed. "Madam." The farmer gave a bemused snort.

She was staring in disbelief. "Lawks! You's *him*." She elbowed her husband. "That's *Mr. Darcy*."

The farmer winked at me. "The Darcys are far from here, woman."

"I am Mr. Darcy," I confirmed.

The wife clapped her hands. She then giggled in a very unbecoming manner. That happened when some women were introduced. I never under-stood why.

Her husband boggled. "Damn it! Deuce it, I mean..." He flopped into a bow. "My Lord."

"I am not a lord," I said. My eyes had a will of their own, drifting to the distant forest he had mentioned. "You have been a gracious host. Thank you."

The wife caught her husband's sleeve. "Did you show him?"

The farmer rubbed his chin, avoiding my eyes. No, his gaze was on the wilting peas. "That's not his business."

"That's *Mr. Darcy*. He might know."

Three nights. I could spare a minute. "Show me what?"

THE PEA PLANTS were tall and scraggly, the leaves yellow-edged and curling. The farmer plucked a pod, bright green and grossly huge, five inches long and thick as my thumb. It was lumpy, as if stuffed with rocks instead of an orderly row of fresh peas.

"Best open it like this," the farmer said. He dropped it on the ground, then prodded it with the toe of his boot until it split. "You tell me."

Sticky black bile leaked, and a long, fat, white grub squirmed free. Sulfurous rot stung my nostrils. The grub writhed, lethargically hunting an escape from the sun.

I squatted to look. Where the black bile rubbed off, the grub's skin was translucent. Shadows of many paired legs were visible. There were folded pincers at one end and stingers at the rear.

"A foul crawler," I said.

The farmer swore. "Here I feared they were grasshoppers." His wife blanched, her freckles dark on pale cheeks.

Georgiana had seen visions of a blight. I had thought it a metaphor for war and conflict. Not so... tangible.

"Send a messenger to Mr. Campbell," I said—*that* was the landowner's name. "Tell him I was here, and that I ordered the field burned."

"Burned!" the farmer cried.

"Do you want them to hatch?" He shook his head, horror-struck at the rows of swollen pods. I added, "They do not yet seem able to sting. Summon your neighbors. Cut the plants, stack them with straw, and burn them. *Today.*"

"They're not mine to burn!"

"I will pay for Mr. Campbell's loss. And yours, if he does not compensate you. If you have paper and pen, I will provide a letter."

I would write to my attorney. No, to Mary Bennet. She would muster Pemberley and tell Georgiana.

"Could you not speak with Mr. Campbell yourself?" his wife asked in a shaken voice.

"I cannot." I crushed the grub under my heel. The skin split, the back splaying oddly. "I have tarried too long already. Fetch paper, then point me to the Blackcoats."

# 10

# TOLERABLE

## DARCY

I crawled belly-down, hidden by ferns and brush, my coat buttons snagging the forest loam.

The Blackcoat camp was forty yards ahead. I had approached from downwind, an unnecessary precaution as they had neither dogs nor horses. Even if they had, my scent would have been overwhelmed by their cookfires and general reek. Animal offal and human waste had been dumped and left to rot.

Ten men, poorly shaven and presented, wandered in flapping black coats. There were two large tents, probably stolen from some festival as the canvas was striped lemon yellow. Those might hold more. And if the camp was more competent at raiding than hygiene, there would be sentries out of sight.

My heart sped in my chest. Coming so close was dangerous but exhilarating. I had found my bait. Elizabeth would find them, too.

Only one thing nagged at me. Why had she not found them already? The first two nights after her return, bands of Blackcoats were ruthlessly eliminated. Then the attacks stopped, leaving only vague rumors of "the angel." If I had found these men ahorse, how did she fail on dragonback?

Perhaps she was gone, flown away. She might be unthinkably remote. France. Ireland.

A tent flapped open, and a woman emerged. I tensed, but she was the antithesis of Elizabeth—blonde, slovenly, and hunched, as unkempt as the rest. She stared at the dirt while a man spoke to her.

I squirmed backward, collecting scratchy dead leaves in my collar, until I was screened by the underbrush. Then I walked a third of a mile through forest to where Escalus waited, tied in a clearing and grazing on lush spring growth.

I buckled my sword and pistol to the saddle and untied his reins from the tree branch. Then I watched his teeth methodically crop grass. My hands bunched the leather reins until they creaked.

What now? Follow the Blackcoats. Assume that, when Elizabeth came, she would see me. Would speak to me.

That plan, which for days seemed sensible, felt like a fool's errand.

Irritated, I turned to mount. The buckle where I hung my sword was empty.

I whirled, expecting a lunging Blackcoat.

Elizabeth stood four paces away, examining my sheathed sword. She still wore Mary's striking black gown, a finely finished garment but fraying where it had been hacked off ankle-short. Her feet were bare. She wore no bonnet, and her nose and cheeks were sunburned and peeling. Her hair was gathered behind her neck with a piece of twine, then fell in a chestnut cascade that brushed her hips. I had only seen her hair loose in our bedroom, and the sight, misplaced and intimate, stole my breath.

She rapped the sword's shell guard, testing its thickness. I carried an English small sword, a gentleman's dueling weapon, lighter and more practical than a military saber. Usually, they were shorter as well. Mine was two inches longer to suit my reach.

Eyes still on the sword, she said, "You have tracked them for two days. Why?"

"To find you. You are hunting Blackcoats."

She looked up, and the words I had prepared vanished at the sight of her brown eyes. I remembered stumbling through inanities when we first met.

She moved one hand to the grip and raised an eyebrow. *May I?*

That was swordsman's etiquette, unsettling from Elizabeth who, to my knowledge, had never held a sword, but it was habit to nod in answer.

She drew the sword and studied the blade, triangular and hollow-ground for lightness, then ran her thumb across the edge. "Not sharp."

"It is a thrusting blade. The point is sharp."

She cast me an amused glance, then tossed the sword to me, a perfect throw that seemed to hang in the air to be caught, which I did.

"Attack me," she said.

"You know me," I burst out. "You remember me. I see it in your eyes."

She smiled lightly, as if I had admired the weather. "Attack me. Perhaps then I will answer."

"I have searched for you for days. I thought you lost when you went into the lake. Dead." My voice broke; I had never confessed that aloud.

She was still for a breath, then said, "I wish to see you fight." The scabbard was still in her hand. She flipped it to a sword-like grip and lifted it *en garde*. Mockingly, she poked it toward me. "Attack, or I leave."

I recognized that tone; she was serious. Could I rush her? Restrain her by force? That image was repugnant, and somewhere a dragon was at her call.

Still, bizarre though this conversation was, it was better than Pemberley. There, she flew away without a backward glance. And oddly, fencing—literally for once, not with words—was not that strange. I had fenced with women before. The Angelo School of Arms, where I trained, had female students.

I tapped the last few inches of my blade against the scabbard, accepting combat. She waited, still as stone. I performed a slow lunge, a teacher's demonstration. She watched the sword tip stop two feet short of her ribs.

"You are better than that," she said. "I watched you practice this morning."

I recovered from the lunge and lowered the sword. "You spied on me."

"A man asleep in a field is common. A man and a *horse* asleep are worth a look." Idly she moved the scabbard through a parry and thrust, the exact riposte I had drilled this morning. "You practiced without clothes. Is that the problem? Must you remove them to fight?"

My cheeks heated. Ridiculous; this was my wyfe. And I had worn my drawers. "I was washing them." The words felt stiff in my lips.

She eyed my wrinkled coat and trousers. One eyebrow rose fractionally.

From nowhere, my lips spread in a joyous grin. That was Elizabeth's wit, familiar and beloved. Giddy relief rushed into me. I resumed my stance and launched a faster lunge.

This time, she watched the sword point stop eight inches shy of her waist.

She sighed. "If you are so afraid of hurting me, aim here." She waved the scabbard in the air beside her, then dropped it on the ground.

Now unarmed, her manner changed. Her empty hands floated by her waist, elbows tucked close. Her knees flexed above her spaced feet, although her skirt made her stance hard to read.

And it was a stance. A fighting stance. The proof was in her gaze. She did not watch my hands, or the tip of my weapon, or my eyes—anything that could feint. Her gaze followed my chest, the center of balance.

"What happened to you?" I asked. She did not answer, so I tried, "Why have you not attacked the Blackcoats?"

"They have a woman with them. I do not understand her. Not yet."

"Why are you doing *this*?" I whipped the sword through the neutral space between us, fast enough that the blade sang. "Is this because of a memory?" Like Georgiana, Elizabeth's power had granted her visions, but Elizabeth's were memories of past wyves of war.

She did not answer. Her eyes were steady and unfocused. The best fencers, the tutors of royalty, had that gaze. They saw their opponent's motion as a whole, not fixating on a button or a collar. Seeing that, an unexpected emotion tightened my throat, the same feeling I had felt at the modest country dance where we met and she offhandedly shredded my self-important conceit.

I drowned in awed admiration.

I lunged, a serious attack but aimed a safe distance to one side. I picked the opposite side from where she had pointed.

She lunged too, toward me, toward the sword, spinning as she moved. Her hand flashed out and knocked the blade aside, then the sword twisted to follow her spin—she had not struck it, she had grabbed it. The base of the blade levered against her hip, wrenching my sword hand past her as she finished her rotation by slamming bodily into me. Only fifteen years of hard practice kept my fingers on the grip.

She ended facing me, fully inside my guard, our bodies pressed together. My sword arm was half behind her back, the blade pulled harmlessly around her, her hand gripping it a foot from the tip.

Her grin was ecstatic. "You are dead, Mr. Dull Blade." A hard point was jammed into the pulse of my neck. She took it away and showed me her two extended fingers, a mock knife.

My sword arm still wrapped her like an embrace. She tugged the blade teasingly, drawing us tighter. "*This* is why you sharpen the edge. So your enemy cannot just..." She wiggled the blade again.

The admiration that had filled me soured. I pushed her away, overly hard. She made a show of staggering, laughing and pirouetting to free my sword.

"Why are you doing this?" I said. "Who are you?"

"Everyone. A hundred hunted women. No one."

"You are not yourself." Elizabeth would not gloat. Well, Elizabeth *would* gloat, just... not like this. Not coarsely. Not over violence.

She became serious. "Who are you? Would pretty Mr. Darcy chase fourteen Blackcoats alone?"

My name sounded strange on her lips. "I am chasing you."

"You found me." She cocked her head, studying my wrinkled clothes. "You are less pretty. That is an improvement. Find me again when your sword is sharp, and I will show you another trick." She turned away.

"Wait! You need me."

Smiling, she turned back and placed her hands on her hips. Waiting.

I tried to think, ignoring my irritation over her jibe about clothes. "You need reinforcements."

She snorted. "*You?* Will you have them form a line, then ask them to fight one-by-one so the others can admire your footwork?"

"You need clothes. A bonnet. A bath. Food." I was throwing ideas randomly, and her eyebrows notched higher with each one. "Tea. Boots."

Her skepticism vanished. "You have my boots?"

"Um... not *with* me."

She laughed and turned away, then stopped mid-stride, toes in the grass, one bare heel lifted. I had forgotten how delicate her feet were.

I tried again. "At Pemberley—"

She held up her hand. *Silence.*

Escalus snorted. He stamped the turf, great head swinging and ears twisting.

A rattle grew in the forest, like a hundred twigs drumming on wood.

Elizabeth yanked her skirt up, exposing a scandalous length of muscular leg and a makeshift cloth sheath strapped to her thigh. She drew the dagger Gramr and let the skirt fall.

"Why are you watching *me*?" she hissed.

I started and turned, peering into the dense forest. Clicks come from every bush and shadow.

A giant foul crawler slipped into the clearing, the clatter of its feet hushing on the soft grass. It was serpentine, four feet long, thick as a man's leg but flattened and low to the ground. A pair of jointed legs sprang from each shiny, armored segment. The front third lifted into the air, questing blindly as if scenting, the finger-length pinchers on the head clacking open and closed.

Elizabeth reached it with one lightning step and stabbed underhand, driving her dagger through the lighter-colored bottom shell. The creature gave a peculiar squealing hiss, writhing on her blade.

"Above you!" she shouted. I looked up as a six-inch crawler fell from a branch. I jerked back. It brushed my thigh, the feet scrabbling but missing their grip. It landed by my feet.

Another crawler, longer than my arm, burst out of the bush and ran at me, legs a blur. I kicked it, as awkward as kicking a rope, and it retreated in a seething mass. The smaller crawler was hissing, so I stamped in the grass and felt shell crack just before the long one flowed out again, faster than a snake. I jabbed it with the sword. The tip skittered off the shell, then the pincers closed on my boot toe, crushing the thick leather and squeezing the bones of my foot. I kicked, a disgusted reflex, and its grip on my boot whipped the crawler like a yard-long rat shaken by a dog. There was a sharp snap, and it fell off, limp.

Escalus whinnied and bucked. I raced to him and stabbed at another long crawler squirming by his feet. Again the blade skidded. Fool. I backed two steps and executed a proper downward lunge—in practice, I hit targets the size of a guinea. The point caught between two segments and slipped under the shell, skewering the thrashing vermin to the ground.

The back of the creature flicked over its head, scorpion-like, the stingers hunting for flesh. Then Escalus's hoof came down, smashing a dinner-plate-sized chunk of the body into shards of shell and mushed, clam-like flesh.

The horse reared again, screaming, front feet sawing the air, and a hoof clipped my forearm with a stinging smack. "Easy!" I shouted. "Down!" I caught the reins left-handed, sword in my right. The pistol on his flank was in reach, but priming it would take an eternity. A blade was better.

The clattering had stopped. There was only Escalus's frenzied panting and my own.

Frightened, I spun, seeking Elizabeth. She was turning a wary circle in the center of the clearing. In her hand, Gramr dripped unpleasant, yellowish gore. Four large crawlers lay dead in the grass around her.

"Where did they come from?" I gasped. My words shook with the strange, harsh tremble that follows combat.

She looked up. Even now, her eyes made my heart stutter. It was Elizabeth's serious, steady gaze.

"That is what she does," she said. "The woman with them. She sends crawlers."

"You encountered this *before*?"

"Twice. They are not dangerous."

"Not dangerous!" Venom was trickling from the crushed crawler. The acrid, sour scent stung my eyes.

"A little dangerous," she admitted. "That is why I do not bring the draca. They cannot fight in *this*." Her hand wafted the venom scented air. She pointed her dagger at my riding boot. The heavy leather toe was pinched and cut. "You see why I want boots."

"This is madness. You must come home."

She considered me. She was not even breathing hard. "No. I was called for revenge, and it is not done. What will you say next?"

"Then I will go with you." The only other choice.

She laughed. "You are no use to me."

I raised the sword and stepped toward her. She fingered Gramr's hilt, eyes narrow. I took another step, then lunged, driving the point a few inches beside her calf.

It was a good hit, exactly between the crawler's pincers and straight into the maw. The blade sank in a foot and a half, spitting half the length of the body. The stingers, which had curled for a last, wounded strike, rattled and fell limp.

I kicked the repulsive thing off the sword, then wiped the blade with my handkerchief and discarded the fouled cloth.

"At least the point is sharp," I said. "Still no use?"

This time, she did not laugh. I could see her turning it over in her head. That lasted too long, a puzzle more subtle than the benefit and cost of another blade and another mouth.

Every mannerism was wrenchingly familiar. Seeing her was joy and loss together. She was Elizabeth. She was not. She was.

"You are tolerable," she said at last.

# 11

# TWO SKETCHES

## MARY

With no word from Mr. Darcy, I had spent the days worrying about Lizzy's state of mind, then reveling in Lizzy's miraculous cure, then worrying all over again in a useless cycle. Irritated, this morning I set a goal: solve the puzzle of the third great item, the flute sought by *la Demoiselle des Parfums*.

The choice was no whim. Since meeting the perfumer, a lost memory had tickled the periphery of my mind like a crooked page in a pristine stack. A page I had been unable to grasp.

Georgiana's table in the Pemberley library was, as usual, buried under a mess of musical scores. A half-dozen French and German books perched on the clutter, serving as paperweights while being read. The French books were risqué romantic novels with innocent titles. The German books were philosophy by Hegel and literary reviews by Caroline Schelling.

Mr. Darcy had a library table as well. His held an ebony writing tray with ink, a blotter, and pens—goose quills for correspondence and crow for fine work. A small stack of ivory notepaper sat on an expanse of ready, bare oak.

Despite the mess, I chose Georgiana's table and sorted inward from the corner, piling manuscripts by musical era until there was enough space to lay the Loch bairn journal open to the page that mentioned the relics:

*For the Great Song, I knowe the three relicks, edged, chayned, and hollow. The Queene holds the edged and chayned, but not the thryd, the hollow relick of Musike bathed in tears of betrayal.*

The journal's pages had yielded no further clues. The passage before described the weather, the passage after a clutch of duck eggs. But this room was suffused with volumes and knowledge. It might uncover whatever lost memory involved the flute.

I relaxed and began from the words in the journal: *edged, chained, and hollow.*

The dagger was edged. The amulet, chained. The item for the wyfe of song would be hollow and, according to the Frenchwoman, it was a flute. But "flute" was a broad label. It included everything from panpipes to piccolos. Still, it would be an old-fashioned instrument, a tube with fingering holes, nothing like a modern flute.

And it would be formed from dragon claw, harder than steel, incredibly difficult to shape or drill. So, it was likely a small, simple flute...

I let my mind wander, my gaze drifting over the shelves of books. Useless memories fluttered, some from Longbourn, some from Pemberley: a treatise on reed flutes, a chart of recorder fingerings, a page of Virgil's *Eclogae* where *tibia*—flute—was repeated over and over.

I let my mind spin from there... flute... music... dance. *Pah.* That was the wrong direction.

Perhaps the Frenchwoman was wrong, and it was not a flute. What else was hollow? Pots and buttonholes and frames flooded my brain like I had split open a peddler's sack of irrelevance.

I dug my fingers into my hair and scrambled it into a mad mess. When I was a child and my brain was over-cluttered, I would scramble my hair then stumble through the house half-blind until Lizzy or Jane took pity and tidied me. Now, the ritual was more nostalgia than necessity, but when I combed my hair with my fingers, my mind was clear.

Follow the theme of the puzzle: music. Lizzy said the dragons' true names were songs. The ancient calamity that broke Fènnù's mind, the fracture, was a corruption of those songs. Music was not merely one of the great wyves' callings. It was intrinsic to draca themselves.

The dagger Gramr, despite being an artifact of war, had been invoked by song. At the London ball, Joane Rees wet the dagger's blade with her own blood to reveal hidden notation. When she sang those notes, Fènnù rose.

I went to Mr. Darcy's table and borrowed writing materials, then returned to Georgiana's seat. On a sheet of thick notepaper, I drew the five lines of a musical staff. Joane had sung soprano, so I wrote the swirl of a treble clef, and the staff lines became tones in my mind, E – G – B – D – F.

When panic erupted at the ball, I had fought to reach Joane through the frightened, fleeing crowd. I heard only snatches of her singing. An isolated A-flat. An E-flat descending to C, a minor third. Not enough to establish a key, although Western keys were likely irrelevant. Georgiana's power manifested through melody, and the modes of her song tended as Eastern as the dragons' names.

But on the shores of Pemberley lake, I had shared Fènnù's ancient memory of three great wyves' attempting to heal the broken song. The stupendous power of their music tore my soul, but I had heard their song through Fènnù's senses. I could not listen analytically as I would with my own ears.

Fènnù's attention had fixed on one melody within the song. That I did recall, and it matched the fragments of Joane's song, although those were so short they would match almost anything.

I dipped the pen and transcribed the melody onto the notepaper. It was largely pentatonic, usually called an Eastern style, but pentatonic scales appeared in the West as well. Gaelic music. Gregorian chant. It was an ancient form. Origin aside, I was certain of one thing: The complete song had been contrapuntal, three equally important parts combined in a harmonic whole.

Stuck and tired of thinking in circles, I unlatched the library window and whistled. After a minute, a lustrous song draca, the loyal one from London, winged to a nearby branch.

I drew a breath, held it—wondering if this was stupendously foolish—then sang the melody from Fènnù's memory.

The song draca cocked his bejeweled head and whistled the notes back. Perfectly. An echo, as he could repeat any tune I gave him.

The earth did not shake. Wings did not eclipse the sky. The song draca, with studied indifference, watched a caterpillar inch along the branch. Even small draca preferred meat.

That was unexciting, but I was not the one with power. I let the ink dry, then set out briskly to find Georgiana.

I entered the grand music room to the sound of her playing Mozart. Two bars later, Mrs. Reynolds hurried in behind me, her elderly shoulders puffing. She gasped in relief and offered me an envelope. Apparently, she had been chasing me.

"A letter for you, madam."

"Thank you," I said and took the envelope. "How is Thomas?" He had been unconscious only a few minutes when struck by the Blackcoat, but his headaches had lingered.

Mrs. Reynolds permitted herself a smile. "Mr. Digweed said, 'Right as rain today.' He is greatly relieved. Even so, Lucy has asked to take a day off to care for him—for Thomas, that is, not the father." Another amused crease joined her wrinkled cheeks.

Then she waited. Georgiana, in snow-white morning dress, had abandoned the Mozart. She arrived beside Mrs. Reynolds and watched me with equal interest.

I realized Mrs. Reynolds was asking permission for Lucy's request.

"Do not ask *me*," I protested. "You know far more about it." Lucy routinely vanished to attend school and, hopefully, to live her life. Embarrassingly, I had never inquired about the details.

"Yes, madam," she said obediently.

The day before Lizzy rose, Mr. Darcy had informed the senior staff of my new status as an heiress. With him gone, the result was a raft of uncomfortably deferent questions. It did not help that this amused Georgiana. She had folded her hands and adopted an innocent expression, but I knew better.

Once again, Mrs. Reynolds was waiting. "Yes?" I said warily.

"The letter is from the master," Mrs. Reynolds said pointedly.

I whipped the envelope up. Mr. Darcy's handwriting. "Why did you not *say* so?"

Georgiana pressed to my side, and I opened it for us both. The seal was intact but thick and layered; he had broken and resealed it.

*"Miss Bennet,*

*I trust you and Georgiana are well.*

*In south Derbyshire, I have encountered a dangerous blight. Crops are infested with foul crawler grubs growing within pea pods and young fruits. The numbers would be overwhelming, but we appear to have discovered it in time..."*

I read on, frustrated. "There is not a word about Lizzy. He says we are to reimburse a farmer for his burned crop."

The bottom of the page held an ink sketch, unquestionably a foul crawler in nascent form. Georgiana frowned at the drawing. "Do crawlers breed in crops?"

"It was *thought* they were subterranean," I said. "Certainly, they have not spawned from entire fields. Hatching that many would endanger everyone within miles. We should inspect Pemberley's crops. And the neighboring estates will need to inspect theirs..."

I puzzled over the problem. Inspecting Pemberley's fields would disrupt farming for several days, a substantial effort. Inspecting the neighboring estates, however, required convincing wealthy and independent gentlemen to make the same sacrifice. Mr. Darcy had the influence to achieve that, but he was not here.

Georgiana was leaning lightly on my arm, studying her brother's sketch and looking delicate draped in her white linen. That was an illusion—she was terrifyingly fearless—but she reserved her strength for private matters. She had never confronted a group of angry, dismissive men. I had, with unpleasant regularity.

"Mrs. Reynolds," I said, "we must speak with Mr. Digweed and the heads of the farming cooperatives. Swiftly. Today. And could you also invite the masters of the neighboring estates to Pemberley to discuss the infestation? Tomorrow would be ideal." Finally, my disconcertingly elevated status had a use, but still I hesitated. "To convince them, you may need to be... vague... about who is issuing the invitation."

"Vague invitations are customary, madam," she said blandly. "The housekeepers often communicate to ensure their masters have not overlooked some matter. The wording might be... '*Confirming your master's attendance at the Derbyshire landholders' assembly to discuss crop infestations. Pemberley. Four o'clock.*' If that time will serve?"

"That is perfect. Thank you."

Georgiana looked up from the letter. "They will not be easy to convince."

"By then, we may have more proof than a sketch."

I flipped over Mr. Darcy's letter, then beamed and held out the page for the others. Georgiana cried out in delight, and Mrs. Reynolds positively grinned.

*"P.S.: May 4. I have found Elizabeth. She is healthy but opinionated. We are traveling together and shall not immediately return to Pemberley. I have left my horse with the aforementioned farmer..."*

The rest of the page frustrated me all over again. "He wrote a full paragraph of instructions to retrieve his horse! They are traveling *where*? Doing *what*? What does 'healthy but opinionated' mean?"

Georgiana was looking through the towering windows, her gaze distant. "The blight is so close now."

"Are you not worried about your brother?"

She rolled her eyes. "Fitz is fine. Fitz is always fine. But I *am* worried about Lizzy."

"Lizzy is always opinionated." I reread the page. "How will they travel if he has left his horse?"

Georgiana's eyes sparkled. "They will fly!"

I scoffed. "Mr. Darcy riding bareback on a dragon?"

"You do not know Fitz. He will clamber up looking proper and stern, but inside he will be cheering like a schoolboy."

"I doubt he is cheering. You did not see Lizzy when she returned. She was... ferocious. She completely refused him."

Georgiana exchanged amused looks with Mrs. Reynolds.

"What is it?" I said.

"Lizzy refused him once before," Georgiana said. "We had to live with him afterward. Let us just say it did not have the intended effect."

I checked the envelope for more addenda and found a smaller sheet, folded and labeled *G*. I passed it to Georgiana. She opened it, then shared it with a knowing smile.

It was another ink sketch, spare and skillful lines swiftly drawn. Lizzy's dark eyes stared defiantly, her jaw set in a way that indicated a sharp retort was brewing. One swirling pen stroke conveyed a mass of hair slung over her shoulder. The mark I had noticed on her cheek was a drop of ink carefully blurred by a fingertip.

"Yes, he is completely lost," Georgiana pronounced cheerfully. "At least he draws well. I hope they sort this out before he resumes composing poetry. *That* was painful."

Mrs. Reynolds gave a choked cough.

Georgiana noticed the other sheet of paper I held, the melody transcribed from Fènnù's memory. Her amusement faded. "Where did you get that? I have heard it before..."

A monstrous, clutching worry had fallen from my mind. Lizzy was alive and with her love. Months of thick dread evaporated like clouds in summer sun.

"A project," I said and folded the melody. "It can wait. We must start the crop inspections. And dinner should be a celebration. Lizzy is safe."

# 12

# FÈNNÙ'S SONG

## MARY

The curtain hooks rattled. Golden morning flooded our room.

I lay curled against Georgiana's back. She slept as hot as a furnace, so on cold nights, I tended to chase her around the bed like she was an elusive foot-warmer. But last night had brought one of the Peaks' sudden chills. With no fire set, she conceded to snuggle.

I cracked an eyelid against the brightness. Our dressing table was a rosewood smudge, my spectacles a golden flicker out of reach. Swift steps passed behind me, and a blurred form crossed the looking glass.

Georgiana groaned theatrically. "Must you open the curtains? Make some music instead. That will wake us up." She wiggled firmly into my arms. Her hair was an inky, braided mass and thoroughly disheveled. The news about Lizzy had spawned two celebrations, the first a festive dinner, the second more intimate. Remembering that, I buried my face in the curve of Georgiana's neck and inhaled lavender and a musky hint of dried sweat. That made Georgiana giggle.

"Your pardon, madam," came a rock-stern woman's voice. "My singing days are past."

Mrs. Reynolds. Georgiana froze in my arms like a startled deer.

In the silence—and into Georgiana's hair—I said, "Where is Lucy?"

"Attending Thomas, as we agreed," Mrs. Reynolds answered coolly. A pause. "It is half seven, madams."

That *was* late. Lucy usually woke us at seven. Of course, Mrs. Reynolds kept a busy schedule. That was why housekeepers did not fill in for absent lady's maids.

Clearly, Georgiana had not expected her. She had not twitched a muscle. I could not even feel her breathing.

I whispered, "Are you alive?"

"I am waiting to find out," she whispered back. Mrs. Reynolds, formidable in the best of circumstances, had served as Georgiana's governess after her mother's death. That authority was not easily outgrown.

Mrs. Reynolds's dry tones resumed. "Young people like to imagine they have invented this or that shocking behavior. I, however, have served in great houses for sixty-two years. If you wish to shock me, Miss Darcy, you shall have to try harder."

Georgiana's braid nodded dutifully. Perhaps she thought it was an assignment.

More gently, Mrs. Reynolds continued, "Shall I lay out your robes until you are ready to dress?"

"Yes, please," Georgiana peeped.

The armoire opened. Cloth rustled. The bedroom door opened and closed, latching softly.

"Is she gone?" Georgiana whispered.

I lifted my head, squinting. "I think so. I cannot see."

I started untangling myself from Georgiana's limbs, but she caught my wrist and pulled me back. "Hold me a moment. That was terrifying!" I laughed and hugged her. She sighed gratefully, then said wonderingly, "I think we *did* shock her. She would never have let me loll in bed by myself. Or... perhaps I am indulged because I am with the mistress of Pemberley!"

"Do not joke about that." The title summoned memories of Lizzy's battles to protect Longbourn from the vultures who descended after Papa's death.

Georgiana quieted, and we lay still while distant birds sang.

Some idle part of my mind unraveled the reason for Mrs. Reynolds's visit. She did not trust another servant to attend us. Whether that was loyalty to Georgiana, or to Mr. Darcy, or simply duty, a rush of gratitude filled me.

I drew Georgiana close. "I forgot to ask if you wished to handfast on Beltane." In the confusion after Lizzy rose and Mr. Darcy rode into the hills, the idea had vanished from my mind.

She snuggled against me. "I could not be more bound to you than I am now."

PROPERLY DRESSED, I examined Mr. Darcy's drawing of the crawler grub. It was neat work; every line portrayed a specific feature. Except the dorsal ridge. He had drawn over that several times, hunting for the correct rendering. The ink was thick and muddled.

Georgiana and I were breakfasting in the grand music room, a glorious space with a towering wall of windows. Georgiana, a famed pianoforte performer, was an equally brilliant technician, so manufacturers sent their new models for evaluation. She tore apart each hapless arrival, marveling at innovations to the escapement or frowning at skimpy dampers, then reassembled it to play.

A year ago this room had eight instruments, but the war had shrunk the collection to four. Two were new models loaned from the Erard London factory. The other two were permanent acquisitions and Georgiana's favorites, eight-foot grands built to order by Nannette Streicher, a great Viennese builder. Their sweeping curves nestled back-to-back in the center of the room.

Georgiana stopped her practicing—some blistering finger exercise she invented—and came over for a bite of toast. She did not allow food or drink within ten feet of a keyboard, so our table was tucked in the corner.

I placed the melody I had transcribed by her plate.

Her attention shifted from toast to paper. "Not your usual style." Her lashes lifted, and our gazes met. "This is like my songs. Music of power. And it is familiar, but I do not know why."

"We heard it in Fènnù's memory. The three great wyves attempting to heal the song."

"Oh... you remember it from *that*?" She nodded with professional approval. "You are remarkable. I was overwhelmed."

"They are connected. The relics, the great song. I think it is a clue."

"Have you played it?"

"I sang it. Nothing happened. But I do not have... oomph."

She had picked up her toast; playing made her hungry. The crust stopped an inch from her lips. "Oomph?"

"You are the great wyfe of song. *You* have oomph."

She set down the toast. "My songs are not written. I do not write them down, I mean. I just sing what comes to me."

"You can sight-sing anything. Will you try this one?"

I waited for her to refuse. Georgiana was cautious about singing. Cautious of the power it invoked.

She lifted the score, scanning through the lines. "I do not know if I should sing another wyfe's music. Not with... *oomph*." Thoughtfully, she handed the score to me. "This may be like my songs, but it is not mine. You understand it better than I. We should perform it together. You play. I sing."

I had not expected that. My own breakfast twitched in my belly. But I sang it once already. I had barely even hesitated. Had I been so confident I would fail alone?

"Will something happen?" I asked.

Her lips curved. "You are the one who remembered it. What do *you* think?"

I had no answer, so I swallowed my hesitation, wiped my fingers, and walked to the second Streicher. We sometimes played duos on the twin instruments—for pleasure, not performance, as I could not match Georgiana's keyboard skill. The instruments had an exquisite, singing tone from high-tension strings in iron-reinforced frames, an invention of the last few years.

I opened the lid to the short stick and positioned the music, then experimented with chords. It would sound absurd to plink out a unison melody while she sang, but more importantly, the great wyves' song was complex and layered. Even if I could not reconstruct all three voices, I could test the harmonies that lingered in my mind.

Georgiana listened dreamily, standing beside the instrument so we faced each other. She did not need to see the score; her second reading had been to memorize it. Already she was lost in the music, imagining how the melody would fit with my harmonies.

I nodded to her and played an opening chord. She sang the first note, lingering and high. I had written no words for the vocalist. Georgiana chose simple syllables, sounds without meaning that fit the flow of the melody.

Music, whether heard or played, had always formed structures in my thoughts, abstractions that nested and resolved, intricate as filigree or roiling like thunderheads. Social nuances might puzzle me, but music embodied Plato's pure forms of emotion: ecstasy, longing, grief, and fury all distilled to their essence and stripped of artifice, innuendo, and imprecision.

But nothing prepared me for this. As Georgiana's voice soared among the harmonies I played, fabulous arches threw themselves into my mind, scaffolding that supported another layer and yet another, each of Georgiana's notes fixing a taller peak, a shimmering sun, hot or magnetic, that coaxed the phototropic, crystalline edifice higher. It was a structure of flawless feeling, and my inviolate love for her infused every truss and beam.

Then the abstract became visible—the music room's towering glass windows blinked out of existence, and I saw the form of music itself, a fairy fortress spun of countless interwoven triumphs and trials. But incomplete. The summit soared, but the foundation gaped where two other musical voices should stand. The fairytale pillars teetered like brittle spun sugar.

From far away, a tremendous presence, feminine and inhuman, launched towards us as fast as thought. Her shadow blackened the castle's trusses, then spread to cover the horizons. Her mind, disfigured and diseased, swallowed us.

Fènnù.

Her voice roared like a mad goddess: *Raise nothing between me and my wyfe of war!*

Like an iron sky falling, her dark weight slammed down. The castle's incomplete foundation shattered, and it crashed in catastrophic ruin. An arctic blast froze my skin to crackling ice, but then the real world—glass windows, polished keyboard, and a single sheet of music—snapped back into view.

My fingers still pressed the keys of the last chord. The harmonics faded from the strings. Georgiana's whitened fingers clenched the edge of the pianoforte, supporting her deep gasps.

"Did you see that?" I cried. "See the music itself? I always see music, that is... ordinary, but to feel its shape and see the shapes build—" I shook my head, annoyed by my own rambling.

"Fènnù came," Georgiana breathed. "We called her."

"She spoke," I said. "She thought we were separating her from Lizzy."

"I heard her as music. Celestial music." Georgiana drew a long, disciplined breath. Her hand, steady now, clasped mine. "Mary, we did that *together*."

"The power was incredible..." I murmured.

Not Fènnù's strength, massive though that was. What shocked me was the power in that castle of song. Emotion, clarified to perfection. It mocked the doubts that circled my heart. Was my home Longbourn or Pemberley? Were Mr. Darcy's promises a rich man's whimsy, cast in a fire as casually as they were inked? Was I wrong to accept them? Was I worthy of them?

"*I* felt powerful," I admitted. Those words felt scandalous. Wonderful.

Georgiana's fingers squeezed mine. Her smile was strained but happy. "You *are* powerful. Have I not told you so, over and over?"

While we stared at each other, a little dazed, a maid announced that Mr. Digweed and the Pemberley farming directors had arrived. After a few settling breaths, we set out to the other wing to meet them.

But I had not gone ten steps before more ideas poured out. "Fènnù heard us because this is her song." I waved the sheet of music; in my excitement, I had brought it along. "And it is a third of the great song! That was the musical shape we saw forming, incomplete without the other two dragon songs. That is what those ancient great wyves were doing, assembling the great song so they could heal it with the artifacts." Another connection formed. "Would that heal the blight?"

"The blight and the broken song are the same," Georgiana said, which sounded like agreement to me.

I was bubbling like a child, and more words flooded. "All we need now are the other two artifacts, and the other two songs, and all three dragons." I frowned, thinking through details. "And they may need to be bound."

"Is that all?" Georgiana echoed mildly.

I caught her arms, stopping us so sharply the carpet runner under our slippers skidded. "We can heal the song. For the first time, I believe it."

"You say 'three dragons' just like that. There is no sign of a third dragon."

Why did she not see? "But it is so obvious. Three artifacts. Three wyves. Three melodies that form a great song."

"It is a pretty solution," she said softly. "A neat structure. I understand why you like it."

That sounded less than enthusiastic. "You doubt it?"

"No, I saw it too. But the blight remains. And Fènnù fought the song. I have never heard her music so clearly." Her brow pinched. "Did you feel how strong she was?"

"Did you feel how strong *we* were?" That left me giddy. Foolishly, I spun, arms waving at the luxurious wainscotting and windows and grounds while half-formed thoughts sprayed out. "You grew up in this. You cannot understand how I feel. All my life, I wanted to *be* something. To be worth something. To be anything other than the plain, peculiar sister, eclipsed in beauty and wit." My laugh came out slightly manic. "Now, when I am literally surrounded by women from legend, at last I feel like I belong. Like I have power."

"That makes me happy," Georgiana said. She touched my cheek, her fingertips rippling like a rolled chord. "But you should feel that way already. You are so exceptional. Look at your compositions. Look at what your Marys achieve in London."

"That is all... mundane. *This* is incredible."

She cradled my cheek, and—briefly—I imagined she looked uneasy.

# DISCOVERIES

## MARY

Than afternoon, the sun spilling through the observatory windows painted the room an angry orange. The Pemberley inspections had found three infested fields. Two were burning. Already, bitter smoke stained the sky, and our meeting with the neighboring landholders was still to come.

"Mary?" Georgiana called from the doorway. "We have been looking for you."

Distracted by the microscope, I muttered inarticulate syllables.

A shadow arrived, blocking the light on the condensing lens, and the eyepiece dimmed. Just as well; I was tired of squinting. I tucked back my dangling hair and hooked my spectacles over my ears. The shadow resolved into two people: Georgiana and young Thomas Digweed, who was thoroughly recovered. Lucy's request to visit him seemed to have been for celebration, not care.

"You are using the microscope!" Georgiana declared, charmed that I had raided her belongings. It had been on a shelf overflowing with palm-sized lenses of crown and flint glass, concave mirrors, and brass mounting loops. Telescope optics.

"Dr. Davenport taught me to use one." He had demonstrated several mind-boggling views—consumptive tubercles, and red blood cells clotting before my eyes—then grumbled that most doctors considered magnification a useless novelty.

"What are you looking at?" Georgiana asked, her nose inches from the specimen tray. Thomas looked from the other side.

"A foul crawler," I said, and Georgiana recoiled. "Or the immature grub of one. It is from the plums." The plum orchard infection had been obvious, the fruit distended and overlarge for May.

Georgiana looked concerned, so I added, "It is thoroughly killed. I soaked it with camphor and alcohol."

"I am not afraid of it," she said. "I am *disgusted* by it. Must you... pick it apart?"

I was brandishing a hatpin to lever up a length of hardened shell, what would be the elytron in a beetle. "Look. Wings."

That made her frown. "Crawlers do not have wings."

"This would, if it hatched." To Thomas—who seemed fascinated—I said, "Did you succeed?"

"Yes, ma'am." He held up the small wicker box I had given him. "I collected them from the broad beans. My father wants to know if we should burn the field now?"

"Not yet. That field will be our exhibit." I took the box to the window and angled it, peering through the mesh as spots of sun penetrated. Nothing unpleasant had emerged, so I opened it. There were two long beans, even more grossly swollen than the plums. They flexed slightly where the sun touched them. "Good. Still alive." With tweezers, I moved each into a separate glass jar.

"Disgusting," Georgiana repeated. "Could you not raise puppies instead?"

"I want to find a way to kill them without burning crops." I covered one jar with a copper lid punched with tiny airholes, then opened a flask of draca essence. "The Loch bairn journal refers to essence as a treatment for crawler stings, but another passage suggests it is repellant to crawlers themselves, or even toxic..."

Georgiana was unconvinced. "We do not have enough essence to douse a field."

"It is an experiment. It is not only our fields. The army is being attacked by huge crawlers. We need options."

I dipped a piece of straw and dripped draca essence onto the second swollen bean. The pod throbbed with disturbing vigor, so I hastily covered the jar with another metal lid. We all crouched down to watch.

The treated bean settled and lay still.

"Is it dead?" Thomas asked.

"We must wait and see." I secured both metal lids with twine, tucked in a note to mark the treated jar, and set the jars on a shelf. "Either way, we will learn what comes out."

THE INFESTED broad beans filled a sloping, odd-shaped tenth acre, densely sown and intended for pig fodder. The plants had grown into a morass of tangled green as tall as my waist, and a bitter reek underlaid the healthy, earthy scent from recent rain. That aside, the day was pleasant. The burns at the other fields were finished, and the fouled sky had cleared to blue.

Georgiana and I tethered our horses to a hazel shrub near the field's edge. The song draca had followed us from the mansion, circling and calling. He flitted to the top of a bush a few paces from me, his scaled muzzle cocked while his bright eyes watched expectantly.

"Not now," I told him. He whistled, mimicking the tune of my words. I had never taught him a song for "go away," so I flapped a hand at him until, affronted, he soared up to perch in a cedar overlooking the field. He chittered urgently. Even that sounded musical.

"Here they come," Georgiana said. "All of them."

A party on horseback rounded the bend, three well-dressed gentlemen I did not know escorted by Mr. Digweed. A good beginning. I had not been sure Mrs. Reynolds' network of housekeepers would convince them.

The three men dismounted and greeted Georgiana warmly, the two older men fond as fathers. When that friendly exchange finished, glances drifted my way.

Georgiana said simply, "Miss Bennet." With both my older sisters wed, I no longer required "Mary" in introductions. This would be the pinnacle of my social status: the eldest unmarried sister.

The first gentleman, Mr. Berrycloth, bowed to my curtsy, his ruddy cheeks framed by graying side-whiskers as stiff as brushes. He pursed meaty lips and looked me over with the unrushed curiosity of a wealthy, old man. Or was it dislike? I suppressed an urge to sneak a look at Georgiana and gauge her reaction.

These gentlemen might be strangers to me, but Bennet sisters were surrounded by rumors. Lizzy's binding of a dragon was tacit knowledge in this area, although her apparent death and the Darcys' influence had kept the news from spreading. Jane and her golden wyvern, although living quietly in Hertfordshire, marshaled a share of envy and mystery as well.

Mr. Berrycloth finished his assessment with a baffled look at my limp, hanging hair. It had not occurred to me to put it up, but it was too late to pander to convention now.

Gruffly, he cleared his throat. "Miss Bennet. The Britons speak of you." He nodded and stepped aside.

Mr. Gastrell rolled up next, his portly belly wrapped in expensive tweed sealed by straining silver buttons. We exchanged wordless dips and polite smiles.

Mr. Spragg, the only one closer to my age than my parents', was last. He snapped a stylish bow and held my fingers too long, reminding me unpleasantly of Wickham. This man was less dainty though, his face rough from sun and wind. A long-healed scar pinched his upper lip, perhaps a childhood accident.

"The Britons departed our property in my grandfather's time," he said. His attention lingered on me with the more practical interest of a young man. "What *do* the Britons say about you?"

"I do not know," I said. "I have not asked them."

He nodded as if that were an answer. "I was surprised to review my appointments for the day and discover a meeting of the Derbyshire landholders' assembly. As I have never *heard* of the Derbyshire landholder's assembly." He flicked a smile. "Will Mr. Darcy attend, or does the assembly simply use a muddy trail on his land for meetings?"

"My brother is abroad," Georgiana said, with a barely audible emphasis on "brother." I was happy to let attention shift to her, but she deftly nodded it back to me.

"Mr. Darcy requested that we meet," I said, in a rather choppy beginning. "There is a grave threat. A threat to agriculture, but also to life. Foul crawlers have adopted a new pattern of spread, based on infestation of fruits and seeds. The mechanism is unclear—"

"Crawlers?" portly Mr. Gastrell interrupted. "We rode all this way for a few *pests?*"

"More than pests," I said. "A deadly risk." He guffawed, so I explained. "The breadth of infestation is unprecedented. That density elevates the risk."

"Slow down, Miss Bennet," Mr. Berrycloth said, not unkindly. "You are afraid of crawlers, is that it?"

"Afraid? No. Not in a personal sense." Now everyone looked puzzled. "The risk is of scale. We must coordinate our efforts in this region."

"Perhaps if we showed them..." Georgiana prompted me. *Reminded* me.

"Yes," I muttered, feeling idiotic. We had agreed to start with a demonstration. How could this be harder than proclaiming women's rights amid shouted insults in a London square?

Mr. Digweed was already busy at the field's edge. He picked one of the bloated, diseased pods, and the gentlemen gathered, serious at last. Even the most pampered gentleman landholder was, at some level, a farmer.

A pair of song draca swooped through the midst of our party. They perched in the cedar. More gleams shifted in the branches. Eight. Ten. I had never seen so many song draca together. They were singing softly, a discordant drone near the bottom of their range that set my teeth on edge.

"Are you calling them?" Georgiana whispered to me. The men were occupied asking questions of Mr. Digweed.

"Of course not." The last thing we needed was draca. Single ladies with draca were, at best, suspected of unchastity. A display like this would prompt accusations of witchcraft.

Mr. Digweed said loudly, "Miss Bennet could answer that better." That was my cue, so Georgiana and I joined the circle of men. Mr. Digweed laid the bean pod on the ground and offered me a stick. "Would you do the honors?"

I took it, feeling rather like a schoolteacher. "As grubs, they seem unable to sting, but keep a safe distance." Muddy boots stepped back. I prodded the pod, trying to open it without injuring the crawler. A live specimen would be more convincing.

The pod slipped in the damp until I pinned it against a stone, then it split. A finger-length crawler squirmed free, the segmented shell gleaming before becoming coated in mud. There was a mix of *hmms* and *ahs* from the audience.

Shell. Not a grub's translucent skin.

Two pairs of delicate, insect-like wings opened, and it churred into the air. Heads ducked as it sailed in a clumsy arc and plunked heavily among the overgrown bean plants. Muffled, angry buzzes sounded, like a wasp trapped against a window.

Surprise turned to excitement. "A grasshopper!" "Too many legs." "Not a *crawler*, not with wings!" "Chunky bastard, whatever it is... your pardon, ladies."

My eyes were on the tangled greenery. A tenth of an acre, five hundred square yards, infested with crawlers. But not like the grub from the plums. Mature crawlers, ready to emerge.

I caught Mr. Digweed's eye. "The field must be burned. Quickly."

"Yes, surely." He pursed his lips, looking toward Pemberley's barns, out of view and a mile away. "Shall I ride to bring men?"

The angry buzz became overlapped buzzes. The plants shivered, and wet pops snapped as pods split. A winged form lobbed head-high and dropped deeper in the field, then a dozen followed. The buzzing swelled explosively, suddenly louder than swarming bees.

A thumb-sized shape flew from the tangled bean plants and plopped at my feet. It was unquestionably a crawler, a pair of pinchers on the head, and a pair of insectile legs on each shiny body segment. Only the wings, webbed and transparent like a mayfly's, were unusual.

The twin stingers at the rear vibrated like greedy needles. Then a lustrous blur skimmed by my ankles, leaving a puff of transparent blue flame inches from my toes—draca flame. Even that tiny breath radiated heat. The crawler's wings crisped to ash. Its body writhed and crackled.

More crawlers lofted from the field, passing between us and over our heads. Mr. Gastrell shrieked and flailed his arm, then stomped on the ground. A crawler flew toward me but was intercepted midair by a swerving song draca breathing fire. The crawler fell, a smoking cinder.

The men shouted warnings as a twisting column of crawlers seethed up like an airborne snake. The mass fell on a horse, swarming like hornets. The horse screamed and threw itself to the ground. Men dodged, cursing, as a thousand pounds of desperate animal rolled, saddle and all, then Mr. Berrycloth was back, swinging his bundled coat at the throng.

Amid that, Georgiana was trying to untie her panicked horse—so it could run; it was too maddened to mount. Crawlers streamed between us, and fear for her cut my breast.

That fear brought clarity. "Call draca!" I shouted to her over the deafening buzz.

She turned, her face pale. "I cannot. It is Lizzy who commands..."

I pulled her to me, wrapping our hands together, and sang my summoning song, that excerpt from my first fantasia. The song for that little draca from London. *My* draca.

And through the cries and insectile whir, answers came. Woodwind whistles joined my voice, some as melody, some in harmony. Then Georgiana's confident soprano rose with mine. Our eyes locked over our clenched hands, hers sapphire and bright, and the mesh of our fingers tightened.

The music expanded my senses. I heard the tune of the living hillside around us, the water and sun singing their endless duet, night and day performing their ageless round, and woven through that, the call and answer of hundreds of draca voices. It was profound. Ecstatic. A joining with something vast.

Jewel-bright wings swirled, fifty song draca in that group alone, and blue flame snapped out in a furious storm. A pillar of crawlers rose, wide and ponderous as cold smoke from smoldering leaves. We sang, the world sang with us, and the crawlers were encircled by spiraling song draca. A hundred small flames met, together so hot that my skin flushed as the pristine blue fire turned dirty orange and black with exploding vermin.

The crawlers were all around us, leaping, flying, scurrying, darkening the air. The draca pursued them. Thousands of bird-like forms raced, unfathomably agile. My next snatched breath came tainted with the bitter citrus of crawler venom, and I broke into hacking. Georgiana's tones held though, and I found the tune again, my eyes smarting.

Slowly, the dark madness subsided. The buzzing faded and stopped, leaving crackles from a hundred small fires. Song draca whirled triumphantly over the field in shifting, fabulous murmurations.

Synchronized by our touched fingers, Georgiana and I ended our song in unison. For a few breaths, we stared at each other. Georgiana's cheek was soot stained and smeared where she had wiped her watering eyes. Smoke and sparks floated between us. The air had a foul stench.

I remembered the others. "Is anyone stung?" I called.

Mr. Digweed stood with two of the gentlemen, coughing and well back from the smoke. They shook their heads, and one said, "The draca protected us."

Mr. Berrycloth did not answer. He was kneeling by his fallen horse.

I knelt beside him as the mare wheezed a shuddering breath. Her body and neck teemed with the paired pricks of crawler stings, already bloating.

"Are you stung?" I repeated, soft but insistent.

He shook his head, then said in a cracked voice, "Have you draca essence at Pemberley?" He was petting the suffering creature. Comforting her.

"We do. That would treat one sting, or two. But this... this is too much."

Mr. Berrycloth choked out a sob and nodded. He fumbled for the pistol and powder hanging from the saddle.

I stilled his fingers and returned them to his horse's shoulder. "There is no need. She is gone." Her last sigh had passed. Mr. Berrycloth's grayed head bent, and he sobbed freely.

I rose to let him grieve. I understood mourning from the hospitals, and a strange woman was no comfort to a weeping man. He might have ridden his horse for twenty years, a deeply personal connection.

That left me facing the other gentlemen. Song draca flitted around and over us, several hundred still. At the peak, it had been far more. Fire flashed as they scoured the infested field and burned the blighted plants. The last beanstalks were collapsing, wilting into a blackish mire.

The bold song draca from London landed on my shoulder. As if that were a signal, others arrived, landing in a loose semicircle around and behind me, filling the bushes and blanketing the ground where they hunted restlessly, prodding any burned or crushed remains of a crawler. It was like I wore a living train of brilliant feathers and jeweled muzzles.

The memory of the song spawned from the hillside hung in my mind, an existence that dwarfed flickering human lives.

Mr. Gastrell was sniffling in blank, rotund shock. Two pudgy fingers picked aimlessly at a silver button.

Mr. Spragg though, the younger man, watched me steadily. I met his scrutiny easily enough. The nerves that jumbled me before had been burned away as thoroughly as the crawlers.

"I do not know what the Britons say," he said, "but I have heard what they call you in London. Mary Bennet. Great Wyfe." He folded his arms. "My mother kept the old ways. When I was a child, she visited Pemberley for the Britons' celebrations. She brought me, too. Dragged me—as a boy, I had no patience for anything but riding and shooting. Then a fever took her in my sixteenth winter, and that door closed." He unfolded a hand toward the smoking field. "You said we must coordinate our efforts. What do you propose?"

RETURNED TO PEMBERLEY HOUSE, I sought solitude in the observatory looking out over spring-green hills.

Inspections were underway at the neighboring estates. One infected field had been found, but there were no reports of mass crawler eruptions. With luck, the broad beans had been the most advanced infestation.

Why here, though? Why Derbyshire?

I remembered my desperate winter flight with Lizzy to recover the dagger. I had confronted Fènnù on a London hill. When black ichor dripped from her diseased wings, crawlers rose from the earth.

Fènnù had haunted Derbyshire for months while Lizzy lay beneath the lake. Somehow, that was the cause. History had no mention of foul crawlers before the black dragon was driven mad. Before the dragons' song was broken.

For once, recalling my meetings with dragons did not make me feel insignificant. Georgiana had said, "You are powerful." The strength of our song filled me, and at last, I believed her.

Still, I had not solved the puzzle that led us to sing Fènnù's song. My memory of the flute remained a nagging flutter beyond conscious reach.

A muffled, irritated buzz sounded from the bookshelf. I had no appetite for discoveries, but, wearily, I walked over.

The untreated bean pod had split. An ugly crawler circled futilely in the jar, delicate wings fraying. The sight brought an acid distaste to my throat, and I considered how best to kill it.

In the other jar, the bean pod I treated with draca essence flexed. Morbidly curious, I watched until, with eerie exactness, it split. No, it was cut, as if by a miniature razor from within.

Gleaming with nacreous lapis and jade, a dragonfly-like needledrac emerged. She perched on the cut pod, airing her wings, a beautiful, perfect little draca.

## 14

# PASSING CHELSEA

## EMMA

I looked out the coach's open door. Mr. Knightley was conferring with our driver. Gusts plucked their coat collars. Watery sunlight and gloom alternated as layered clouds crossed the sky.

The driver nodded and climbed back up to his seat, his boots thumping the coach wall behind my head. Mr. Knightley returned to sit across from me. He gave an ironic shrug. "We agree that it will soon rain and that the inn is ahead, somewhere. Whether it is a mile or five is hard to say."

Before we left Pemberley, Mr. Knightley had arranged rooms at an inn in Berkhamsted. That would lodge us only twelve miles from Netherfield, the Bingleys' home. So, I had started two letters to Harriet, crumpled them half-written, and finally sent a short note explaining our plan and suggesting we call on her.

But we were arriving two days later than I had said, delayed by peculiar weather and detours around Blackcoat bandits. When the scheduled date passed, I began inventing unpleasant outcomes. Harriet had replied and suggested we shop in Meryton, then stormed off after waiting for hours. Or worse, she sent a cutting missive refusing any contact.

Muffled voices sounded as the driver and the Pemberley footman, who served multiple duties as coachman, security, and chaperone, dug out their rain gear. The driver whistled, and the horses sped to a brisk trot.

Another gust rattled the coach, and the windows dimmed alarmingly. I straightened a seam on my glove, aligning the embroidered stitches in a neat row.

"You are counting threads again," Mr. Knightley said. He smiled. "I have noticed that you dislike night travel."

Having my secret discovered made me want to deny it, but his expression was so sympathetic that I admitted, "You are right. I am not fond of dark coaches. But it is an old concern. One I have overcome." I held out my hand, and he reached across to take my fingers. "You see? Steady as stone."

"Impressive." Politely, he released my hand, just a touch between friends. We had such easy friendship now. I fixed a suitably friendly smile on my lips to hide the warmth that his touches stirred in my belly.

Thinking about dark coaches cooled that quickly enough. Nighttime rides were vehicles for memories of Mr. Elton. When we reached Highbury, I would encounter him; that must be why the dimmed windows bothered me. It had been a coach like this where he shouted claims of courting me, as if a few weeks of unnecessarily gallant manners and abundant sighs justified the violence that followed.

Mr. Knightley had also courted me, but invisibly, as if courting could be as simple as two people muddling together through an upended, frightening world. I ended that when I rejected his understated, gentlemanlike inquiry. At the time, I fancied that rejecting him was self-sacrifice, a noble decision for his own good. Now, it seemed self-absorbed. I had been insensible of his merits, insolent enough to presume that my defects were beyond redemption merely because I alone had not had the strength to overcome them.

But a repented choice is still a choice. Repented consequences do not vanish.

"What are you contemplating so intently?" Mr. Knightley asked, his eyes catching gleams of lamplight through his black lashes.

"Choice and consequence," I said lightly. "Which reminds me, you must prod me to find the amulet when we arrive. My projects at Hartfield will certainly drive it out of my head."

"You do not fool me. You talk about the amulet every day. I will remind you of Hartfield, instead. Reclaiming your life matters also."

That seemed friendly, so I reused my suitably friendly smile.

Uneven plinks sounded on the roof. Raindrops. The wind swirled, rocking the cab on its springs. Mr. Knightley lit a thin wooden spill from the heater coals and held it to the lamp wick. He trimmed the lamp and shrugged apologetically, as if he were the one afraid of dark coaches.

"Strange weather," he said. "An English spring."

The next gust sheeted rain across the windows. The plinks became a drum, and the windows darkened like midnight. I tried to look out, but water sluiced over the glass. I could not even make out the road. "Can the driver see?"

"Better than us. The lamp blinds us. But it is cold work driving in this weather. I told them to seek a farmhouse or other shelter if it grows bad."

That was also unlike Mr. Elton. On that winter night, he had ordered his driver to halt for an eternity while soft snow fell on us like ash.

The wind strengthened, tugging at the walls. The wheels skidded sideways, then steadied. The rain fell in sheets, rhythmic as ocean waves, and the drumming sharpened to the clatter of hail. Mr. Knightley frowned.

The driver banged twice on the roof: almost there. The coach slowed and turned, rocking precariously as we left the main road, then gravel crunched beneath the wheels, and we stopped. Mr. Knightley opened the door a few inches. "This is the inn. Wait. I will return." Holding his hat, he ducked into the squalling rain and pushed the door closed behind him.

Alone, I listened to the storm. The wind was inconstant, first from one corner, then another. Peculiar, distant thunder thrummed in slow beats.

Then I understood.

I had no person to touch, no illness to focus my skill, but the storm itself was like a raging wound. Pretending that, I stretched my awareness and found, very distant, the aged awareness of Fènnù prowling the sky.

Had she followed me? No; there was no sense of her attention, merely her tireless hunt, disgruntled and frustrated. The storm was seeded by her mood and chased her path.

Lamps approached, golden blurs through the streaming windows. Mr. Knightley opened the door, hung a lamp on the hook, and handed in a gentleman's great coat. "Wear it," he shouted over the moaning gusts. Water poured from his hat brim. "It is a river out here."

While the driver and footman carried in our travel chests and boxes, I pulled on the oversized coat, an awkward process without room to stand. Mr. Knightley offered his hand, and I held it tight, balanced in the doorway and squinting to find the step in the freezing rain. Then I was swept off my feet and carried over the squelching mud and through the inn door.

Mr. Knightley eased my feet to the floor in the receiving hall. The great coat was drenched, my bonnet dripping. Warmth tingled where my side had pressed him, my hip, my thigh, my breast.

"Pardon my not asking permission," he said.

I nodded, unable to think of a clever reply.

Our poor coachmen shed layers of soaked coats by the fire while the innkeeper greeted Mr. Knightley as an old friend. The innkeeper's wife fussed over me, a habit of all innkeeps when a lady is damp, and showed me to my room.

"Right beside mine and my husband's," she said, "and my two daughters are across the hall, so you call if there's a need during the night. The lads have a room in the servant quarters. Mr. Knightley we put upstairs. Not so far away..." She drew that out, curious why a single lady and gentleman were traveling together. I simply thanked her and let her wonder.

I did have a question though. "Did you receive a letter for me?"

"No, madam. Not a thing."

No reply at all from Harriet. That was the one outcome so outlandish I had not considered it.

THE INN'S breakfast was very nice, thick slices of toasted oat bread, fresh churned butter sprinkled with salt, soft boiled eggs, and thick rashers of bacon. There was an earthenware pot of good strong tea and another of hot water. The sun shone cheerily after yesterday's storm.

"This is what Papa and I called country breakfast," I said to Mr. Knightley. I dipped my toast in the egg yolk and took a bite. "It is a relief after Pemberley. One should not have to decide things on an empty stomach. Tea or coffee? Rolls or toast? And four types of preserves. It made my mind spin."

"A woman of simple tastes," Mr. Knightley observed with a smile. His plate was emptied to crumbs. He leaned back comfortably in his chair, folding his arms and looking positively rakish after vertical Mr. Darcy.

I considered his comment. "I would not say 'simple.' Uncluttered? No, that is not right. Wait until you see the front hall at Hartfield! I just feel that one can choose the best things instead of everything."

"Are these my instructions? The care and feeding of Miss Woodhouse?"

"Perhaps," I said playfully. "I do not require feeding now, though. This has been very solid."

The inn's other table held an older married couple in country dress, the man's graying whiskers surrounding an unfortunately red nose, his wyfe—I sensed her bound ferretworm outside—plump and apple-cheeked. They had been glancing at us and whispering all through breakfast.

Our comments prompted a fresh exchange of whispers. That erased Mr. Knightley's smile, and he straightened, very much the proper gentleman. That felt a little dull after his rakish tilt.

I leaned closer and whispered, "Do not assume the worst of people." He raised a skeptical brow, so to distract him, I made a show of considering the last bite of toast and of bacon. "If I eat the bacon, I shall not need luncheon."

Mr. Knightley relaxed in his chair. "I imagine the Bingleys will convince you."

I had forgotten that I mentioned my plan to him. I ate the bacon, dwelling on Harriet's silence. "I do not think we should visit Netherfield. Harriet has her own life, now. She has not invited me. And I hardly even met Mr. Bingley and Jane."

"I am sure Miss Smith would welcome you. And my impression is the Bingleys welcome everyone."

"Let us not," I said softly. "I prefer that she asks first."

I expected him to press, but his reply was distracted. "As you wish." He seemed to be working through some other thought. What emerged was, "Then we might reach Chelsea today. I could show you my home."

That surprised me.

It was certainly a brave offer—touring a gentlewoman through a loft, or whatever lodging a musician could afford on the fringe of London. But I knew Mr. Knightley was brave. He routinely risked his life to aid others. Social awkwardness likely seemed trivial.

However, it was a significant offer. It was not improper to visit a gentleman's home. The Pemberley footman would accompany us; he had come for just such situations. But touring a single man's home provided insight into his living. The ritual implied a... practical interest. Or was this a display of concern? Mr. Knightley might not believe I could recover Hartfield. Was this a prelude to repeating his prior offer?

That flustered me, and my fingers tangled in my lap. But I was reading too much into it. We joked constantly about madcap musicians. Doubtless he regularly invited gentlemen to drink brandy and opine on music. Why not a lady? Or ladies. Or might a handsome musician meet actresses?

"Perhaps it is better to press on," Mr. Knightley amended. "Surrey will only grow more dangerous. Haste is wise."

By this point, I had mentally assembled a bacchanal of dancing beauties, sloshing brandy, and swirling pipe smoke.

"It is," I agreed, relieved.

The other couple rose to depart and walked toward our table. Mr. Knightley straightened again—he looked positively grim—but they passed without a word.

AFTER BREAKFAST, I went for a stroll in the inn's modest garden alongside the lane. Mr. Knightley had been out here before breakfast for his exercise, a strenuous routine of rolls and fierce athletic poses. I had watched him once at Pemberley, but not since. For all the dance-like precision, the motions summoned memories of the short and lethal fight I had witnessed between him and a repulsive American slaver in Pemberley's hills.

Having circled the little path twice and peered down the lane, I accepted the innkeeper's suggestion and took a seat by a garden table that he toweled dry. The plants were prettily raindrop-jeweled, although the hail had broken twigs and stripped spring blossoms of their petals. The older couple from breakfast emerged and sat at the other garden table, and we exchanged pleasant nods.

Distantly, I could hear Mr. Knightley practicing his violin—his travel violin, as his good instrument was safe in its cherrywood case at his home. His diligence made me feel idle, but a traveling lady has few options for productivity. Once I reclaimed Hartfield, there would be fifty tasks to do.

A young man strode down the cottage lane. He spied us, slowed, and entered the inn's garden. He was cleanshaven and well-dressed, a respectable working man on an errand. He eyed the older couple, then to my astonishment, he walked directly to me with a smile.

"For you, ma'am," he said, holding out a sheet of paper.

I took it in blank confusion. Had Harriet hired a messenger for her letter? No, of course not. This was printed. It had the smeared, cheap look of the advertising sheets posted in London. But people did not wander through the countryside handing advertisements to ladies.

*Our incredible movement stands STRONGER than ever!*
*Help us fight the lies!*
*KING ROSDAN calls all Pure Men...*

The rest was even more bizarre.

"A donation would be appreciated, ma'am," the man said. "A penny. Perhaps a shilling..."

"Who is King Rosdan?" I asked. Was that one of those Scandinavian royal families who kept switching sides in the war?

"The *rightful* King." I looked more puzzled, and the man switched to a broad, understanding smile. "Mr. Rosdan Tinsdale."

With a cold start, I understood. "We have a King. And a Prince Regent."

"No, ma'am. That's the lies, you see. The royal family died in the fire from those dragons. A sad end, but it was God's retribution for their betrayal of England's True Faith. Now, Parliament is refusing to crown the rightful heir—"

"I *saw* Prince George," I insisted.

"An imposter," he said smoothly.

"I do not think so. I had coffee with him." I did not say it was at Pemberley; that might still be secret. But this was ludicrous.

"Get out of here, you filth!" The older gentleman had stormed over. Ramrod straight, he confronted the young man. "We have no use for rawgab-bits! Take your nonsense away."

The young man gave a mocking bow. "Just spreading the word, sir. Ladies can be patriots, too. They have their part to play in purging the low blood. Like the Southern Alliance in America. They know how to do it." The older gentleman growled, and the young man grinned. "I'll post this in the stable, then. The working men are with us..."

Mr. Knightley emerged from the inn's door, looking questioningly at me, and the young man's grin thinned. He strolled off without another word, over-long black coattails swinging insolently.

The sheet felt dirty in my fingers. I set it on the table. The older gentleman picked it up and crumpled it. Then he offered his hand to Mr. Knightley, who, after a pause, shook it.

The gentleman bowed to us both. "My apologies that you should encounter that. You two go right on showing those slaver sympathizers what English freedom is about." He excused himself and returned to his wyfe.

Mr. Knightley took his seat looking thoughtful.

"You see?" I said. "Do not assume the worst." But my words felt hollow with that vile paper crumpled on the ground.

# 15

## FAITHFUL AND BOLD

### DARCY

A rabbit sizzled on greenwood spits. The sunset stretched purple and violet across the sky. Elizabeth sat on the far side of the fire, staring unblinking into the glowing coals or, with her gifts, seeing far beyond.

The Darcys have a family motto: *Fidelis et audax*. Faithful and bold. It appeared in 1683, a few Latin words decorating signatures and embossing plaques. But, *ex nihilo nihil fit*—nothing comes from nothing. An ancestor of mine chose those words. They aspired to those values.

I chose to honor them.

When I lost both parents in quick succession, boldness came easily. I was ambitious, confident, self-righteous. My father had drilled me in business, and I used his lessons to purge the grotesquery of slavery from our holdings, a moral bankruptcy he had refused to recognize during his life.

The other half of our motto—faithful—seemed easy as well. I devoted my life to Georgiana, a child then, and to protecting our household and estate.

Five productive, stultifying years trickled past. Faithfulness calcified into duty. Boldness thinned into pride. Then I fell in love with Miss Elizabeth Bennet, and it was like a tempest blew the walls from my stifling prison. And, incredibly, she loved me, too.

But when the person you love no longer loves you, what is faithfulness? Is it bolder to press yourself on them, or to walk away?

"Darcy."

I jerked, guilty for my thoughts. Elizabeth was holding out half the roast rabbit wrapped in a handful of bay leaves.

I had learned her new rules. Never approach her. Never touch her. Do not presume intimacy.

Had I imagined her speaking my name?

"I did not hear you," I said, hoping she would repeat herself, but her hand hung silently. I took the food, hot juices dripping, and thanked her.

After fighting the crawlers, Elizabeth had declined to ride Escalus—she rarely rode when she could walk—so I led him as we left the woods and then, at the farm, arranged for his lodging and amended my letter to Mary.

Elizabeth had waited in silence. She was Elizabeth to me, but the farmer and his wife were awed and whispered in her presence. Would they tell stories of a wordless, unkempt woman in bare feet? No. It would be the angel.

Now, we were camped on a rocky slope dotted with brush and sketchy trees. The rabbit, freshly caught, had been laid at Elizabeth's feet by a ferretworm. The pair of cream firedrakes had visited for a silent communion, then rose in pearly spirals, more glorious than swans. Around our camp, an endless pilgrimage of draca watched in a reverent circle.

I tossed a rabbit bone into the fire and broke the silence. "I would not think these fields could support so many draca."

"Some came a long way," Elizabeth said, cleaning her fingers on a handful of plucked grass. She had, as politely as feasible under our circumstances, devoured her portion of rabbit. I used to tease her about her hearty appetite.

I tipped my chin toward the ring of draca; there must have been twenty. "Draca did not gather around you before. Before the lake, I mean. Are you more powerful?"

"No." A line furrowed her brow. "I suppose I no longer forbid it."

Speaking of the lake summoned a memory: Yuánchi falling like a bloody spear, wings tucked close, then the pillar of spray. The despair I had felt then returned like a chest full of broken bones, even with Elizabeth safe a few paces away.

"Do you remember going into the lake?" I asked, my voice rough.

Her lips pursed. "I remember hugging Yuánchi's neck, and his wings wrapping me. I heard us hit the surface—it was a tremendous crash, like breaking stone—then the water rushed in, cold as ice. We sank like an anvil until his wings opened and I floated free. I liked that. I wanted to see daylight one last time, but my eyes were ruined. There were only blurry gleams. Sun shattered by froth and waves. Then all the light vanished, and I was wrapped round and round in warmth." She smiled, bemused. "It felt like a blanket."

Her smile relieved my remembered despair. "Mary theorizes that draca wrap themselves in the finned form they use for water hibernation, then discard it afterward, like a chrysalis. Could Yuánchi have wrapped you somehow?"

She shrugged. "I cannot say. I only dreamed after that. Dreams from a hundred lives."

"Was our life one of them?"

Her smile flattened. "Do not ask that."

I had broken the rules. Still, I had heard no rule against bribery. "What about getting you boots? We could make a stop at Pemberley." The familiarity of home might restore her.

She thought about it before shaking her head. "Too many people. And I cannot go until I decide about the Blackcoats. About the woman with them."

The woman in their troop was all that had saved them.

"You can find them whenever you wish," I pointed out. "You have draca watching them. How long would it take to collect boots?" She gave me a level stare—*I already said no*—so I changed topics. "Why do you hunt the Blackcoats?"

"They hurt Mary. They are why she called."

"The men who hurt Mary are dead. You are not bound by some fairytale pact." She eyed me. In truth, I had no idea what drove her, but I forged on. "You are Elizabeth Darcy... or call yourself Elizabeth Bennet, even. Whichever name, you always chose your own path."

She hugged her knees and leaned nearer the fire. "Fènnù's anger chews at me. Her fury... it is like jaws around me. I must rid myself of it. Spend it, so she does not take me."

"The Blackcoats are vile enough, but they are mere thieves and bullies. War rages in the south. Why does that not interest the wyfe of war?"

That straightened her back. She looked flustered. "Are you suggesting I go to war?"

"I wish to understand what you want."

"I waged war enough in my dreams." Her words came quick and fierce. "I lived a hundred women's lives, all shattered until, in fury or desperation, they chose to fight. But the wars all turned out the same: bloody, then forgotten, then a generation later, fought anew. Two thousand years only heightens the futility of it."

That passion was Elizabeth's. The words were uncanny, the speech of an angel. A god.

"Then why chase Blackcoats?" I said.

She blew a frustrated laugh. "Were you always so annoyingly persistent, or am I only noticing now?"

"I was. And I am certain you noticed before."

She stood, restless in the dusk. "I was destined to bind a mad dragon. If I *had* bound her, I would have been overwhelmed long before this. Like the wyves of war before me."

"If you were destined for the black dragon, then fate intervened. You bound Yuánchi instead." I hesitated, wondering if this would violate a rule. "*We* bound Yuánchi."

She did not notice my presumption. "And Fènnù's poison corrupts that binding. That is why I must purge her fury. If I break—if she takes me—I will see war soon enough."

"Fighting the French and the slavers?"

She shouted, "Destroying it all!" in a cracking cry, her hands clenched, knuckles white.

I was standing as well, so close I could have gathered her to my chest with the slightest reach. "You would not do that. I know you. You would never be overwhelmed by Fènnù's madness."

Her trembling shoulders calmed. She gave me a sardonic glance like when we bantered at breakfast, and I said something overly sentimental.

I ached to hold her. But I had concealed love for Elizabeth Bennet before, and I could do so again. I clenched my fists, knuckles aching.

Try something simpler. Bribery. "What about Longbourn? Did you leave boots there?"

She turned away, but it was to look up at the darkening sky. The circle of watching draca cowered, pressing their bellies to the earth.

Yuánchi's colossal form exploded from behind the ridge, the wind of his passage flattening the flames of the fire, then drawing them into an envious swirl. He landed a hundred yards behind us.

"I have boots there," she announced abruptly. "We will go to Longbourn tomorrow."

My sleep was tossed by evil dreams of war and thunder.

Dawn had the chill of a late-spring morning, cold but soon to warm. Elizabeth was awake when I opened my eyes, standing in her black gown and watching the distant forest. The ever-present ring of draca had vanished. The fire was dead.

Her pose had the stillness of a long wait.

"Did you sleep?" I asked.

She shook her head. "Time to go." She walked from the camp, her eyes over-bright, her posture brittle.

I had left my meager equipment with Escalus at the farm, keeping only sword and pistol. I strapped those to my belt and strode after her.

Yuánchi waited at the top of the ridge, his sightless head aligned to the rising sun. In the rose light, his mismatched colors were garish—scarlet simmering like hot coals beside swaths of midnight. His scales, whether black or red, were glossy, and they shimmered with the motion of his tremendous breaths.

The pair of cream firedrakes watched me, one perched in a tree, the other atop a boulder a few paces from me.

"You mount first," Elizabeth said crisply. Perhaps I had imagined her over-bright eyes. She added, "If you fall off, I do not want you dragging me with you."

I looked up at the dragon's towering form. "I have never touched him. Will he speak to me?" He had done that in the past, or at least let me listen when he spoke to Elizabeth.

"He no longer speaks. Not since he rose—" Her voice caught.

Was that due to Fènnù's corruption of their binding? Or was it a symptom of a more profound change, that blackness spreading over Yuánchi's hide?

I placed my palm on the front of his wing. Seen in the sky, Yuánchi's silhouette looked as delicate as a firedrake, his wingspan more than twice his body length. This close, the rounded bone leading his wing was like a ship's mast, eight inches across. The scales, two inches long, were dry and textured, not slippery like a fish.

I had seen how Elizabeth mounted at the lake, so I stepped onto the knurl of his wing joint and, like balancing on a log, walked up the wing's front, the tip of my scabbard clicking his scales when I crouched too low. At his shoulder, I waited for the lull in the bellows of his breath, then stepped onto his back. The center was decorated with a series of knobby ridges as tall as my boots, but a six-foot span near the base of his neck was smooth. I sat there astride, bracing my back against a ridge and leaving as much room in front of me as possible.

Like thunder from an ancient storm, Yuánchi's voice filled my mind:

*The broken song corrupts me. Save your wyfe. I cannot.*

Rattled, I wet my lips and twisted to see Elizabeth. Her eyes were narrowed impatiently. She had not heard him.

"Yuánchi no longer speaks?" I asked her.

"No," she said tightly.

Did he choose not to speak to her? Or could the wyfe of war no longer hear the scarlet dragon of healing?

She mounted. Her lithe ascent would have mocked mine except it was too effortless, a master horseman who sweeps into the saddle without breaking stride because he has forgotten how else to mount. She walked casually around me, stepping over my leg, and settled into the natural saddle at the base of Yuánchi's neck.

That left two feet between us. She frowned over her shoulder. "If we dive, you will slide forward across the scales. That direction cuts." Her gaze settled where my crotch straddled Yuánchi's back. "I imagine that would be unpleasant." She slapped directly behind her. "Sit here."

Apparently flying relaxed the rules. I waddled forward, rocking on my rear to avoid shredding my trousers. When there were inches between us, she pulled my arm around her waist. "Closer. Hold tight. Or fall off now and get it over with."

Her back settled against me. We had touched more intimately than this every day of our wedded life, but her slim figure made my heart pound. Without petticoats, her dress was a single layer of fine linen. I could feel every contour of her skin. Elizabeth had always been fit, a tireless walker, but now her waist was ridged with muscle.

Tense muscle. Her back and shoulders were rigid as well. For all her brusque directions, she was as uncomfortable as I.

That made my responsibility clear. I adopted her businesslike tone. "I am ready."

In answer, Yuánchi stood. Our heads rose level with the tops of some good-sized trees, not unthinkably high but very different from standing on a structure. Yuánchi embodied living balance and inhuman power. It was like being astride a racehorse, but a hundred times more. A thousand times more.

"He is incredible," I said. "Unbelievable."

His wings unfolded fifty feet to each side, stretching high while his body crouched, muscles the size of oxen bunching in his haunches. The two fire-drakes shot past arrow-swift, one on each side, then we leaped into the sky. The wings drove down. Elizabeth leaned with a rider's anticipation, and I followed her motion. The world tilted, treetops flashing beneath a stroking wingtip, then leveled.

We climbed toward the forest. The world flattened to a painter's landscape. Wind sang in my ears and forced my eyes to slits. Elizabeth's rigid tension vanished. One of her hands rested lightly on a knob of Yuánchi's neck before her, the other atop my forearm around her waist.

"This is beautiful," I cried. She did not answer; I was not sure she heard over the wind. But we were flying north, the wrong direction, so I shouted, "Are we going to Longbourn?"

She must have heard that, but she did not answer. Her small frame was warm against mine, as familiar as my own body, and I felt her tension return. Was she afraid to go home?

Yuánchi's wings stopped their massive strokes. We glided for a minute, then he tilted in a wide turn, his inner wing dipping. Elizabeth leaned, studying the ground, and I followed her gaze.

The forest below was hazed with blue smoke. Two full acres had been burned to glassy, bare rock. Patches still glowed sullen red, and a metallic scorch filled my nostrils. The surrounding woods were gone; there were a hundred yards of cinders before tree trunks resumed, blown down like twigs, the smaller branches and leaves missing.

In that ash and devastation, a strip of lemon yellow fluttered from a broken branch, a charred fragment of canvas from the Blackcoats' tents.

Elizabeth finished her inspection. She shouted, "We will go to Longbourn."

Yuánchi's wings snapped us through a cruel curve, wind tearing and hissing. Weight crushed me into my seat until the southern sky swung into view.

Miles away, a huge black form flapped from a rocky hilltop and followed us —Fènnù pursuing her wyfe of war.

16

# LONGBOURN

## DARCY

We descended, and the wind sharpened. Countryside sped by unfathomably fast a hundred yards below. Ahead, Yuánchi's shadow raced along a winding country road, his wings eclipsing entire swaths of trees. Houses became more frequent—we dropped lower yet, perhaps seventy yards up—then a picturesque town appeared, a handful of streets filled with rising faces and pointing arms.

"Meryton," Elizabeth shouted, twisting her head so I could hear, the town out of sight before the word was done.

We cleared a copse of tall ash trees. The twin cream-colored firedrakes tucked their wings and dove like stooping hawks, and we followed in a dizzying descent that made my stomach flip. The ground roared up—my body braced for collision—then Yuánchi reared like a stallion, his wings scooping and pounding the air, the force pinning us to his inclined back until we settled. The sudden quiet was profound, like a hurricane had been snuffed out, then the sounds of nature—birdsong, breeze—returned.

Longbourn House, a well-made country home of two stories and fourteen rooms, was beside us. One firedrake alighted on a chimney. The other found the iron perch on the old draca house, a waist-high stone kennel twenty steps or so from the main house.

Elizabeth watched the house, her shoulders taut as a bowstring. "This is dangerous."

I looked around the slightly overgrown garden, snug windows, and quiet countryside. "Why?"

"I am dangerous."

Rules be damned. I leaned closer, my lips brushing her hair. "I will stay with you." She nodded, a single jerk. There was not even a sardonic glance.

Yuánchi shifted to lie flat, wings folding, his chest and lower neck coming flush to the ground. We were still higher than a horse, six or seven feet from the ground, but Elizabeth stood and jumped. I followed, my bootheels cutting divots in the turf. I smoothed my coattails, and my fingers caught threads torn loose by Yuánchi's scales. If we kept riding this way, our clothes would fall to shreds.

Instead of following the path to the door, Elizabeth took stiff, swift steps to the draca house. While the cream firedrake watched from the perch, she touched the slate roof tiles. "It began here with Longbourn's drake. I saw through his eyes, and he feared me. Feared that the wyfe of war would enslave him."

The Longbourn front door flung wide and Mrs. Bennet, her hair threaded with strands of gray, ran out crying, "My dear Lizzy!"

"Mamma," Elizabeth said, sounding very much an over-absent daughter.

Mrs. Bennet swept her into a huge hug overflowing with frills from a floppy housecoat and a highly decorated at-home cap. That stilled into an intense motherly clasp and hushed sobs. At last, she stepped back, wiped her eyes, and caught Elizabeth's cheeks in her hands. She tilted her head one way and the other. "Look at you. Oh, what a state! We shall fix that up in a moment."

Mrs. Bennet saw me waiting a few steps behind. I bowed, "Madam," then I was hauled into an equally huge but substantially less expected embrace of my own.

"You wonderful man," she cried into my soiled neckcloth. "Mary wrote to say you found her. And to think that people used to call you disagreeable!"

I knew quite well who had called me that, but I smiled above her filly cap. "Mary deserves the credit for her return, not I."

She stepped back and plucked at my wrinkled sleeve. "And you as well! Whatever are young people doing these days? It comes of riding dragons, I suppose. We should make you both presentable, but you are such a tall thing.

At least it is a laundry day. Come on. Come on!" She headed toward the house, beckoning.

Elizabeth's sister Kitty emerged. She passed her mother on the path and gaped blankly up at Yuánchi, who swung his sightless head around until his muzzle was a few feet from her. "Goodness," she exclaimed. "I was starting to think I dreamed I met him. But his poor eyes! And why is he turning black?"

"Kitty!" Mrs. Bennet scolded from the doorway. "Stop gawking and bring Lizzy this moment."

"Yes, Mamma," she replied, then frowned at her sister. "It is good to see you. I never believed you were dead. But gracious, you look *dreadful*."

THE WOMEN MILLED IN THE BENNETS' parlor. I stood by the front window, one hand resting on the back of the same straight chair in which I once sat, watching sparkling Miss Bennet and cursing my inability to master any rudiment of social grace.

For a modest country household, an impressive crowd had gathered. Elizabeth was visible in fleeting snatches. Occasional exclamations penetrated the din: "Why wear *Mary's* horrid clothes?" "Madam, your mother is insisting on a bath." "You can take one of my bonnets. You are very nearly freckled!"

A housemaid arrived at my elbow, blushing furiously and explaining that Mrs. Bennet wished my coat ironed, but I remembered the promise I made to Elizabeth when we landed. I declined and edged through the swirling thicket of skirts until, at a loss how else to intervene, I caught Elizabeth's fingers. She turned, and we faced each other in the center of a suddenly silent crowd, like a couple frozen mid-dance at a crowded ball.

"Is this too much?" I asked.

"It is so many... I had hoped to see—" Some unseen signal snapped her attention to the front door. It opened, and, dressed in buttercup yellow, Jane Bingley stepped in to behold her dearest sister. They each took a step, then ran to embrace. Tears dampened Elizabeth's cheeks, and I relaxed.

"Hush, everyone!" Mrs. Bennet said in a penetrating whisper, although nobody was saying a word. "Give the girls a minute."

Another woman, an older servant whom I had seen somewhere before, stepped carefully over the threshold. She held a sleeping baby—the Bingleys' daughter, I thought. I met her when she was a few weeks old, but I had no knack for distinguishing infants. The woman craned her neck to look back through the open door and announced in a Scottish brogue, "The scarlet dragon is turnin' black as the earl of hell's waistcoat!"

Mrs. Bennet's restraint failed, and she rushed to her daughters, launching frilly chaos.

The servant turned to watch the sisters' reunion, her red cheeks rounded by a happy smile. Hearing her accent helped my memory: she was a washerwoman who served at both Netherfield and Longbourn. More than that, she had provided draca lore to Elizabeth that saved Jane's life.

I eased around the perimeter and greeted her. "Mrs. Bruichladdich."

"Mr. Darcy," she said, flustered to find a gentleman bowing. She curtsied, child and all.

"Is that Jemma?"

"Aye, sir. Isn't she a wee darlin'? Mrs. Bingley felt her sister coming—through her wyvern, ye ken—so we came galloping here in the carriage."

"My wyfe spoke very fondly and favorably of you," I said.

The washerwoman met my gaze for the first time, her old eyes pleased. "Your wyfe is a grand lassie." She looked at Lizzy among the bustle of women. "*Banrigh nan Dràgon.* 'Tis like being in an old song, except for her being English of all things... your pardon, sir. I mean na' offence. 'Tis only that everyone knows the great wyves were Scottish."

Her Gaelic reminded me of late nights with Rabb, the Pemberley gamekeeper murdered by the Wickhams. He had regaled me with Scottish history over tumblers of peat-steeped whiskey. *Banrigh nan Dràgon* was their name for a great wyfe.

"My gamekeeper told me of the Scottish great wyves," I said. "Repeatedly, in fact." She watched me uncertainly—England had a poor record of respect for Scottish heritage—so I added, "It is history worthy of pride."

"Aye." Her toothy grin returned. "A Scot carries their fair share of pride. Your wyfe springs of Scotland, if ye ken. The Bennets at least, far back."

"I have heard that also. I am privileged by association."

"Och, you're a good lad." She frowned and pinched my wrinkled cuff. "Were ye rollin' in a puddle?"

It seemed unwise to tell a professional laundress I had attempted to wash my own clothes. "A mishap at a brook." She eyed my collar skeptically.

"Darcy!" a man's voice exclaimed, and Charles Bingley strode in dressed for bird hunting. He thumped me on the back. "I saw the dragon flying..." He spotted Elizabeth. "It *is* her!"

He dragged me into an embrace, pounding me even harder. His unreserved happiness broke some restraint of my own, and tears stung my eyes. The long days of pursuit and the strangeness once I found Elizabeth had made me neglect my miraculous luck.

"You are a good friend, Charles," I managed between thumps.

Charles pushed me back and gripped my forearms. "Mary wrote us a letter. Only a few lines. It was as short as one of mine! She said Lizzy returned and flew away, and you chased after her like the romantic fool you are!"

"I suppose," I said with a rueful grin.

The ladies' reunion had calmed, and Kitty announced, "Let us help Lizzy dress." She, Jane, and a housemaid tugged Elizabeth away and upstairs. Elizabeth looked back, her glance meeting mine before she disappeared. The ease from her reunion with Jane was gone; she looked anxious.

Mrs. Bennet stayed and fussed at the other staff until they hurried one way or another. Then she dithered, visibly torn between following her daughters and some other purpose. At last, she came to me, her usual, flouncing smiles absent.

"Mr. Darcy, my daughter is not herself. What has happened to dear Lizzy?"

A mother deserved what truth I had. "Elizabeth has survived a trial I do not fully comprehend. It left her... haunted or possessed by memories of past great wyves." Mrs. Bennet set her lips in a determined line as I continued, "Those women led violent lives, and their memories affect her. I brought her here because I hoped home would help her. And it has. *You* have helped. I thank you."

"That is what homes are for," Mrs. Bennet said briskly. She squeezed my arm. "And that is what husbands are for. Bless me, but Mr. Bennet always set me straight when I got in a flutter."

The baby stirred grumpily in the washerwoman's arms, and Mrs. Bennet took her. Jemma quieted while Mrs. Bennet adjusted her granddaughter's knit cap. "The older one gets, the more one understands that young people are what matters. Lizzy's home is with you, more than a silly old mother or an old, creaking house. You must care for her."

Yuánchi had said almost the same thing: *Save your wyfe. I cannot.*

"I swear it," I answered, and the words lodged in my heart.

Mrs. Bennet smiled, now her customary, bustling self. "I must go help Lizzy dress. Her hair is such a tangle!"

She passed the baby to Charles, who received his daughter with evident skill. Mrs. Bennet trotted up the stairs, and delighted feminine noises erupted. Charles and I exchanged the well-practiced glances of gentlemen captive to ladies on errands. He chose a comfortable chair, balancing Jemma on his knee and preparing for a wait.

The Scottish washerwoman had not curtsied to withdraw. Her fingers pinched nervously in her apron. "Begging your pardon, sir, but might I have a look at the dragon?"

I understood her nervousness. "He is safe to approach."

"Aye, thank ye, sir," she said, curtsying and hurrying out with such alacrity I wondered if I had misinterpreted her hesitation.

"The wyvern is prowling, too," Charles observed good naturedly. "That beast follows Jemma like a puppy. Jane has to scold her to keep her out of the house—her claws slice the rugs to pieces. Everything is confused with Harriet gone. School children lurk in every cupboard, and I am useless at helping with them, as you could guess."

After the dragons' battles razed miles of London, Elizabeth had relocated the city school to the safer locale of Netherfield. That did not satisfy the headmistress, who resigned and fled even farther north, so Elizabeth chose Harriet Smith as her replacement. Miss Smith had proved herself efficient and unflappable, skills I had not recognized in the shy girl I first met in London.

However, a headmistress and her school were usually in the same spot.

"Miss Smith is gone?" I asked.

"Only for a week. She hired a teacher to help. I gather she heard from her long-lost mother down in Surrey, but you would have to ask Jane for the details. I cannot untangle all those Woodhouses and Smiths."

Harriet's mother. That would be earthshaking for Harriet; she had never known her.

Had Emma known when she departed to Surrey? I thought not. She acknowledged Harriet as her sister, accepting whatever scandal that caused. If Emma had expected to meet the woman who bore an illegitimate child with her father, she would have told us.

"Mrs. Bennet has been a godsend, though," Charles continued, cradling the baby with one arm and stretching the other. "She takes Jemma every afternoon. You and I are lucky fellows to have such a mother-in-law."

I found, with some surprise, that I agreed. Then I settled in another chair to wait.

THE LADIES RETURNED. Lizzy was bathed, travel grime gone, and dressed in a white muslin country frock, the hems decorated with an oak-leaf pattern in green thread. I recognized the dress from an eternity ago when we had strolled through Longbourn's gardens. Her dark brown hair was up, grown to a thick, less-than-fashionable mass, but utterly beautiful. She had found her boots, the brown leather well broken-in. Other than some peeling sunburn and the rose-colored blemish on her cheek, she looked her old self, although subdued.

The other ladies, though, were more than subdued. They were silent. Kitty cast nervous glances at her sister, then at me, then back.

Something had happened. Nothing dire or dangerous, just... unsettling. The dagger Gramr was visible, strapped to Elizabeth's thigh, the shape more apparent under white cloth than it had been under Mary's black gown.

Elizabeth walked directly to me. "We must go." Perhaps unconsciously, she touched a finger to the blemish on her cheek. This would have been her first glimpse in a looking glass.

I wanted to ask "Go where?" but that seemed wiser without an audience, so I nodded and followed her to the front door.

Mrs. Bennet hugged her hard, then held her out at arm's length. "You let Mr. Darcy take care of you, you hear me? And do not fly too high. I worry you will fall off."

"I shall not," Elizabeth said, and I wondered which statement she had answered. She held Jane, and they exchanged whispered words. Kitty handed her a hand-trimmed spring bonnet and received a wordless embrace in exchange, then Elizabeth returned the bonnet saying apologetically, "The wind."

Outside, curious locals had gathered a hundred yards distant on the approach to the manor. Yuánchi waited impassively in a grassy area past the front gardens, a sightless god cloaked in mottled scarlet and ebony, his tail wrapped cat-like around his feet.

The Bingleys' wyvern was perched on a sturdy fence and gleaming bright as a fresh-minted guinea. She launched with one powerful stroke of her wings and glided silently over our heads to land protectively by Mrs. Bennet, who was holding the baby.

The Scottish washerwoman was a few paces from Yuánchi but bent almost double as if the ground were more fascinating than a dragon. She straightened when Elizabeth arrived, then dropped to a low curtsy. "*Banrigh nan Dràgon.*"

"It is good to see you again," Elizabeth said, smiling.

"Aye, lassie." She rose and grinned back. "Who'd have thought you'd be astride this beast? But I knew ye from the first when I saw ye commandin' your drake."

"You did," Elizabeth admitted.

"Your dragon is turnin' black. 'Tis nae good. Black is war."

The woman held out her hand, offering something from the ground. A scarlet scale. Others were scattered in the grass.

Elizabeth took the scale from the woman's wizened fingers. Her reply had the sound of a quote, but unknown to me. "'A cage dusted with fallen scales, like stars.'"

"Aye, ma'am. That was the story. I don't know of dragons, but I know a draca sickened by a fouled binding."

Elizabeth nodded. The washerwoman curtsied again and hurried away, leaving Elizabeth and me alone.

The secret I had kept, from what I thought to be pity, now burdened me. "Yuánchi still speaks. He spoke to me. Either you do not hear him, or he does not speak to you."

Elizabeth was still a long time, turning the fallen scale in her fingers. I saw the voids in the dragon's coat now, exposed spots of unhealthy leathery hide.

"Yuánchi is the dragon of healing," she said. "He was never meant to bind the wyfe of war. I am poisoning him."

"You cannot know that."

"I do know that. Yuánchi has seen a hundred human empires rise and fall. Our lives are as fleeting as sunbeams to him, yet he will not survive binding me." She looked up at me, her brown eyes level and serious. For all that Elizabeth was a woman of humor and wit, this seriousness—this decisiveness—was the real Elizabeth of old. "Fènnù makes it worse. She is twisting my mind, and her venom flows through me to Yuánchi. I must escape her."

"How? She outflew Yuánchi at Pemberley."

Elizabeth studied the southern horizon. Ponderous thunderheads were swelling. "If we go north..." There was a silence. "Would you come with me?"

*Fidelis et audax.* The answer should be simple.

Instead, I asked, "Why north?"

"Fènnù is drawn to war, to the south. If we go north, we escape her."

"And... hide?" The word reeked of dishonor.

She abandoned the horizon to watch me. "What happened to 'I will stay with you'?"

I could feel my loyalties tearing, one half bound to Elizabeth, the other to England and the war, to trust in Georgiana and duty to those risking their lives.

"We need the great wyves together to heal the song and end the blight." My words had started wooden, but my conviction returned. "Georgiana has seen it. She says the war and the blight are connected."

"She is right. The blight is subtler than blackened plants and rot."

"Emma and Knightley are retrieving the amulet. It is a dangerous venture, but Emma is strong. She will succeed, and then we will have two of the three great items. We must be prepared to act when we find the third. England's survival is at stake." I realized we were having a coherent conversation—planning together—and that I had never asked a crucial question. "The third item, the one made of claw, is a flute. Do you know where it is?"

Her overly pale skin blanched under the healing sunburn. As if from a great distance, she recited:

> *"To sound our claim,*
> *the three wyves came:*
> *Of healing, wise.*
> *Of song, who cries..."*

That was not the end of the quote, but she stopped.

"You do know," I said, amazed.

"In the north, a wyfe of war held the flute," she whispered. "But the memory ends... swiftly." When her gaze met mine, it was veiled. "Is that enough to bring you north?"

It was a path to the flute. My split duties converged, and my conscience cleared. "North, then. Where you go, I go." *Fidelis et audax.* But I remembered her veiled gaze, and the motto rang hollow, the resolution too convenient.

Elizabeth, though, actually smiled. Then she reached down and hoisted the tail of my coat, suspending it with a finger hooked through a two-inch rip. "We must make a stop first."

# 17

# PEMBERLEY BY STEALTH

## DARCY

"I should have kept Mary's dress," Elizabeth whispered, brushing irritably at her white sleeve. "This is too visible."

We were hiding in a lush grove of sapling oaks. Pemberley House was ahead, shadowed by the deepening evening twilight.

After a harrowing, treetop-brushing flight that hugged ravines and valleys—all aboard a blind steed—Yuánchi had landed two miles from the house. Elizabeth and I had walked from there, choosing the most obscure paths.

I did not comment on her clothes. I was too busy scheming.

Our visit to Longbourn had restored her more to her old self. She no longer felt like a stranger. This was Elizabeth, only moody and guarded. So, when she proposed visiting Pemberly—raiding it, really—I wholeheartedly agreed. The familiarity of Pemberley could only restore her further.

"There is no need for secrecy," I pointed out, again. "We can walk through the front door. Mrs. Reynolds will gather everything we need." That was a scheme, of course. Elizabeth would be mobbed when we appeared.

"We only need the saddle." Elizabeth dashed off, sprinting across fifty yards of meadow and vanishing into the shadows behind the stables. I hurried after her, expecting to hear a shout of recognition, but, incredibly, not a soul was in sight.

That was no more incredible than the rest of our trip. Like many country ladies, Elizabeth had been raised tramping through wilderness, and being an adventurous woman, she had even explored the roughest forest at my aunt's estate, Rosings. Now, though, traveling with her was like being guided by a master hunter. For the second time today, I thought of Rabb. Elizabeth had the same awareness of her surroundings, every rustle, every sightline, every snapped twig. I was not sure if her skills were gleaned from memories of past wyves, or if she augmented her awareness with unseen draca.

She was intimidatingly fit as well. When I reached the back of the stable, puffing, she was inside. I slipped in and found her greeting the small mare she sometimes rode.

Escalus scented me and whinnied from his stall. I hurried to quiet him. "Good fellow," I said while he pranced excitedly. "Mary certainly retrieved you quickly." Feigning a sudden thought, I turned to Elizabeth, "It was good to see Jane and the baby. We could—"

"I do not wish to speak with Mary," she said.

Apparently, my schemes were transparent. More relieved than anything, I tried honesty. "She will be desperate to see you."

"She does not know we have come, and you informed her I am well." That sounded dismissive, but her gaze was earnest. "Mary is safe at Pemberley, safer away from me, and safer yet when I am gone." She pointed across the stable. "There it is."

Yuánchi's saddle hung on a far wall. It was a large affair, rigged for two riders with room to spare. With tack, it would be heavy and awkward—far too heavy for two people to carry for miles.

Elizabeth had considered that. She opened the mare's stall. "If we strap it loosely, I think she will carry it. If not, we can find a cart."

"That provides our seating. But we will need more than the clothes on our backs."

"So you can look pretty?" she asked while leading the mare to Yuánchi's saddle.

That felt uncalled for; I had looked like a feral hound for days. "A gentleman presents himself properly." And if on occasion I was fastidious, that was to honor my mother's reliance on pristine clothing. A reliance shared by Miss Woodhouse, for that matter.

When Elizabeth did not answer, I added, "I thought you *liked* that I dressed well," which sounded unfortunately peevish. But her jibe about "pretty" had lodged in my head. Could she have been teasing?

I realized she was staring at the saddle. A folded sheet of notepaper was pinned to a strap and addressed in angular script: *Lizzy*.

Reluctantly, Elizabeth unpinned it:

*"Talk to me before you go, or I shall not forgive you.*

*—M"*

FIVE MINUTES LATER, Elizabeth announced, "She is coming."

I was tired of endlessly asking "How do you know?" so I simply nodded, as if one sister summoning another without lifting a finger were perfectly normal. That drew an assessing glance from Elizabeth, relieved or annoyed that her parlor tricks no longer merited surprise.

Mary exited the conservatory door carrying a lantern, her black satin almost lost in the onset of night. One of the small, feathered draca that followed her flew celebratory figure eights in the air—a messenger, presumably.

Mary entered the stable, noted her sister, nodded to me, and hung the lantern from a hook. The small draca fluttered to her shoulder, and she said, "He began pecking at the window. I thought it must be you. You are not here to stay, clearly."

"I cannot," Elizabeth said. Mary waited, and Elizabeth added, "The changes to me are harming Yuánchi. We must escape Fènnù, and the war, and the... temptation of violence."

"So you will just leave," Mary said tightly.

"I have no choice—"

"You have a choice!" Mary shouted, then seemed shocked that she had. She closed her eyes for a breath. "Lizzy, it is a miracle you are alive. You were passing through death's door. With you returned, we can heal the song. We *must*. That is the cause of all these disasters. The foul crawlers. Fènnù's madness. The madness that impinges on you and Yuánchi."

"That madness is consuming me. Do you know what will happen if Fènnù claims me as her wyfe of war? She will lay waste to England, searching my own memories for targets, burying us in a yearslong winter. All while the black blight spreads."

Mary shrank under her sister's assault, arms clutching herself. But when she spoke, she straightened, and her tone was proud. "I *do* know. I have read accounts. When there are allusions to Fènnù rising, famine and war follow. Realms are erased. Even the historical record falls to fragments. But Lizzy, you must understand: Georgiana and I have achieved something miraculous! We sang Fènnù's song. It is one voice of three that make up the great song. If we find the others, we can heal it."

"You sang Fènnù's song?" Elizabeth said in disbelief.

"Georgiana sang. I played. But I *saw* the song."

Elizabeth shook her head. "The great song is beyond us. You must not try."

"I did not try. I *did* it!" Mary retorted angrily, then she waved her hands in frantic apology. "I am saying this all wrong. Lizzy, I do not want you to go. You were gone for so long. It is hard without you."

Elizabeth was silenced by that, and I used the pause to offer a calming hand. "There is no disagreement between you. No conflict. Elizabeth and I are leaving so we can *find* the flute and heal the song. Our goals are aligned."

"Why did you not say so?" Mary said finally. "You know where to find the flute?"

Elizabeth seemed stymied by the question. Her gaze flicked between me and Mary before she answered, "Only a clue. It was in the north. Far in the north."

Mary sagged. "The arctic?"

"What?" Elizabeth burst out laughing. "No! Scotland. I am sure I can write you a letter."

Mary drew a relieved breath and smiled back. She turned to me, her spectacles circular gleams in the lamplight. "And you are going with her. I am glad for that. But what about Pemberley? You cannot imagine what was required to convince the other landholders to hunt for crawlers."

"That sounds like you succeeded," I noted. "Georgiana and you are worthy of Pemberley. Trust yourselves. Do what is right."

I added no qualifier, no "until we return." When a person accepts responsibility, it is churlish to trot out conditions and limits. But hearing my words, the phrasing felt right.

I understood the cause of the sisters' argument. Fear. Fear that I shared.

England was being ripped asunder by war. In the face of that disaster, the English ideal was to pretend normalcy—to trust in calm and competence, to persevere, and to return to an unchanged life. But that ideal had been exposed as a myth. The American War of Independence shook the British Empire, and the weight of this war pressed deeper, not only because battle was being waged within our own shores but because it was aided by rifts in our politics and society. The soldiers dead or maimed, the families fleeing or broken by hate—they had no unspoiled life to resume. To pretend that English constancy waited for Elizabeth and me was self-deception. To pretend our lives were safe was a lie. And I abhorred dishonesty.

Even now, while war raged, I was being dishonest, trying to ingratiate myself to this incredible, altered woman as if our old life were a play that she could be tricked into performing by parading the halls of Pemberley. In truth, I had no idea what life awaited us, only that it would be changed.

"It would be unwise to leave without supplies," I said to Elizabeth. "I will fetch them. You need not come, but I must speak with Georgiana before we go."

She watched me, her thoughts hidden, then nodded.

I left her with Mary and strode to the house, every seam of the stone path known to my boots even at night. The windows of the grand music room were dark, so I entered through the conservatory door that Mary had used and set out for Georgiana's room.

Shimmering candlelight and clavichord notes came from her adjacent music salon. I knocked on the half-open door.

"Fitz!" she exclaimed and ran to embrace me. "How did you arrive without an uproar?" She drew back, frightened. "Is Lizzy not with you?"

"She is," I reassured her. "She is in the stables with Mary. She did not want a crowd. She fears that her presence endangers those around her." In a few words, I explained Yuánchi's illness, and Lizzy's plan to fly north to escape Fènnù and search for the flute.

"What of the war?" Georgiana asked, after a moment.

"It is like a poison to her, and to Yuánchi."

"It is a poison to us all. The blight *is* the war—it is a darkness corrupting minds and morals, affecting life itself. Have you read of the horrors in the occupied south?" Her finger touched a reading table stacked with rumpled newspapers.

"We can do nothing without the flute."

"Yuánchi could turn the tide of battle in a day."

"And Fènnù would claim Elizabeth." I smiled to reassure her. "Others can fight the war."

"*Others*," she echoed, disbelieving. "That does not sound like my bold brother."

The passion on her face, the challenge, filled me with unexpected wonder. We had a rare relationship: two parentless siblings who, due to age and circumstance, were almost like father and daughter. A year ago, Georgiana had seemed girlish and cloistered to me. Now I saw, or finally recognized, that she had been transformed by our trials.

"Elizabeth needs me," I said, "and I am faithful to her. Until we return, you must be the bold Darcy."

I RODE Escalus while Elizabeth and Mary followed in the pony cart. In the forested vale two miles from the house, I packed supplies into Yuánchi's cavernous saddlebags: clothes, both mine and Elizabeth's; spare shoes and weatherproof outerwear; rye bread with a chunk of cheddar—I, at least, was hungry. To prove we were civilized, I wrapped up a bottle of whiskey from an upstart but promising distillery in Oban. In my coat pocket, I carried every guinea and half-guinea from Pemberley's coffers. English banknotes were worthless in Scotland, but gold was valued everywhere.

Elizabeth handed me a pair of the flying goggles she had commissioned. She fastened hers, tightening the strap that drew the leather frames snug to her temples. Looking like a caricature of a woman in spectacles, she said, "Now we can fly fast."

I suppose that meant we had been flying slowly.

"Thank you for helping," I said to Mary. "And for staying with Georgiana. For being with her."

She seemed unsure how to respond. Finally, she said, "You look much better."

A snort issued from Elizabeth's direction. My valet had greeted me with a rueful shake of his head, then worked wonders while Mrs. Reynolds gathered the supplies.

"You still have Gramr?" Mary said, resuming her customary brisk delivery, and Elizabeth nodded. "The French seek for it and for the amulet, but they approached *me* about the flute. They think it is connected to the Bennets—"

"What?" Elizabeth said, so sharply I wondered if she had remembered something, but her tone was normal when she asked, "Why?"

"I do not know, but the journal calls the flute the 'hollow relic of music.' It will be inscribed with the third song." Mary snatched a breath. "It is strange that our family journal mentions it. Ask about Bennets—"

Elizabeth stopped her with a touch on her shoulder. "I will. But we must go. It is time to move the horses back."

Mary led the mare with the pony cart twenty paces distant. Escalus, his lead tied to the cart, followed, looking reproachfully at me and challengingly at towering, saddled Yuánchi.

Elizabeth turned to me and removed her gloves. "Fènnù is west of us, a half hour's flight. She stays close to track my binding to Yuánchi. I must hide us so she cannot follow." She offered her bare hands. "Hide *both* of us. Yuánchi bound you, too."

I removed my gloves. She crossed her wrists to take mine, her left hand in my left. The pose felt formal, and memories of our Beltane handfasting whispered. Her fede ring of knotted gold gleamed, a sight so familiar that I only now noticed she still wore it. Was that significant, or was her request that I travel north simply practical? Desired or not, Yuánchi's binding linked him to us both.

Elizabeth closed her eyes. Escalus shivered and neighed. Yuánchi drew straight, his wings rustling, and his scythe-like claws cut into the forest loam.

I felt... a coiled heat in my breast, spooling like a ship's line.

"It is done," Elizabeth said and opened her eyes. "It will not last long. Fènnù will feel the absence. We must be far away before she arrives to search." She called to her sister, "Hurry on your trip back. Stay at Pemberley. It is safe."

Elizabeth climbed the stirrup-like footholds to the saddle. I settled in the rear seat and followed her example, fastening the leather belt over my lap.

She pointed to the northern sky. "*Tiānshū*. The pivot star. We will fly like the wind and leave the war for those in the south."

# 18

## SURREY

### EMMA

We had come so close to Hartfield.

"How long until the road *is* open?" I asked the officer. Arguing had achieved nothing, so I tried a helpless smile and peering through my lashes. "I really *must* return home."

That made him tidy his scarlet lapel with its brass buttons. He looked young for an officer, perhaps younger than I, and I remembered Georgiana mourning young, dead soldiers.

Unfortunately, a tidied lapel did not change his answer. "It was unwise to travel in the first place. All residents in the south parish were told to remain at home. There is a war."

"Of course, there is a war. But it is not *here*—"

"It is enemy agents that concern us. Blackcoats, infiltrators, and spies. There are reports."

I looked entreatingly at Mr. Knightley. Thus far, he had watched in silence.

"I am sure the captain knows his business," Mr. Knightley said gravely.

That was either a subtle message or singularly unhelpful, but I had no idea which.

"If you will excuse me," the officer said. He bowed smartly and crossed the road to harangue a pair of soldiers who had lit a pipe.

"I told you this might be difficult," Mr. Knightley said to me.

We stood beside our stopped coach, stranded on Donwell Road, just north of Highbury village. Hartfield was south of the village, two miles farther.

I watched twenty soldiers march past in a double column, their red coats grimy, oily muskets at their shoulders. Others blockaded the road to prevent anyone from crossing.

"Did you encounter this sort of obstacle on your last trip to the south?" I asked.

"At times."

"How did you get past?"

"I did not bat my eyelashes and smile." That earned him a cool look, and he admitted, "I was on official military business. Sanctioned by the War Council."

Beyond the marching soldiers, the village looked perfectly normal. "Do you think it is dangerous?"

"I cannot judge. This seems a heavy-handed tactic to root out spies. But armies are not renowned for moderation."

I angled my head, shading the sun with the bonnet's brim. "People are walking about in the village. I can see them. What is the point of keeping us from crossing this one road?"

"Armies are not renowned for logic, either."

I considered that, then batted my eyes at Mr. Knightley. "I am sure the captain knows his business. Shall we turn the coach around?"

WE HEADED BACK NORTH, but at the first junction, I knocked on the front panel and signaled the driver to turn right.

"Where are we going?" Mr. Knightley asked.

"I cannot bring you all this way without showing you the sights."

"Would these sights be in the southern parish?"

"Now that you mention it, I believe they are." I looked through the rear window to ensure the officer was not watching, then turned back and met Mr. Knightley's frown. I frowned right back. "Oh, do not try *that*. You crossed the line of battle. I doubt you convinced the enemy by waving a letter from Lord Wellington."

After a half mile, the road entered the orchards. Apples and pears rained blossoms like butterflies. I signaled again and pointed to a farmhouse, where the coach stopped.

We walked to the house and were met by a joyful collie. I petted him, then knocked. Mrs. Hewitt herself answered. The Hewitts had a maid of all work, a parish orphan they took in, but she would be busy scrubbing, not answering doors.

Mrs. Hewitt was a welcome sight after so long, and she clapped in delight when she saw me. "Miss Woodhouse! Glory, what a relief. Are you here to send that nasty man back to London?"

She launched into a spirited recital of my brother-in-law's faults, not least his refusal to purchase proper Hartfield cider. I nodded along cheerfully, adding I-told-you-so glances to Mr. Knightley at the best parts.

When she wound down, I said, "I must ask a favor, though. This is my friend, Mr. Knightley." He bowed, sweeping his black topper with panache, and Mrs. Hewitt hurriedly curtsied. "We wish to visit Donwell Abbey, but the road is closed. May we leave our coach here? You need not pay it the slightest attention. Mr. Knightley's men will watch over it."

"Oh..." She peered at the coach. "What a fine coach. Where are you from, sir?"

"London," Mr. Knightley answered. Mrs. Hewitt frowned, and he amended, "Chelsea, more properly. I have an apple orchard, myself." I thought that was a clever invention.

"Oh, well then." She smiled, her eyes flicking between us. "Certainly, a coach is no bother. You go have a walk with your gentleman." She waved us on our way and winked at me, eyes twinkling.

That left me self-conscious, and I stewed while Mr. Knightley arranged matters with the driver and footman. At last, he joined me.

"Shall we bring the footman?" I asked, striving so hard for a light tone that I sounded quite inane.

That surprised him. "Do Surrey ladies bring their footmen on walks?"

"No..." I suppose it hardly mattered if Mrs. Hewitt thought this was a courtship. Mr. Knightley knew better. Still, I felt my ears turn pink. I turned to study the trees. "There is a footpath in Donwell Abbey. It leads most of the way to Hartfield. We can cut through the orchard to reach it."

We walked among the apple trees and their masses of bloom. The weather was nicely cool. When we reached the hedgerow at the edge of the orchard, I showed Mr. Knightley the stacked fieldstones for climbing over. "These keep the sheep in their place, but goats go over, and we shall too." The stones provided two tall steps, each a stretch, but country ladies are practical about hems and glimpses of ankle. He held my hand for balance, and feeling happy, I jumped down the far side, skirt flaring. The ground thumped harder than I remembered. I had been twelve the last time I jumped instead of descending sedately, and rather smaller.

Mr. Knightley scrambled up with no trouble and jumped beside me with a huff and a grin.

"These are the Abbey grounds," I said. "It has been abandoned for centuries. Nothing is left but fallen stones. I like to imagine it looks like Rome."

He gazed over the grassy field. Blocks of golden Bargate stone, a sandy rock much harder than it looked, lay at odd angles in the greenery. A few ragged sections of wall remained, none taller than a man, all of them rough-topped with stones and bricks poking out from crumbled mortar. The Abbey stones were very large and heavy, or they would all have been taken for building long ago. Ivory arum lilies and pink masterwort filled the marshy, eastern side.

"It is a beautiful setting," he said. "The drainage needs repair. Why is the land not maintained?"

"There was a disagreement over who owns it. A duke died without an heir, the Church made a claim, then other debtors argued. That was hundreds of years ago. I imagine it is still a tangle." He nodded thoughtfully, and I set out across the uneven meadow. "I had an adventure here with a draca. I think that was when I realized I had some affinity for them."

"A feral draca?"

"No, she was bound."

Bound to Miss Bates, a local spinster who was at least forty. Miss Bates was widely assumed to be silly, harmless, and thoroughly unromantic—certainly I had thought so. Learning she was a widow, let alone secretly bound, was a shock. She had confided her story to me: eloping with a soldier, being disowned by her family, then being widowed and penniless.

I understood her choice of secrecy. Bound widows risked terrible persecution. Draca usually left when a husband died, so a widow who kept her draca was suspected of harlotry or even witchcraft. There were only a handful of bound widows in England, all of them wealthy and influential enough to fend off the Church's disapproval. Although, now that I thought about it, if Miss Bates was secretly bound, other bound widows might hide their draca as well. Perhaps publicly bound widows were wealthy and important because only rich women dared admit the truth.

Mr. Knightley and I walked for a time, and I thought about secrets. Finally, I said, "I feel something is changing with my affinity."

Mr. Knightley's answering look was hesitant. "Should you discuss that with Mr. Darcy? Or Miss Darcy?"

"You mean, instead of you?"

He nodded. A few black locks had gone astray when he doffed his hat, and they stuck out around his ears. If he were Harriet, I would reach over and tuck them in. I could even picture doing it, the heel of my glove resting on his cheekbone beside his dark lashes.

Shocked by my own musing, I concentrated on swishing my boots through the grass until we reached a row of old building stones. I stepped up on the first one and began walking along them, one step for each.

"If I discuss my affinity with the Darcys," I resumed, "it is instantly serious. War. Lost wyves. Dragons. Dusty books are opened, and armies readied. I just want to talk about it."

"Then I suppose you must tell me. How has it changed?"

I reached the end of the row and rested my gloved fingers in his to step down. "I do not think I can express it." He burst out a laugh, and I had to smile. "I said I *wanted* to talk about it, not that I knew how. Can we wait here for a moment?"

The Abbey ruins were as familiar to me as Hartfield's gardens. I did not even remember my first visit, I had been so young. They had always interested me—for imaginary games, and later to paint or just to wander. I had seen the vines climb and die, the tree leaves rain down in all colors, the swallows nest in high corners. The ruins stayed steady through it all, an anchor while nature surged and changed.

I took off my gloves, steel gray that matched my muslin walking gown and feather-trimmed bonnet. For color, I had a dark rose corded spencer over top. I packed this outfit to be intimidating when I reached Hartfield, but it was warm, so it was pleasant to feel the cool air tickle my fingers. I crouched and rested my palm on one of the gold-hued stones, a foot tall and three feet long. "The Abbey's history is all layered, like an oil painting covered over and over." I lifted my face to the sun and closed my eyes, flooding my eyelids with scarlet glow.

So far away that I could not comprehend the distance, I felt the tug of Yuánchi's binding. He was moving. Swiftly. "Yuánchi is flying again." I had felt him move several times in the last few days, in the quiet moments when I was very calm.

Mr. Knightley's clothing rustled. His watch chain jingled; he had crouched beside me. "With Mrs. Darcy?"

"I still am not sure. He is so far, I cannot make out her side of the binding." The binding was changed, too. The black streaks I had noticed at Pemberley were more pronounced, like a sheet of paper dropped on hot coals and charring before it bursts into flame. "I am not sure," I repeated. "It is very frustrating. I hope they sent a letter to Hartfield."

"That is a mundane hope for a woman who can sense dragons." Mr. Knightley sounded quite impressed.

I opened my eyes, and the sensation faded. "Ink and paper are easier to interpret."

My fingers rested on the stone. The blocks were coarsely dressed, but the texture was smoothed by age. They were also dirty. I rubbed my gritty fingertips together, wondering why that did not distress me. I did not want it on my gloves, though.

"There is something reassuring about this place," I said. "It was not a ruin when Queen Mary ruled. Then it was a fortress."

Mr. Knightley bounded to his feet. "Miss Bennet thought your connection to Yuánchi would help you find the amulet. Could it be here?"

"That *would* be nice! Just lying in the grass. But I think not. The ruins have been picked over a thousand times. It is something else about this place. Draca rarely come here, but I feel like there is a residue of binding, an echo soaked into the earth."

"Is that the change you meant? That you sense their past presence?"

I closed my eyes, seeking the calm I had before. The impression of Yuánchi had vanished, but there was a resonance around us like the hum of bees in a flowering garden.

"I suppose so," I said, unsure myself. "Draca bindings have become more tangible to me. Like they can be touched."

I brushed off my hands and put on my gloves. The start of the footpath was in view, so we set out.

There was another half hour's walk until Hartfield. I had left Mrs. Hewitt's house happily confident, but the approaching confrontation hatched little flutters in my stomach.

"Tell me something clever about yourself," I said.

"Clever is a high standard," Mr. Knightley protested.

"I need a distraction. Anything I do not know."

We entered the path, side-by-side in the shade, and he began, "As a young man, I traveled to Vienna for my musical studies. There, I made the acquaintance, and then the friendship, of the composer Herr Beethoven. He was an irascible man—a truly ferocious temper. At the time, I thought him very old." He chuckled. "He was in his early thirties, and already famous throughout Europe." His smile ended. "It took six months before he confided that he had lost most of his hearing and that the condition was worsening. That is a curse for anyone, but for a musician, it is catastrophic, and for a genius who had barely begun his ascent, it was cruel in its irony.

"He had many dark nights of the soul. He was too proud to confess his struggles, but I saw his pain. His daily life was hard as well. Fear of ridicule and of pity prevented him from announcing his disability. To him, the word deaf —*taub* in German—was terrifying. But after he confided in me, he regained a measure of hope. His brilliance remained a pure thing within him. He could create even while his body sealed him away in silence."

"That is very sad." My view of the path had turned watery. It was all too easy to imagine the loneliness of hiding his disability.

Mr. Knightley's hand touched my forearm. "I did not intend to upset you. I suppose I had some thoughtless idea that it was relevant. A gifted person fighting private battles, then confiding in friends who help. But it is a poor analogy to your situation."

"I am not irascible," I pointed out and dabbed the tips of my gloved fingers beneath my eyes. "Nor do you think me very old."

The corner of his mouth twitched. "True."

I felt he had not finished his story. "What happened with you and Herr Beethoven?"

"He wrote a sonata for me, and we performed it together. He could just manage that if I played loudly. We went to a bar to celebrate, and he admired a pretty woman singing folk tunes. I told him her singing was offkey—the crowd was noisy, so he could not hear her, only see her. I had to shout before he understood, which embarrassed him. Her, also. I had drunk too much. He became enraged, and we never spoke again."

Mr. Knightley's steps fell heavily. His cheeks and lips were furrowed with regret and shame.

"I am sorry it ended poorly," I said, "but you helped him before. That help is what matters. I think you will meet again, and he will take your hand and call you 'friend' in German."

"*Freund*," Mr. Knightley supplied, his thoughts far away.

"You are in good company with me. You cannot imagine how foolish I was when I was a young woman." That made me laugh. "Actually, I am sure you *can* imagine! You criticized my project to remake Harriet. Think how insufferable I was at eighteen." I could see Mr. Knightley puzzling over how to answer that, so I rushed on. "I lived through so many years that left no mark on me at all. Then suddenly, I was caring for Papa, and every day changed me. And then the challenges after he was gone." I hesitated but felt it was cowardly not to finish the thought. "The six months that you and I have known each other—those have affected me a great deal."

I had drifted to a stop on the path. Mr. Knightley halted at a proper distance, his posture as perfect as any Darcy although, seeing him framed by equally straight tree trunks and with the sunlight dappling his fitted coat, I had no complaint.

"May I ask how our knowing each other affected you?" he said.

A stone wall was visible through the trees. Long years had led my feet along a path that passed the vicarage, home of Mr. Elton. The thought of meeting him was like freezing hands had clamped my torso.

I willed that away, set my heels in the earth, and forded several yards of thistles to reach another path. I smiled back at Mr. Knightley. "We are almost at the village. This way is better." He nodded slowly and followed.

I walked swiftly until the trees thinned into the small park of Highbury square. It was empty. That was unusual. Several hundred people lived in the village. The captain's warning had an effect after all.

But the emptiness was an opportunity. "There is an old engraving here. The Witch of Woodhouse—"

Mr. Knightley, though, was looking north. "Did you hear guns?"

I listened but heard only birds. "Hunters?" Then it came, a peppering softened by distance. Many shots together.

"Not hunters," Mr. Knightley said. "That is volley fire. Troops."

"Could they be practicing?"

"Perhaps." His tone said *No*. "We should take shelter."

"Hartfield is not far. Another ten minutes."

"What if we are not admitted?"

I did not like considering that, but he was only being cautious. "We could call on the neighbors. The greatest risk is that we shall be invited to dinner. But I do wish to try Hartfield first. I... I am a little nervous about it, you know."

Then I had a happy thought. "If the army warned people, John will have fled to London. I cannot imagine him facing a scrap of danger."

We hurried south. Hartfield was always described as being within the village, which rather enhanced the reputation of both, but the southern parish was sparsely settled, all modest meadows and isolated cottages with rambling gardens. I led us along a remote footpath away from the road.

"There!" I cried triumphantly as the house came into view, forgetting that Mr. Knightley had seen it already.

The house had grown even prettier. The ivy was flourishing on the two-story walls—the gardener said it pockmarked the cladding, but Papa and I never had the heart to tear it down. The walls, faced with ancient Caen stone, glowed cream and gold in the sun. Hartfield might look modest beside a behemoth like Pemberley House, but it was the greatest manse in these parishes, with four-and-twenty rooms, a stylish courtyard, and acres of park and gardens.

It used to be more. The original estate was hundreds of acres, both park and farmland, but parcels had been sold, and the sum shrank to seventy in my grandfather's time, then twelve in my father's. Papa justified each sale by grumbling about how he despised managing land, but after his death, I discovered that the sales were financial necessity—necessity, but also a strategy. Papa did not fritter away the funds on gambling or poor investments. Instead, he pooled them for my inheritance, enough to maintain Hartfield for a generation or, with care, for two. Or if I married well, as he had hoped, forever.

Six months ago, I departed these doors, hiding my symptoms and determined to accomplish Papa's deathbed request that Harriet, my dearest friend and his unacknowledged daughter, be elevated to gentry. That day seemed so remote. War had come to England. Fènnù rose. Lizzy fell. And Harriet was a teacher.

"Are you ready?" Mr. Knightley asked gently.

My shoulders were tight, but I gave him a bright smile. "I am just thinking how much has changed. Harriet might still marry a wealthy gentleman. She will be listed in the next *Debrett's*, you know."

Mr. Knightley's laugh was curt. "If there is a next *Debrett's*."

"If you say things like that, I will have to scold you again about assuming the worst." I took a bracing breath. "I am glad you are here, though. John hurt my elbow the last time we met."

Mr. Knightley's lip bent, but it was not a smile. He offered his arm, and we proceeded.

The front garden was nicely trimmed and weeded. I usually kept a few field flowers in the brass vase beside the front entry, but it was empty. The first difference.

I stopped at the door. The house was quiet. No one was visible through the windows.

When I returned from outings in our carriage, James, our coachman, would open the house for me. Or if I was simply out for a walk, I would stroll to the kitchen door and find it open, or wave to Serle through a window and she would let me in. Ladies did not carry a key to their own house.

Even if this door was unlocked, it was considered improper—or inadvisable, at least—to barge in on servants unannounced. They deserved a minute to prepare themselves. And what if John had replaced them? I might encounter strangers.

"I cannot believe I am unsure how to enter my own home," I said.

"Permit me," Mr. Knightley said as if my confusion were perfectly natural. He knocked.

After a minute, light steps approached. The door opened and a wonderfully familiar face peered out under a maid's cap.

"Teresa!" I exclaimed. "Oh, what a relief. I was afraid you would be gone."

"Miss!" she gasped. She curtsied, half-stumbling in shock.

I stepped over the threshold, but Teresa blocked me from going farther, lifting her trembling hands with fingers splayed.

"What are you doing?" I said, confused.

"You must not come in," she whispered desperately. "Go. Just *go*."

"I know John is here," I assured her.

Her hands flew up to clap her cheeks. "And you *came*? Oh, Heavens." She fumbled a dusting cloth from somewhere and began sniffling into it.

Anger rushed into me. "What has he done?" Then weighty steps thumped down the hall, and John strode into the entryway.

Now it was his turn to stare. Only his lips were animated, sucking frantically on his pipe like an excited fish. The house reeked of his tobacco, an obnoxious concoction that somehow involved cherries.

"I have returned," I announced. That sounded grand.

He fumbled the pipe from his mouth. His empty lips puckered twice more, then unexpectedly split in a wide smile. "What a welcome surprise." His head ratcheted toward Mr. Knightley.

"May I present Mr. Knightley," I said. It seemed best to pretend their prior, brief meeting had never occurred.

They shook hands. The contrast was very gratifying, Mr. Knightley's athletic grace, perfect dress, and solid shoulders beside John's stooped, wrinkled, pudgy form. But a civil greeting was not what I had expected. Nor what Mr. Knightley expected. He uttered a terse "How do you do?" and gave me a mystified glance.

"You should have sent a letter that you were coming!" John exclaimed, seemingly manic with delight.

"I wrote many times," I said, skirting the question. My earlier letters had not been answered, and it had seemed unwise to announce this visit.

John waved his pipe jovially. "The mails are hopeless. The letter carriers blame the war, but that is nonsense. It is pure laziness." He scowled at Teresa. "Go! We will use..." He stopped and gave me a disconcertingly stretched smile. "What am I thinking! This is *your* home. Where would you like to recover from your trip?" He pulled out his pocket watch and squinted at it.

"The sunroom," I said to Teresa. The parlor would feel like I was a visitor. "Tea, please. And sandwiches, if Serle has something to hand. We have had a long walk since breakfast."

Teresa remained frozen, watching me with wide eyes, the fingers of one hand knotting in her apron. John tore his gaze from his watch and snapped, "Go!" at her before she hurried away.

John gestured for us to precede him down the hall. As we entered the sunroom, he muttered, "I will just check..." and scuttled away down the corridor. A distant door slammed.

I stood, thinking.

Mr. Knightley walked a tense circuit of the room. He ended facing me and said, "I owe you an apology. When I first called on Hartfield, your brother-in-law's behavior led me to believe—"

I quieted him with a touch. "I have no doubt that he claimed Hartfield. It is *this* behavior that confuses me. He has never been deferential. Or even civil." I examined the sunroom. The decor was homey—a quartet of linens embroidered by me and a few friends, an exceedingly amateur watercolor I painted when I was fourteen, and several screens woven with dried flowers. But the linens were hung in a different order. The flowers on the screens were crushed. And something deeper tickled inside my mind—wrong, wrong.

"Perhaps the law foiled his plan," Mr. Knightley suggested. "Might he have found instructions from your father saying that you should have Hartfield?"

"If John found those, he would burn them." Here, the tobacco reek was acrid enough to make my eyes water. A brass plate was heaped with what must be a pound of tobacco ash. Why would a man who despised crafts smoke in a room that even Papa called excessively frilly? "Something is very wrong. Teresa was frightened. And Serle should have come running the moment she heard I was home."

I left the sunroom and led Mr. Knightley through the dining room to the kitchen. The kitchen door was closed. It would not budge when I turned the latch; it was barred somehow. A bitter scent pricked the back of my throat.

I listened. Silence. The kitchen was never quiet.

I backtracked to the sunroom, almost running now, and tried the garden door. That opened, and I drew a relieved breath as we burst into the rear courtyard, surrounded by shining sun and birdsong.

We followed the flagstone path beside the house around to the kitchen. The windows had been boarded up from the inside. The dirty glass revealed nothing but rough-fitted planks.

"There you are!" John cried behind us, huffing as he jogged awkwardly around the corner. He pulled out a handkerchief to wipe his sweaty forehead. "Oh, you discovered the kitchen renovations. That was to be a surprise—"

"That is absurd," I interrupted. "What are you really doing? Where is Serle?"

John pasted another unsettling grin on his face and reached for my shoulder. The gesture stopped abruptly midair. Mr. Knightley had caught his wrist, the motion so deft his hand seemed to materialize from nowhere.

"Do not," Mr. Knightley said simply.

John's grin drained like whey through sour curds. He pulled his hand back and patted his disarranged coat, eyeing us both. For the first time, he looked authentic—irritated and self-important.

"You were always clever, Emma," he said grudgingly "Very well. I will speak frankly. But inside." He turned and stomped away.

"What do you wish to do?" Mr. Knightley asked, crossing his arms and watching my brother-in-law's retreating back.

"I wish to speak frankly," I said and followed John.

JOHN HAD CLUTTERED Papa's study with magazines and loose papers. The odor of pipe smoke was less intense, but the stale undertones were sour. John collapsed heavily into Papa's chair. Mr. Knightley drew out a chair for me, then took a seat himself.

"First," John announced, wagging his finger at me, "remember that I have been working myself to exhaustion. While I hardly sleep from worry, you gallivant about spending money willy-nilly."

I was not sure how to answer that. "You have not provided a penny for my survival in a year. A penny that would come from *my* funds."

He glowered from Papa's chair. "You nagged enough, though. You and Isabella are the same. Do you think I withhold money for selfish reasons? Nothing could be more untrue."

"Why, then?" I asked.

He dug out his pocket watch and plunked it on the desk, then spun it like a top, sulking like a child.

"He has lost your funds," Mr. Knightley said, his tenor voice as cold as a judge pronouncing punishment. "He has lost everything. He only lacks the courage to admit it. Look at his coat—secondhand, not even re-tailored. Or his watch. Copper plate."

John plopped his fleshy palm over the watch, but not before I noticed the dirty fringe of verdigris. "I did not *lose* the funds! They were as good as stolen from me. It is those miners and weavers extorting their exorbitant pay. They infect workers with unreasonable expectations. I have written an excellent letter to *The Times*—well, I plan to write it—explaining that the government must rise to the occasion and assist gentlemen investors who selflessly assume risk..."

My swelling emotions washed his words away. More than once in the last months, I had found myself holding a forgotten book or ignoring a conversation while privately considering the unthinkable: John had stolen my fortune. Discovering that the Woodhouse fortune was literally destroyed provided icy finality... but strangely, the emotion rising the quickest was relief. If the money was gone, John no longer had power over me.

He was now ranting about Luddites. When he took a breath, I said, "I am reclaiming Hartfield. It is time you left."

"No!" John cried desperately. "Not yet! You have not heard my plan! Our fortune can be restored!"

Mr. Knightley shifted to the edge of his seat. He seemed eager to assist

John's departure. That was tempting, but the nagging sensation in my mind had returned—*wrong, wrong*.

Like the sunroom, this room was disarranged. The books on Papa's shelf were out of order. Some were even upside down.

An ephemeral black rope flickered through the room's wall and vanished.

Nobody else batted an eye. Was this some new form of the miasma?

I had not answered, so John resumed talking. He seemed unable to abide silence. "The complication is that Isabella refused to come to Hartfield. She whined about exposing the children to war. I do not understand it. She is usually such an obedient creature, but she argued endlessly."

That did not surprise me. Isabella obsessed about her children's safety. But I had forgotten that she and her children were victims as well. I would need to reach out to her through some channel that John could not intercept.

John's chin was flushing from his desperate chatter. "Women do not understand that war is a tremendous boon for all parties involved! The Crown opened their vaults. Military spending is sky high. Why, commodity prices have risen—"

Mr. Knightley, apparently, could no longer listen in silence. "And yet, you lost your fortune and another that was entrusted to you."

John sputtered, "In hindsight, anyone can see that prices rose. But at the time, the very best gentlemen at my club agreed that Parliament's spendthrift policies would cause a glut. The speculative opportunity was tremendous."

I was thinking about my sister. "Why is Isabella's absence a complication?"

"Oh." John blinked furiously. "I had promised to bring her. When she refused, I had no choice but to come alone. That... uh... disappointed people."

"At last, something I believe," I said. "I do not wish to hear any more. I think you should return to my sister. And you had best confess to her, as I shall visit."

John fell silent. Then, with surprising dignity, he rose. He retrieved his pocket watch and tucked it into his waistcoat. "Do not think you have achieved a victory."

He strode out of Papa's study. Mr. Knightley and I exchanged a look and hurried after him.

We caught up at the front door, where John turned and said, "I promised you frankness, so here it is. Isabella had one merit. She was born a Woodhouse. When she refused to come, I had to barter whatever value I could find in your precious Hartfield. That was yet another disappointment. The search turned up nothing." He smirked. "However, there will be no 'confessions.' Because you came. The *other* Woodhouse."

Again, an inky rope slipped through my vision, twining like the questing tentacle of a sea creature. This time, I recognized it. It was a binding, like those pent up within unbound draca, but perverted. Diseased. The untethered tip crept close to my breast, then shied away as if burned.

The twitching root led toward the kitchen.

"What did you search for?" Mr. Knightley asked. His voice was deadly soft.

"*They* searched for an amulet." John opened the front door.

Armed soldiers had filled the carriage drive—French troops with their elaborate white crossbelts and tall plumed hats, and, standing to one side and scowling in gray uniforms, American soldiers from the newly formed Southern Confederate Alliance.

# 19

## CAPTIVE

### EMMA

The French soldier herding us said, "*Attendez ici,*" and tapped his bayonet on a polished corner of Hartfield's front parlor floor. I moved there, tugging Mr. Knightley when he stopped stubbornly short. He had been deadly quiet since John's betrayal, his gaze flickering aggressively among the soldiers. I did not want him to try something foolish, so I stood close, ready to take his arm at the first hint of bravado.

This was one of Hartfield's larger rooms. There were two fireplaces, each with chairs and a comfortable sofa. Tea tables and decorative screens partitioned the rest. When we still had parties, our cleverer guests had used those to chart paths around the more tedious conversationalists.

Mr. Knightley jerked his jaw to indicate one of the Southern Confederate soldiers. "That is an Overseer, an officer in their army. His title is copied from the men who drive and punish slaves on plantations. In Brighton, the army Overseers are forcing slaves to build fortifications."

"Where did they get slaves?" I whispered back. Slavery was illegal in England.

"They purchase kidnapped Africans from slave traders. And they have captured Black Englishmen—free Englishmen."

Fear chilled me, but I tried to reason it away. They would not have sent soldiers to Highbury hunting for Black gentlemen.

The Confederate uniforms were familiar from the newspapers: gray coats with two rows of buttons and upturned collars, butternut trousers, and peculiar small caps with a front brim. The Overseer's coat was longer, stopping just above the knee and made of expensive charcoal-gray wool. His lower sleeves had elaborately knotted patterns of gold braid, an insignia of rank. He was solidly built with a bushy black beard and mustache, and when he left the parlor, his eyes studied me and Mr. Knightley.

Mr. and Mrs. Otway, a gentry couple in their mid-forties from east Highbury, were escorted in by a French soldier and positioned in the adjacent corner. That was too far to speak with, but they watched us with terrified, questioning expressions. I wondered where their daughter was. Then Mr. and Mrs. Weston were marched in, and my heart fell further. They were very dear friends; I had rather cleverly encouraged their marriage. Mr. Weston was an older husband who had been widowed, and he glowered at the soldiers through his graying whiskers. Anne Weston was red-eyed and teary. She clutched their two-year-old daughter who, thankfully, seemed to be asleep.

Carefully, I nodded to Anne. She dipped her head feebly. She had been my governess, starting when I was five and ending when I turned twenty. By then, we were like sisters.

"Why are they collecting gentlemen and ladies?" I whispered to Mr. Knightley. Even if it was the most horrible explanation, seeking slaves, these were hardly the most able-bodied workers.

Mr. Knightley shook his head, unsure.

The French officer appeared in the doorway, assessing Mr. Knightley and me from a distance. The Overseer stood beside him, and John hovered behind.

The Overseer pointed at me. "Is that the Woodhouse?"

"*That* is French business," the officer answered in superb, barely accented English, but with a scornful French curl to his lip. His gaze remained on me. Like all French officers, his uniform was magnificent. His coat and hat were layered with heavy gold braid and his sword hilt gilded.

"She is or she isn't," the Overseer persisted. "These others are useless."

"They are *la petite noblesse*, the gentry," the French officer replied stiffly. He did not seem to enjoy the conversation.

"Old and married. Useless. Are you French too stupid to understand orders?" He waved toward me. "If she's not *your* Woodhouse, she's what we want. Young. Fancy. Those are the ones who bind." His gaze shifted from me to Mr. Knightley. "We'll take him, too, while we're at it."

The chill of fear in my belly boiled into panic. "I should never have brought you here," I whispered to Mr. Knightley.

"I was about to say the same to you," he whispered back. "Do not worry. I have faced worse circumstances."

I doubted it.

John squeezed past the Overseer to face the French officer. "How many times must I repeat that she *is* a Woodhouse. I expect your government to honor our agreement. I have invested substantial effort—"

The officer silenced him with a lift of his hand, then he crossed the room to us and bowed. "I am Capitaine Louis Fournier. You are prisoners of the French army." Mr. Knightley bristled. The captain waited with professional detachment until he quieted, then he addressed me. "Answer truthfully. Are you who that man says?"

"Of course," I said. "I am Emma Woodhouse. You are standing in *my* home."

"You see!" John cried out behind him. "Summon the perfumer. She will—"

The French officer turned on him. "You met *la Demoiselle des Parfums* once. Are you such a fool that you wish to meet her again?"

That punctured John's confidence. He tugged at his collar, his ruddy cheeks draining of color. Sullenly, he said, "I wish to be paid and to have this matter resolved. It is unpleasant enough already. That is my wife's sister, after all."

The French officer looked appalled. One of the French soldiers muttered darkly, "*L'anglais.*"

On this subject, Mr. Knightley apparently agreed. He was watching John and clenching his hands rhythmically. I could hear his knuckles creaking.

"This is your house?" the officer asked me. "This... infernal place?"

That was insulting, but at the edges of my vision, fouled tendrils were slipping through the walls. What obscenity had they hidden at Hartfield?

"I have just returned," I said. "It was stolen from me."

The officer unfolded a sheet of paper from his coat pocket. "We know this is here. Tell us where, and you will save yourself."

The page held a precise, almost scientific drawing of an amulet. The center was an oval labeled *rouge brillant*. The setting was elaborately carved jade, every whorl painstakingly rendered.

"What safety can you offer her?" Mr. Knightley said suddenly.

"On my honor, I will send you both on your way. You can run north. I have seen too many women taken already. And too many of *les Noirs*, men like you.

147

This war they wage"—he jerked his head disdainfully toward the frowning Overseer—"it is not *la guerre française.*"

"I believe him," Mr. Knightley said to me. "Tell him."

"It is not here," I said. Mr. Knightley gave me a sharp look, but I shrugged. "I have seen nothing like this in my entire life. I would know if it were at Hartfield. I sorted everything after Papa's death."

The French captain held the paper higher, waiting for me to study it more carefully. Or to reconsider. I shook my head. He bowed stiffly and left the room. The Overseer and John followed, bickering.

Boots began tromping through the hallways and stairs. Thumps and crashes sounded. They were searching the house, less gently than before.

"Is the amulet here?" Mr. Knightley whispered to me.

"No. I told the truth."

What if I had known? Would I have kept it secret? I was not even sure the amulet mattered anymore. The dagger Gramr had woken Fènnù from her sleep, but the amulet was paired to Yuánchi, and Yuánchi had risen on his own.

Would the amulet let the French control Yuánchi? I wished I knew if Lizzy had returned. Her binding to Yuánchi was unimaginably strong. I could not imagine anyone overcoming that.

Mr. Knightley resumed whispering. "You must escape. Or we must bargain for your release. They do not know you are a great wyfe. If they discover that, they will take you south."

"I do not think I matter that much." I said it lightly, but I meant it. My life at Hartfield was lost unless the French advance was turned back, and Lord Wellington's comments at Pemberley were not optimistic. And I had not the slightest idea where the amulet could be. This entire trip seemed a dismal failure and extraordinarily dangerous, particularly to Mr. Knightley.

The search reached our parlor. A pair of French soldiers methodically dumped out every drawer. Treasured letters and keepsakes spilled across the floor. A porcelain inkstand smashed to wet, staining shards. A tiny crystal draca gifted to me by Papa shattered, one little leg skittering past my boot.

Anne's crying shrank to silent fear, her arms tight around her child. I sent her hopeful looks and wondered if they would shoot me if I crossed the room to speak with her.

A sensation plucked my awareness.

The Westons had bound a broccworm when they married, quite a prestigious binding as it was Mr. Weston's second marriage; remarried husbands often failed to bind at all. At least husbands could try, though. The Church did not even perform the binding ceremony for remarried wyves.

But Anne had no particular affinity, so like most draca, their bound broccworm roamed, often gone for days at a time.

However, a roseworm had just crept into the parlor to sit at Anne's feet. That was what I had sensed, and it was very peculiar. Why would a bound draca sneak into Hartfield to visit a strange wyfe?

The soldiers ignored it. Being French, they had little experience with draca. They probably assumed the roseworm was bound to the Westons.

I concentrated, and the roseworm's binding overlaid my vision, rose-red and stretching outside, well beyond Hartfield's front gate. The draca was watching me now, which was unsurprising. Lizzy had said that great wyves shone gold in draca's vision.

The sounds of the search ceased, and the French captain marched back in with the Overseer in tow. The pair of them came up to me with an unpleasantly decisive attitude.

Capitaine Fournier asked, "Have you remembered the amulet?"

Should I lie? I was frightened; my heart was pounding. That seemed to block inventing a story.

"You had better answer," the Overseer warned. "Mr. Elton'll be here soon."

I blinked at him, so puzzled that I forgot my fear. I would much prefer to avoid Mr. Elton, but how could an American know that?

Mr. Knightley, understandably, was mystified as well. "Who is Mr. Elton?"

"Our vicar," I said automatically. Which did not adequately convey the situation.

Mr. Knightley straightened with his own decisive air. "She knows nothing of the amulet," he told the French captain. "Free her. Ask this Mr. Elton to escort her north." To the Overseer, he said, "I will remain."

"Absolutely not!" I exclaimed. "You cannot invent foolish plans without asking me first."

"A clergyman can cross the line of battle," he said doggedly. "He is the safest escort—"

That drew a ragged laugh from me. The Overseer guffawed at the same time. We eyed each other, as if wondering how we knew each other's secrets.

The French captain, however, was nodding gravely, as if Mr. Knightley had been noble and sensible. What if he agreed?

"You cannot separate us," I announced desperately, and then I knew what to do. I raced through my memories of meeting John: Mr. Knightley's introduction, everything that followed, everything that was *not* said...

"We are married," I announced. My cheeks instantly heated, but that was charming in a new bride. I grabbed Mr. Knightley's hand and threaded my gloved fingers through his, which required a bit of a shove. Then for good measure, I stepped closer so our arms could touch. A little too close—my hip rubbed his. My blush heightened.

"*Married?*" the Overseer said. The French captain looked skeptical as well. Mr. Knightley's flabbergasted expression was certainly not helping.

But I had proof.

Across the room, the little roseworm was lying with her feet tucked under her body, dog-like. Her eyes, two gleaming ink drops, watched me. I met her gaze and threw my soul into a voiceless appeal: *Please come to me.*

The roseworm startled like she had heard a clap of thunder. Then she got up, stretched with maddening laziness, and trotted over.

"See who finally found us, darling," I said happily to Mr. Knightley, and bent to pet the roseworm as she gamboled around my feet.

## 2 0

# MISS BATES

## EMMA

S oldiers and broken ornaments are sad, but friends celebrate a marriage, and Anne and her husband rushed over to offer their sincere, if surprised, compliments. The Otways followed more cautiously, but that drew the French captain into our impromptu celebration. He shook Mr. Knightley's hand, offering congratulations in his native language, and bowed to me. A few soldiers touched their hats and smiled.

"You have set us on our back foot!" Mr. Weston continued heartily, neatening the tips of his mustache with two pinches. It had been drooping before.

Anne bobbed her child, who was looking around blurrily, woken by the fuss. "Were you married in London?"

"No," I said exactly as Mr. Knightley answered, "Yes." I stiffened, but he chuckled handsomely and explained, "In Chelsea. It is very rural, so Mrs. Knightley is correct."

I looked around our little group, then realized that was me.

"And *when*?" Anne asked breathlessly.

"Ah," Mr. Knightley began expansively. He seemed to have gotten into the swing of things. "It was three—"

"—weeks ago," I finished firmly. I was afraid he would say months. That would have been terribly rude of me, as I should have told Anne immediately. "I am sorry I did not write to you. I thought it would be amusing to appear in person. And then there was the war." I pouted, and Capitaine Fournier had the decency to appear abashed.

Anne plucked my sleeve, pulling me aside for a private conversation. "You said you would never marry! What happened?"

"We danced on a ship that was frozen in the Thames." Really, that was romantic.

"He is very handsome. Does he have money?"

"Not a penny!" I answered cheerfully. She giggled—I was being very improper—but I meant it... although, *how* did I mean it? It was true, or true enough by the standards of rich Miss Woodhouse. But I was rich no longer. How would we survive? We were not *actually* married, of course, but it was an irritating thought. "He performs," I added. "Music." Could we live off that?

Mrs. Otway joined our ladies' discussion, and wedding topics proceeded. The giddy rush of my invented marriage dimmed. I answered with smiles; suddenly, fabricating details tasted sour. The discussion drifted to recollections of other weddings, and my mood turned pensive.

We were still prisoners, even if the French soldiers were amused. The Overseer had stalked off after my announcement. That, at least, worked as I planned. A bound woman did not interest the slavers. Nor, for that matter, a woman who was not gentry. And I doubted the French captain would rip Mr. Knightley from the arms of his weeping bride, so he was safe as well.

The French captain, though, had left the parlor to speak angrily with the Overseer in the front hall. John was there too, glowering at me through the parlor doorway. He had heard the happy news.

John shouted, "Everyone must proceed outside!" That meant everyone; the French captain barked a command, and the French soldiers left before us at a trot. A pair of Confederate soldiers forced us out with rude prods and pushes.

Outside, the cheery mid-afternoon sun clashed with the scent of gunpowder on the breeze. At the top step, Mrs. Otway broke away and ran to where her daughter Caroline, only sixteen, stood shivering and frightened, held by a gray-clad soldier.

"I am sorry," Caroline burst out, "I tried to see where they took you..." Her mother wrapped her in a silent hug.

There was one other new arrival. A middle-aged lady in a frowsy blue-and-white dress and a slightly tired cotton-lace cap was chattering at the soldier from his other side. The roseworm, who had loyally followed me outside, perked up, watching her.

Miss Bates.

I concentrated and saw the rose-hued binding between her and the rose-worm. Of course, the draca would be hers. There was no other bound rose-worm in twenty miles. I had only discounted that because her roseworm was so secret. She never let her be seen in public, let alone visit people's houses.

Meanwhile, Miss Bates, a committed conversationalist, was proceeding full blast to her captive audience. "—and I always say that a soldier is a fine sight, for you know I can hardly tell the difference between soldiers, what is a blue or a red jacket after all, with the navy in blue anyway, and now gray ones too, so really how can one expect a simple woman to know? Although if I may say, gray is a very dull choice. Do they let you pick?"

The soldier was displaying the same glazed expression I had worn myself on occasion, so I took advantage of his stunned silence to call, "Miss Bates!"

She beamed at me. "Miss Woodhouse! What a delight. Only two days ago I was reading a letter from my niece and thinking, if only Miss Woodhouse were here to enjoy it with me!"

"Shut yer face," the soldier said as he pushed her, Mrs. Otway, and Caroline into a clump with Anne and me.

"Miss Woodhouse is Mrs. Knightley now," Anne said to Miss Bates, nodding toward Mr. Knightley, who had been placed with the gentlemen. I was glad he had not been singled out, but he looked dangerously angry.

Miss Bates, who had ended her patter with an affronted "Well!" shot a highly perceptive glance at me that flicked to her roseworm by my feet. I had seen this side of her before—the real Miss Bates, far more intelligent and serious than the bumbling persona she presented in society. And far more knowledge-able of draca and their lore.

Miss Bates put her head by mine and whispered, "We are preparing a rescue. I am here to give the signal."

My heart leaped. "*Who* is preparing a rescue?" I whispered back.

"The widowed wyves. But we must wait for Kent."

Her short sentences were as baffling as her long ones. Were there more bound, widowed wyves? And who was Kent?

The six French soldiers had assembled in a two-by-three column. Their captain approached me.

"The amulet?" he asked bluntly.

"I do not know."

"Then we search elsewhere."

My relief from my wedding ploy turned to a sodden mass in my belly. "You cannot leave us with that slaver. Please do not!"

His gaze mixed frustration and regret. "I do not wish to, *madame*. I am a husband. I have a daughter. But my orders are from the Emperor himself." He bowed, his regalia gleaming, and marched his soldiers away from the house.

At the same time, a two-horse coach was rattling up the other side of Hartfield's circular carriage drive. A coach I recognized. The sodden mass in my belly turned to lead.

"Oh," Miss Bates gasped like she had been struck. "He is early. *Where* is Kent?"

The coach was met by more soldiers, and a narrow-shouldered, overly pretty young man stepped out wearing a clergyman's white collar with a belted black coat. He greeted the Overseer with a smug smile and familiar handshake.

Mr. Elton. My apprehensions lurched to life.

A woman wobbled down the coach's step behind him. Her head was lowered, her features concealed by an oppressively deep-brimmed poke bonnet, but her dress was English and extremely overdecorated with cheap ruffles and draped beads. That unfortunate style could be only one person—Mrs. Augusta Elton, the vicar's wyfe, married a year ago. She had been touted as an impressive match, having a substantial fortune, but then failed to bind, a grating embarrassment to the vicar which I had privately celebrated.

An unpleasant clicking drew my gaze to her feet. A grossly oversized foul crawler had slithered out of the coach, following her like a sullen housecat. It was three feet long, flowing in a rattle of shell-wrapped segments.

Mr. Elton finished shaking hands with slavers and strode toward us. Augusta shuffled in his wake. A short length of rope was tied around her wrist, and one of the soldiers picked it up, tugging her when she drifted the wrong way.

"I hoped it was not true," Miss Bates whispered, her breath harsh with outrage. "He has made his wyfe one of their horrors." She clamped her eyes shut, hiding the scene. No. She was drawing sharp, focused breaths, building her resolve. "We cannot wait any longer."

Her hand drew something small and glittering from her skirt pocket—a glass vial. The cork fell into the lawn. Hiding the vial in her palm, she tossed the contents in her mouth and swallowed with a choked cough.

The roseworm at our feet hissed as a sour, bitter odor stung the back of my nose. I knew that scent. When an American slaver had forced Harriet to use the black dagger, he drugged her with that to strengthen her control. Crawler venom.

"Are you mad?" I whispered to Miss Bates.

She was unnaturally still and silent.

"Emma," Mr. Elton announced in surprise, halting a few steps from us.

I said coolly, "Mr. Elton."

I had dreaded meeting him, expecting to be frightened. Instead, the fear that had filled me receded. He looked far less consequential than I remembered, rather skinny and superficial.

John hurried to shake Mr. Elton's hand, bobbing like an ingratiating fool. "Welcome, welcome. Is all proceeding to plan?

"The True Church rises in Highbury," Mr. Elton replied. His eyes were locked on me.

John noticed his attention. "Ah, yes. I managed to bring Emma after all."

"That is very excellent," Mr. Elton said. "All together, again."

"And I do not believe this marriage nonsense for an instant," John scoffed.

"Marriage?" Mr. Elton echoed. He stepped closer, examining me and the roseworm. "You cannot marry."

I felt an irrational edge of pride. "You are mistaken." Defiantly, I picked up the roseworm. Roseworms are small but solid, with a draca's gem-like scales, dense bones, and musculature. She curled into the crook of my arm like a warm brass sculpture.

"You certainly cannot bind," Mr. Elton said with a lopsided smirk.

John, though, was staring at the roseworm in my arms. Others were also; Mrs. Otway was wide-eyed. A wyfe with strong affinity might handle her bound tykeworm—they were unusually tame—but holding a roseworm was exceptional, almost myth. A roseworm was dangerous. One tended to forget that after meeting dragons.

"The truth will out," Mr. Elton said idly. "The Emperor has cleansed the English Church of centuries of corruption. God's Truth is revealed so that our hands may wield His strength for the Empire."

That sounded highly un-English to me. Also, very unlike Mr. Elton's usual preaching. In services, his rare moments of rhapsody had been to praise donations to the vicarage roof repair fund.

He clicked his fingers, a hunter summoning a dog, and the gray-clad soldier dragged his wyfe forward. John and the others gave the crawler behind her a wide berth.

Something unpleasant was scritching at the back of my mind, but my nerves obscured it. I breathed through closely pursed lips, a calming exercise I had practiced with Mr. Darcy, and bindings became visible.

The black linkage between Augusta and the crawler was thick but ill-formed, a coarse mimicry of the elegant connection between draca and wyfe. The crawler's binding looked like a greasy rope twisted from dirty rags. It also looked like the seeking tendrils that had emerged from the back of Hartfield house. That was what John hid in the house. Unbound crawlers.

But that was not what had raised shivers on my neck. The binding between Miss Bates and the roseworm crackled and seethed with unhealthy energy. That was the effect of crawler venom—it strengthened a wyfe's binding. It was also intoxicating, addictive, and eventually deadly.

Whatever escape Miss Bates had planned depended on using that strength to command her draca. The roseworm was squirming, so I set her down. She hunted around our feet, dashing in one direction then another, then screeched at the crawler, who hissed threateningly. Draca and crawlers were mortal enemies.

"Time for business," the Overseer said with an ugly grin. He took the rope tied to Augusta, then shoved her at young Caroline Otway, who was cowering by her mother. "Test her first."

"No," Mr. Elton interrupted. "*Her*." He pointed at me.

"She's bound," the Overseer protested. "Can't bind her twice."

"We shall see," Mr. Elton said with a hair-thin smile.

"That is foolish," John blurted out. His eyes darted between me and Mr. Elton. Had we reached a crime he could not stomach? More likely, he lacked the courage to watch. He plucked at his waistcoat, frowning. "She is a Woodhouse, not chattel. The perfumer will want her."

Augusta wobbled toward me, her face shadowed. The crawler, though, refused to follow her. It seethed in place, thin legs tapping the dirt. Its insectile eyes were impenetrable, their direction impossible to gauge, but watching it, I felt a flickering connection, much like I felt with a draca when our gazes met. But where a draca would have been attracted, the crawler redoubled its resistance, rearing in a knot of clattering shell segments, torn between obeying Augusta and fear of me.

"Make it move!" the Overseer snapped at Augusta. He pulled his long coat aside, revealing a short, coiled whip fastened to his belt. She cringed, but I felt the black binding between her and the crawler harden with command.

The crawler advanced a foot, then stopped again, twitching. Impatient, the Overseer stomped on the segmented body with his hobnailed boot. He pressed down. One of the jointed legs was caught at an awkward angle, and it broke with a *snap*. The crawler hissed pathetically.

"Do not hurt it," I cried. Everyone, English or not, looked at me like I was mad.

Miss Bates burst out a triumphant laugh, and her binding to the roseworm lit like a coral sunrise. The roseworm heard her command and darted forward, chest swelling. Blue flame shot from her mouth. It was not aimed, or at least it struck nobody, just a spray of ferocious heat that incinerated lawn and left smoking earth.

The soldiers scattered, cursing, but the Overseer laughed and kicked the crawler, sending it flopping toward the roseworm. "Make it fight," he ordered Augusta.

The crawler had landed in burning grass a few feet from the roseworm. It hissed, scrambling out of the flames, then whipped its paired stingers up and over its head. A spatter of venom almost hit the roseworm. She retreated, her graceful motions turning jerky. The mere scent of crawler venom was enough to stun a draca.

The soldiers whooped and gathered to watch, leaving Augusta ignored, a pace from me.

I yanked off my glove and dropped it, then caught her wrist in my hand, skin to skin. Her pain burst into me—pain twice over, horrid whip cuts on her shoulders and back but also the crawler's injuries through their binding. I was close enough to make out Augusta's face inside her overhanging bonnet. Her cheeks were blotched and tear-stained, her hair a greasy mess, her teeth bared in an endless grimace.

The impotent, enslaved fury of the crawler climbed my arm. The binding, rough-made and twisted, filled my consciousness. But it was not the perversion it had appeared at a distance—it was infected, ugly like illnesses could be, like the sores on Papa's legs or little Nessy coughing blood before the healing strength of Lady Anne, the prior great wyfe of healing, had briefly filled me and saved her.

I had no power to heal, though. Augusta's injuries and the crushed leg and burns on the bound crawler were beyond me. But the binding... that was intriguing. It might be a shadow of a true draca binding, but it was still a living connection pulsing with jealous, desperate strength.

The illness I sensed, the flaw, was where it touched Augusta. A draca's binding flowed gracefully into the bound wyfe, as organic as a stem to a flower, but this binding was lodged in her chest like a barbed hook. That was different. That *mattered*. This had been forced without consent, and without consent, a binding was not pure. It was a violation.

As if my thoughts were hands, I grasped that weakened point. I tugged it with no effect, then yanked with no more success, then—distantly, I heard a scream tear through my throat—my entire being sank into it, saturating it. Healing it.

The binding lodged in Augusta disintegrated. Whip-fast, a fizzing erasure sizzled back the entire length to the crawler, like a fuse I once saw at a fireworks display in Sydney Gardens.

Augusta drew a massive, surprised breath, then fainted. Her wrist tore from my fingers as she fell. My own scream had wrung the air from my lungs, and I staggered, head spinning.

The fight between the roseworm and crawler had continued while my mind was in the realm of draca. The soldiers were cheering as if a deathmatch between two creatures were sport. The roseworm had lost—she was a limp, pathetic shape caught in a loop of the crawler's body. The crawler's poisonous spines were at her small, rose-hued throat, ready for a deadly strike.

The spines hung, glistening with venom. The Overseer strode closer, his eyes crazed. "Get on with it!" He kicked the crawler. The segmented body rattled but did not respond. He turned to us and yelled, "Make it..." then stopped. He had seen Augusta, collapsed on the lawn.

His fevered glee broke in stages: surprise, confusion, then his lips parted in fear. "Shoot it—" he cried. The word stopped with a grunt. He looked down.

The crawler had whipped its venomous tail high, sinking both curved prongs their full two-inch depth into the Overseer's thigh. The tail arched once, quivering, then the paired stingers relaxed and withdrew.

"Ya got to shoot it," the man muttered. He grabbed the arm of the staring comrade beside him. "Ya got to..." Above his bushy beard, his face blanched like paper, and he tipped woodenly to the ground, his muscles spasming.

The other soldiers pulled pistols. I caught a glimpse of skittering, greenish-brown shell, and another man screamed, falling and kicking, the crawler wrapped around his calf like a python. A pistol fired. Another.

Searing heat lit the garden as draca fire blew a laurel bush into roaring flames. The roseworm? No, she lay where she had been dropped by the crawler. Miss Bates was dodging panicked soldiers to pick her up.

Two other small draca had entered the garden. They were not prestigious breeds, probably ferretworms or broccworms, but they moved with a draca's predatory exactness.

My spinning head had eased. I knelt by Augusta and wrapped her wrist in my fingers. I could perceive her health—alive but unconscious, more from exhaustion than any new harm—but my thoughts fluttered oddly. Some reservoir within me had been drained by breaking her binding.

Then I recognized the real danger. Her sleeve cuff was undone.

I fumbled to fasten it, but the button had torn off. Broken cotton threads hung in a hideous tangle. I felt in the dirt, finding only pebbles, my panic growing as gleams of miasma bled from the earth.

The heat of draca fire flooded my side amid more yells. A pair of hobnailed boots ran up, nearly stomping on my seeking fingers. I looked up at a furious gray-coated soldier. He shouted, "Go inside!" just as a garden shovel clanged the side of his head. He keeled over, leaving Mr. Knightley, holding the shovel like a club.

"We must run!" he shouted.

"I cannot leave her," I said, pinching to keep her sleeve closed. "I cannot find her button!"

He cursed and hauled her out of my grasp, the ruined sleeve ripping from my fingers. He slung her over his shoulders like a yoke for hauling buckets, then grabbed my hand and yanked me to my feet.

Miss Bates dashed by, shouting unintelligibly but pointing, the Otways behind her. The miasma spilled in vile pools in their footsteps. Mr. Knightley followed, dragging me and oblivious to the danger. I cried out, pointing to the shimmering puddles, terrified that he would step in one.

We entered the trees, the east path. Shots fired behind us, and a bullet buzzed overhead, snicking off a branch. "Where to?" Mr. Knightley shouted. Someone answered, and he ran, Augusta bouncing on his back. His pace was slow, and I followed him easily enough, trapped between the seeking miasma ahead and the pursuit behind. More bullets whizzed, clipping leaves or hitting trunks with loud *whacks*. Mr. Knightley stumbled; this time, I caught his arm. His eyes were grim.

We almost collided with the others, who had stopped cold. Everyone had escaped: the Otways, the Westons, Miss Bates. But the older people were spent

—Mr. Weston had sat down in the dirt, his head hanging. Anne was panting while clutching their squalling child.

But two new women were here, elderly widows from the poorer north district of town. I knew them, but I had to look away, their clothes were so disarranged. Everyone's were. I fixed my eyes on a gnarled root instead and pulled off my remaining, asymmetrical glove, discarding it behind me.

The shouting behind us grew louder, joined by the baying of dogs.

"Do not stop." Mr. Knightley begged the group, but he was bent almost double under Augusta's weight, his legs shaking.

Miss Bates's face was locked in a drugged rictus of a smile. She gasped, "Kent," as if that was an answer. "The widowed wyves of Kent have come."

A majestic, gray-haired woman stepped around her. Her clothes were not patched and worn. Greedily, I fixed my eyes on perfect silk seams.

Lady Catherine de Bourgh saw me and offered a regal nod. "Miss Wood-house. I do not forget a face. I am, however, disappointed in Surrey. It has become far less tolerable."

Her bronze wyvern trotted up beside her, sparkling in the dappled sunlight. The miasma had caught us now, and it poured down, condensing from every forest leaf, but the drops vanished in the shine around the wyvern. Her prismatic eyes met mine, and through the closing walls of my exhaustion, words chimed:

*healer. you must bind for strength*

She spread her wings, and with a spray of leaves, launched herself low to the ground. Her powerful, compact wings steered her between tree trunks, deft as a hunting goshawk, and she vanished toward the pursuing shouts.

# 21

# BUN ILIDH

## LIZZY

The stars burned pinpricks through the pre-dawn sky, the bitter air raked my cheeks, and I wondered how much longer I could lie to Darcy.

A thousand feet below, the churning surf glimmered in the faint light, outlining the shape of the coast.

*Slow now.* I visualized a falling feather to the drakes, and they swayed to and fro, shedding height and speed while Yuánchi cupped his wings to follow. We floated lower. My goggles had fogged from the cold, so I loosened the leather strap and let them dangle from my neck.

"Are we landing?" Darcy called from behind me.

The wind had eased enough for conversation, and my mind had calmed as well. There were no longer a hundred prior lives condemning Darcy's presence —that was a comfort—but his touch confused me with longing and guilt.

"Soon..." I answered.

Yuánchi stretched his wings, trimming the lay of his scales, and we glided soundless as a hunting owl. I closed my eyes and found the vision of one of the drakes. Even moonless, the world came alive with the etched, violet precision of draca eyes under night sky.

A prior wyfe's memories knew the shape of this shoreline, but those images had faded like childhood memories. I caught glimpses as we followed the breakers, the crashing foam sparkling and glowing in the starlight. A deserted mile flowed beneath Yuánchi's wings. Was this the wrong place? No, there it was, the glistening cold silver of a river winding into the North Sea.

"The river Ilidh," I called back to Darcy, the Scots Gaelic name simultaneously familiar and awkward on my tongue.

We circled, and I saw a castle had been raised on the hilltop. It used to be a wooden fort. A castle would mean guards... too late, I bit back the thought, then waited for the rush of Fènnù's anger that followed any halfway military observation.

Nothing. Was I beyond the black dragon's reach? That would be why my feelings were no longer dominated by dispassion and violence.

We landed beside the castle on a windswept, elevated point overlooking the juncture of river and sea. The castle was in ruins, unoccupied and abandoned. The timbers supporting the main roof had caved in, and the walls were missing stones.

A blue morning glow fringed the eastern horizon. I undid the lap belt and stood on the saddle, toes perched on the highest lip so my head was above the castle walls, then turned a slow circle, adjusting my balance when Yuánchi rocked to stretch his wings. I finished facing the brightening sea and rested my hand on his neck. The pulse of his great heart, quickened by the long flight, thudded almost as fast as a person's. At least his neck scales were scarlet and firm, not yet corrupted by the evil spreading from Fènnù through me.

The castle, old though it was, was new to me, as was a stone bridge farther up the river, but the shadowy dips and peaks of the hills were unchanged. This was the hill I remembered from long ago. The great inland strath, a vast grassy valley spreading from the river, was the same as well, although without a single lamp or lit window. That was unexpected. Even long ago, there had been farmers who woke before the dawn.

When we left Pemberley, I had hid Yuánchi's binding. That was an ancient tactic, one used when fighting other wyves—I had forgotten that detail until now, and the realization spilled an ugly chill into my belly. The trick had lapsed, though. Like compressing a carriage spring in my bare hands, a powerful binding could not be concealed forever.

Carefully, I opened my awareness and sought Fènnù. I stretched, straining at the edges of my perception. Nothing.

Darcy had clambered down the stirrup ladder to the ground. I stepped off the saddle and dropped beside him. The rocky earth smacked the soles of my boots while my thick wool pelisse billowed.

"Fènnù did not follow us," I said. With my mind opened, the endless pressure—that dark influence—had lifted. Even speaking felt different. I could bare my thoughts effortlessly instead of checking and rechecking that I was not saying something distressingly violent.

Darcy stamped his feet, rubbing his arms and working stiff fingers. "How are you not frozen solid?" He stilled, a dark shape facing me. "You sound more like yourself."

The wyfe of war must have no husband.

In defiance of that, I offered my hand. "I am glad you are here." He took my fingers, his grip strong and trusting. Also cautious, the way one would be with an invalid or a madwoman. That made me smile in the dark.

When I did nothing more, he let go and studied the castle's ragged stone walls, vague and inky in the pre-dawn, then looked down at the village by the river mouth. "Where are we?"

"The village is Bun Ilidh. That just means the foot of the Ilidh river. The castle is new, so I do not know, but this hill had a name. Helmsdal."

"Helmsdale Castle," he mused, modernizing the pronunciation. "It is famous."

"Famous?" I squinted at it again. It would have been an efficient fortress in its day, but it was not extraordinary. Not in obsessively fortified Scotland. Longbourn House was bigger.

Darcy picked his way across the dim ground and patted a stone block. "This place inspired the last scene of *Hamlet*. An aunt wanted her son to inherit, so she poisoned the earl and countess, but she was careless and poisoned her son as well. Betrayal and tragedy together, all within these walls."

The story was a coincidence, but "betrayal and tragedy" prodded my uncomfortable conscience. I took a breath to buttress my deceit.

Darcy looked as inky as the castle. I was suddenly desperate to see him and flicked to a firedrake's perspective. Darcy's high cheekbones and expressive brows became clear, but his face was unfathomable in the peculiar colors of draca sight. His posture, though, was achingly familiar. He was studying Yuánchi and distinctly dissatisfied.

"He is hungry," Darcy reported.

Relying on Darcy for reports about Yuánchi frustrated me. Cautiously, I reached for Yuánchi's thoughts myself and felt a grating, ill-fitted contact, like shoving a chisel into a finely crafted lock. But that was better than at Long-bourn. There, Yuánchi's mind, usually inhumanly potent, had crumbled under my touch.

Count your successes. The isolation from Fènnù was helping, and with the war drawing the black dragon south, she was too distant to sense Darcy or Yuánchi. The search for the flute would keep Darcy occupied. The rest of our family should be safe in Longbourn and Pemberley, far from London and the war. I could not save everyone, but it was a start. A token.

A boot knocked a loose stone, and the firedrake's inhuman vision snapped from Darcy to the darkness of the half-fallen castle. A man's voice called, "Who's there?" as a figure stumbled into view, his sleepy hand rubbing tousled hair. In the draca's sight, the man's face was painfully lean. He squinted at Darcy's vague but well-dressed shape, then he lifted a farmer's scythe like a weapon. "Ye cannae hae the stones!"

"What stones?" Darcy asked.

"The Pictish stones," the man replied in a wary, but calmer, Scottish brogue. "Thought ye were Sellar. The *factor.*"

Factor was the Scot's name for a land manager, the sort who organized a grand estate, and the man all but spat it.

"I am not your factor," Darcy said simply. "I am Mr. Darcy." There was a pause while the two men watched each other, then Darcy asked me, "Is this the place? Is the flute here?"

A razor-thin slice of sun cut the horizon, illuminating his features for my human sight. That made lying hard, but a clever answer could be truthful.

"My memories from the wyves of war flow through Fènnù," I said. "We have escaped her—my mind is beyond her reach—so the memory has faded. But the flute was here."

The man listened, eyes wide. He repeated, "The flute?" Then the rising morning sun caught Yuánchi's hulk. The man pivoted, and his jaw hung. "Ye rode the scarlet dragon." He thumped down on his knees in front of me. His improvised weapon, the scythe, clattered onto the stony hilltop. "Ye heard us. Ye *came!*" He stabbed the fingers of his right hand at his heart. "*Banrigh nan Dràgon.*"

THE MAN INTRODUCED himself as William MacLeod while he led us down a steep hundred-yard path to the river. The village was on the far shore, the houses simple dwellings with thatched roofs and rough, unpainted plank walls, not the turf walls that usually insulated homes in this climate. They looked new, the wood not yet weathered, and were placed in peculiarly regular rows, each with an identical, inadequate strip of farmland as if the village had been built to some miserly plan. Three single-masted fishing boats were anchored along the river's mouth, and the wind carried a strong scent of herring.

Some warlike habit of mine inventoried draca. Six were bound in the village. That would be an impressive count for a mid-sized English town, but this village had a mere twenty or thirty houses. They must bind like the Britons, ignoring human restrictions of class.

People ran out of the houses as Mr. MacLeod rowed us across the river. They gathered and chanted *"Banrigh nan Dràgon,"* the Scottish name for a great wyfe. Eager arms pointed out Yuánchi across the river.

A cry roared as we clambered out of the skiff and joined the mass. Mr. MacLeod all but danced ahead, shouting, "She has come! *Banrigh nan Dràgon!*" Fording the flood of greetings, we followed him to the largest house. That proved to be a community building, laid out like the turf-and-stone long-houses I remembered but built with thin, chilly plank walls. There were three long tables with bench seats, enough for the entire village if they packed in, which they proceeded to do.

Darcy and I were ushered to seats across from each other at the center table. The villagers eagerly settled, some sitting backwards on the benches to watch us.

"What do they expect?" Darcy asked me, his words buried in the din.

"A great wyfe," I said, not sure how else to articulate the history—and the responsibility—that title carried in the Highlands.

The man's wyfe, Mistress MacLeod, took a seat beside me and waved hushing gestures at the room. When it quieted, she said, "We read stories sayin' a dragon burned London. 'Course the newspapers are filled with nonsense, aren't they? But here ye are, a dragon and a great wyfe."

Exclamations swept the room, and boots pounded in a rough, regular stomp. Her husband cried out, "'Tis the legend reborn!"

"Where did ye fly from?" Mistress MacLeod asked, quieting the room. She was not the eldest wyfe in the village—I would have placed her in her mid-twenties—but her title "Mistress" signaled authority. Perhaps that reflected her binding. We had passed their lindworm in the street, a rare breed, this one a ruddy oak-brown.

"Derbyshire," I answered. "We flew all night."

"All night! Have ye broken yer fast?" When I shook my head, she fell back in her chair with comic dismay and cried, "Shall we feed the poor lass?"

"Ayes" resounded.

Women ran out and returned with several round, crusty oat bannocks, three battered tin plates of smoked herring, a stone jar of sheep butter, and another of soft cheese. The food was divided between the tables. A small dish of dried berries and apples was placed for Darcy and me, likely a treat at this time of year.

I had expected a raft of questions, but absolute quiet fell other than reverent murmurs of "Pass the butter" or "The fish, please." Darcy and I exchanged a look but joined the meal; it would have been insulting to refuse. We had landed mid-flight and eaten bread with cheese, but I was starved and wolfed down a chunk of the griddled oat bread slathered with butter. I avoided the herring—I had developed a petty distrust for fish that stared back at me ever since I was startled by a splashing draca in a river. That seemed silly now, a childhood fancy, but it had been less than two years ago. Darcy had steadied me that day—held me, really, as much as propriety allowed. We had known each other a month.

I watched him compliment the bread, and my dishonesty prickled my conscience.

The food, not much for so many, vanished in two minutes. A peculiar disquiet climbed my shoulders. I pulled back my hair, tying it—any trace of style had been blasted away by the gale of Yuánchi's flight—then recognized what made me uneasy. The villagers' cheeks were sunken, their necks thin... every face was gaunt. This village had survived a hungry, hard winter. A young girl near me was picking crumbs from where the bannocks were sectioned, and I regretted taking a slice.

I turned back and met Darcy's gaze. He inclined his head infinitesimally to the emptied serving plates. He had noticed also.

Mistress MacLeod introduced herself formally and nodded to Mr. MacLeod, seated beside Darcy. "That firebrand's m'husband."

Her husband grinned. "Fire is good for the soul, wyfe, whether it be 'tween a man and a woman or for roasting mutton." His eyes glittered in his weather-creased, freckled face. "A dragon, though. That's a fire that'll put me in my place!" The other men chuckled agreement, and Mr. MacLeod capped it by shouting, "And put others in their place, too!"

"Haud yer wheesht," his wyfe snapped. Her husband grinned.

"What're those?" the girl who had been picking up crumbs asked me, pointing at the goggles dangling from my neck. She was about nine.

"They are like spectacles," I said, "but to block the wind when we fly."

"By golly." Her lips blew an inexpert whistle. "Ye ride in the sky? Like a flying kelpie?"

"What is a kelpie?" I asked, resisting an urge to attempt her Scottish lilt. It was terribly infectious.

"A water horse," Mistress MacLeod answered for her. "This girl loves those bonny stories. In the old times, they talked of all manner of creatures rising from the lochs. Folk dinnae ken it was draca sleeping in the water, so they dreamed up nymphs and kelpies. But it's all nonsense." She ruffled the girl's hair.

The girl, evidently her daughter, squawked "Ma!" then asked me, "Is yer dragon hungry, too?"

The answer was yes, but I did not want to say it. I had seen a few goats in the village, but after a long flight, Yuánchi could have downed them all as a soup course. We could not strip these people of their livestock.

Mr. MacLeod, firebrand or not, had been listening to his daughter with a fond smile. He gave a wry snort. "Does yer dragon like sheep?" He pitched that to carry across the tables, and laughs rose.

In truth, sheep were not Yuánchi's favorite—the wool caught in his teeth— but he would eat them. "He does. But you have been generous already. We cannot eat your flock."

Mr. MacLeod rubbed his hands together with glee. "Och, but we're arse deep in sheep! The more he eats, the merrier." There were scattered "Ayes" again, but Mistress MacLeod frowned.

"Why are ye come here?" she asked.

The meal had been quiet, but now there was true silence. Every breath seemed to stop.

"We seek something from the past," Darcy answered, choosing his words carefully.

The expectant quiet soured into shuffling feet and disappointed expressions.

"The *past?*" Mr. MacLeod blurted in disbelief. "What about the present? Yer astride a bleedin' dragon!"

"Hush," his wyfe scolded. "What from the past?"

Darcy hesitated, looking at me for guidance.

"They're seeking the flute," Mr. MacLeod broke in flatly. "Said so by the castle. It's the legends come true! *Banrigh nan Dràgon* heard our call. She'll bring justice." Boots pounded throughout the room.

Mistress MacLeod rose, and the noise stopped. "Justice is cool headed. We've a right to anger, but a fist swung by anger is revenge, not justice." She flapped her hand at the audience. "Look at ye gawking. Naught more'll happen today. Time's wasting. Get on with ye."

The crowd filed out with curious glances and whispers, leaving the MacLeods with us.

Mistress MacLeod sank to the bench and rubbed her temples. Her thinned face was shadowed by the morning sun pouring through the open door. "Never seen a dragon afore today, and the sun is bare risen, but I'd be hard pressed to say if that creature you ride is scarlet or black."

"He is the scarlet dragon, Yuánchi," I said. "He is... ill."

"Scarlet. But ye carry the dagger, lass."

"I am the wyfe of war," I admitted.

Mr. MacLeod slapped his palm triumphantly on the table.

His wyfe waited until the clap had faded. "Hard to imagine a wyfe of war satisfied by stories, but stories is all we have of the flute."

"We would have your stories, if you will share them," Darcy said.

"The story is told by the stones. I'll hae to think on it."

THE MACLEODS INSISTED on hosting us as their guests, scoffing good-naturedly when Darcy offered to pay for lodging. There was no space for Yuánchi to land in the village, so Mr. MacLeod hiked up Helmsdale hill with us to retrieve the saddlebags.

At the top, he stared slack-jawed at Yuánchi's bulk. "The *size* o' him." He shook his head as if rattling his brains, then barked a laugh. "Feeding him's nae problem. There's big flocks inland a few miles." With a grin, he pointed. I imagined the distant sheep, and Yuánchi was in pursuit the next moment. We braced against the hammering gusts as he powered off the hill's edge, led by the pair of firedrakes and following the river upstream.

Back in the village, the MacLeods' bound lindworm waited by their threshold. I rested my palm on his scaly head in greeting, and he returned a muscular, steaming yawn. The home itself was a long, narrow rectangle, the rooms placed one after another. There was a parents' bedroom with an alcove for a baby, then a combined kitchen and eating room heated by an open and smoky peat fire, then another tiny bedroom used by their daughter. She cheerfully presented it to us, rescuing her cloth doll off the pillow before moving to her parents' room. That left us a single, narrow bed buried in homespun wool throws and a strip of empty wooden floor about a pace wide. There was a window the size of a book with blurry, cheap glass polished scrupulously clean.

Mistress MacLeod bid us to settle in, adding, "Rest ye after yer travel. It'll be a long day tomorrow," before departing.

That left Darcy and me alone. Darcy's posture was over-exact, a tall man in a small room. My own hands clasped awkwardly. Since the lake, we had barely touched each other. When we first met in that forest clearing, dodging his blade had been a delightful game, a contest that left me amused and excited. That memory felt foreign now, but the thrill heated my thoughts, like the private glee I had felt sparring words with proud Mr. Darcy when he first arrived in Hert-fordshire. I had an unpleasant suspicion that some poorly repressed part of me thought assaulting men, verbally or otherwise, was flirtation.

But contests between us were in the past. There was no person in my life I trusted more, no one with whom I had shared more intimacy, in mind or in body.

"I will leave you to rest," he said abruptly, bowing formally.

I blinked. How long had I stared at him silently? "Do not go. It is morning. I am not tired."

A smile released the tension in his cheek. "You are quite literally swaying on your feet."

"We can be together here. Away from Fènnù." I was not sure what that meant. In this room, with its tiny pane of cheap glass so faithfully washed? In Scotland, with its ruined castles and gray seas?

He stepped closer and, hesitant as a new groom, stroked his fingers over my shoulders. It was the first intimate touch we had shared unless I counted briefly holding his hand on the hilltop.

"By my count, you have not slept for two days," he said. His fingers steered me gently onto the bed like a child. "You are blinking at me like a roused owl. Rest. I will wake you."

I WOKE MYSELF, sensing Darcy's quiet movement in the room. The sun was casting low, orange beams through the window. Sunset came late this far north. I had slept long.

I lifted my head groggily, and Darcy said, "I did not mean to wake you. The MacLeods have retired for the evening." He cocked an eyebrow in sympathy. "Fishermen rise early."

He had spread a blanket on the floor. Preparing to sleep there.

I was curled atop the bed's covering wearing everything but my boots. I did not even remember removing those. Darcy must have eased them off while I slept. The dagger was under my pillow, loosened in its sheath. That, I had done.

I sat up on the side of the narrow bed, no longer exhausted but still pleasantly sleepy and ready for a proper night's rest. A breath later, that relaxation was replaced by the edgy, acute vigilance that had possessed me since I returned from the lake.

"I do not want to be a wyfe of war," I said dismally, the balls of my feet braced on the floor as if an armed assailant might burst through the door at any moment.

Darcy sat on the bed beside me. "Then do not." He left a foot of empty, rumpled covers between us. Understandably. I had done little but push him away since I returned.

A chorus of voices from the past whispered: *The wyfe of war must have no husband.*

"I wish I could not," I said, "but those women's lives—their wars—are woven into my heart. It has driven out all the pleasant things I used to enjoy. A pretty shawl. Laughing at a ridiculous person."

"I am certain we will meet ridiculous people," Darcy offered gamely.

I was not in the mood for jokes. "All that evil history existed before. The world did not change while I was submerged. All that changed is I am aware of it." I laughed shortly. "Mary once accused me of complacency, and she was quite right. I miss my complacency. Awareness confers duty. Do you understand that?"

He nodded.

I blew an exaggerated sigh that puffed my cheeks. "What did you do while I slept?"

"Talked with the people. Asked about the village."

"Something is wrong here. These homes are fresh built, but the people are starving."

The planes of Darcy's face flattened. "The homes are new, half of them unfinished. Mr. MacLeod was chinking gaps in the walls while you slept. They do not trust me enough to say what happened, not yet, but I have suspicions."

He offered nothing more, and I knew he would not until he was certain, so I asked, "Is Yuánchi fed?"

That drew a chuckle. "He returned with his belly bulging and enough wool snagged on his scales to knit a pair of socks. The firedrakes ate, too. They fished for herring, diving like seabirds. The entire village watched that, except for Yuánchi, who was asleep atop the hill. He has claimed that as his roost. The villagers are in awe of him. And of you."

"I am glad you are here," I said, and remembered I had already said that. I must stop repeating it, or he would become suspicious.

I reached across the gap between us and laid my hand on his. Light glinted on my gold fede ring. Darcy had it crafted for me after our Beltane handfasting. The finespun gold depicted a woman's and man's linked hands, the muscles and tendons minutely sculpted to convey the strength of their grasp. It was the sole possession that survived my sleep in Pemberley lake—it and the dagger, if that artifact could be called a possession.

Darcy wore my father's posy ring as his wedding ring. He had asked the jeweler to copy its message into my ring, but the old letters were too worn to decipher. For me though, the message of Papa's ring was clear: on his deathbed, he had pressed it into my palm, granting his blessing—and his firm advice—to marry Mr. Darcy, the sole man he knew who could make me happy.

Again, the past voices whispered, *The wyfe of war must have no husband.* Portents filled my mind, memories I had not confessed to Darcy. Feeling guilty, I lifted my hand from his.

Darcy immediately stood. He shrugged his muscular shoulders out of his coat, folded it, then untied his neckcloth. Without meeting my eyes, he said, "We should sleep. Our hosts will rise early." He lay down, arranging his long frame under the coarse blanket on the wooden floor.

I lay on the edge of the bed atop the wool throws, some edged with reused fabric scraps cut like draca wings. The sunset turned scarlet, then mauve, then indigo. Cold night air infiltrated cracks in the unfinished walls. Through all that, Darcy lay unnaturally still. Finally, I whispered his name, but he did not answer.

# 22

## THE MEMORY

### MARY

T he needledrac alighted on my outstretched finger. I lifted her near my spectacles. Her four crystalline wings tilted, tiny sails balancing in the breeze from the observatory's open window.

Her two legs were tiny but muscled like a draca's, not shell-wrapped like an insect's. The lapis and jade colors came from gleaming scales wrapped around her body like miniature plate armor. Her claws gripped the skin of my knuckle. Each foot had three foreclaws and one hooked rear claw, all as black as night, as fine as needles, and long enough to inflict a bloody scratch as I had discovered in yesterday's encounter. Or perhaps she made the discovery; today her grip was feather-light.

Needledrac consumed only nectar from the draca breath flower, so the claws were defensive, like a bee's sting—

I realized I had given her my right hand as a perch, so I could not write notes. "Drat," I whispered. Her wings flicked, compensating for my breath.

This needledrac had hatched from the infested broad bean I treated with draca essence. The other broad bean, untreated, hatched a winged foul crawler. That meant crawlers were some brethren of draca, so I had moved the crawler to a larger container and given it water and food, but it died in less than a day, the mayfly-like wings shredded and the segmented body desiccating amid dozens of curling legs.

The needledrac I let fly free, but she returned daily. I did not know why. I had hoped to see her again and gathered fresh draca breath flowers as a lure, but she ignored them. Draca breath had bloomed riotously this spring, so she found food easily enough.

Lizzy's communication with draca extended to needledrac, although she said their tiny minds rendered it simple. Still, as I watched this gem-like creature leave my finger and explore the observatory, hovering to study her distorted reflection in the telescope lens, I envied my sister's gift.

I had other, less whimsical projects than visiting with needledrac. On the table, four medical syringes lay in a row. Syringes were simple copper tubes with a plunger and nozzle. We used them to suction liquids or apply ointment, but any person who handled one learned, sometimes comically, that they could spray the width of a room.

I had filled these syringes with draca essence and sealed the tips with wax— sealing wax, in fact, in the Darcys' shade of burgundy. If I had correctly trans- lated a thirteenth century scrawl I found in the Loch bairn journal, I had created my own defensive sting.

One project frustrated me: my lost memory about the third great item, the flute fashioned from a claw of the mysterious, missing third dragon. I was certain I had forgotten some fact about the flute, but I had not found the trigger for recollection. Idly, I looked around the observatory, testing unusual objects, but no revelation leaped to mind.

"Miss Bennet!" a young man's voice called outside the window, "we found one!" I waved acknowledgement to Thomas Digweed, then grabbed a steel-wire bird cage and a syringe and hurried for the stairs.

"It is a huge crawler," Thomas said breathlessly as we exited into the south-west garden toward the stables. "As long as my foot!"

Two gardeners armed with rakes were pointing excitedly at one of the baits, a putrid dead chicken. Crawlers were attracted to carrion, the rottener, the better, and while I would not harm sentient animals, spoiled chickens discarded by the kitchen were convenient for science.

We arrived, and the gardeners lifted their rakes in a salute to me, like guards with poleaxes. The story of Georgiana and me summoning song draca had flown through the household. Their respect reminded me of the power that had stormed through me, and I savored a tingle of pride.

"Do not harm it," I reminded everyone. Before, I had considered crawlers the worst of mindless vermin, but the needledrac's emergence promoted them to moral ambiguity, creatures either derived of draca, or draca's precursor, or draca diseased.

Keeping the syringe in my right hand, I set down the cage, borrowed a rake from a gardener, and gave the chicken carcass an awkward, left-handed prod. Flies buzzed up, and the shell of a squirming, olive-green crawler came into view.

It *was* a big crawler. Moral arguments aside, the twining segments raised hairs on the back of my neck. The armored body was nearly as wide as my wrist, the jointed legs as long as my ring finger. It looked too large to be concealed by a chicken. Perhaps it was stout but short.

A year ago, a crawler this large would have been a fictional horror, but since Fènnù's return, crawlers had grown. Even ignoring the monsters serving the invading army, six- or eight-inch lengths had been spotted on Pemberley's grounds.

A large crawler complicated this test. They moved faster. Their stings killed quicker. I patted my reticule, feeling the stoppered bottle of draca essence I carried as a last recourse.

I passed the rake to Thomas. "When I tell you, push the chicken aside."

He nodded, gripping the handle like a spear, then blurted, "Will you call the draca birds?" The gardeners nudged each other expectantly.

"No," I said. "This is an experiment. I have read that draca essence has an effect on crawlers. It may stun it or slow it."

"Slow it?" Thomas echoed uneasily. That was less impressive than summoning fire breathing draca.

"Or stun it," I said firmly. Although early Middle English was not my best language, I had consulted multiple dictionaries and grammars while translating the journal. "If that fails, I will call draca." Remembering that remarkable summoning lent conviction to my tone, and Thomas nodded, reassured.

I aimed the syringe, then used my free hand to snap the sealing wax off the nozzle. "Move the chicken!"

Thomas gave the chicken a shove. It flopped aside wetly, and a cloud of flies rose.

The crawler unwound, the front pinchers snapping. A dozen more segments streamed out of a freshly dug hole in the ground. It was longer than I expected, as long as my forearm.

I pushed the plunger. Draca essence sprayed in two crooked streams, wetting empty spots of grass. A fragment of sealing wax was still in place, blocking the nozzle.

"Drat!" I exclaimed, forgetting that cursing had been a private experiment. I pried at the broken wax with my thumbnail while draca essence dripped from the nozzle.

Instead of returning to its meal, the crawler advanced toward Thomas and me, the dozens of legs falling in a rhythmic pattern that was viscerally unpleasant—spiderish, but more so. We backed away hurriedly.

The fragment of wax came out. I aimed and pressed the plunger again. A spurt shot straight, then the plunger struck the end of the tube. Empty.

Had I hit it? The crawler was hissing.

"Get behind me," I said to Thomas. I dug the bottle of essence from my reticle and uncorked it. "Everyone stay back."

"I could whack it with the rake," Thomas offered.

"That will make it angry." Even small crawlers were hard to kill. The shell on this one looked thick.

"It *is* angry," he pointed out.

The front three sections lifted in the air, and an unpleasant, slug-like appendage emerged between the pincers. A tongue? It wriggled, as if tasting the air. The body dropped and crept nearer.

I set my feet, held the bottle of essence at arm's length, and waited. But I must not use it all. There was no longer a shortage—the Britons were making new batches regularly—but the rest of my supply was in the syringes. If someone was stung, I would have to dash up four flights of stairs to the observatory—

The crawler shot forward like a striking snake. I yelped and dumped the bottle, dousing my shoe, spraying my skirt, and—I was certain this time—splashing the crawler. I scrambled back and collided with Thomas. We untangled, separating left and right, and he raised the rake like an ax.

The crawler was writhing, the body coiling and twisting in endless figures. That slowed to quivers and a sad rattling sound, then stilled.

I edged closer. The crawler was not completely still. There was a slight, rhythmic flexing. Respiration.

I took the rake from Thomas, hooked a prong under the crawler's body, and lifted it, dangling, into the cage. I pulled the lid down with the rake, then gingerly locked it.

"It worked," I said, rather relieved given that not everything went according to plan. "The essence does affect it." I knelt on the grass and peered through the steel mesh. Seeing a large crawler this close was like viewing a specimen under a microscope. Already I saw fresh details. There were twin rows of pin-prick holes along the body's shell segments—supplementary breathing? Tiny flutters affected the legs in unison, like a team of oarsmen.

"Will it turn into a draca?" Thomas asked, kneeling beside me. He had been fascinated by the larva's transformation to a needledrac.

"I think that unlikely. The larva we treated was in metamorphosis, so the essence could affect its development. This crawler is mature." The pincers had folded into depressions in its head, but they were beginning to wiggle and click. "The passage I read says the effect is temporary—"

"What are you *doing*?" Georgiana cried behind me.

I scrambled to my feet, brushing grass off my skirts.

Georgiana had worn no bonnet—her hair was loose—and she had bedroom slippers on her feet. She must have run from the house. Her hands were clenched, the tendons standing like wire.

My stomach tilted with irrational guilt. "Do not be angry."

"I saw through the window," she said, angrily. "You could have been *killed!*" The word rasped. I had never heard her voice break like that.

"It was perfectly..." I almost said safe, but that was untrue. "It was a necessary risk. I needed to test—"

"You did not *need* to do anything. Not without me."

My guilt transformed into a healthy dose of irritation. "I did *not* need you. It is an experiment to determine the effect of draca essence on crawlers. I read that—"

Georgiana interrupted with a snort. Something sharp lodged beneath my sternum.

I took a breath, trying to settle a surge of hurt and anger. "Are you going to scold me for reading, like Mamma does?"

"I am scolding you for taking risks." She pointed at the caged crawler. Her finger was shaking. "That is a monster. What if you were stung?"

"I have treated crawler stings. I would treat myself as best I could. Soldiers are dying from these. They need defenses. This is not a time to shy from risk."

She was silent for a breath, then, "What if Thomas were stung?"

"You are angry about me, not Thomas." That much I was sure of. Thomas was witnessing this, which must be unpleasant, so I said to him, "You did nothing wrong. Will you excuse us? Georgiana and I will discuss this privately."

"Of course." He bowed, suddenly mature and channeling his father's calm assurance. He left at a measured pace. The gardeners fled in his wake.

Georgiana's arms were folded in disapproval.

Frustration and confusion swirled in me, but I had discovered a pattern in the last few days. "What is bothering you? I hear it in your voice when I talk about the great song. When I describe the power that I touch. When I confess that it makes me strong."

Something I said struck home. She unfolded her arms, a gangly unwinding for such a graceful woman.

I was struggling to imagine an explanation for her anger. "Are you jealous?"

"Oh," she gasped, a sobbing half-laugh. "Never, Mary. You know that I love you." Her sapphire irises filled with tears.

*Memory flickered—the lost memory, vivid as life:*

*I held a sheaf of paper in my left hand. A book? My throat stung. Georgiana faced me, her hair disarranged, a lock hanging by her cheek, tears streaming—*

The memory shuttered as she resumed speaking. "I have not known how to—"

"Stop!" I threw out a hand, blocking my sight of her eyes, blocking her words, grasping at that edge of recollection, but the memory folded to nothing. I looked around wildly, as if it might have lodged on a clod of dirt or a fence post. "I almost had it..."

Georgiana had drawn back, stricken. Some combative corner of me notched that as revenge for her snickering at my reading, then remorse overwhelmed me. I lowered my hand. "I am sorry. But we did this before. This is the memory I lost! About music..."

I closed my eyes to concentrate. It was gone.

"Music?" Georgiana's voice said uncertainly.

"Madams," called Mrs. Reynolds. I opened my eyes and saw her trotting across the grass. "A messenger has arrived, an aide-de-camp of Lord Wellington. He says it is urgent."

Georgiana sniffed and wiped each wet eye, then we exchanged cautious nods —agreement to defer—and hurried for the house.

INSIDE, and with Georgiana's hair swiftly pinned by Lucy—Mrs. Reynolds stated that even military messengers could wait two minutes for a lady to be presentable—we entered the front drawing room.

The aide-de-camp was a uniformed officer in his early twenties. His coat was smudged with soot, his left forearm bandaged and bloodstained. He was flushed and smelled of horse, his trousers sprayed with mud from riding at a gallop.

He rose the instant we entered. "Ladies. Your pardon for my appearance. I am Lieutenant Colonel John Fremantle. Lord Wellington dispatched me from battle. I am to deliver this letter to the hand of a lady of Pemberley House and wait for a reply."

He held out an envelope. I recognized Lord Wellington's slanted script.

"To whom are you to deliver it?" Georgiana asked, her eyes on the envelope. It was addressed: *The Great Wyves, Pemberley House.*

The colonel recited, "To Mrs. Darcy, or to Miss Darcy, or to Miss Bennet, or to Miss Woodhouse."

Georgiana's lips thinned when my name was included, reawakening my mystification at her reactions. But she took the letter, broke the seal, and unfolded it between us where we could read together:

*"Ladies, I write this letter in haste and with hope that it will reach Mrs. Darcy, but I cast this plea to you all.*

*Our soldiers in Surrey have been overmatched by a vile force. The enemy has marshaled hundreds of monstrous crawlers, and their perfumer strikes from the air. I cannot judge if such evil is natural or supernatural, but it is an assault beyond what brave soldiers and cavalry can withstand.*

*By the time you receive this, Surrey will likely be ceded to the enemy. I send this plea because the heart of London is but twenty miles farther, and the enemy drives toward it like they are possessed. We have no weapon to halt this foul tide.*

*If London falls, England falls. I will say simply that we require a miracle.*

*Wellington"*

"How does the perfumer strike from the air?" Georgiana asked.

The colonel shifted uneasily. "I have only heard her in the distance, a roaring whir like the winds of hell." He had a Hertfordshire accent; it reminded me of home. "I have seen the crawlers, though. They are controlled by enslaved English wyves, who are driven and beaten by Overseers. That is bad enough, but"—his voice caught—"in the worst of it, when soldiers were dying, some of the men tried to shoot the wyves. Shoot Englishwomen. Lord Wellington forbade it when he heard. And now, the French conceal the wyves where even cannons cannot reach while the crawlers advance."

"That is abhorrent," I said. I was not even sure which part. All of it.

Georgiana said softly, "The miracle he seeks is a dragon."

That was evident. Also impossible. "We do not even know where Lizzy is. And she must not use Yuánchi to fight. Violence attracts the black dragon. Fènnù's madness would consume Lizzy and Yuánchi."

Georgiana was rereading the letter. "What if Fènnù fought?"

That shocked a laugh from me. "That is *worse*. When the black dragon is unleashed, history itself fractures. Entire civilizations vanish. Fènnù is not a weapon. She is an apocalypse." Georgiana was watching me with a brilliant, focused intensity, like I was a keyboard score thick with accidentals, so I argued on, "If Lizzy commands Fènnù, if their minds connect, Lizzy's mind would be consumed. Since the song was broken, every wyfe who ties herself to Fènnù has become a vessel for her fury." Georgiana said nothing. Did she not understand? "Besides, which dragon is irrelevant. We cannot contact Lizzy."

"I can do it," Georgiana said.

That surprised me. "You can speak to Lizzy?"

Georgiana shook her head. "No. But I can summon Fènnù. I could command her to fight."

That was so preposterous, I should have laughed louder. Instead, dread infused my veins. Fear for Georgiana.

I blinked and held fast to logic. "You have no way to summon Fènnù. Lizzy has the dagger. The wyfe of *war* has the gift of command, not you."

"I am the wyfe of song." Georgiana spoke slowly, testing each word. "After you remembered Fènnù's song, we sang it together. Fènnù heard us."

The dread in my veins chilled colder. "But her power was monstrous. It crushed us."

"It crushed the tower you built. That tower of music."

Georgiana's voice, always melodic, was toneless. She was hiding something. My dread congealed, hard as ice. "We built that tower together."

"I know," she whispered. "That is why it fell."

The pieces of an ugly puzzle were assembling in my mind, but I refused to see it. "You *cannot* command Fènnù. She is beyond human strength. Even Lizzy cannot command a dragon against its will. Fènnù would consume you."

"That is how it will end. But England might be saved first."

"No." I shook my head like a child. "No. I refuse it. I will not allow it."

"Mary—"

"No! I will not give you the music. I will burn it!"

Georgiana smiled a pitying smile. She had sung it. The wyfe of song remembered every note she sang.

In a flash, I was on a different path. "Even if you could summon her, you could not control her. Together, you would wreak senseless destruction. We would all be consumed."

"Not at first. Not for a time. I am stronger than you know."

"No one is that strong!"

She took my hands in hers. "Do you remember the power in the hills when we summoned the song draca? The strength when we sang together and you built that crystal palace of music? Mary, you are not feeling some ancient force or mystical song. You are feeling *me*." The puzzle in my mind snapped into unforgiving clarity as she continued, "I did not know how to tell you. The strength you have been celebrating, the power that makes you so proud... it is mine." Tears brightened her eyes. Her fingers clutched mine. "I should have told you. Can you forgive me?"

All my nascent pride, all the selfish importance I had collected, collapsed. It had been delusion, alms from this woman whom I loved and could never equal. Who occupied a realm I could barely perceive, let alone enter. I had only been too ignorant to understand.

"There is nothing to forgive," I grated out. "I was a fool."

"Mary, I swear that you have your own power—"

"Please do not." I managed that with a steady voice, but it was hard. Being comforted, whether from love or guilt, hurt more than the truth.

Finally, a pooled tear penetrated Georgiana's lashes and sped down her cheek.

*The lost memory woke:*

*Georgiana, crying. A sheaf of papers in my hand. Smoke, raw in my throat. A panicked crowd surged around us, but earlier, there had been music and dance.*

*This was the ball, the London ball where the dagger was stolen, and Jane's wyvern killed Miss Rees, and Fènnù woke from centuries of sleep.*

*I ratcheted the memory back through time:*

*The papers I held were not a book; they were scholarly notes for a lecture on the dagger. The museum researcher had found me, sent by Mr. Darcy. Mystified, I had leafed through the sheets, and amid the flutter of words, glimpsed an illustration...*

I blinked, leaving memory to fall into Georgiana's tear-filled, sapphire gaze.

"The British Museum has the flute," I said. "It has a *catalog* number. It is in London!" A city that would soon fall to Napoleon and the invading slavers.

It took seconds before Georgiana's throat worked and she said, "I do not understand."

"I found my lost memory of the flute. It was... overwhelmed by the chaos of the London ball." Overwhelmed by grief. Joane Rees had just been killed.

Georgiana had a wondering expression, but skeptical, too. "If it is in London, why did Lizzy fly north?"

I dismissed that with a flick of my hand. "She only knew it *had* been in the north." The implications were locking into place, a fortress of logic to defeat this deadly spiral. Relief overwhelmed me. Georgiana did not need to be brave. She did not need to sacrifice herself. "Lizzy has the dagger, and Emma will find the amulet, and the flute is in London. That is all three items. I will get the flute, and you can heal the song. This madness—the corruption of crawlers—will end. This *war* will end."

"We will go together," Georgiana said immediately.

I shook my head. "London could be captured at any moment. The great wyves must stay safe to heal the song. Lizzy will return when she does not find the flute. *Keep* her here at Pemberley. You and she cannot risk being taken."

Georgiana grabbed my hand. "Then you cannot go!"

I stretched my mouth into a semblance of a smile. "Of course I can." The conundrum had resolved itself, like a problem in composition where the right chord bridges two passages that appear irreconcilable. "I am not important. You are."

"Mary, that is not true—"

Clumsily, I pressed my fingers to her lips, stopping her words and reveling in her tender skin. It was madness to show intimacy with strangers present, but I no longer cared.

"Promise me that you will not summon Fènnù," I said.

181

She tangled my fingers in hers and pulled them to her cheek. "I will not if you stay safe."

"Calling Fènnù would not save me. If she had your power, she would destroy us all."

Georgiana drew a stubborn breath, then let it out reluctantly. "If we are to heal the song, we will need Emma, too."

I had considered that problem, but there was nothing to do about it.

"Perhaps she has found the amulet. Perhaps she is already returning."

# 23

# CELLARS AND COVENANTS

## EMMA

"Steady," Mr. Knightley said, his arm guiding me through a squat, vaulted doorway of old stone. The trim on my bonnet grazed the rock as I ducked.

Lady Catherine's wyvern was ahead, shining in the gloom. We were in a long, wide cellar as ghostly as a catacomb. Thick columns of ancient brick rose every few yards, the tops merging in shared arches like a forest canopy.

"These are the Abbey ruins," I said, emerging from my daze. I hardly remembered walking here.

"If you say so," Mr. Knightley replied. "Miss Bates led us here. She seems to be managing our escape. I must go help her with Mrs. Elton."

That cleared my stupor. "How is Augusta?" She had collapsed after I broke the infected binding between her and the foul crawler. I remembered Mr. Knightley slinging her over his shoulders.

"She has recovered enough to stand." His hand tightened on my elbow, drawing me to face him. "How are you? You had one of your... episodes."

"That is a polite description," I said, forcing a smile. I still felt the effects. Miasma was pooling in the distant corners, but it was ephemeral, a stage illusion that could be dismissed with rational effort, not the terrible, gut-churning threat I felt when obsessions ruled my mind. "It is passing, though. Very quickly. I am not sure why..."

Was it the wyvern? Her presence had not helped me when we met at the London ball. Although Mr. Darcy had helped then by standing close to hide the visual madness...

Mr. Knightley was steadying my left elbow, so I turned to him and rested my other hand, ungloved, on his chest, almost like when we waltzed on the frozen ship.

Mr. Knightley was not as tall as Mr. Darcy—my eyes were a few inches below his, not staring into his neckcloth—but even if he were, his clothes would not have provided the solace of perfection. He had sprinted through wild forest carrying a full-grown woman. His coat was rumpled and strewn with burrs, his neckcloth undone, his hat lost. Tangled spirals of black hair hung to his shoulders. The disorder should have distressed me, but, as I felt a shaky breath lift his chest—apparently he was not as recovered from running as I thought—he looked dashing and disheveled, like a pirate captain in a play.

"I wondered if our touching was helping," I explained, belatedly.

In answer, he rested his fingers on the back of my hand. I felt the calluses from his violin strings, so unusual on a gentleman. My touch and his made an intimate pose, but, after dodging death together more than once, it seemed excusable.

"I should see to Mrs. Elton," he said after a minute. "If you are recovered?" I nodded, and he bowed before hurrying outside.

I was not sure exactly where we were, but it was one of the larger old cellars, as big as Hartfield's drawing room. We were not buried, though. Shadowy sunlight trickled through slots in the roof. The light was fringed with green from foliage above, and I heard birdsong. Most of the Abbey cellars were over-grown like this; they looked like hillocks of meadow from outside. I had thought them grand secrets when I was a child, doubly so because exploring them was forbidden. A rule I frequently forgot, naturally.

With my senses and mind calm, I recalled walking here after we met Lady Catherine and her wyvern. Walking, not running. There had been no more need to run.

The wyvern's scales shimmered in the scattered light and seemed to blaze as I approached her.

"Did you kill the men who chased us?" I asked.

*i fought those who fought me. the hounds were wiser. they fled*

Her four-inch claws glistened against the stone floor. I had seen the inhuman ferocity of a wyvern's attack before at the London ball. Our pursuers, the slaver soldiers, had certainly been killed. I had trouble summoning regret.

John and Mr. Elton would be safe, though. They were likely congratulating each other on avoiding the tiresome effort of running, particularly after it turned deadly.

"You must not approach her," Lady Catherine said reprovingly as she ducked through the doorway and saw my proximity to her wyvern.

"Your ladyship," I said politely and moved a few steps away. The wyvern's muscled, stout neck swiveled, following me.

Lady Catherine observed that with an uneasy frown, an emotion that seemed out of character. This woman had, without batting an eyelash, dispatched her wyvern to wreak bloody murder. That required both an uncommonly strong binding and ruthless confidence.

Miss Bates entered next, cradling her roseworm. Once inside, she staggered, closing her eyes, her face ashen.

I hurried to her. Her roseworm greeted me with an alert *cheep*. The draca, at least, had recovered from her fight with the crawler.

"May I take your hand?" I said to Miss Bates. Weakly, she opened her eyes, then let me press her palm between mine.

The crawler venom she drank still coursed through her body, pulsing vilely with every heartbeat. It was diminishing, though. I had sensed far worse when the slavers dosed Harriet to the brink of death. Then, I had been able to purge the venom, but only because I had borrowed strength—the mysterious gift Lady Anne Darcy left for me in the keeping of her wyvern. My own skills sensed injuries but were completely useless for actual healing.

"I have a terrific headache," Miss Bates muttered. "But for a time, I felt... wonderful."

"You must not take the venom again," I warned. "It is addictive. A weaker wyfe would have been killed by the dose you drank."

Her affinity was certainly strong. The unnatural boost from the venom had ended, but her binding shone a brilliant rose. It was no match for the blinding power of the Darcys' binding, but by any other standard, it was impressive. I had spent much of my life dismissing Miss Bates as tiresome. Really, I must have been shockingly self-absorbed not to recognize her qualities.

Lady Catherine's wyvern trotted over to nuzzle my skirts. I could not see her binding at all. That was odd. Were my skills not recovered after all?

I squeezed Miss Bates's hand and smiled. "You were tremendously brave."

"I was thoroughly terrified," she said. "But the widowed wyves do not stand by while women are enslaved. This place"—her bloodshot gaze scanned the brick pillars—"is where the widowed wyves were founded. Widows were consigned to the Abbey as nuns, but in secret, some remained bound to their draca. They met here and swore to shield women from persecution. There are chapters in all the counties. Lady Catherine heads the Kent widowed wyves." She frowned and busily adjusted her shawl. "I admit it is rather dank in here."

A wavering light was approaching from an opening in the back wall. A short, rounded gentleman in a clergyman's black suit and white collar emerged beside a lady bearing a candle.

"Mr. Collins," Lady Catherine snapped with no hint of her earlier unease. "Wherever did you vanish to?"

"Your ladyship!" the gentleman exclaimed, scurrying forward and performing a frivolous bow that displayed prematurely thinning hair. "I took it upon myself to investigate this shadowed abode to ensure there was no lurking danger to your esteemed personage. But the longer passages proved exceptionally difficult to navigate..."

"My husband's candle blew out," the lady beside him explained with equanimity. "I went to fetch him." She was a straightforward looking woman a few years older than me, tastefully but not extravagantly dressed.

In tones of profound disappointment, Lady Catherine introduced the gentleman as Mr. Collins, rector of Rosings Park. More positively, she added, "Rosings Park, naturally, is mine. And this woman is Mrs. Collins."

"Please call me Charlotte," the lady said, and I introduced myself. I had lost my gloves, so she removed hers to shake hands. Our touch revealed nothing. Had she not bound when she married?

This absence of bindings was becoming a puzzle. I stretched out my awareness, and the gloomy parts of the cellar gained a pretty, blue glow—that was new—but I saw only Miss Bates's binding, nothing for Charlotte or Lady Catherine. Surely that was wrong.

Once, the loss of my affinity would have seemed a blessing. Seeing bindings was occasionally interesting but more often distracting and dangerous. However, if it broke the vile connection forced on Augusta, my affinity seemed to have a use after all.

As if she heard my thoughts, the wyvern's voice chimed:

*the one you call lady anne had the gift of healing flesh. yours is the gift of healing spirit*

Lady Catherine was scowling at me with narrowed eyes, so I tried a trick of Lizzy's and replied silently in my head, *Does healing spirit mean healing bindings?*

*spirit, binding, song. all are one. lady anne saw the rise of the three wyves and knew her gift could not heal the song. she passed her duty to you. you must bind for strength*

The ghost of Lady Anne's wyvern had said something similar: *you are as she thought you would be. the heiress to her skills, but stronger.* Lady Anne's history seemed woven with mine: Mr. Darcy had taught me her lessons, and I carried the red lanyard from her journal. Despite that, I had never learned what happened to her, only that she sent her wyvern away and died, and that my symptoms—and my skills—appeared soon after.

And then there was that last part, *you must bind for strength.* That was a tiresome refrain with wyverns. But if there were more captives like Augusta, they might be right. The effort of dissolving that vile connection had drained me.

Mr. Knightley returned with a small crowd: Mr. Weston and Anne, who was carrying their young child; Augusta Elton, who gave me an unsettled look but was standing on her own two feet; and the Otways, wide-eyed in the dim cellar. Augusta's face and hair were tidied, although her gown was still garish. I suppose I could not blame the slavers for that.

The required introductions proceeded, complicated by Mr. Collins's silly flourishes and repetitions. Anne finally stepped in to introduce Mr. Knightley and me to the Collinses. I had already met them, so I was preparing a clever comment when she proudly named us "Mr. and Mrs. Knightley."

I had forgotten that. Again.

Charlotte, calmly, offered her hand for a second time, but she cocked an intrigued eyebrow—I had introduced myself as Miss Woodhouse five minutes before. Mr. Knightley cast me a questioning look while Mr. Collins's hand fluttered, ignored, in mid-air.

I suppose we could not just continue pretending to be married. Eventually, it would be ridiculous.

"In fact, we are not married," I announced brightly, as if it had all been a tremendous lark. Anne uttered a long, understanding *Ohh;* she had witnessed the threats from the Overseer. But she looked disappointed, so I hastened to add, "We are..."

Then, I could not imagine how to finish the sentence. Friends? That choice wrenched something within me. I looked questioningly at Mr. Knightley, as if trying to invent a new fanciful story together, and found he had a very serious expression.

"Pardon us," he said, and offered his arm. As the only option for privacy were the brick columns, we took a few steps and stood behind one of those. There was not much room, so we huddled close.

I was still trying to express what we were to each other. "I never thought I would enjoy being married, but I... it felt nice to pretend, did it not?" His face tightened, and the air thudded from my lungs. I had blundered. I bit my lip until I could speak. "Your pardon. I forgot my situation is changed." Gentlemen did not marry penniless ladies.

He took my forearms in his hands. "You mean your lost fortune?"

"I understand perfectly," I said bravely. My fingers stroked the buttons on his sleeve, so neatly sewn. "You need to buy your beautiful coats..."

"Your fortune means nothing to me," he said dismissively.

His tone stirred my pride, but pride belonged to lost, rich Miss Woodhouse. *Nothing* was a very accurate word. "I really do understand."

"You are not even listening," he exclaimed. "Emma, you do not need a fortune for me to wish to marry you."

With our arms intertwined, we were so close I could have shifted one toe and leaned against him. That closeness had grown on our trip, flourishing in the stories we shared and our quiet walks while resting the horses.

"Well, then why do we..." I started again. "We seem to be endlessly dancing around each other."

With some emphasis, he said, "Because you said you did not wish to marry!"

"I only said that because you *asked* me to marry you," I pointed out. "Or you almost did." That was not a very reasonable response, so I tried a different one. "You have not truly asked me, you know. Not properly."

He drew a deep breath and, in a plain, gentlemanlike manner, said, "Miss Woodhouse, you are the most extraordinary, beautiful, and wonderful woman I have ever met. Would you do me the great honor of becoming my wyfe?"

My heart stuttered, and then I said, "I would." The words felt outlandishly joyful, and they raced around my body until I was feather-light.

Our linked hands tangled inexpertly until we both laughed. We let go and held each other. I wrapped an arm around the small of his back and the other behind his neck, burrowing fingers into his hair. My cheek pressed his shoulder.

His solidity felt wonderful, and our embrace lasted until, self-consciously, we sorted ourselves out and walked back around the column.

The entire group was watching with tremendous interest.

"We are engaged," I explained to Anne.

She clapped her hands. "Engaged! Oh, you were so *clever* with those horrible soldiers!"

There was a round of congratulations and good wishes, which was generous as most of these people had already congratulated us once. When the happy babble diminished a little, I said to Mr. Knightley, "We should marry swiftly. The wyverns keep pestering me."

He was shaking Mr. Weston's hand. He gave me a smiling nod, then a more serious one. "*How* swiftly?"

"Very," I said.

The other widowed wyves had been coming and going this whole time, bringing young, unbound ladies. The cellar was a haven for those pursued by the slavers. Another returned now with a pair of ladies at greater risk because of their dark skin.

I squinted uncertainly in the dim light and said, "Harriet?"

She spun and cried, "Oh, you are safe!"

We ran into an embrace. I hugged her tight, blinking away tears, then pushed her to arms' length to get a proper look at my sister. "I cannot believe you are here!"

"I heard that you were!" she said, grinning. "I did not expect to find you so easily, though."

We said a few sisterly things, and she greeted the others swarming around us, then we settled in for better explanations.

"Oh, the trip has been nonstop terror," Harriet said, beaming, "but also *so* exciting! When I arrived, I called at Hartfield to trade news with Teresa, and your horrid brother-in-law marched out, all stiff and mean. So I said 'Why are *you* here?' and he said some nonsense, and I told him that you would throw him out! That was before I knew what he had done..." For the first time, her smile faltered. "I was so worried when I heard you had come. Have you been to Hartfield?"

"Briefly," I said. "Enough to know that John has done something evil with crawlers."

Miss Bates, who had narrated our reunion with irrelevant anecdotes and clucks and nods, shifted to her more serious persona. "They are using Hartfield to bind crawlers to young ladies. And, we think, to grow those oversize monsters. He and Mr. Elton have some treasonous alliance with the enemy."

At that, Augusta burst into sobs. Miss Bates sent a few clucks in her direction and offered a lacy handkerchief.

"But why are you in Surrey?" I asked Harriet.

"Oh," she said shyly. "I did not wish to write to you until I was sure. I am, now."

She squeezed my hands and led me a few steps to the other new arrival, a lady of around forty years dressed in yellow linen. She had beautiful dark eyes and wore a stylish bonnet with a long, yellow feather. Her skin was an even deeper shade than Harriet's, as if dusted with fine coal.

"Mrs. Prince," Harriet said, "this is Miss Emma Woodhouse, whom I have told you so much about. Emma, this is my mother."

"Miss Woodhouse," she said with a delicate curtsy.

I returned it, my mind spinning. Harriet's mother. That was incredible. But that meant...

"You knew my father," I said. The words fell harsh and flat from my lips.

There was a silence.

"I did," she acknowledged.

Unbidden, my brain ticked through dates. I was four years older than Harriet, give or take. My mother died soon after my fourth birthday. So, had Papa... had he known this woman before or after my mother's death? My reeling brain could not solve it.

"Mr. Woodhouse was extremely proud of you," Mrs. Prince said. "He was a good man."

I swallowed and pushed away my mental calendar. "Not good to you, I am afraid."

Papa told me he had sent her away. I did not even know how. Bribed her? Threatened her? A pregnant, unmarried woman was an easy target. Whatever his strategy, he regretted it later.

At my answer, she had gone tense and still, unreadable, but her eyes were bright with emotion. I drew a deep breath and continued, "I am very thankful for your daughter. For my sister. Harriet is a true lady and a dear friend. Papa was proud of her as well."

"That pleases me," she said. "I am also, very much."

"Goodness!" Harriet exclaimed. "The two of you sound completely foolish. We are *family*."

"We are," I said. I managed another settling breath and stepped in for what became a messy, three-person hug. It was sincere, but short. Mrs. Prince and I had much to think through.

"You have not heard the *other* news," Anne said to Harriet with a mischievous smile and a tilt of her head toward Mr. Knightley.

"Are you finally engaged?" Harriet asked matter-of-factly.

"Oh, you are lucky we are sisters!" I declared. "I would not forgive that from anyone else. But you arrived just in time. We plan a... brief engagement." Mr. Knightley, looking handsome in a satisfied way, was watching, and I asked him, "If you are willing?"

"Haste is important?" he confirmed.

"Very much so," I said, remembering the wyvern's words.

"Then we should proceed apace. Tomorrow?" I bit my lip, waiting, and he tried, "or... *today*?" and I nodded.

That peculiar man, Mr. Collins, unexpectedly joined the discussion. "Nothing delights more than bearing witness to the impetuosity of love! And I am honored to provide my humble services"—reluctantly, I realized that Lady Catherine's clergyman was the only choice to officiate—"*however*, the Church requires preparatory steps. I must counsel the gentleman on... proper husbandly conduct. And the banns must be called for three Sundays—"

"Heaven and earth!" Lady Catherine interrupted. "The Church continually grants exemptions from the calling of banns. It is simply a matter of giving the Church money, which I have done in abundance."

Mr. Collins stopped, lips pursed and eyes wide. He *hemmed* several times and resumed, "Exemptions may occur in necessary circumstances, but the bishop must first pray for guidance on worthiness—"

She gave a stentorian snort. "Worthiness is *money*. I have attended a dozen expedited weddings. The common factors are wealth and a firstborn who follows at breakneck speed. Rest assured, the bishop will concur." She squinted at me. "*You* are not, are you?"

"With child?" I said, so amazed by their conversation that I simply finished, "No."

"Then you are more worthy than most." She scowled at the clergyman. "Mr. Collins. Do you intend to *argue* with me?"

He hauled his rotund profile into a marginally taller oval. "Never, your ladyship."

"Very wise." Her steel-blue gaze returned to me. "I trust this speed is not frivolity. You do not strike me as the sort of woman who would choose marriage in a cellar without good reason." Her gaze drifted to her wyvern, a few feet away. "It seems a time when wyves must show independence and strength. The widowed wyves have always protected a wyfe's right to bind. Therefore, *you*"— her bejeweled finger shot out toward Mr. Collins—"shall provide no counseling. I will educate Mr. Knightley and Miss Woodhouse on the necessary technique."

"Thank you, your ladyship," I said. Any respite from Mr. Collins was a relief. Although Mr. Knightley now looked faintly terrified. I had assumed Lady Catherine meant the speaking of vows... had I misunderstood?

Harriet observed all this with a happy smile and a sisterly dash of amusement. Now she spoke up. "I am delighted it will be soon as it is very overdue. But there is no need to marry in a *cellar*."

# 24

# THE WYFE'S HUNT

## LIZZY

I woke to morning brightness, surprised I had slept. I remembered watching Darcy lie on the floor, too still and too straight, and then when darkness shrouded him, listening for him to move...

I looked over the side of the bed. He was properly asleep now, sprawled in his customary fashion, head cushioned on a bent arm, hair a tousled mess, jaw stubbled, the blanket twisted but tucked tight around his torso.

Tight because it was *cold*. I pursed my lips, and my breath steamed. A May morning in the Highlands.

I eased my woolen covers off, feeling determined to behave less morosely than last night. However long our journey lasted, it was senseless to waste it in self-pity.

Dodging a sleeping man in a tiny room was unexpectedly easy with a hundred lives of martial training. I collected the dagger from under my pillow, tucked the toes of one foot in the notch between the bed and Darcy, then balanced stork-like before leaping soundlessly over him to where my boots and shawl waited.

Our hosts were gone, their bedroom curtain open and the house empty. With the dagger tied to the dress loop that usually held my reticule, I went outside and found father, mother, and daughter gathered by a small cookfire in a rock-lined hearth.

"Good mornin'," Mistress MacLeod said, curtsying and jabbing two stiff fingers of her right hand savagely at her heart. It was clearly a gesture of respect, although a disturbing one I did not recognize. Their daughter wobbled a more traditional curtsy while her husband bowed with a rough-voiced "*Banrigh nan Dràgon*." This morning, his hard-worn fisherman's clothes had been replaced by Highland garb, including the brightly colored tartan trousers called trews. I had seen those worn by Scottish officers visiting the Meryton militia, a show of nationalism that was currently admired but, as recently as my parents' lifetime, would have earned them a six-month sentence in an English jail.

"Good morning to you," I said, curtsying showily to the delighted daughter. "Mr. MacLeod, I hope we have not disrupted your schedule. My husband thought you would be fishing."

"No fishin' today." He fiddled with his tartan scarf, his sheepish smile revealing a sliver of uneven upper teeth.

"We've called a feast day," his wyfe explained. "Beltane is a week past, but it was a poor celebration. With a great wyfe in Helmsdale, there's more cause for cheer."

She beckoned me to the cookfire. A wide iron pan had been placed on the coals, and a bannock was browning. It was shaped more elaborately than the breads served yesterday, with nine pointed rays around the perimeter, each a handspan in length.

"The Wyves' bannock," she said. "Thrice three draca teeth to honor the three wyves, the three dragons, and the three relics. 'Tis part of telling the story of the Wyfe's Hunt." Her finger sketched a circle above the smoky hearth, pointing out the nine rays, the ends of which were crisping to tooth-like black spikes.

Darcy emerged from the house; perhaps I had been less stealthy than I thought. He joined us, unshaven but with his neckcloth elegantly tied and his coat pristine. I found myself smiling up at him—it was so in character that he would appear perfectly dressed after sleeping on a wooden floor—then I felt a ridiculous girlish flutter in my breast when he smiled back. That sensation deepened into a more mature, aware yearning. I missed my husband and the joy of our young marriage.

"What of the story of the flute?" Darcy asked. "We believe the flute was connected to the Bennet family, long ago."

"What know ye of Bennets?" Mistress MacLeod asked, surprised.

"My wyfe is a Bennet."

Mr. MacLeod grinned, but that news darkened his wyfe's mood. Frowning, she slid a soot-stained plank under the bannock, lifted it from the fire, and set it to cool on a cloth. "There're Bennets all about the north, but nae here. Long ago, though, that's another matter..."

Darcy stiffened like an English Pointer scenting a bird, but my stomach twisted. Foolishly, I had assumed the history of Bennets was forgotten.

"We'll feast tonight," she said finally, "and tell the tale of the Wyfe's Hunt. Then we'll see about tales of the flute."

"Not much of a feast," her husband muttered. "We'll be chewing shoe leather. That bog bleatin' factor..." He spat into the fire.

"Enough," his wyfe said.

"Sellar's not done with us," Mr. MacLeod burst out. "There's still crofters in the hills. He'll come for them." He waved at me. "It's a *sign* that she's here. A sign for vengeance!"

"Stop that!" his wyfe snapped. "Do ye nae see she carries the black dagger? Think what you're saying. They'll be no talk of vengeance."

Darcy watched their exchange. I could practically see the gears turning in his head. Finally, he rubbed his hands in the brisk air and asked Mr. MacLeod what form of net he preferred for catching herring. In a minute, they had set out to visit the boats. The MacLeods' daughter begged her mother's permission and ran after them.

"Off to pry the truth from m'husband," Mistress MacLeod observed as the men vanished.

"Darcy worries about people. He wishes to help."

"He's a proper gentleman. He'd be a bonny clan chief if he were not so stiff and English."

"He would be flattered to hear that." Darcy held the Scots in high regard and would have merely nodded at being called "stiff and English."

Mistress MacLeod wrapped her cooled bannock in a cotton cloth, careful to preserve the spiky rays. "I've a cartload of cooking to do. For the feast, ye ken? Will ye be fine by yerself?"

For all that I had grown up in a frugal household, I had a lady's education, and my culinary experience was a few frivolous childhood projects while Barbara, our cook, alternated laughter and theatric despair. So I nodded and, dismissed, found a path to explore the unfinished homes and insufficient farmland.

The village, whatever its struggles, bustled with a festive air. Wyves and men passed me carrying dishes or returning from the fields with fresh-picked greens, tubers, and flowers. The men all wore tartans; I saw several designs. Some wyves had tartan caps, and the younger, unmarried women had thin strips of tartan cloth tied ribbon-like in their hair. Everyone smiled at me, curtsying or bowing, and the women stabbed two fingers of their right hand at their hearts. I smiled and curtsied back.

No urgency drove me. The endless crush of Fènnù's violent attention had vanished. My anger at the Blackcoats who hurt Mary felt... resolved. Yuánchi was asleep; I sensed his resting presence and did not probe further for fear I would hurt him. Even Darcy was out of sight, so I did not have to teeter atop yearning for him and fearing that yielding would hopelessly complicate what came next.

Directionless, I followed the salty air toward the sea but stopped when I spotted Darcy with the fishermen. A net had been spread on the short dock, and he was in animated conversation with a half-dozen kilted men. When I first met Darcy at the Meryton ball, I would not have imagined he would mingle like that, a proud gentleman so "stiff and English" at ease with tradespeople. But Darcy admired frankness and competence, whether from a cobbler or a duke, and he swiftly gained the confidence of both. It was social pretense and hypocrisy he abhorred.

Some wrong had been done to this village, and he was determined to unearth it. He would win their trust, and then he would set out to remedy it, preferably invisibly and unthanked. It was a Darcy pattern.

One of the young, unmarried women, red-cheeked with a cheerful step and an armload of green heather shoots, stopped to curtsy while offering her *"Banrigh nan Dràgon"* and driving two fingers viciously at her heart. When I stood rather aimlessly after my own curtsy, she offered shyly, "Would ye care to help braid the decorations?"

I was far more accomplished at braiding than baking, so we set off together, the dagger bouncing on my hip.

THE CELEBRATION STARTED as the setting sun touched the low hills. Benches had been dragged from the common longhouse to an open area at the village's edge, tables added to hold dishes, and peat fires lit. Our braided decorations rested on the tables, local plants and flowers twined with different tartan strips, a centerpiece for each clan in the village.

The food was country fare: grain gruels seasoned with sea salt and herbs, unusually large savory puddings boiled in sausage casings, and herring served every way imaginable—smoked, fried, pickled, even stewed in raised pies with thick, shining crusts.

There were three loaves of bread, all crusty bannocks with nine sharp, black-crisped rays, what Mistress MacLeod had called the Wyves' bannock. Instead of being served, they were placed prominently on an oak stump, untouched.

With a minor flourish, Darcy drew his bottle of whiskey from a cushioned chamois bag and presented it to the MacLeods. Enthusiasts crowded, studying the bottle and asking about Oban, a village on the other side of Scotland and apparently as remote as the far side of the moon. Geography was then replaced by questions of copper stills and levels of peat smoke, all beyond my knowledge but fielded authoritatively by Darcy.

The MacLeods sat at a table with us, and when the unopened bottle finished its rounds and was cradled in Mr. MacLeod's arms, he pursed his lips and said, "We'll keep it for the Wyves' tale. That's the time for a dram." He stabbed a wooden spoon to open a solidly crusted raised pie. Steam, redolent of herring and sheep's cheese, swirled free.

Night fell. The smoky fires shone crimson on faces and hands and the men's bare ankles beneath their kilts. The glowing peat blocks reminded me of a smith's brick-lined forge, although this heat was pleasant, not the eye-watering inferno of hard coal fanned by a bellows. The food was solid and good, if salty, and I tried the savory pudding, called a haggis. It was tasty but rich.

With the meal done, tables were pushed aside and the benches dragged into two rough rows. The bound wyves' draca wandered around the periphery, an unusual show of interest from the creatures. A half-bottle of sherry was shared, and tea. Mr. MacLeod asked Darcy to uncork the whiskey, then he doled it out in drams indeed, little more than wetting the bottom of each glass. Two dozen villagers took a taste, and there was much sniffing and tilting of glasses while arguing whether a few drops of water would open the flavor or flatten it. Finally, the whiskey was sipped and declared a bonny batch, indeed.

Mistress MacLeod, in a wool cap decorated with tartan and a shawl to fend off the cooling air, walked into the cleared area in front of the benches.

"Now we tell the tragedy of the wyfe Brynhild," she cried out, "and of the

hero Sigurd, and of the Wyfe's Wild Hunt." She moved to the side of the improvised stage.

A woman strode out dressed in a gray riding cloak. She was my mother's
age, with a few wrinkles and streaks of gray.

"The wyfe Brynhild was a noblewoman," intoned Mistress MacLeod,
"strong of arm and mind and terrible to cross." The woman posed like a
warrior, shoulders square, and her years fell away. She looked young and strong.
"She was courted by a hundred men, but they may as well have been chasin'
their tails, for one of the hundred was Sigurd, a hairy bull of a man who would
melt any lass's heart."

A stocky, balding man, his skin tanned by sun and sea, rose from a bench
and came forward grinning, surely the woman's husband as they shared a
private smile.

The woman called out, "I, Brynhild, know that a great draca lives in these
hills, unbound for two hundred years. I will bind that draca, but I need a grand
lover. A hero." Brynhild and Sigurd approached each other and trailed fingers
across each other's shoulders, the image of youthful, carnal attraction. My
cheeks flushed as some men hooted approval.

Now, the red-cheeked woman who invited me to braid decorations joined
the performance. Serious as any actress at Covent Garden, she stole forward
dripping deceit. "I am Gudrún, and I'm as bonny a lass as Brynhild. I should be
the one t'bind the great draca." She circled Brynhild then whipped Brynhild's
riding cloak free—the crowd hissed—and wrapped it around herself, hood
forward to hide her features. "With this disguise, I'll steal into Sigurd's bed."

In pin-drop silence, Gudrún approached and embraced Sigurd. They
turned in slow circles, hands on each other's hips, half a dance, half lewd
mimicry. Under the blackening sky, the audience began a slow stamp, one
thump each time the lovers circled in the flickering red firelight.

The emotions of the performers and audience spread to the world of draca,
and in the shadows, feral draca joined the bound watchers, their eyes reflecting
the crimson of the fires. Then, as the turning couple quickened, a firedrake
scaled dark as iron strutted into the firelight. Most people lived their lives
without seeing an unbound drake, but only one young child exclaimed.
Everyone else continued their relentless stamp, quickening with the spins of the
actors.

The firedrake's gleaming black eyes fixed on the writhing couple as if it were
a true consummation—a consummation and a betrayal, for Brynhild was

watching Sigurd's seduction, and the wyfe playing Brynhild was watching her husband in life with another woman. Her face, whether in performance or truth, was filled with fury.

Abruptly, the red-cheeked woman's back arched, and she screamed in ecstasy and triumph. The iron-dark drake opened his wings wider than a tall man's spread arms, and the thumping stomp ended.

I startled as a hand fell on my shoulder. Mistress MacLeod whispered in my ear, "Come away, lass. I would speak with ye."

Darcy was engrossed in the performance. I tapped his arm to signal I was leaving, then with a few swift steps, Mistress MacLeod and I threaded between the benches until we stood behind the audience.

"Do ye ken the story of Brynhild?" Mistress MacLeod asked me as the play continued.

I shook my head. "I have heard the names but not the story."

"Brynhild has been betrayed." Her eyes glittered. "What d'ye think will happen?"

I had read enough fables to answer. "Revenge. Disaster."

The crowd reacted to the play by bellowing an animalistic, rolling snarl. Brynhild's shout reached us. "With the black dagger I summon the Wild Hunt. Rise, river dragon! Freeze the land in bitterest winter!" Steam hissed as people threw water on the peat fires, and the red light dimmed near black.

Mistress MacLeod's eyes never left mine. "Revenge, aye. 'Tis the story of the north. Honor is valued over life. This village is awash in honor, like oil poured on tinder awaiting a spark. Hae the men come to ye yet?"

"The men who are plotting violence." Without Fènnù's presence, my past selves had faded to shadows, but those wyves remembered their own starved villages. Famine always bred war. "Not yet."

"They will, lass."

From beyond the audience, a woman's voice carried, "Through dark and ice, across frozen turf and dying trees, the draca led Brynhild on her hunt. And when the sun rose, feebled by ice, she caught Sigurd and deceiving Gudrún..."

Mistress MacLeod grabbed me, her fingernails digging into my forearm. "Ye carry the black dagger, lass. Did ye burn London?"

I shook my head. "The black dragon attacked London. She seeks me, but I do not command her."

"If Helmsdale rises up, it'll be a hot fire but a short one. There'll be naught left but ashes to mark our graves. Will ye set that fire, wyfe of war?"

"No," I said. "I swear it."

Her grip eased on my arm, and she nodded. "Tomorrow morning, then, we'll read the stones. Yer husband will hear the truth of the flute." Her gaze bored into mine. "I think a wyfe of war, and a Bennet besides, already knows the tale."

She tugged my hand, hustling us through the crowd while tossing over her shoulder, "Hurry up, lass. Time to see how revenge turned out."

Uneasy, I found Darcy in the crowd and sat beside him on the bench, wrapping my arm in his.

On the stage, Gudrún was cowering before Brynhild.

Sigurd stepped toward them, hands beseeching. "Brynhild, ye wielded the dagger. Ye commanded the dark dragon. Now show a wyfe's mercy. Spare fair Gudrún, who is but a lass."

Silence stretched. Brynhild raised something sharp and black above her head, and even though I would know if Gramr were touched, my hand reached to check the hilt was secure.

Brynhild spun and stabbed Sigurd. Darcy started up as if to intervene, his arm stretched in hopeless intercession, but the black point did not strike like a blade—it folded in Brynhild's hand, a prop. Sigurd, the woman's husband in life, collapsed in a credible stage death.

Mistress MacLeod strode onto the stage, narrating, "Then Brynhild saw what her fury had wrought. As her love died, she repented, and her sorrow lifted the black dragon's winter from the land."

Thin-split kindling was tossed on the half-doused fires. Sun-yellow fire bloomed, and warm light spread.

The audience passed the Wyves' bannocks hand-to-hand. Each woman tore a burned ray from the breads. Even the elderly wyfe beside me took one with a toothless grin before passing the half-used loaf to me.

Around us, wyves stabbed their husbands with the mock-knives. Young, unmarried women chased young men. They yelled, tripped, and collided. Each stabbed person shuddered their death then miraculously recovered and embraced their attacker. The red-cheeked woman who had played Brynhild caught a bearded young man. He did not put up much of a fight.

The embraces turned passionate. Pairs fled, hand-in-hand—toward houses, into the secluded night. Only the children remained, watching the adults vanish as if this were perfectly normal. Then the older children got up and began collecting plates and cups.

"Are ye nae going to stab yer husband?" the MacLeods' young daughter asked me. Her parents had rushed off like the rest. I turned the burned knife of bread in my hand, and she explained seriously, "It means yer fond of him, ye ken?"

I nodded that I understood. When I did not immediately disembowel my husband with the crust, she rolled her eyes and trotted off with a bored expression.

My other senses, my draca senses, vibrated. The passion of hidden lovers was like whirlpools churning a rising sea. I closed my eyes. Draca of every breed moved through the village. The iron-dark drake flew in pursuit of the red-cheeked woman and her man, and through his alien mind, their arousal trickled down my spine like hot oil.

"A strange play," Darcy said. Flushed, I opened my eyes as he continued, "It does not match what we know of Fury and Gramr's history, nor what I recall of the Völsunga saga, but there are connections. The origin must be Nordic or Germanic..."

"Leave the scholarship to Mary," I said hoarsely. The draca around us were fueling a sensuous awareness of Darcy's closeness, of his scent. The two cream-colored firedrakes crisscrossed in the sky above, waiting, watching us, two heated bodies in their vision.

Awkwardly, Darcy raked back his hair. Despite his dry topic, the mood had affected him. His pupils were huge, his pulse quick in his throat.

"Tomorrow," I said, "Mistress MacLeod will take us to the Pictish stones and tell the story of the flute." This escape, this pretense, my parade of lies would be exposed. How could it end but disaster?

My despair must have shown on my features, and Darcy's brow furrowed. "I know you are troubled about the flute. What are you not saying?"

"Quiet," I whispered and pulled him to me.

# 25

# NEARING LONDON

## MARY

Colonel Fremantle, Lord Wellington's aide-de-camp, and I stood in front of our stopped coach. The road to London stretched ahead, a packed misery beneath a smoke-reddened sun. Tens of thousands were fleeing the city, a northward flood that spilled into the adjacent fields, plowing them to impassible mud.

London's skyline was visible as low notches on the southern horizon. I compared it to memories from other trips... we were eight miles from the city's outskirts. After that, it would be two miles to the museum. At least it was on the north side of the city. Chathford House, the Darcys' London home, was south of the Thames and likely unreachable.

A man staggered by, his lips gray and his arm crudely wrapped in bloody muslin. I dug my nails into my palms and did nothing. Passing this uncountable humanity felt like when Dr. Davenport first walked me through the slums of London. I had wept, and afterward he provided a cup of tea and his first lesson: You cannot help them all. Choose carefully where to spend your strength.

"This is a horror," murmured the colonel. He was unshaven and red-eyed. "It is like witnessing the flight from Athens when Xerxes burned the city."

"You read Herodotus?" Perhaps military history was required for officers.

"In translation. My uncle gave me a copy." His lip twitched. "I was miserable at Greek."

"You do not need the Greeks for accounts of razed cities. The crusaders ravaged Jerusalem in 1099. Two years ago, the Americans massacred the Indians at Prophetstown." The colonel gave me an uneasy look, and I grimaced. "When I am tense, I tend to be... academic. You are right, this is a horror. That is why our errand for the flute must not fail."

We were traveling in a post-chaise carriage, a stripped-down military express that the colonel commandeered for his return trip by waving the signature on Lord Wellington's letter. The army kept four-horse teams in reserve every twenty miles, so we had raced one hundred and forty miles in twenty-odd hours, not once slower than a trot. The jolts from the bench had bruised my calves, my shoulders, and very definitely everything in between.

Distant, punctuated thunder rumbled. Cannons. Some illusion made the sound seem to rise from the earth, as if the war raged in Hades.

We had met the first fringe of this exodus ten miles back. For a while, our military standard and livery opened passage, but that slowed as the crowd grew. Now, we had halted to consider tactics while the driver watered the horses.

A passing woman, sweating through fine clothes unsuited for walking, her hair threaded with gray, started when she saw the iridescent song draca perched on my shoulder. I stopped her with a finger on her arm. "What have you seen? Are the French in London?"

"I have seen nothing with my own eyes, but I heard men shouting in the street. Enemies on the brink of London, they said, the French army and the slavers. And there are creatures in the air..."

My exhaustion vanished in a tingle of fear. "Dragons?" Had the French captured one of the artifacts?

"Not a dragon." The woman shook her head definitively; Londoners knew dragons all too well from Fènnù's attacks and battles with Yuánchi. "Something different, swift and vile. It flew over me. The roar hurt my ears."

She was pulling north, eager to leave, so I bade her good travel. She slipped into the dusty crowd, lost in a blink.

Our driver, his scarlet infantry coat caked with gray clay and dirt, reported to the colonel. "The team is fresh enough, sir, but I don't know what to do about the crowd. There's no way to find headway in this." He squinted at the people, chewing his lip, then offered uncertainly, "If I laid about with my whip..."

Colonel Fremantle frowned. "Not that. We will consider other options." The driver nodded and went to calm the nervous horses.

"I must reach the British Museum," I said.

"And I must find Lord Wellington in Surrey."

"Do you even think that possible? At least the museum stays still."

The colonel's lips compressed in a mirthless smile. "I suppose I shall wander, looking for soldiers who are unreasonably cheerful. It has worked before."

"He has that effect on morale?"

"When all seems black, yes." The colonel's mirthless smile became an honest chuckle. "In Spain, I once followed a stream of happy gunners and found the duke at an improvised ball. I even danced with a Spanish lady. She was astonishingly beautiful. Sadly, I could not speak a word of Spanish."

Since I had fallen in love, I had discovered a soft spot for romance. "You could learn. It is easier than Greek."

"My father died when I was four. I have no fortune to tempt foreign beauties into marriage. That is why I enlisted, to earn a few pounds. And any marriage would be difficult with me gone to war for eleven months of every year." He watched me with curious eyes, then ventured, "Do you worry about Miss Darcy when you are apart?"

It was my turn to smile. "Georgiana is like a demigod from a Greek myth, imbued with divine grace—in England, that is money—and beyond that, at her innermost self, stronger than us poor mortals." I remembered the intoxicating reach of her song. "I suppose I worry she might do something foolish."

The colonel rubbed his hands decisively. "We could unharness the horses and ride. A horse and rider can force a path where a carriage cannot."

I looked at our four-horse team, prancing, skittish, and wild-eyed. I was reasonably comfortable on a horse, but that was on country paths. These did not even have saddles. "I doubt I could handle a horse in this press."

The colonel nodded. "Probably for the best. They are not cavalry mounts. They might bolt."

I worked my neck, loosening cramps and studying the smoky sky. "If only we could fly..." Colonel Fremantle produced a dutiful chuckle that choked when I continued, "but I cannot summon a dragon by myself."

He eyed the song draca on my shoulder, so still and unbirdlike amid the chaos. "Miss Bennet, I do not wish to pry, but... I know Lord Wellington's message, and I could not help but witness your and Miss Darcy's discussion. What powers will you gain from this flute?"

"Me? Nothing. I have no power. But if I deliver the flute to the great wyves, they can end this war."

I unfolded a scrap of linen and cleaned my spectacles while I thought. Could we walk? Eight miles was three hours on good roads, but against this tide it must be six or more, and dangerous among a desperate crowd. It would be fully dark when we arrived, and I doubted carriages would be for hire in a besieged city.

And when I recovered the flute—persuaded the staff to loan it to me, or claimed it in the name of the King, or stole it—how would I return?

"What if I need your aid when we reach London?" I asked. "Lord Wellington sent you to us."

"To be frank, that would put me in a difficult position. Lord Wellington did not instruct me to aid your... quest. I have been left to guess at his intent. My duty is simple. Return to him."

The song draca chittered, the points of his claws digging into my shoulder. I replaced my spectacles and blinked bleary eyes. "Do you see something new? Something dangerous?"

The colonel's head pivoted, then he pointed. "To the west. Is that one of those flying creatures?"

Miles distant, a dark shape climbed on powerful strokes of colossal wings. Recognition wiped the cobwebs from my brain. "That is the black dragon, Fènnù."

"The demon of the Thames," Colonel Fremantle whispered. "Saints preserve us." When I did not answer, he looked more alarmed. "I hope *that* is not our ride!"

"Nobody rides Fènnù." She was miles distant, but I felt her gaze focus on me, then her awareness pressed my mind. The song draca on my shoulder flew away with an alarmed screech. "She must have sensed I was near. She will come. Stay close to me." I called to our driver, "Come here, quickly."

The crowd had seen her, and the Londoners who lived through Fènnù's attacks cried out. People ran, northward on the road or scrambling over the fences into mud and rough brush.

Fènnù was closing at a phenomenal pace, sweeping through a curve that intersected the packed road two miles south of us. Where her shadow touched, the crowd seethed in panic. She swept lower, following the road, her wings driving for speed, low enough that dust rose behind her, then lower yet so the wind of her passage knocked people off their feet like wheat in a storm. A windy howl became audible, the deepest pedal pipes of a celestial organ played in discordant madness.

Behind us, the horse team whinnied and fought their traces. The driver turned to go to them, but I grabbed his wrist. "She seeks me because she wants my sister. You are safest here."

Incredibly, the road in front of us had emptied other than dropped bags and packs. Fènnù's dark shape grew. Already her wingspan filled my eyes, eclipsing the sky, surely atop us although the shadow of her wings was a quarter mile distant. But no black cloud billowed behind her, that omen of her destructive breath. Her approach was intimidation. She would turn aside.

A hundred yards away, her scaled feet untucked, and her hooked rear claws, the longest, caught the earth like a pair of razor-sharp plows. Dirt and rock exploded in her wake, a barking cacophony that shook the ground. The colonel shouted something inaudible and fell. The horses screamed. I had one heartbeat to think *I was wrong; we are dead* and then her feet flashed past, bracketing us with the roar of twin landslides. I threw myself down, shielding my head as gravel and rocks stung and dust coated my throat with grit. There was a meaty thump and a smash of wood and glass, then a hurricane blast as her wings carried her up. Each gust slid me across the torn dirt.

Coughing and spitting grime, I struggled to my feet. Colonel Fremantle and the driver were shrugging off inches of debris. Two massive furrows had been ripped down the road, strewing rocks, soil, and boulders...

The horses were unrecognizable gore splattered among the wrecked flinders of our coach. The iron scent of blood joined the dirt in my nostrils, and unpleasant scenes filled my mind's eye: a mid-thigh amputation I had observed with clenched teeth; the violent death of Joane Rees.

My rational mind was reeling. Despite her devastation of London, I had invented a delusion that Fènnù, named a deity of death in the broken records of ruined civilizations, was somehow... fond of me? Tame? Harmless unless commanded by the dagger?

The driver was gibbering, pointing at four thousand pounds of gutted horse and the remnants of the carriage. Then he broke and fled, tripping and stumbling to the north.

Across the fields, Fènnù's wings angled as she turned to return.

I screamed—at the air, at her—"Why kill horses?" Our transport was destroyed, my supplies gone, but the horses seemed... arbitrary. Spiteful. "Why?" I shrieked.

"Run!" the colonel cried. He was pulling me, his arm linked through mine as if we were on promenade.

"I will not." My error, my blithe trust and naiveté, had turned to anger. I scrambled to a less ruined patch of road. The colonel followed, tugging with aimless resistance.

Fènnù hung in the air, black and growing.

My lips were too crusted with dust to whistle, so I sang the summoning song. The song draca returned to my shoulder, settling his feathers as if nothing were wrong, then another winged in from the field beyond, and then another. Those others did not land but circled in the air around and above us. More joined them.

Fènnù's awareness caught my mind again, cajoling me with whispers of vengeance and death. I sang an answer, fitting makeshift words to my little tune, "I am no wyfe of war. You do not tempt me."

Her wings flared, darkening half the sky. Leaves stormed, turned white with frost, and my skirts twanged and shivered like sails in a tempest. She settled fifty yards away. The furor stilled. Her scaly head descended, and her faceted eyes reflected red hues from the sky. Black bile dripped from sores on her jaw. The reek of her corruption, acidic and biting, burned my eyes, and I recognized volatile scents shared with crawler venom.

Dozens of song draca circled the colonel and me, a flowing shield high and low, too many to have been in the local fields—they must have followed from Pemberley. Fènnù's head twisted, tracking their motion, then the turbid swirl of her gaze fixed on mine. Maddened visions entered my brain: Lizzy floating in the depths like drowned Ophelia, then Lizzy's face with brown skin decorated with Egyptian kohl, then Lizzy nude and writhing in passion.

Words came, stuttered and uneven: *Where is my wyfe of war?*

"Gone," I cried. "Escaped."

A vise crushed my mind. *Yield! Where is my queen?*

I could not force words through that pressure, so I sang the summoning song again, and the song draca joined in harmony. Like parody, as a challenge, I threaded in fragments of Fènnù's song—a half bar of melody here, a modulation there.

Fènnù roared, not the weapon of her frozen breath, just deafening noise. She crouched, then leaped. With one downsweep of her wings, she passed over our heads, scattering the song draca. I turned to watch her climb and shrink in the distance.

The colonel was moaning, curled on the ground like a child in a nightmare. I was trembling as well... no, I was shaking from cold. There was hoarfrost on my gloves. The ground was slick with steaming ice. A whorl of half-submerged leaves stood up from the surface, trapped in mid-spiral.

I knelt and shook the colonel's arms, knocking ice off his coat. "We must move out of this cold."

His moans quieted, and his wide eyes latched onto mine. "How are we alive?"

"Fènnù resumed her search for my sister. She tried to force her whereabouts from me, but I... refused." It occurred to me that she had no reason to let me live after that. Perhaps the delusions that confused her had saved us in the end.

We slipped and slid off the ice. The road was still empty, but muddy heads were popping up behind distant bushes and rocks.

"We should walk," I said. "Make haste while the road is open."

"Haste," the colonel echoed tonelessly, but he followed as I started south. Motion felt good, restoring sensation to my freezing toes and loosening my myriad stiffening bruises.

The song draca returned, twenty or so, swooping and circling. They looked uncanny, so I pulled the hood of my black cloak forward to hide my face. For once, superstition might be useful. "Perhaps the crowd will make way for a witch."

Colonel Fremantle's officer's bearing returned. He had campaigned in the Peninsular wars after all, a far bloodier field than this. He caught up, striding apace with me, and his hands inventoried sword, pistol, powder. His methodical check reminded me to inspect my reticule. The syringes with draca essence remained, their brass tubes securely sealed.

It was some time before he spoke. "I thought you had no power."

"That was nothing. You should see my sister."

Still, he had a point. I had faced Fènnù again, heard her voice, and for the first time, without a great wyfe beside me. And Georgiana swore I had power.

"I may have some peculiar talent," I admitted.

# 26

# TO BIND

## EMMA

"I will find a ripe one," Harriet insisted, bent to the ground.

I peered doubtfully at the half-wild vines. "It is early for strawberries."

"They ripen first at the Abbey, and this is a southern slope..."

Our party had left the underground cellars and, staying on neglected paths, reached what Harriet and I called Berry Hill. It was a remote, brambly part of the Abbey grounds and highly unlikely to interest an invading army. Mr. Knightley excused himself on some mysterious wedding errand, and the Otway and Weston families were wandering the slope, recovering from fear and flight, so that left a few ladies—Augusta, Harriet and her mother, and me—to plan the ceremony with what odds and ends were on hand.

Considering my own wedding was being prepared with a few hours' notice, I was surprisingly idle. Mostly, I watched Harriet bustle. But I was happy, a ferocious joy that sang in my ribs despite my treacherous brother-in-law and his violent allies.

Harriet plucked a berry from the vines. "Here! Not perfect, but mostly ripe. There will be good bites." Shyly, she showed it to her admiring mother, then laid it on my palm. It was luscious red except for a white fringe around the stem.

"I am amazed!" I said. "But may I give it to Mr. Knightley? I have no wedding present for him. I cannot imagine what would be better than the first strawberry of the season."

"Certainly! But then I must find the second strawberry for you." Harriet resumed her hunt.

That left me and her mother facing each other. We managed awkward smiles, then found other things to watch. I was still unsure what to make of our family connection. It seemed Mrs. Prince was, too.

Augusta Elton had ignored the entire exchange. Her face was pallid and her eyes haunted. While we walked here, she had silently and savagely ripped off every ruffle and gilded bead on her overdecorated gown. That made me regret my prior scorn. Perhaps the fashion had been to appease her husband's fixation on status. If so, it failed. Mr. Elton had handed her to the slavers like chattel, expensive dress and all.

When life returned to normal, we would visit a dressmaker together, and if she chose something even more gaudy, I would applaud. It would be for herself, at least.

I touched her hand, but she did not stir. I had lost my gloves during our escape, and she had none. When our skin touched, I saw an ash-like shadow, a scar of the false binding I had broken between her and that crawler.

"You have escaped Mr. Elton," I said. Her half-lidded eyes swung, wary as a woodland creature, but she listened as I continued, "He betrayed your trust. He hurt you. He has broken every vow of your marriage. You are your own woman now, a free wyfe."

"I do not feel free," she said. "I feel ashamed. Dirtied."

I leaned close. "That is his method. He blames his victims for his sins. Deny him that." She smiled tentatively, then fiercely, and suddenly offered to help pick strawberries.

I bent to help too, but the strawberry beds, wild with fuzzy mouse-ear weed, muddled my eyes. The shadows under the plants flickered with the blueish glow I had seen in the Abbey cellar. It was not the miasma—I felt that too, lurking in a recess of my brain, stubborn but contained even though Augusta's gown had a dozen fringes of torn threads. The blue glow was something else. It rose from the earth, a force for harmony, not for illness.

"You chose well, Miss Smith," Lady Catherine pronounced as she paraded up, rigid in her cinched dress stays. "I am regularly named an exceptional judge of natural beauty, and I find this hill most suitable for a wedding." Her gaze landed on me. "I have told Mr. Collins to prepare the ceremony. Now, Miss Woodhouse, you and I shall speak." She strode away.

I gave Augusta a farewell pat and followed her ladyship, bemused by her quirks.

Lady Catherine led us past a lime-washed cottage, home of the Abbey drainsman, an ancient position funded by a withering endowment of twenty pounds a year. Because those funds were woefully inadequate to maintain miles of medieval ditches, the drainsmen traditionally supplemented their income by selling strawberries, not to mention the whortleberries and dewberries that flourished in the marshy hollows.

Lady Catherine chose a patch of meadow bordered by dog rose and elm and studied me with her habitual scowl.

Charlotte, the sensible half of the Collinses, had taken me aside to warn me about Lady Catherine's "technique lecture." Charlotte did that with such calm humor that I decided she would be a wonderful friend, and if I had questions about the marriage night, I would certainly have asked her rather than her ladyship, who was old enough to be my grandmother.

However, two winters ago I had investigated this on my own, at least the pressing issues—how to recognize conception, and how soon one could tell. All that had required was carefully crafted, wide-eyed questions to local widows. They reminisced at length, so it was a wide-ranging education.

"Your ladyship is gracious with her advice," I said, "but I sought out my own knowledge on the consequences of the marriage bed. It seemed important for a lady on her own."

"Good," Lady Catherine said shortly, her eyes narrowing. She inhaled a stupendous breath. "But that topic was a pretense. I wished to speak without interruption, and the specter of an old woman describing lovemaking keeps curious ears away."

"That is clever," I said, impressed. "You have surprised me."

"When I can no longer surprise young ladies, I will consider myself tiresome."

"What do you wish to discuss?"

"You knew my nephew's wyfe, Elizabeth."

*Knew*, as if she were dead. That was the public report. Mary had been the first to realize that Lizzy survived, but when I left Pemberley, that was secret. And though I had felt Yuánchi rise, I had no idea what that meant for Lizzy, not with half of England between us.

I settled for a nod. If Mr. Darcy had not told his aunt, I would not.

A nod seemed sufficient, and Lady Catherine resumed, "I will share that my relationship with Elizabeth was not close. When she was Miss Bennet, a rumor about her engagement to my nephew led to... an estrangement. Oh, we were polite after the wedding—my nephew is nothing if not polite—but before that, Darcy had been like a son. I had feared losing him to an upstart, inferior woman. Instead, a rumor"—her mouth wrinkled—"my *reaction* to a rumor drove him away. But it drove him to a different sort of woman than I thought."

She was quiet then, perhaps waiting to see if I would comment on what sort of woman Lizzy was. I waited too, a picture of attentiveness.

"Then," Lady Catherine said, "Elizabeth died. Suddenly and mysteriously. I felt..." She sighed, considering.

Gently, I offered, "Remorse?"

She straightened. "Certainly not! I felt *regret* that I had not investigated her more thoroughly."

More coolly, I said, "And what has this to do with me?"

"When Elizabeth died, a lady with golden hair was a guest at Pemberley. Pemberley has a loyal staff, and Darcy battened down the hatches after Elizabeth's death, but I have sources, and the name 'Woodhouse' reached my ears. I remembered you, a woman who, at the museum ball in London, was impossibly at ease with my wyvern. A woman who was so trusted by the Darcys that she was invited to Chathford House even after that horrific evening."

On the path below us, Mr. Collins bustled into view, looking very ministerial with a bible in one hand and his ceremonial tippet folded in the other. He saw Lady Catherine, fluttered the tippet in an obsequious wave, then noticed I was with her. Even at thirty yards, I saw him blush. He ran back down the path.

Lady Catherine smiled at his fleeing back, then aimed her gaze at me. "While my nephew mourned, you remained at Pemberley. That was unusual. You remained for months, unchaperoned by your family. That was... provocative. Darcy began to be seen with you, an hour or more each day in private conversation."

I did not like this. "Are you accusing me of something?"

She scoffed. "I am not suggesting a tawdry affair. I would not care if there was, but it is not in Darcy's nature." She leveled a finger at my reticule where I had tied the red, plaited lanyard from Lady Anne's diary. "My sister wove that. I doubt even Darcy would think that a token from his dead mother was a romantic gift. His interest in you is different."

"Madam, I am not enjoying this conversation. I must excuse myself—"

"Not until you summon my wyvern," she said.

I had turned to leave, but that stopped me. I presented a smile. "I beg your pardon?"

"Do not pretend, woman. My late sister, Lady Anne Darcy, could summon draca. That headstrong girl, Elizabeth, was capable as well, when she was not chattering about bolts. Heaven and earth, there were *dragons* flying above Pemberley." Lady Catherine held out her hand, but the gesture was imploring —desperate, not commanding. "I know that you can. I saw you at the ball. I merely wish... to see it once more. To know that great wyves exist. That my sister was one, and that she was... extraordinary."

I had only ever called draca that I could see, but Lady Catherine's wyvern shone so brightly that I sensed her, high in a tree a few minutes' walk away. It was her ability to bind I sensed; without the distraction of sight, that potential, pristine within her, was vivid.

The wyvern was not bound. She had never been bound.

My shock must have shown. Lady Catherine drew herself into a pose of dignified acceptance. She had expected it.

"Call her," she whispered. "Call her the way my sister summoned her when I failed to bind."

Spring breezes whispered in the elms' young foliage. For twenty heartbeats we watched each other, then the bronze wyvern glided to a landing between us.

*healer,* she acknowledged me, then her head swiveled, pinning Lady Catherine with her scintillating gaze. Lady Catherine backed an involuntary step. Her hands clenched and unclenched.

"What a lie I have lived," she said at last.

"She is loyal to you," I said. "She protects you as few draca do their bound wyves. What does it matter if you are bound?"

"Binding is a force of women." Lady Catherine's voice was hoarse. "And I was unworthy."

"Your sister believed you were worthy." I untied the lanyard from my reticule and offered it. "You should have this."

She closed my fingers over it. "Keep it. Present it to your husband at your wedding. My sister wove it as a symbol of her handfasting, a great joy of her life." Her voice firmed. "And when you do, tell Mr. Knightley he may stop hiding from me. I have no intention of lecturing him. The man is a professional musician and resides in London. We may assume he is properly educated in love."

Wondering about that, I tucked the lanyard away.

As we headed back down the path, Lady Catherine said, "There is only one reason a single lady must comprehend the consequences of the marriage bed."

I did not answer, but after such a revelation about her life, I did not deny it either.

Somewhat farther, she asked, "Was it by your choice?"

I remembered the dark coach, the falling snow as smothering as ash, and Mr. Elton shouting how I had encouraged him, how he would die if I refused him. Then he seized the bodice of my gown in his fist, and the cloth tore, and I realized that refusal was not an option.

"No," I answered, because it felt good to say it.

"Then it does not matter. It is choice that matters. That, and love."

HARRIET WAS WEAVING strawberry runners dotted with green berries and white flowers into my hair. She tucked a few sprigs into my feathered bonnet, stepped back to judge the effect, and smiled.

"You must wear gloves," she added, retrieving hers from her dress pocket and placing them in my hand.

I thanked her. They fit well, and the white brightened my steel-gray gown. For better or worse, my clothes were what I had worn on our visit to reclaim Hartfield. The ensemble was darker than a typical wedding outfit, but it was dramatic and had a striking bonnet.

Mr. Knightley returned and bowed with solemnity and a nice air of admiration. I returned a curtsy, and the first hint of nervousness quickened my heart.

"You were gone a long time," I said, striving for a light tone.

"I needed to fetch some things. I visited our coach at Mrs. Hewitt's orchard."

"That was dangerous!"

"I was careful. The line of battle has moved north, perhaps even to London. French troops are patrolling the town, but I saw none in the countryside. They can hardly guard every inch of Surrey."

I folded my arms, illogically frightened even though he was standing in front of me, unharmed. But he had crossed enemy lines many times before. I suppose that would be my husband's peculiar hobby, the way other men collected butterflies or snuff boxes.

"Is Mrs. Hewitt safe?" I asked.

"She saw troops, but they did not visit her. I took the liberty of telling her our news"—his serious expression broke into a hearty laugh—"honestly, I could not hold it in. She sends happy regards and a gift for the bride." He lifted a corked, clay bottle of cider. "The Pemberley footman and driver are gone. They hid the coach behind the house, then headed north on foot ahead of the advancing troops."

"I think they were wise."

He glanced at the lowering sun. "My trip took longer than I thought. If we wish to marry while it is light..."

With that, everything became a rush. The group assembled, fifteen of us as none of the captives who escaped Hartfield had dared return to their homes. There was Harriet with Mrs. Prince; Mr. and Mrs. Collins; Anne, Mr. Weston, and their two-year-old girl; the Otways with their teenaged daughter Caroline; Miss Bates, her roseworm at her feet; and Lady Catherine, wearing a dramatic turban with an ostrich feather and flanked by the bronze wyvern.

Mr. Collins, his dark coat and trousers transformed into rector's garb by his draped tippet, directed the modest crowd with unexpected efficiency. He approached me and Mr. Knightley. "Is it your wish to bind draca when you marry? I feel compelled to point out that her ladyship, Lady Catherine de Bourgh, feels *most* strongly that all ladies should bind."

Mr. Knightley looked at me, and I nodded. This was what the wyverns kept nagging about—*you must bind for strength*.

Mr. Collins nodded as well, visibly relieved. "Then we shall begin with the binding-of-gold." That was the old ceremony to prepare a couple for binding. Some said it predated Christian marriage. He added, "And have you marriage gold?"

"Oh," I breathed in dismay. I had forgotten.

At my sister's and my christenings, Papa had set aside binding offerings: two virgin-struck gold guineas for each of us, the custom for a gentry lady. But Papa's offering for me was at Hartfield—or stolen by the soldiers, or even by John.

"Emma," Mr. Knightley said. I looked up and found him smiling. "Considering the inconvenience of war, I wished to offer you this." He held out his hand, and nestled in his palm were two brilliant, unmarred golden guineas— marriage gold, far more valuable than normal currency.

"Is *that* what you went to fetch?" I asked.

"One of the things," he confirmed, pleased. He continued formally, "Wilt thou accept this gift, unencumbered and requiring no duty of thee?"

Those were the ritual words when offering marriage gold to a bride so destitute that she could not afford her own.

"I accept thy gift as mine own," I said, completing the ritual, then I ruined it by saying, "but you must keep one for *your* offering!" Two guineas of marriage gold was worth more than forty pounds. I could not imagine how he had raised that much money, let alone... "Why do you even *have* these?"

"I acquired marriage gold last year, before I visited you at Pemberley." He licked his lips. "We spoke that day, but I... expressed myself poorly. Afterward, I found I could not part with the gold."

"I remember every word," I said. "You were eloquent. The fault was mine."

Mr. Collins cleared his throat to break a lingering silence. "Then this matter is... settled?"

"It is," I said and took the coins.

THE BINDING-OF-GOLD IS A SIMPLE CEREMONY. Harriet would be my bridesmaid for the wedding, so she stood as green wyfe. None of Mr. Knightley's London friends were present, so he asked Mr. Weston to serve as green husband. The two of them held hands behind us, symbolizing the consummation of marriage, and although Mr. Weston was too old to look romantically handsome beside Harriet, his military bearing made him dashing, and Harriet fairly glowed with beauty.

Anne Weston's contribution was mistletoe and a leafy branch of oak, so those and a cotton kerchief served as our binding bowl. The husband and wyfe do not touch until the wedding proper, so we knelt carefully side-by-side while Mr. Collins recited scripture and then, in a surprisingly powerful voice, chanted the old Gaelic texts to an ancient Celtic tune. I placed my two guineas of gold in the kerchief. Mr. Knightley—I still struggled to think of him as George—added his contribution. His landed with the rustle of many coins and sank the kerchief through the mistletoe, which frustrated me as I had become curious what else he had fetched from the carriage. But our marriage gold was now property of the Church, so that would remain a mystery.

The wedding itself followed the binding-of-gold. Dusk was spreading, so Miss Bates lit the lantern. Caroline Otway asked, "Will the French see it?" and that was enough to launch Mr. Collins into a breathtakingly accelerated service. I had barely blinked and removed my gloves before we were hand-in-hand and had repeated the vows.

Mr. Knightley placed a slim, gold ring on my finger and recited the husband's pledge, "With this ring I thee wed, with my body I thee worship, and with all my worldly goods I thee endow." His fingers were tender in the cooling air, and the import made me light-headed. I was *marrying*—clever and rich Emma Woodhouse, so certain she would never bother. I let the words flow past until Mr. Knightley caught my attention with an ironic eyebrow. Mr. Collins was speeding through one of the archaic passages about wyves submitting to husbands. Her ladyship punctuated that with a dismissive huff.

A cry of congratulation rose as Mr. Knightley and I turned to each other, holding each other's hands tight, and in a daring display for a Surrey wedding, touched our lips. The sensation was unexpected, nothing like pecking Papa on the cheek, and it kindled a heat which trembled and spread, heightening my senses until I realized draca had gathered all around our hillside, watching and guarding.

"I thought about playing for you," Mr. Knightley said, "but I think we should wait until we will not attract an audience of soldiers."

"You retrieved your violin?" I asked. He nodded, and I pictured him laden with parcels, not to mention a gold ring, while he hiked back from the coach. "Did you fetch my luggage while you were at it?"

"I tried lifting one of your travel chests, but apparently they are full of bricks. The hatboxes were lighter, but I could not choose between so many beautiful bonnets, so I am afraid you will have to do without."

That felt provocative before a wedding night.

HARRIET HAD CHOSEN this setting because she and I often visited the drainsman on our picnics. He was a reclusive soul, happier examining a basket of fruit than conversing with ladies, but he insisted that Mr. Knightley and I accept a loan of his cottage for the night. After apologizing for the housekeeping, he headed off to visit his cousin's farm.

It was a cozy, country place, with a feather bed and an iron stove, unlit in the warm spring. Harriet had arranged the two ripe strawberries on the table with a wreath of leaves. I placed my strawberry-decorated bonnet beside them and ran the tip of my finger through their delicate, rough-textured foliage.

"Emma..." Mr. Knightley said.

I had to stop my usual response, then smiled. "The problem with short engagements is that I have not practiced saying 'George.'" I considered him across the small room, Lady Anne's lanyard decorating his buttonhole. "George. It is a nice name."

He did not smile. "In the rush—in the madness we have faced—I have relied on my own feelings and trusted you to know your mind. But here, I feel selfish. I know this is a duty you were told to perform, part of your role as a great wyfe. I feel no shame in aiding you; most people marry for duty or fortune, and you—you are like a queen or a princess, burdened with responsibility beyond the rest of us. So I can accept—"

I had reached him by then, and I lifted his hand, our bare fingers tight and pulling him so close that our knuckles brushed each other's chests. "That is a very kind speech, and very ridiculous! Do you think I am so selfless that I would marry a man I did not love? I spent years happily planning for a single woman's life. Even twenty nagging wyverns could not overcome *that*." I thought about it and added, "I admit I planned to be a single woman of good fortune, which naturally makes one respectable and sensible and pleasant. So, I had better reclaim Hartfield. But if we must be poor, I will try to be good natured and poor, and you can remind me when I forget."

He was smiling by the end. "That is unlikely."

I found I was empty of clever words, so I lifted his hand to rest against my cheek. The touch, skin to skin, felt intensely precious, as if I was starved for contact. When we kissed at the wedding, my senses had wheeled wide, skating over the hills and the shining draca around us. For this kiss, I closed my eyes, reveling in touch, my fingers exploring his muscular shoulders and his coiled, soft hair, my lips his softness, my face brushing his chin, now clean-shaven. He must have collected a razor when he visited the coach. I felt a sliver of regret about that. It seemed I was the sort of lady who admired a ruffian's shadow on a gentleman.

When the kiss ended, I turned to show my back. "Will you undo my dress? It is awkward to do alone." Deftly, his fingers freed each button. I let it slip off my petticoat and pool around my feet, thinking it was like when he removed my pelisse before we danced on the ice-locked ship.

Just in case, I looked down at the dress, hunting for a shimmer or shadow of miasma, but there was only cloth. And then his elegant fingers encircled my waist and turned me to face him.

Later, in bed, I arched in ecstasy, and the shining brightness of draca surrounded us. Broccworms and tunnelworms, drakes and tykes, all reached out their bindings in reverent offer...

And, even dazed with passion, I thought, *No*, and the draca withdrew.

The next morning, Harriet called on us. We were dressed and waiting; the plan had been to meet early. Reality could not be dodged forever. This was a shire occupied by an invading army.

Harriet, eyes twinkling, met me with a delighted "Mrs. Knightley" and then peered expectantly around my feet. Rather like my husband had done this morning.

"We did not bind," I said. "It is not time."

I had always been told—Mr. Elton had shouted it at me when I confronted him in his vicarage—that only virginal ladies bind, and only on their wedding night. Now I knew that supposed rule was an accident of passion and emotion and, importantly, expectation. For draca, binding was a vow that must be entered knowingly. A wyfe must both seek and consent to bind, and for most wyves, that occurred only once while also at the pinnacle of profound love.

"I suppose you will know when the time is right," Harriet replied doubtfully. "When you saved Augusta, that was like something Lizzy or Georgiana would do. Like magic." She frowned. "But I thought the entire *reason* you married was so you could bind?"

"I thought so, too, but I was wrong." I smiled shyly at my husband, who grinned roguishly. He looked handsome with his coat smoothed and dusted, although a little wrinkled from the last two days, and I had cleverly distracted him so he forgot to shave. "I suppose the wyverns will be cross with me," I continued. "The only thing they ever explained clearly is that I must bind, and here I have ignored them."

"Well, whatever the wyverns think, you are married," Harriet observed. "I came to find my mother, and I have, but I do not like being surrounded by French soldiers or those slavers, who are worse!"

"Where is your mother?"

"I asked Mr. and Mrs. Collins to take her home. It is on their path and away from the fighting. The Collinses are taking Lady Catherine's carriage, which is very intimidating and has two footmen. I do not think she can be much safer than that."

"And Lady Catherine?"

"She and Miss Bates went off with the widowed wyves, and Augusta is at the Westons. I was there last night, too. Mrs. Weston insisted. She is so loyal to you, Emma, and her husband is delighted to be sheltering fugitives. When I left, he was marching around their house insisting we call him Captain, as if he was still in the militia. It was rather funny, but it is serious too. The Otways went to stay with their cousins, but Augusta has nowhere to go." She pulled out an envelope. "Lady Catherine asked me to give you this."

I broke the seal:

*"Mrs. Knightley,*

*After our conversation, I found myself reconsidering certain moments of my life. That is an unfamiliar sensation which I abhor. I am remedying it by assisting the widowed wyves, as I find this exceedingly satisfying.*

*Assuming your and my survival, I expect you and Mr. Knightley to visit me at Rosings Park. A stay of six weeks will be sufficient.*

*Lady Catherine de Bourgh"*

"Was she rude?" Harriet asked.

"Not exactly," I said. "I am sorry for her."

"What will we do?"

"Escape north," Mr. Knightley offered bluntly. "We can swing westward to avoid London. That will be the focus of battle. Perhaps Mrs. Elton can accompany us. We certainly cannot let her fall into her husband's hands. But once we are north of the fighting, Emma and I must make speed to Pemberley. You accomplished your quest, Miss Smith. We did not, and we must tell the others of our failure."

"Mary trusted me," I said, and the words tasted sour. The terrible things I had pushed out of my mind returned—the slavers' crimes, the theft of my fortune, John claiming Hartfield, the lost amulet. I summoned a smile for Harriet. "I did not come to Surrey to marry. We were seeking the amulet." When Harriet screwed up her nose in confusion, I explained, "That was a discovery after you left Pemberley. After you... found your own way."

"Oh," she said.

There was a moment of mutual embarrassment; she and I had hardly been speaking then. As hurt feelings can, it seemed foolish in hindsight. I took her hand, and she held tight.

"Why an amulet?" she asked.

"It was made with one of Yuánchi's scales, and it can help heal what has gone wrong—the blight, perhaps the war. It was sent to the Witch of Wood-house, so Mary thought it might be an heirloom, but Papa never mentioned it. The French tore Hartfield apart looking for it. All they accomplished was breaking things." I remembered shards of ornaments spraying across the floor.

"So, it would be red," Harriet mused, "and old fashioned. Is the setting jade? With a lot of..." She twirled her finger in little whorls very like the drawing the French officer had shown us.

There was a silence. I looked at Mr. Knightley and met his disbelieving stare.

Harriet was grinning now. "If it is so important, should we not collect it before we go?"

"Where is it?" I cried. "How do you know?"

"I know because..." Her smile faltered. "Do you remember, when I was a student at Mrs. Goddard's, a tradesman visited pretending to be my father? The man who was hired by Mr. Wood—by our father."

I remembered. "With whiskers and a bent hat..."

"He was a bad pretend father, but he gave a pretty speech about regretting leaving me alone. He said it very carefully, like it was memorized, and at the end, he gave me a gift. He called it an heirloom. An amulet of jade and shining red. Red that is exactly like Yuánchi's scales."

"Papa wished you were a Woodhouse," I breathed. "He just was not brave enough to share his name." A rush of relief made me giddy. "I cannot believe I did not *ask* you!"

"Well, nobody *else* did, either," she said, casting a look at Mr. Knightley.

I grabbed her fingers. "Please tell me you did not throw it in a river or—"

"Of course not!" she scoffed. "It was beautiful. And the chain is *gold!*"

"Where is it?"

She winced. "This is where it is difficult. It is at Mrs. Goddard's school."

In the center of French-occupied Hartfield.

# PICTISH STORIES

## LIZZY

This Scottish morning I woke far warmer, my back curled into the heat of Darcy's chest, the woolen covers tucked over us both. Even pressed this close, I had perhaps a spare inch in the narrow bed.

Darcy's forearm, wrist, and hand were outside the covers. I lay my arm beside his. His wrist was wider and thicker than mine, all thrusting bone and thick tendon, the build of a tall and athletic man. Mine looked positively delicate by comparison. I had even managed to regain a little feminine softness since I rose from the lake, but it was skin-deep; I knotted my fist, and lean, hard muscle rose in my arm.

I reached with my mind, probing for Yuánchi, and found him east of us, tens of miles out to sea. Clearly, he had recovered from the punishing flight and gorging on sheep. He and the two drakes were reveling in the stiff winds; through the firedrakes' vision I saw their spirals and turns.

"Ermph," Darcy murmured.

"Good morning," I whispered. The curtain to our room did not afford much privacy, but it had been enough. After the villagers' passion-laced performance of the Wyfe's Hunt, Darcy and I stumbled to our tiny room, touching each other with every step—a held hand, a brushed hip, a kiss—and when we arrived, it was loudly evident that Mr. and Mistress MacLeod had their own distractions.

An intimate night had not been my plan when we came. But it changed nothing.

"Are you happy?" I whispered.

Darcy stirred fully awake. His torso flexed as he lifted his head and shoulders to see me. "An odd thing to ask. War is raging. We are on a desperate quest for a mythical artifact." I waited, and he admitted, "Yes, I am happy."

"I am, too." My memory drifted to, of all moments, Charlotte laughing at me after Darcy asked me to dance at the Netherfield ball.

He shifted his hand to hold mine. "You said the wyfe of war may have no husband."

That ended my idle remembrances. "Did I?"

"Twice. When you first emerged from Pemberley lake, just before you complained about my being 'prettily dressed.' Then again last night, when you... cried out..."

I felt a flush in the hollow of my throat. "I recall now." His chest rose and fell before I answered, "It is a lesson for wyves of war. A lesson proved in many lifetimes. A husband is a target for enemies. A strategic weakness." Darcy was very still while I finished, "A wyfe of war brings no happiness to those she loves. Our lives are short."

"That depends on circumstance. We are in a civilized era—"

I laughed bitterly. "All eras call themselves civilized. None are. No wyfe of war lives long." I took his hand between mine, winding my fingers through his. "But I am a selfish woman. I do not regret this night. This is why we are here. To be together."

His fingers tensed. "We are here to find the flute." I was not sure if he was reminding me or had become suspicious until he sat up, full of energy. "The MacLeods are stirring. Today, we hear the story of the Pictish stones."

The last bits of my happiness skidded into guilty dread.

We dressed and greeted the MacLeods, at breakfast with their daughter. They served us bowls of steaming porridge, a mishmash of split peas and wheat groats, modest portions eyed hungrily by their daughter. I claimed to be overfull from the feast and offered her half of mine, which she accepted with astonished eyes before wolfing it down. Her mother watched every bite, unreadable. What did she feel? Bruised pride in the presence of a guest? Guilt and grief because her child was hungry?

We walked to the river, and Mr. MacLeod rowed the four of us across. The sky was overcast but bright, the northern sun occasionally visible as a muted, moon-like orb veiled by flowing clouds.

Halfway up Helmsdale hill, Mistress MacLeod stopped and gazed at Helmsdale with its houses in their regular, too narrow plan.

She pointed inland to the long, broad valley that followed the river. "Ye wondered what happened to our people. That's the Kildonan strath. It's hard land, but it was ours. Every stone and stubborn strand of grass lived in our hearts. The people of the strath have lived here longer than anyone can say. Now, though, we've been 'given' this." She flicked her hand, disgusted, to the ruled lines and tiny farms of the village.

"The landholders bought you out?" Darcy asked.

Her husband burst out a laugh, and Mistress MacLeod gritted a harsh smile. "*Bought?* Nae. The rich don't *buy* things. They take them. We came home one afternoon to find an eviction notice nailed on our door. Claimed we had debts. We've never borrowed a penny in our lives. Turns out *everyone* had these 'debts'."

"Did you seek legal recourse?" Darcy asked. He knew it was a naïve question —his jaw was set. But even angry, he was a thorough man. Darcy understood the weapons of wealth. Even if he did not stoop to using them himself, he was assessing his opponent's strength.

Mistress Macleod resumed walking, climbing the hill while she spoke. "The law here *is* the factor. He runs these lands, every rock and bush as far as ye can see. They made us pay to build those shacks"—she jerked her head toward Helmsdale—"and he made a tidy profit selling to us, I promise ye that."

I asked, "Did you fight?" A less naïve question.

"'Course we fought!" she snapped. "We blockaded roads. We kicked the factor and his bully men off our land. We fought, and blood spilled. Then they brought the army to beat us and arrest us. Some gave up then, or were done with fighting after broken arms and legs, or decided not to risk their little ones. They moved. The factor was spinning a grand tale of how these 'improvements,' kelping and fishing, were businesses that'd make us rich as kings." She snorted. "But most of us didn't believe him, or were too stubborn to change our ways if we did, and we went on the way we had. Until one afternoon, while the men were away tilling the fields, they came for us. Dragged me and our girl out, screaming. Burned our croft and everything in it. Clothes, food, tools, seed. Ye could see pillars of smoke risin' all across the strath, home after home going up. That night, it was beg to huddle in one of those shacks down there, or watch our young ones and old folk freeze."

"We can help," Darcy said. "We can speak to the landholders. I cannot promise to right the wrongs, to restore your land, but wealthy men may be ignorant of the hardship their policies impose. And even if they are indifferent, we can aid the people of Helmsdale. Help you find a way to prosper."

Mr. MacLeod answered, but he spoke to me, not to Darcy. "Would ye fight for us?"

Mistress MacLeod turned to watch me, the promise I made reflected in her eyes, but that seemed more distant than the pool of anger simmering in me. This story could have been any of countless past lives, wyves with their homes taken, their livelihoods stripped away, their families killed...

"We are not here to fight," Darcy answered for me.

"What good are ye, then?" Mr. MacLeod asked me, not even angrily. Just wondering. And the dark pool in my heart lapped higher and whispered of war.

We emerged on the hilltop. An old memory stirred: my sisters and me standing in a wary triangle on this windswept point. There was no castle then, only our swirling power. Not sisters by blood. Great sisters. Great wyves. A guilty pain wrenched my spine and shortened my breath. The ruined castle flickered into a fantastic outpost, an enemy. I had to clench my teeth not to summon Yuánchi, to see him drive and destroy—

"Elizabeth?" Darcy asked carefully.

I forced my jaw loose and tasted the bloody sting of a bit lip. I nodded in answer, not trusting my voice.

What just happened? I had not felt that sort of violent impulse since we flew north. Chilled, I walked after the others.

Mistress MacLeod led us through a fallen wall into the ruins of the castle. Her husband whistled, and a man emerged from the shadows to meet us.

"We keep a guard on the stones," Mr. MacLeod explained. "Sellar, that's the factor, he's after them. Rich folks collect 'em."

Mistress MacLeod walked on, but my steps slowed. My past selves had recognized the unspoken exchange between the guard and Mr. MacLeod—the flick of eyes toward a concealing pile of rocks, the suggestion of a nod. Now the guard's eyes followed me, angry and hopeful.

These were the men planning to fight. There would be more in the village. Their weapons were stashed in this ruined castle.

Darcy's hand touched my elbow, hurrying me forward.

We passed into the castle's interior. The roof was long gone, even the supporting beams vanished, but heavy stone walls remained on three sides, one of them massive and three feet thick, part of the fortified central keep.

The Pictish stones were standing upright in the fresh spring grass, two of them, each as wide as my shoulders, as high as my chest, and carved with runes. They had been moved here recently—I saw crushed grass—but they had an air of stupendous age, the carvings deeply incised then smoothed by the centuries until they seemed drawn by rain and wind.

Mistress MacLeod fell onto her knees before them, an almost religious observance. "See here the auld stones."

"How old?" Darcy asked.

"A scholar would tell ye they're before the Picts were Christian folk, and that'd be true. Not that the Picts ever let go the old ways, Christ or not." She brushed a few bobbing seed heads aside, clearing the face of the leftmost stone. "These hail from a Britain with gods of briar and bog. My *seanmhair*"—she glanced over her shoulder—"my nanna that means, she taught me to read them, for the story is told only at the stones, and the mistress of the strath must be the one to read it."

Reverently, she touched her fingers to her forehead, then to the first stone. "The Wyves' Stone." Sharply, she stabbed two fingers at her heart, then touched the second. "The Stone of Betrayal. Together, they tell the tragedy of the flute."

That word, "betrayal," stung my guilt, then a colder realization drowned that. This was *the* story, the very history I had concealed from Darcy. The story that had played out on this hilltop long ago.

On the Wyves' Stone, Mistress MacLeod's finger traced the top row of symbols. "Three ovals for three leaders. Those are the Scottish great wyves."

That interested Darcy. "The pre-Christian Picts lived a thousand years ago."

Mistress MacLeod nodded. "So I'm told."

"Then the dates do not match. The great wyves fought in the Scottish wars. That would be five hundred years."

She snorted. "That's the *English* story. The great wyves never fought England. If they had, there wouldn't be an England, would there? It'd all be Scotland."

"That is a bold assertion—" Darcy began, sounding irritated, academic, and rather like Mary. Perhaps that was why they got along so well.

"The great wyves united would have defeated England," I said, silencing him, "but the Scottish wyves were dust long before England existed."

"Mind ye," Mistress MacLeod added, "the wyves did fight. We've no lack of wars in the north."

Her words were brightening my own recollection. Helmsdale hill seemed to roll back through time. Despite the dull, overcast sky, sea wind lifted my hair. Salt bit my nostrils.

I knew the story. Pretense was pointless. "The Scottish wyfe of war was a Bennet."

Mistress MacLeod's gaze found me. "Aye. Her clan name was an old form of that."

"It sounded almost French..." I sifted through the past. "*Bénet.*"

Darcy was confused. "You knew this?"

"I knew before we left Pemberley." I made myself meet his gaze. "I lied to you there."

I had expected anger or hurt when the truth was revealed. Instead, his confusion ended. His tension eased, leaving only a swordsman's alert balance.

"I thought you had not told me everything," he said. "I only wondered why."

"You would not have come if I told the truth."

He shook his head. "Nothing could keep me from your side. Nothing could keep me from seeking the flute..." He trailed off, watching Mistress MacLeod. He was beginning to suspect.

She resumed her story by touching the last row, three elaborate symbols. The first was a sinuous draca intertwined with a bent arrow: "Command, for the wyfe of war." Then came a Celtic knot: "Binding, for the wyfe of healing." Last, there was a stylized rod in two parts: "*Duiseal*, the flute, for the wyfe of song. This stone recounts the great wyves allied on Scottish soil. They stood on Helmsdale hill. The Wyves' Stone is a proud stone."

Darcy grated out, "What is the Stone of Betrayal?"

"Well, as happens, there was a war." Mistress MacLeod moved to the second stone, laced with moss and lichen. "A battle of two great clans, north and south, as tends to be. Blood was shed aplenty, and the north paid the higher price, but the northern clan had the great wyves, so their chief asked them to aid the fight. The wyves met to decide, aye or nae, on Helmsdale hill."

I remembered stretching my arm like a banner to the south, to the lands to conquer. "The wyfe of war, the Bennet, wanted to fight."

"Aye. But the wyfe of healing, she was a wise wyfe, she said nae, and the wyfe of song supported her. That dinnae need to stop the wyfe of war—she could fight alone—but she wanted the great talisman that had found its way to the north: the flute. The wyfe of song held that, and when she refused to give it up, the wyfe of war took it from her. Took it by force. One bound wyfe fighting another."

"Our draca fought," I said. "I had a lindworm, she a drake. Hers died."

Mistress MacLeod recited familiar words:

> *"To sound our claim,*
> *the three wyves came:*
> *Of healing, wise.*
> *Of song, who cries.*
> *Of war. Arise."*

That song was this story, but... "The words are wrong," I said. "Her fire-drake fell, torn and smoking, and the wyfe of song's binding broke. That should have stunned her, but she was too strong. I had to wrench the flute from her hands. Even then, she stood tall." I found Mistress MacLeod's steady gaze. "The wyfe of song never cried."

"What then?" Darcy asked, the words sharp and separate.

A voice called outside—the guard—but my memory shone bright, so I continued, "I led the northern clans to battle. The south had four times our warriors, but a wyfe of war laughs at those odds. And I held the *flute!* Its power sang. I thought it would summon a tide of draca, but when the battle began, it... hushed. I struggled to wake it. I obsessed. I ignored the fight. Then an arrow struck me." I clutched my left shoulder, feeling that barbed point drive below my collarbone. "It hit hard as a hammer and cut deep. They had breached our line. I fought, but my sword tangled in a warrior's mail, then a rush drove me to the ground. An ax swung. I lifted the flute—it was a reflex, to block—and the flute shattered..."

The vision ended with a splitting shriek in my skull.

"The song's words are true," Mistress MacLeod said in her brogue. Her finger circled the final symbol: roaring flame. "The two clans built a pyre for the wyfe of war, and the wyfe of song laid the shards of the flute in her dead arms. They burned wyfe and flute together while the wyfe of song wept."

I did not remember that, but it sounded like what she would do.

My lips formed a ragged smile for Darcy. "This is why you would not have come if I told the truth. My own ancestor destroyed the flute. That is the legacy of the Bennets, our mysterious Scottish heritage. The French are chasing a fable, some obscure mention of the Bennet name, but the flute is lost. The three items will never be united. The song cannot be healed."

"I do not believe it," Darcy said.

"I remember it," I said simply. "It broke in my hands."

"Then I do not *accept* it. We could repair it. Replace it. The great items did not fall from the sky. They were fashioned by people. We could learn how."

"It took years to craft them. Fènnù's sanity, what there is of it, will break in days. That is the purpose of the French advance, to trigger her apocalypse. Fènnù will abandon her search for me and unleash destruction. Our petty war will be eclipsed." I took Darcy's hand; I had to pull through his resistance. "But Fènnù has a weakness. She is drawn to conflict..." The next words hurt—I knew what Darcy would think—but I would not lie any more. "If she cannot find me, if she does not have my memories to focus her, her destruction will fall on the south. Longbourn and Pemberley will be safe, above the tide."

Darcy's fingers were wood in mine. I counted thudding heartbeats before he said, "You cannot surrender half the country to destruction. It is amoral."

"Amoral, how? Is destruction in one place better than another? I lost a sister and a father. I lost Denny. We both mourn Mr. Rabb. I will not lose more people that I love. *You* matter to me. My family matters. Georgiana matters. If you and I escape, if we *hide*, Fènnù will hunt endlessly amongst the southern war. Without me, she... she might even give up. Return to harmless sleep..."

"If you believed that," he said icily, "you would have told the truth at Pemberley."

Until now, I had been pleading. Anger cut that away. "I did not tell the truth because you are sentimental. You would not accept the truth."

"What truth? That you have abandoned duty?"

"That we have lost! We are in retreat from a superior foe. When I am near Fènnù, she poisons me, drags my mind into her mad violence, and through me, her madness poisons Yuánchi. To save Yuánchi, I had to flee, and if I left you behind, Fènnù would find you instead. Yuánchi's binding touches you too, and the black dragon is jealous. She would kill you in idle pique and resume her hunt." An old lesson returned. "'A general must retreat without fearing disgrace.'"

Without hesitation, Darcy recited the full quote, "'A general whose only thought is to *protect his country* must retreat without fearing disgrace.'" Into my surprised silence, he added, "When did you start reading Sun Tzu?"

I remembered an ages-dead general so respected that he defied custom and taught his daughter the art of war. He dictated thirteen chapters while I transcribed them, holding the brush perfectly vertical as he had taught me, always standing, never sitting—father said writing was a dance, like swordplay.

"My father told me," I said, but these bursts of ancient knowledge felt suddenly too real, too frighteningly uncontrolled. Despite the risk, I reached out to Yuánchi to steady my mind... and could not find him. It was like I had thrust my hand into a mountain of snow, silent and soft and impenetrable.

Darcy's eyebrows had risen in disbelief, so I forced my attention back to him. "All that matters is that you and I remain here. That we wait."

"Wait for England to *fall*?"

"*Everything* falls. War always wins. I have seen it over and over." I knew the savagery of it, the inevitability of humanity's self-immolation. It was like my mind had been raised to a godlike perspective, dispassionate, staring down, judging...

"You are not hearing yourself," he cried. "Would you make me choose between England and you?"

"There is no choice! England is lost. You are here."

"I can go south. Buy a horse. Buy a ship. Walk."

"Do not joke."

"Do I look like I am joking?" He shouted it, his face ashen, cheeks flushed, eyes glittering, but when he resumed, his voice was deadly soft. "You lied at Pemberley because you knew my answer. No, I will not hide. I will find a way south and then I will heal the song, with or without the flute. If that fails, I will battle the blight. If that fails, I will don a uniform, shoulder a musket, and fight. But I will *not hide*. And the woman I love would not hide, either."

"That is fantasy. If you even reached the south, Fènnù would sense our binding..." The rest faded from my lips. At the word Fènnù, the anger in me had twisted into malevolent, raw fury...

"Then I will die," Darcy said.

"Stop," I whispered. A darkness folded, wrapping my soul. A voice caressed my mind, *wyfe of war, arise.*

"I will *not* stop—"

I reached out blindly, palm skidding over his vest buttons. "Stop!" I gasped, and this time he did. "Something is wrong... something is coming..." My vision dimmed like ink had spilled across the sky.

A well-dressed man walked around the ragged wall into the castle. Three husky roughs with wooden cudgels followed, dragging the beaten guard.

"What hae ye done?" Mistress MacLeod cried.

The well-dressed man touched his hat in recognition. "Mistress MacLeod." He noticed her husband. "And mister."

"What madness is this?" Darcy said, striding toward them.

The well-dressed man squinted at him. "Who're you?"

"Mr. Darcy." He spoke it as a threat.

"I'm Patrick Sellar," the man responded, "factor for this land. Ye best be keepin' accusations of 'madness' to yerself. We're arresting the MacLeods. They're troublemakers, and now they've overstepped to thievery."

"Och! I'm not a thief, ye thief!" Mr. MacLeod exclaimed.

Sellar laughed. "Ye poached a half-dozen sheep. Says so on my warrant." He patted his pocket.

"*They* did not poach your sheep," Darcy said contemptuously. He faced the men holding the guard. "Release him!"

One man actually let go. Another sneered and gave the half-conscious guard a shake for good measure.

Two new men from the village ran into view around the corner. When they saw Sellar, one raised a heavy belaying pin. Every hand reached for a cudgel or knife.

"Stop it, ye fools!" Mistress MacLeod shouted. "Do ye nae see she carries—"

The villagers charged, screaming. Mr. MacLeod attacked the men holding the beaten guard, swinging hunger-thinned arms still tough with sinewy muscle. He punched one man in the eye, who swore and staggered.

Darcy was shouting explanations. "They did not take your sheep—"

A crazed laugh skidded through my throat. As if facts mattered. As if the law were not just another weapon.

Sellar strode to Mistress MacLeod and shoved his wooden cudgel crosswise, banging her shoulder and jaw. She fell back a step and spat blood. Mr. MacLeod, grappling with one of the men, went berserk trying to reach her.

A voice caressed my mind, *wyfe of war, arise.*

Like a loosed hound, I was on Sellar. My skirts whipped as I dragged his cudgel behind his back, ripping it from his fingers. The cudgel came free, and I swung. His shin crunched and buckled, but I had already discarded that feeble weapon, wheeling gleefully to the real fight—

Darcy towered in my path, blocking me. He grabbed for my arms. Endless defensive drills reacted quicker than thought. I caught his weaker, left hand in both of mine and twisted. His elbow jammed into his side. Bone grated as the joint locked.

I had not cranked hard enough to break anything, but pitiless instructors had demonstrated this hold on me, and it *hurt*. Darcy, though, barely grunted. His other hand grabbed my upper arm and, with typical stubbornness, held like a vice when I tried to yank away.

Mr. MacLeod, the villagers, and the other toughs had descended into furious battle. That was what I wanted. Not this delicate dance.

"Let me fight," I snapped.

Darcy was struggling to free himself. Warily, I shifted stance as he thrashed. He was stronger and twice my weight, but this was not fencing, and he did not know how to break the hold. He reared up, trying to use his height, a bad choice. That wrenched his arm, and he cried out. An answering cry spilled from my lungs, and I let go. Then I stared stupidly at my empty palms—why let go? —before he lunged and wrapped me in his arms, lifting me up on my toes, trapping my hands at my sides.

"Do not fight," he shouted. "Do not give in!"

I feigned falling to one side, stretched the other way when he shifted his balance, and drew the dagger.

"Let me fight," I whispered and pricked the tip into his thigh.

"Fighting achieves nothing. When we pay for the sheep—"

I laughed. "You think the sheep *matter*?" I leaned back as if to see him. He lowered his head, and I drove my forehead into his jaw. He staggered, and I was free.

The mad voice came again—Fènnù crooning, *My wyfe of war...*

The gloomy gray clouds swirled and tore asunder, replaced by sky-spanning black wings. My emotions tore with them and fell away, reduced to exaltation.

I threw my arms high and screamed a joyous cry of welcome. Wind blasted, snapping my hair back, flattening grass and kicking grit from the stone walls, drowning the terrified cries.

Fènnù's huge feet landed on the thick walls of the castle keep, her claws piercing rock, her weight smashing the stone down inch-by-inch. Rocks rained, thudding into the dirt. The keep swayed under her weight, dust streaming from crushed mortar and spinning in wild swirls as her wings worked, seeking balance on the shifting footing.

Frustrated and bellowing, she took to the air again, circling Helmsdale hill, faceted eyes fixed on me, then she twisted imperiously in the sky, wings taut. A rumble built, climbed to the shriek of an infernal demon, then her jaws opened and the world turned to ear-splitting thunder. Blackness darker than midnight streaked over our heads and pounded into the keep. Thick walls blew apart. The foundation tore away. The castle walls were dragged into the rush like mud in a torrent, stone blocks that weighed hundreds of pounds rolling and disintegrating to gravel. The black breath blew through them and down to the valley below.

After an eternity, or seconds, it ended. My exposed skin, my lips, hands, eyes, all stung from the unnatural radiant cold, like a frozen sun had risen to destroy warmth.

"Control her!" Darcy screamed at me. Somehow, he had kept his footing in the maelstrom, but he sounded muffled and distant; I was half deafened. "You have the dagger! Use it!"

I looked at the dagger in my hand, an artifact built to summon the black dragon, to tempt her with humble offerings for her wrath. Through my eyes, Fènnù studied it also. Her amused mind twined around mine, drawing me deeper into her clutch.

"Nobody controls the black dragon," I said.

His hands grasped my shoulders, shaking me. "No wyfe of war has been as strong as you. Use the dagger!"

I ducked away and ran across the frosted stones and dirt. Mistress MacLeod was shouting at her husband while she dragged Sellar, gibbering with terror, off the frozen, poisoned earth. I passed her and the rubble where the castle's outer wall had stood.

Helmsdale came into view. Fènnù's breath had missed the village, but the bay was a slurry of blocky ice and choppy seawater.

Gusts slammed as Fènnù returned, landing in the cleared ground that had held half the castle. Even then she had to jockey for position, careful not to crush me with her wings. She was a skilled predator. She understood the fragility of flesh.

I walked toward her, but Darcy caught up and grabbed my hand. "Elizabeth! Resist her!"

"Why?" I asked as Fènnù watched us, curious and waiting. "I am her." I turned to her, riotous joy straining my lips. I reveled in her judgment, her fatal condemnation of upstart, unworthy humanity—

Then my joy faltered, interrupted by... music.

It was a few notes, not even heard—my ears rang too loudly to register such delicacy—but the draca senses, the old senses, responded. The certainty of purpose that had consumed my mind faded. Doubt slipped in.

The tune swelled, unthinkably beautiful, powerful and exquisitely performed. A woman's voice, singing.

Fènnù's head lifted to the south. Listening.

I had heard this song before, sung at the ball in London when Miss Rees read the melody embossed in Gramr's blade and invoked its power to wake Fènnù. But that had been an ordinary wyfe, ordinary singing. This was ancestral tones rising from the earth. Notes storming from the restless sea. Music shining from the countless dusks and dawns stacked beyond the horizons. The forces that ruled the world of draca, forces rooted in nature, were being folded into melody.

Only one woman had that power. "Stop!" I shrieked. I turned toward Pemberley, hundreds of miles distant. "You cannot have her! She chose me. *I* am the wyfe of war!"

Fènnù's wings spread, and she leaped into the sky. In seconds, she was shrinking into the south.

Like an iron chain stretched beyond its limits, the madness filling me groaned, bent, and shattered. The cold shroud erected to block my link with Yuánchi fell.

Trembling with shock, I fumbled the dagger into the sheath on my thigh. Its touch burned my skin. Ashamed and terrified, I looked up at Darcy.

He cradled my hands in his. "You did it. You commanded her."

He had not heard the music. "No. Fènnù had taken my mind. I was lost. She was summoned by another..."

His head turned to watch her fading silhouette. "Who could summon Fènnù?"

"The wyfe of song. Georgiana is singing her melody. Calling her."

He grabbed my arm. Hard. "*Why?*"

"I do not know, but we must stop her. She has the power to summon Fènnù, but the wyfe of song cannot hold the black dragon. Fènnù will break her, and consume her strength, and pour it into destruction."

For the first time since I rose from the lake, the fears that had driven me, the fears that had led to indecision and hiding and running, were gone. Now the contest was clear. And even with Fènnù's influence removed, I remembered my lifetimes of training. Wars were not won by running.

With the cold shroud gone, I reached my thoughts out to Yuánchi.

*Your mind is clear,* he answered in tremendous relief. I fell into his welcoming senses, sightless but rich with other awareness, the flows of air, the sound of waves cresting hundreds of feet below, the peculiar abstract imagery shared by the two firedrakes.

*Fènnù found me,* I thought. *She hid her approach—hid herself from you and me until she was upon me. She is stronger than ever. Come. We must save the wyfe of song.*

Below, stunned people congregated on the frozen shoreline of Helmsdale. Behind us, Mistress MacLeod and her husband, both bloodied, staggered out of the sprayed rubble of the castle. They were supporting Sellar, who was dragging one leg. He saw me and reeled back, wild-eyed and terrified.

I took Darcy's hand—his left, which made him wince, but I forced that guilt aside. There was no time.

"We must fly," I said as the scarlet of Yuánchi's wings became visible, streaking above the gray sea. "Race south as we have never flown before. We must stop Fènnù before she breaks the wyfe of song."

# 28

# PEMBERLEY, SHROUDED

## LIZZY

When I tricked Darcy into fleeing, our flight north had been an exercise in nighttime stealth made clumsy by my lost connection to Yuánchi's thoughts.

Our return was a brazen, daylit sprint. Yuánchi's mind and mine were joined again, our path so high above the earth that the air thinned until my heart pounded between straining lungs and the sun glinted from Yuánchi's scales with unnatural brilliance.

I rode pressed flat to the leather of the saddle, head tipped just enough to peer through my goggles at the horizon. Through my eyes, Yuánchi read the ever-changing wisps and roils of cloud, an atlas of drafts and currents. The cream firedrakes, who usually flew ahead on each side, took turns perching on the saddle below my right knee to rest, hooking their claws to a sturdy iron ring, their neck, body, wings, and tail flattened into a gleaming, drop-like form that effortlessly split the air.

My human body was far inferior. The wind pummeled my shoulders, forearms, and fingers like tireless fists until my grip shook with exhaustion. Pinprick gaps in the seams of my riding coat admitted icy needles of air. But all that was nothing compared to the pain in Yuánchi's ox-sized breast muscles as he drove his vast wings beyond endurance.

When we donned our riding gear, Darcy had asked one question, "Can we beat Fènnù to Pemberley?" I shook my head and saw the bitter compression of his lips. My scheme had taken us far from home. Now Yuánchi paid the penance for my failure, spending his impossible strength in reckless pursuit.

Forests passed below. The sun shifted. The Highland mountains shrank to hills. We overflew a tremendous bay beside a coal-smoke-wreathed city—Edinburgh. Yuánchi, even blind, steered us with a draca's awareness of place, senses so inhuman that I understood only his reactions, a wing dipped to correct for a crosswind, a burst of effort to ride a higher, fortuitous breeze.

What would happen when we arrived? Had Georgiana already fallen to Fènnù? I closed my eyes and stretched out my senses. Georgiana's song filled my bones, its beauty intact, its power uncorrupted. All was not lost. But that did not answer what we would face.

I was so exhausted and awash in inhuman senses that Darcy spotted our destination before me. He tapped my hip, then whacked me when I did not stir. I twisted my head to see him—conversation was impossible—and saw his arm point forward.

An unnatural storm squatted on the horizon, shaped like roiling thunderclouds but as black as tar. I checked the landscape, less familiar from this direction. The ridges matched: the blackness engulfed Pemberley.

*What is that?* I asked Yuánchi.

His answer was slow. *Fènnù's strength grows.*

Wings spread wide, he descended in a hunter's glide until we were level with the highest hilltops. The wind lessened to a mere rush. I unfolded to sit upright in the saddle, hips and back groaning. The firedrake fell away from the saddle then winged ahead as the two guides took their accustomed positions. A muddle of emotions engulfed me—guilt, regret, resolve. I reached a gloved hand behind my back, and Darcy squeezed it.

The blackness approached, a strangely featureless wall across the sky—my mind perceived it as a storm and expected thunder and rain, but it was still. *I do not need your sight to find Pemberley,* Yuánchi thought, and we crossed into the dark.

Light vanished, a lurch into blackness. I felt no change in the air, there was no scent, but the skin around my goggles tingled. As my eyes adjusted, vague features emerged. The inky sky was not uniform; it had cracks of lighter sable. When a hill passed on our right, the trees flickered like columns of sulking soot. Then the sound of wind over Yuánchi's scales brightened, echoing from some flat surface below, and I heard falling water ahead. Yuánchi flared his wings and settled in what I barely made out as Pemberley's north garden, overlooking the lake.

Darcy and I slipped down Yuánchi's heaving chest to the ground. The garden was weirdly silent, no birdsong of day, no insects of night, no hint of the endless industry that occupies a busy estate.

"Where is everyone?" I whispered.

"Where is Fènnù?" Darcy whispered back.

I closed my eyes, seeking with draca senses. Georgiana's song blossomed within me, but when I reached farther, I struck a barrier—a cold shroud like what had isolated me at Helmsdale Castle.

"Fènnù is here, but not close. She has screened Pemberley. I cannot push through to find her." It was strange to be near the black dragon but not feel her crushing my mind. There was a reason: her focus was elsewhere. "Georgiana is at home." I pointed to the shadowy mansion, the direction of the song.

Darcy ran, sure-footed on the familiar paths, and I followed. Pemberley's front entrance stood open, the impressive door unattended. In the vestibule, a single candle flickered in a glass lamp. The warmth of natural light was a relief.

I called out, "Mary?" If Georgiana was here, she must be as well.

Darcy cocked his head in the silence, then he took the candle and stepped into the entry hall. He shouted, "Georgiana!" Her name rang from the walls, but there was no answer, nor any sound of music. I could sense her song, though, and led him through the house. After a few turns, it was clear we sought the music room, and he ran ahead.

The heavy, carved doors were closed and did not budge when he shook the handles. A girl's voice sounded inside. "Who is there?"

"Lucy," I answered, "it is Mr. Darcy and I."

There was a rattle and scrape of heavy furniture. The doors split to reveal Lucy's worried face. Darcy raced past her into the room, but Lucy caught me in an unexpected embrace. She was as tall as me now, but she clung like a child, burying her face in my shoulder. "Thank goodness you are back."

Georgiana was seated at one of her tremendous grand pianofortes, her fingers resting on the keys but still. She wore her red-and-gold silk dress, a Chinese garment with illustrations of their dragon lore. Her hair hung wild, fallen from its morning dressing. Her face was tilted back as if studying the sky, but her eyes were closed.

Mrs. Reynolds stood at her shoulder, a candle in one hand, an iron fire poker clenched in the other like a sword.

"What happened to her?" Darcy asked.

"Miss Darcy ordered us away," Mrs. Reynolds said. Her old voice sounded steady, but the poker, forgotten, slipped through her fingers and clattered to the floor. "She assembled the household and told us to proceed into the hills." Mrs. Reynolds pulled a cloth from her pocket and dabbed at Georgiana's neck; she was slick with perspiration. "Lucy and I... chose to stay. We hid in the hall. Then, Miss Darcy began singing. You know how she sings to draca. It was glorious for a long time. Then her voice weakened, and the windows darkened. She did not answer, so we forced the lock. It was as dark as night by then, and she was like this, and the air felt like..."

"Like death," Lucy whispered.

Darcy's hand found the pianoforte's side, his knuckles white.

"She is not silent," I said. "Not to draca. In her mind, she is singing Fènnù's song over and over." I felt it, a peculiar melody that had been infused with the nature and life I associated with Georgiana's power, but it was streaming away like fog in a gale, sucked into the shroud around Pemberley.

Gently, I lifted her right hand from the keyboard. It came unresisting, her long fingers slim, wide-spaced, and strong from endless practicing. I wrapped it between mine, remembering how she had evoked her power to help Emma, and reached my awareness toward the glowing song I sensed within her, the way I would cast myself into a draca's mind.

Her lips parted. She whispered, "Lizzy. You should have come sooner. I could have gone to her."

I did not understand that, but I said, "I am here. Georgiana, you must stop the song. It is being taken from you. Fènnù is... consuming it." The people watching us were motionless, but a shoe rasped nervously on the floorboards.

Georgiana's eyes roamed under closed lids. "I thought the song could order her mind, help her reason, but melody cannot command. It is like singing to a glacier while it slips under my feet, fed by endless snows, carrying me away..."

"*Why* did you call the black dragon?"

Her answer was suddenly, savagely strong. "To save Mary!"

I looked around the music room, realizing how strange my sister's absence was. "Where is she?"

Georgiana's slim throat worked, then she sang, "Gone to London," her pure soprano placing the words in flawless harmony with her endless, silent performance of Fènnù's song. A rush of power slammed my draca senses. Brilliant sapphire lines hammered the shroud, making it shudder, but the darkness sealed itself, oily and vast, leaving only sable streaks.

"Why is Mary in London?" Darcy pressed.

Georgiana whispered, "To find the flute."

"The flute is destroyed," I said.

Her drawn breath was a gasp, then she slumped sideways off the bench. Darcy caught her and laid her on a sofa by the fire, the red of her silk gown as dark as pooled blood in the candlelight, her brunette hair a tangled mess on the pillow.

Her silent song had faltered as well. The shroud around Pemberley surged inward until she resumed, now shaping the silent syllables on trembling lips. The shroud ground to a hungry halt just outside the manse's walls. When it was still again, she began fitting spoken words around her inaudible song. "I am frightened for Mary. She sang to Fènnù..."

"*Mary* sang?" I said.

A smile eased Georgiana's lips. "What I am to melody, she is to form. I heard her, even here. But she is stalked by malevolence. Blight." She grimaced. "Lizzy, fly to London. Evil pursues her, and you must save her. I thought I could master Fènnù and protect her, but Fènnù is taking me..."

"I am with you now," I said. "You and I will drive Fènnù away, then we will find Mary together. Fènnù will not hurt her."

She arched and cried out, "It is not Fènnù who hunts her!" then fell back, limp.

I settled my mind, seeking my own strength. So near the black dragon, thousands of memories arrayed themselves from an army of past wyves. I hunted through their experiences while seeking a way to push back Fènnù's shroud, but my attempts were like pressing my fingers into smoke. Instead, I tried supporting Georgiana's song, to be a foundation for her shining melody, but the music slipped past me, ephemeral and glorious but beyond my under-standing.

Darcy was watching with his hands locked behind his neck, arm muscles straining against nothing, face ragged. When he saw my frustration, he said, "The dagger was created to control the black dragon. Can you use it?"

I remembered it burning my fingers when I forced it into its sheath. "The dagger was created to call the black dragon. It strips my protections and merges my mind with hers. I might command her once, convince her to free Georgiana, but she would win control in the end, as she did at Helmsdale." I almost offered to do it, unfair as that choice would be to Darcy, but some ruthless past self refused; uniting the black dragon and the wyfe of war would unleash annihilation. I searched for another way. "We must strengthen Georgiana. The black dragon can steal her strength, but they are not intended to pair. She can resist Fènnù better than I. My skill is command, but command is a human thing, a weapon. Georgiana is song, the essence of draca themselves. She needs *that*." I turned to Mrs. Reynolds and Lucy. "Do either of you play?"

"The *pianoforte*?" Lucy exclaimed, aghast.

"I do," Mrs. Reynolds answered.

"Play something she knows." That was meaningless; the wyfe of song remembered every note she heard. "Something she knows from childhood."

Mrs. Reynolds took a seat at the keyboard, straightening her cuffs, her posture as proper as ever. "Her mother played this to her when she had bad dreams." She began, not a child's lullaby but an introspective, melodious baroque aria.

I sent a silent summons for draca. It reached the two firedrakes before being quashed by the shroud. "I summoned the drakes, but we need more draca."

"I will bring them," Darcy said. He ran out the doors even as the firedrakes arrived, winging cautiously in the building's interior. They settled by Georgiana, one on the floor, one perched on the back of the sofa. I shared a mental image of Georgiana singing but tiring, and they began to croon, not Fènnù's melody, but other tones... they had joined the music Mrs. Reynolds was playing. Georgiana heard; subtly she adapted her inner song so the rhythms and harmonies interleaved. Outside, a deeper tone added an inhuman basso, Yuánchi's own slow thrum.

Faintly, through the towering, double-paned windows, I heard a horse whinny. Hooves pounded away, galloping despite the dark.

"Where is he going?" Lucy asked.

I did not know, but I smiled for her sake. "Where he will find aid. He knows Pemberley better than anyone."

I took a seat by Georgiana and held her hand, lending reassurance if not strength, and her fingers tightened on mine. My draca senses shivered from the unseen battle, Fènnù pressing in and Georgiana resisting with song, although that was a shallow name for what surrounded her—it was the endless music of seasons, of intermeshed stars and planets. I remembered the nights she spent with her telescope, observing the motion of the heavens. "Help is coming," I whispered. "Hold on so we may go to Mary."

The drakes crooned over Yuánchi's deep pedal tones. Mrs. Reynolds reached the end of her piece and began again. Lucy, learning the melody, began to hum along.

The hooves returned and came nearer than the stables, somewhere in back of the main house. A door banged and hurried steps approached; Darcy had ridden to the conservatory entrance, a few rooms away. He burst into the music room with Aggy, one of the wyves from the Briton village. She held her roseworm, forest-brown and rich-red.

"More wyves are following," Darcy said. "Escalus outran them, but they will be here soon. What should we do?"

"Just... gather," I said to Aggy, who fell to her knees beside me, staring in dismay at Georgiana's drawn face. "Encourage him to sing," but her roseworm had already joined with a pure, bird-like tone that danced above the crooning drakes.

Two more bound wyves arrived, and the draca chorus grew. I closed my eyes and, unbidden, their vision replaced mine, the darkened music room lit in brilliant violet, our living bodies glowing with the warmth of life, Georgiana and I shining with the gold aura of great wyves. Georgiana's song flowed, buttressed by the draca, but Fènnù's shroud pressed down harder, as if mountains were being stacked on top. The sable cracks, remnants of Georgiana's resistance, began to seal, each thud like a closing tomb.

"I do not understand this fight," I whispered to Darcy. "It is too foreign. I do not know what to do."

He rested his hand atop mine and Georgiana's. "I called someone who will." Voices approached in the hall, and he shouted, "Edward! In here!"

Mr. Digweed, the gray-haired headman of Pemberley's Briton clans, hurried through the double doors, aided by his young son, Thomas. Mr. Digweed uttered one pained exclamation when he saw Georgiana, then he strode over. He felt her damp brow, his face grave.

"What see you, wyfe of war?" he asked me.

"Fènnù's shroud presses in on her. Her song holds it back, but she tires. I have been trying to aid her... my power is no use."

"*Teine eigin!*" he said, and I recognized the words from our Beltane wedding—make fire. Thomas ran to the fireplace and stoked it with wood, then blew at the banked coals until the smolder burst into flame.

Mr. Digweed moved to the head of the sofa and held Georgiana's hands high in his. "*Druí wide*, join us." The Britons held hands to form a circle with him, including Darcy and Lucy who had a deep connection to the Briton's faith. I hesitated, but at his nod, joined as well. Mrs. Reynolds continued to play.

Mr. Digweed began a gruff, melodic chant, words that felt as hoary as mossy oaks and as solid as bedrock. A tiny, glowing light flew into the room, then a flurry of them—little needledrac glowing in blues and greens despite the dark. They swirled around, dancing near the warmth of the fire and dodging in and out of our circle.

Georgiana drew a hard breath, then began to sing with her human voice— Fènnù's song. When I first heard those notes, they stabbed me like icy knives, but now it was part of something greater that shone like sunrise. In the world of draca, the song flared as blazing sapphire. The shroud twisted and tightened, a black iron vise struggling to contain it.

The windows rattled, then more violently. The thumping thunder of Fènnù's wings grew louder.

"Fènnù will not relinquish this power," I warned. "She will kill us all first."

Mr. Digweed bent to Georgiana, his voice almost lost in the strength of the chorus. "Daughter of Bel, beloved of Pemberley, scion of a great wyfe. Gather our song into yours. Sing. Proclaim yourself!"

The musicians, human and draca, reached a climax, then the disparate melodies resolved in a meeting of perfect, pure unison. I felt a crashing tear open in the shroud, then it split, folding away into itself like a punctured soap bubble. The darkness outside appeared to spatter with sparks, then beams of sunlight ended the false night.

Like a person waking from a nightmare, Georgiana flew up to sitting, her eyes wide. She reached to the window, to the south, and shouted, "Mary!" Everyone crowded around her, reassuring her.

Everyone but me. At last I could sense Fènnù—and her surging anger. Her malevolent presence looked down from on high, assessing tiny, fragile Pemberley, the shelter for a lost prize, a frustration she could blot out of existence. I ran through the conservatory, knocking treasured plants aside while summoning Yuánchi, hopelessly, to fight. But even a minute might draw the battle away from Pemberley and save the others.

Bursting out the conservatory doors, I entered the south garden. Fènnù's gaze penetrated me like an icy lance, but this time, her strength did not crush my mind. The brilliance of Georgiana's song was fading but not yet gone, and it held Fènnù's mind at bay, a fleeting advantage, one I could use.

But as Yuánchi winged in, steel-strong fingers grasped my arm. Georgiana, staggering, had half-dragged Darcy across the garden to catch me.

"Do not fight her," she said, her voice worn and cracked. "Do not drive her away. The pestilence is the enemy. Fènnù must be healed to cure it. We need her close."

Yuánchi landed at the garden's edge, furrowing the earth and obliterating decorative hedges in his blindness. But I looked another way, seeking the black dragon.

From the clouds, Fènnù dove on Pemberley. I no longer felt even the shards of her broken sanity. She had succumbed to fury.

*Stop!* I commanded with all my strength, but no human could command a dragon. Black darkened her wake as her breath primed. Out of time, I abandoned strength and reached for the memory of when our minds had merged in Scotland and I entered her abyss of despair and loneliness.

*Wait*, I called. *Wait until I join you.*

Her wings flared, braking her plummet, and she shot over Pemberley with a thump of wind that knocked slate tiles off the roofs. But that was all.

*My wyfe of war*, crooned in my mind.

"You commanded her," Darcy cried. "I knew it. You saved us." He pulled me against him, supporting Georgiana with his other arm.

I was not sure what I had done.

With daylight restored, I saw the garden properly. The hedges, the flowers, even the towering oaks were stained a lifeless gray. That leaden darkness extended to the hills, to all the forest in sight. Withered leaves were dropping, coating the ground with oily decomposition. Young, green branches softened, drooped, and spattered down as mush. The only growth that survived were the budding flowers and fruits. The rosebuds, poppies, even the green acorns were swelling, bloating with infestation.

Beyond sight, Fènnù coasted into a turn and began a patient circle. Not leaving. Waiting for me.

Georgiana's iron grip tightened on my arm. "We have not saved everyone. Take me to London. *Now*."

## 29

# THE MUSEUM

## MARY

"Mary," a woman's musical voice sang while a cracked cello buzzed and whined.

An ill-favored dream: Georgiana struggling, her slight body shrouded in frost-rimed music scores longer than bed sheets. I clawed at the freezing bonds, found I held a fistful of woolen blanket, and woke to blink owlishly at a hovering, blurred face. I felt for a nonexistent dressing table—no, not Pemberley—then retrieved my spectacles from the shelf above the bed and slipped them through my tangled hair.

Rebecca Spoon's pretty, serious face came into focus, a delicate twenty-two-year-old woman with wispy eyebrows and bones as fine as the clavichord music she composed.

"Did I startle you?" she said. "The maid would have done it better..." She gave a helpless shrug. Her maid had fled. "You said an hour of sleep, but I could not make you stir. Colonel Fremantle said to wait. It has been two hours."

The window behind glowed dull gray. I found my watch. Three o'clock in the afternoon.

Yesterday, the colonel and I walked until jammed refugees and sightings of Blackcoats forced us to detour eastward, finally entering London at Stratford. It was dark by then. The cobblestones were strewn with broken carts and luggage. The omnipresent nighttime poor fought over the abandoned goods while distant cannons rumbled and nearer gunshots barked. We ran, hid, and retreated until the morning light drove away the scavengers, then I spotted a familiar street and followed it west to Rebecca's residence, the Marys' emergency shelter in north London. Exhausted, we thumped on the door at noon, and Rebecca herself answered.

"Has your brother returned?" I asked now. This was his home; a single lady did not reside alone in London.

"No," she said, an awkward chirp as if she meant it lightly but her throat could not sustain the sound.

I had slept in my clothes, having nothing else, so I dragged a few knots from my hair and followed Rebecca into the parlor.

Colonel Fremantle, washed of the worst road dirt, was looking out another window. "Did it wake you?" he asked. "That infernal sound."

"The buzz? I only dreamed of it."

"Like nothing else on earth," he muttered. "A roaring whir like a monstrous machine. It means the perfumer has come. She is in London."

"*La Demoiselle des Parfums* has a machine?" Steam-powered machines were fiddly, heavy contraptions. They had ruined many honest professions, but I could not imagine machinery being useful in war.

"She is a demon, not a *demoiselle*, and I do not know what the roar is, only that it is unnatural. None who see her live to speak of it."

I rubbed sleep from my eyes. "More reason to reach the museum and be done with London."

"May I come?" Rebecca asked suddenly.

"You are safer here," I said.

"I do not think so. Robbers broke into the home beside us yesterday. My brother has been gone for two days. He said it would be an hour. Something horrible has happened, I know it. There are no markets, no food..."

Rebecca was one of the ladies of good family abducted last autumn by Tinsdale and his slaver allies. The slavers had sought a potent wyfe to raise the black dragon; Lizzy and I had rescued her but after vicious maltreatment. She was a brave woman and recited her litany without tears, but each word frayed some thinning restraint within her.

Feeling clumsy and a poor friend, I blurted, "Yes, you should come. But after the museum, we will need to plan. Perhaps another shelter house is staffed. I must return north with the flute, and the trip here was... I would not wish that on you."

She nodded, blinking, her arms crossed and her hands clutching her elbows.

Carrying valuables would draw thieves, so Rebecca fit a few coins and mementos in her reticule, then the three of us set out, sharing the last of a bag of stale cobnuts.

The streets, sparse of traffic before, were utterly deserted. A humid haze veiled spires and bridges, draping us in uncanny, pastoral calm. For luck, I whispered a line from Virgil, *"Incipe Maenalios mecum, mea tibia, versus"*—Flute, sing with me Maenalian songs. The loyal song draca flapped to my shoulder, a sapphire gleam in the city's grime. A handful more followed as we set off at a hurried walk toward the museum.

"It is good to be out," Rebecca said. Her imprisonment had been in a dark, sealed cellar. Since her rescue, she always proposed meeting under open sky, even when the weather was foul.

A half mile banished the illusory calm. Raucous ravens whirled as we entered a rundown district called Bagnigge Wells, the subject of futile and heated debates on civic improvement. The junction was a scene macabre. Eleven English soldiers lay in painful poses, their skin livid with death and picked at by the birds.

Colonel Fremantle muttered a prayer, the religious observance at odds with his angry tone. "I have seen this in the south. The perfumer's work."

"It is a large war," I said, kneeling by one of the bodies, a slender, fair-haired man. "She cannot be everywhere."

The colonel's head swiveled as muskets sounded to the south. "We should move. Ministering to the dead is a swift path to join them."

"I wish to know why they are dead. They were not shot." Rigor had peeled back the soldier's lips like he was shouting a final warning. Behind his rigid jaw, the exterior jugular vein bulged, distended and cyanotic. I lifted his collar and saw twin punctures an inch apart, the skin torn as if struck in passing. "A sting. This could have been any of the enemy with a captive wyfe to control crawlers." But the torn skin was unlike other stings I had seen.

"Or the perfumer," Colonel Fremantle repeated. Through the frenetic night, he had been collected and professional. Now he twitched at every sound. "She has killed hundreds. They say she is as beautiful as an angel, but under her clothes, she is half crawler and has pincers for hands."

This must be how myths begin. "Her hands are perfectly normal—"

"Mary, rise slowly," Rebecca said. "There is a crawler behind you."

Not at all slowly, I scrabbled to my feet. A thick-bodied crawler was squirming out from under one of the bodies. Its sharpened feet scraped for purchase while the soft, slug-like horns on its head extended to scent the air.

Colonel Fremantle drew his pistol, but I signaled to wait. "Too loud. Let me try something."

I took one of the syringes from my reticule, this time careful to remove every scrap of sealing wax. I squinted to aim and pressed the plunger. Draca essence splashed over the crawler's head and body, and it spasmed and curled into a heap.

We formed a cautious triangle, looking down at the shivering creature.

"What is that liquid?" the colonel asked.

"Draca essence. I have two left." I offered him one of the syringes, but he shook his head, patting the butt of his pistol. I gave it to Rebecca. "Break off the wax first." She examined the tip as if it were a novel embroidery needle.

Colonel Fremantle raised his boot and, before I could protest, crushed the crawler's head. Perhaps that was for the best. He would have argued if I said the crawler was blameless, a pathetic distortion of draca, while we were surrounded by the dead.

THE BRITISH MUSEUM was as still as the streets we had passed through, but the sounds of war were nearer, a more disciplined and deadly chorus than the cacophony of the night. The museum's main entrance was unattended, the doors ajar. The colonel, a gentleman even here, held them for us with a brief bow. The song draca flew away before I entered.

The museum's foyer, abandoned, felt even larger than usual. The ceilings were cavernous, the pillars looming.

"Where now?" the colonel asked, peering into the first, large exhibition room.

"I hoped to have help." Loudly, I called, "Is anyone here?"

There was a metallic, ringing *bong* followed by a man's dismayed exclamation. We headed that way and found a tremendously thin, young gentleman, one of the curators and the precise person I had hoped to meet. I was not surprised. He either worked day and night or lived here.

He looked up while snatching at a rolling brass pitcher on the floor. "Miss Bennet!" He straightened with a smile, then began brushing at the smears of heavy dust on his disarranged coat. He appeared to be packing the exhibit into a crate. "Whatever are you doing here?"

"I could ask the same thing. However, I am only happy you have stayed. Is there no one else?"

"They all left," he admitted. "A soldier came to say the French are close. But I am sure the Prince will send troops to protect the museum. He is very fond of the Egyptian collection." He noticed Colonel Fremantle's uniform. "Is that why you are here?"

"No," the colonel said. "The English army is stretched thin, and I have other duties. You should depart as well."

"Not yet," I interposed hurriedly. "First, I need your help." Inspired, I changed that to "The *Prince* needs your help. We must save not only the museum, but all England."

"Oh," the curator said, straightening his shoulders.

"You remember the museum ball, the night when the black dragon rose? You showed me notes for a lecture on the dagger Gramr. There was a catalog number..." I closed my eyes, visualizing the sheaf of papers in my hand. Images of pages flickered, most with the nondescript blur of material I had not actually read, but the drawing had caught my eye, and the caption beneath returned in a crisp, mental reconstruction of the curator's scholarly hand. "1756-1-3-17."

He nodded. "The Scottish flute. That is a museum number, not a catalog number. Although that particular classification is contested. The acquisition notes proposed moving it to the Sloan collection, as he was present on the expedition, but I am proposing the Asian collection—"

"Is it here?" I interrupted. "Can you take us to it? It is most urgent."

He rocked on his feet, thinking, then wandered off. I hurried after him, excitement lifting hairs on the nape of my neck, and Rebecca and the colonel followed. We passed through the public halls, several with exhibits that had been transferred to straw-lined crates, then through a narrow archway into an equally narrow corridor. A door marked *1750–1766* opened into a crowded storeroom. The curator stopped for a beat, then went to a stack of drawers and removed one, about the width and depth of my hand but long. He set it on a worktable.

"The Scottish flute," he announced.

The drawer held a blackened, round tube the length of my palm.

"You have the wrong drawer," I pointed out.

He examined the box. His finger tapped the round piece. "This is it."

"There was a drawing." The words felt awkward; my lips were dry. "An end-blown flute, like a recorder. Thirty inches long, at least."

He beamed. "My artistic rendering! That was for the laypersons at the ball." He took the blackened piece from the drawer. "I had to imagine the intact instrument, but the scholarship is sound. You can see the mouthpiece is end-blown, and made of a rare wood, black bamboo." He wagged a finger. "*Not* native to Scotland! Hence my recommendation to move this to the Asian collection. We are having a tussle over it, but scholars' arguments aside, it is a Chinese end-blown flute recovered in Scotland, which is what I drew. They call it a *xiāo*. The Chinese that is, not the Scots."

He offered the mouthpiece; I took it numbly. The wood was deeply charred in spots, smooth in others, and unusually dense. It had not been broken off a longer instrument; the bottom ended in a narrower joint intended to slip into another piece. Around the joint, a ring of symbols was inscribed. Mechanically, I rotated it in my fingers. Half the joint—half of the symbols—was burned away.

The top of the mouthpiece, where one would blow, was split. I could fit my little finger into the gap. Splinters pricked my skin.

Rebecca and the colonel had watched in silence. The colonel asked, "Could it be played? If one added a bottom tube."

No.

The curator *hmmed*. "I am not a musician, but it seems unlikely."

The mouthpiece was trembling violently, tied to my heart which pounded as if to flee my chest, every beat driving a pulse of pain in my temple. I had been so certain I had remembered something crucial.

I forced my hand still, turned the mouthpiece again, and touched the ring of symbols. "What are these? They are not Chinese characters."

"They are no known language. Decorations. The flute's design, however, is undoubtedly Chinese, a mouthpiece and body joined by an annulet. The acquirer noted the body was destroyed." The curator frowned at me. "Are you well, Miss Bennet? Shall I take your arm?"

"No, thank you," I replied, an automatic reflex. Men were obsessed with taking ladies' arms.

The symbols did not look decorative; they did not repeat in a pattern. They were systematic, distinct marks placed to follow rules. I concentrated, committing them to memory. The shapes were unfamiliar, but the rules teased at something...

I closed my fingers around the mouthpiece and held it up as if to play. The splintered gap pinched my lip.

I whispered, "I did not know it was damaged."

The feathery song draca whipped in through the open door. He circled the ceiling, then landed on my shoulder with a strident *cheep*.

The curator's mouth fell open. He bent until his nose almost touched the song draca's scaled muzzle. "You have a hitherto undocumented breed of draca on your shoulder."

More song draca swarmed in. They settled on boxes and drawer handles, filling the room with flutters and alarmed churrs. The curator turned a full circle of amazement. He finished staring at me.

"May I take this?" I asked, holding up the mouthpiece.

"To save England?" he whispered. His eyes were wide.

I licked my dry lips, wishing to say *Yes*, wishing to believe that this ruined remnant mattered, but logic forbade the word. *Yes* rationalized an error, rationalized my choice to pursue this wasteful quest that endangered myself and others. *Yes* rationalized abandoning Georgiana. The pounding in my temple grew to a painful buzz.

Do not invent another self-aggrandizing delusion. Once was enough. Do what you are best at. Be literal. Be accurate. The flute is worthless.

The colonel was shaking my shoulder. Startled, I looked at him, and he shouted, "We must run! Do you not *hear*?"

The painful buzz in my temple was a deep, chopping whir. Low pitched enough to penetrate the walls of the museum. I felt it in my toes. Drawers were clattering in sympathetic resonance.

The colonel yanked Rebecca and me out the door. The curator refused, shaking his head and beginning some explanation. We abandoned him. The song draca—frightened, I realized at last—churned before and behind.

We reached the main exhibit hall, and the terrible whir ceased. In the hush, the colonel cried, "Which way was it?" Rebecca and I shook our heads. It had seemed to come from every side. He ran to the main doors and checked outside, then summoned us.

We hurried down the steps, the song draca skimming so close they made my hair float. They soared high over the courtyard, a large, paved square bounded on three sides by the museum's main and side halls. So large, I did not at first notice the slim figure on the far side.

I saw her and stopped. Rebecca and the colonel looked back at me, then saw her as well.

*La Demoiselle des Parfums* had abandoned her token disguise of English clothes. She wore an emerald gown of satin brocade, the collar raised, the bodice cut in the French silhouette that had driven English waistlines high. Her neckline was French too, lacy and lower than an English lady would choose. Thirty yards away, she stood alone, elegant and incongruous. She smiled at me beneath her sweeping bonnet, the broad smile one uses to be visible at a distance, and started toward us.

"A friend?" Colonel Fremantle asked. He did not know her. A soldier might imagine a lethal woman, a temptress betrayed by pincer hands. It was another matter for a gentleman to meet a lady whose every tailored seam and refined pose announced her aristocracy.

"Mademoiselle Bennet," she called from twenty yards as I said, "The perfumer."

The colonel yanked his pistol from his holster, cocking the hammer with a sweep of his left palm while he raised it to arm's length, sighting down the barrel.

Behind us, a high-pitched tone like the biting insects of the Thames marsh sharpened to a braying whip. It stopped with a sodden thud, and the colonel's head snapped forward. He toppled, sprawling across the hard paving stones, the pistol clattering away. The back of his head was collapsed in bloody ruin. Shell-like fragments protruded, and four ripped, translucent wings quivered at crooked angles, ten or twelve inches long. He had been struck by a flying crawler, kin to the swarm that attacked Georgiana and me at Pemberley but bigger and bullet-swift.

Rebecca grabbed my wrist with the strength of shock. My medical training, that bloody gauntlet of surgical amputations and childbirths, slammed into place, suspending my bodily reflexes—do not vomit; do not faint—even while mourning and panic overwhelmed my thoughts.

The perfumer had not broken stride. She stopped four steps away. Cloying citrus and musk spilled through the air. She frowned at the colonel's body. "*Quel dommage.* I do not like to lose the flying ones, but your soldier was quick, and a sting is..." She waved a satin-gloved finger, hunting for words, then settled for, "not quick."

"*Salope,*" I enunciated carefully, an obscenity I had never heard, only read in one of Georgiana's cheaply printed French novels.

The perfumer tapped her palms together, an ironic clap muted by cloth. "*Bon français!* But we are told always how English ladies are polite." She looked past me at the museum doors. "The Great Wyfe visits the great museum. Why?"

I did not answer. Wild thoughts raced. Run—but Rebecca was petrified. Fight—but I had no concept how one fought. The pistol lay a few steps away. The hammer had closed, but it had not fired. I did not understand the mechanism well enough to know if it could be reset.

And the perfumer had killed a skilled soldier. Effortlessly. In a heartbeat.

"What is in your hand?" she asked, and pointed to the flute's mouthpiece, clutched and forgotten. Childishly, I moved it behind my back. She arched an eyebrow. "I think we visit for the same reason."

French soldiers were entering the courtyard, running single file in the concealing shadow of the west wing. More. Twenty. Thirty. An officer marched to the perfumer, stopping uneasily some distance away as if afraid of her scent.

"*Cherchez à l'intérieur*," she told him.

"Do not harm the curator," I said. "He knows nothing."

The perfumer watched as the officer selected four men. They propped the museum doors wide and ran inside. The officer shouted flamboyant commands after them, a performance that allowed him to put several more steps between himself and the perfumer.

Be literal. Be accurate. The flute is worthless. I held it out to her. "I found the flute. You may have it."

Strangely, that made her suspicious. She angled her chin toward Rebecca. "*Qui est-elle?*" Who is she?

"A friend," I said. "I am helping her leave the city."

Rebecca released my arm. I hazarded a look, and our gazes met. Her eyes narrowed as if to convey some message, but I had no idea what.

The perfumer took two steps closer, toes in line like a dancer. At the limit of our combined reach, she stretched out her hand. I passed the mouthpiece to her. She retreated and examined it, nose wrinkling when charcoal marked her glove.

She shook her head. "*Non.*"

"It is the flute," I said. "All that remains. *Il n'y en a plus.*" There is no more.

She displayed the split end, the charring. "The Emperor will not accept this." She shrugged and slipped the mouthpiece into a pocket of her gown. "That is sad. I need a proper gift. A gift that ensures victory. A great gift."

She sank her hand in another pocket and tossed something on the ground

—a handful of wriggling, finger-length crawlers. They scurried aimlessly. After so many monsters, common crawlers seemed a trifle, but that was foolish. The smallest crawler was lethal.

"The Emperor learned much from your Lydia's books," she continued. "He orders that the great wyves never unite. So, I see my great gift. The death of a Great Wyfe."

The crawlers skittered forward.

The artificial calm of my medical training had held. My fine muscles were relaxed, what Dr. Davenport called surgeon's focus. I pursed my lips and whistled the summoning song. Beside me, Rebecca was desperately scraping the sealing wax from her syringe of draca essence—she must have had it ready in her hand—but faster yet, the song draca arrived, streaming between us and the perfumer like a sparkling brook, singing harmony to my melody while their blue fire snapped, burning the crawlers to smoldering crisps.

The song draca spiraled up, an airborne flock of shimmering aquamarine and sapphire. The loyal one assumed his perch on my shoulder.

The perfumer watched with professional interest and a certain grudging respect. "*Les presages. Vous êtes devenue une grande sorcière.*"

"I am no sorceress."

"Then your songbirds will not save you."

Rebecca shouted a grating, female battle cry and raised her syringe like a warrior's crossbow. Draca essence squirted twelve feet, dousing the perfumer's face and soaking the bodice of her gown.

The perfumer made a disgusted grimace. She wiped her face, smearing inky kohl and red lip paint, then looked at her luridly discolored gloves. "*Merde.*"

A discordant whine began around the courtyard. The French officer, who had sidled even farther away, turned and ran. His men followed.

The whine rose to a throb, and Rebecca took an uncertain step closer to me. An insectile shape blurred between us, and she clapped her fingers to her neck. She drew them away, puzzled, then showed me her bloody fingertips. "Mary?"

She could not see the twin stings on her neck. "It is nothing," I said. Dr. Davenport also taught when to lie.

The whine crescendoed. The flock of song draca seemed to wilt, finding perches on the walls or settling on the ground. The loyal one on my shoulder tucked his wings and hunkered down.

*Defend us*, I thought, imagining Lizzy commanding draca. I stared at the perfumer, trying to push my thoughts into the flock of song draca. *Swarm her. Immolate her.*

Rebecca wobbled. Very carefully she knelt, hands fumbling unsteadily for the ground. Without a sound, she rolled onto her side.

Tears drowned my vision. My useless concentration broke. I was no wyfe of war, no avenging Lizzy. But as my anger hollowed to grief, my skidding, disjointed thoughts found a focus. The summoning song, that first composition over which I toiled for months, became a trifle from a vaster whole, like the ditty of a child that shares harmonies with a grand symphony. For the first time, for a moment, I glimpsed a path to the celestial music of Georgiana's song.

A song draca fluttered. Another trilled. A few took to the air.

"*Non*," the perfumer said and raised her hand.

Flying crawlers erupted, a storm that darkened the air. Amid the howl, I saw one clearly, its ten-inch segmented body sheathed in gleaming olive shell, the pairs of translucent oval wings buzzing, twin stingers flexing as it sprayed. The burned, sour citrus of crawler venom saturated the air, and the song draca tumbled from my shoulder.

Something grooved and hard clouted my temple, bending my spectacles and cutting my ear. A sunburst of pain whitened my vision. Another smacked my shoulder, knocking me off balance. Not stings—these were blows, hard as stones. I cried out, arms shielding my face as they rained in. I collapsed and huddled on the ground beside Rebecca.

The assault ended. The winged crawlers settled on the ground, seething over and under one another. Among them, song draca lay at stiff angles, unmoving.

The perfumer's gown swayed as she threaded a path to me. Her shoes were as emerald as her gown. She removed her gloves and bent to examine me. "And so, the Great Wyfe dies."

My belly spasmed—absurdly, I was laughing. I huffed until I could speak. "You think a great wyfe dies like *this*? You have no concept of a great wyfe. I am an afterthought, a nobody. You will know when you meet a great wyfe, for you will be crushed." I pried my bent spectacles straighter, wincing as the frame uncoupled from my bloody ear, but I wanted to see her one last time. "My sister will hunt you, and she will *burn* you."

The perfumer was still for a long time, one oily, anointed fingertip touching her lips as if preparing to share a secret. Then she walked away. The huge, low-pitched buzz we heard inside the museum returned, and a monstrous crawler, stout as a bumblebee and longer than a horse, entered the courtyard. It hovered on blurring wings, blasting a gale in every direction, then settled. The perfumer climbed onto it—it was saddled—and they rose into the air. The sea of flying crawlers around me flew after her like a swarm of locusts.

Beaten muscles shivering, I dragged myself across the rough paving stones. Rebecca was unresponsive but alive, lungs snatching air in shuddering gasps, heart racing and weakening. My fingers were too weak to break the wax on the final syringe, but my teeth stripped it. I dripped draca essence into her mouth, stroked her throat until she swallowed, then gave her another dose, and another. The final teaspoon I emptied into my palm and worked into the bloody stings on her neck.

Her eyelids fluttered. She groaned. Her fingers pushed my hand away from the swollen skin. Good. Excellent.

I lay back, sky spinning, and imagined I heard dragon wings.

# 30

## MRS. GODDARD'S SCHOOL

### EMMA

Mr. Knightley, Harriet, and I were hiding in the overgrown back of Highbury square, our shoes squelching in the spring-fed earth but the rest of us nicely concealed by waist-high bracken and dangling branches from the square's white willow. We had a good view along Broadway, Highbury's main street. It was a large street, wide enough for two coaches to pass but perilously crowded with French and Confederate troops.

"There were fewer soldiers before," Mr. Knightley said grimly.

"Why so many?" I wondered. There were senior officers among the French, or at least officers with very elaborate uniforms. The Confederate coats and caps were, by comparison, dull gray and rather dirty. The two groups eyed each other with distrust.

Harriet blew a frustrated sigh. "The amulet is right inside! Mrs. Goddard sent me my clothes after I left, but I did not trust the post to carry gold. I wish I had known sooner. We could have called on her and collected it over tea."

Mrs. Goddard lived in a three-story country home that had been in her family for generations. She was widowed young, and being an enterprising sort, she had the bedrooms partitioned and the drawing room and parlor merged into a teaching room. It was a successful school, boarding and educating girls aged twelve to seventeen from several parishes. A handful of unmarried young ladies, ex-students like Harriet, lived there as well to assist instruction and shepherd girls to and fro.

From Highbury square to the school's front door was perhaps fifty yards, but twenty soldiers milled on that path.

Harriet straightened resolutely. "In London, you said their kind cannot impede proper ladies."

"I was referring to some pro-slaver louts," I said, "not soldiers."

"But look." She pointed to a pair of Mrs. Goddard's students, girls of fifteen, being escorted through the confusion by a French soldier. He opened the door to the school, the girls entered, and he returned to his troop.

"They went in. They did not come *out*," Mr. Knightley noted.

"If I can get in, I know a way out the back," Harriet said. "Waiting and watching will only make it worse. Soldiers keep coming."

Mr. Knightley shook his head, his lips pressed bloodless. "It is exceedingly dangerous."

"Harriet is right," I decided. "It will only get worse. And I must go with her."

Mr. Knightley turned to me, the foliage dabbing light on his black hair. I expected him to protest, perhaps even attempt to impose husbandly authority. Instead, his features were tight with worry. That damaged my resolve far more than any argument.

"Why you as well?" he asked finally.

"The students travel in pairs," I said firmly to hide my misgivings. "And the slavers will harass Harriet if she is alone."

"You cannot pass for a student. Not even a boarder. You are too—" His mouth started to shape "old" but he switched to "elegant" instead.

Oddly, that little kindness restored my confidence. "My advanced 'elegance' aside," I said dryly, "the soldiers, the French at least, are professionals. They seem to be gentlemen, or whatever a French gentleman is called. If Harriet and I walk with assurance and say we are returning home, they will let us pass. What else could they do? Send us away? Shoot us?" I could not help adding, "And I am only four years older than Harriet."

He held out his hand. I took it, and his thumb stroked my skin. I felt the muscles work in his palm and fought a blush. The physical aspects of marriage had been bursting into my thoughts at inopportune times.

"Our quest for the amulet is supposition," he said. "We have no idea if it still matters. But we do know the enemy has gathered here. That is an opportunity. If they have deserted the countryside, we can slip away."

"We came for the amulet. What if it helps end the war? Ends *this*?" I gestured to the foreign troops occupying lovely Highbury. "Besides, I promised I would find it. Wyves have duties and honor, just like husbands."

Reluctantly, he smiled. "Then be cautious. Do not tarry. I will keep watch." He picked up the long wooden case he had retrieved when he went for his violin, the Baker rifle given to him by Mr. Darcy. I could not imagine what good it would do. "If you cannot safely return here..."

"Meet us at the Westons," I suggested. "The others are there. Their estate is Randalls, on the way to Hartfield." He nodded.

Harriet and I checked each other to ensure we were presentable. I fixed her bonnet with a flick of a finger; it only needed a few stray willow leaves removed. For some reason my efficiency amused her, and she made an elaborate show of shaping every crease on mine before grinning her most buoyant grin. "It is a fine afternoon, Mrs. Knightley. Shall we call on Mrs. Goddard?"

We set out along the street as if returning from an afternoon lark. Soldiers' faces turned, whiskered and bearded in foreign fashions. The Confederate troops eyed us, their gazes on Harriet.

"Swiftly," I whispered to her through a smile. We were halfway already.

Twenty steps from the door, a French soldier stepped into our path. In a thick accent, he said, "Halt. Who are you?"

"Miss Smith," Harriet blinked at him with immense innocence. "We are returning to the school, and I am sorry to say, we are very late. Are you having a parade?" I thought that was overplayed, but he looked us over and wordlessly gestured to proceed. He followed us to the door and rapped sharply.

It was opened by an Overseer, one I had never seen, a compact, scrabble-faced man with pronounced cheekbones. Brusquely, he directed us inside. That was frightening, but Harriet, unflinching, curtsied and turned to the staircase to the boarding rooms.

The Overseer held out his arm, blocking her. He pointed down the hall to the teaching room. "That way."

That was one too many complications. Harriet cast me a frightened glance that loudly announced—*wrong direction*.

"We have been walking for hours," I said. His unshaven chin swung to scowl at me. Not knowing how decorous American ladies communicated this, I bounced on my toes with a slightly desperate expression.

He rolled his eyes. "Hurry up."

We fairly raced up the stairs, which I suppose aided the pretense. At the top, we ducked around the corner, and Harriet thumped back against the wall. "I thought we were done," she whispered.

"Not yet," I said.

She shook herself and set off, passing the boarding rooms, attractively decorated despite tiny windows and the folding partitions that crowded the beds. We climbed more stairs to the top floor. Harriet touched a door as we passed—"My old room"—then stopped at a bigger door at the end of the hall. It had a simple painted sign, *School Mistress.*

Harriet knocked. Stillness. Behind us, a man's voice was dimly audible, rising through the stairwells from the bottom floor. Or so I hoped. The cadence of the voice seemed familiar.

Harriet's knuckles hovered over the door, unsure whether to knock again.

"Just go in," I said.

She gave me a scandalized look. "It is Mrs. Goddard's room!"

I tried the doorknob, and the door opened. Harriet took a big breath and strode forward. I closed the door behind us.

It was a lady's bedroom, with a pleasant bed nicely finished with a yellow lace cover. A dark-lacquered armoire stood beside a matched dressing table with a looking glass, brushes, and other feminine items. There was a wooden chair and a cedar wardrobe chest.

Harriet considered. "She kept a box for valuables for each of us, and she retrieved them from her room, so they are here somewhere. But I hate to search."

I did not think a lady would keep boarders' belongings in her wardrobe or armoire. "What about there?" One corner had a narrow, almost invisible door, the sort used for servant passages. We tugged it open and found a storage room lined with shelves.

"This is it," Harriet said immediately. She ran her fingers along a row of identical birchwood boxes, each large enough for a pair of shoes. They had handwritten labels in brass holders. She found one marked *Harriet Smith* and offered it to me.

"It is yours," I said.

"Take the lid off, at least," she said nervously, so I did.

The light was dim, but the amulet's gold chain caught a faint gleam. In the center, an oval of scarlet seemed to glow.

"Is it the right one?" Harriet asked.

The color was unmistakable, exactly Yuánchi's glorious fire. But this artifact was made for the wyfe of healing. Mary had thought I would sense it or feel affinity to it. I felt nothing. I saw nothing, not the immaterial streaks that revealed bindings, not the diseased fantasy of the miasma.

I removed my gloves and lifted it by the chain. It spun, the jade whorls on the setting exactly like the drawing the French officer showed me. "It is what the French sought at Hartfield." I stopped the spin with a finger on the jade, then touched my thumb to the scarlet—

*I SAW three great wyves crowned in shining auras of gold. They wore ceremonial, thick-soled sandals. Their wraps of silk were radiant with silver thread and pearls. They waited on a lakeshore of white pebbles fouled with streaks of black wrack where the poisoned waves washed.*

*The first wyfe's outstretched arm held a gleaming black dagger. The second's raised hand held an amulet that shimmered scarlet. The third stood simply, her empty hands spread and welcoming.*

*From the wyfe with the amulet, the wyfe of healing, Yuánchi's scarlet binding stretched.*

*From the empty-handed wyfe, the wyfe of song, a dazzling sapphire glow spread. The wyfe with the dagger, the wyfe of war, was unbound.*

*The wyfe of war raised the dagger and slashed her bared forearm. The bloodied blade smoked, and a summons formed, an immense black ribbon seeking the sky. The wyves sang music, ancient and inhuman, and the summons rose like a ship's unfurrowing sail.*

*The summons snapped taut. Rhythmic thunder hastened the surf, then blackness shrouded the sun. The singers' voices cracked and strained, and I felt the wyfe of healing exert her power. She reached up along that ribbon, drawing forth from the black dragon a black binding...*

*The ribbon of summoning shivered, tore, and blackness drowned them all.*

*Seasons revolved.*

*Centuries spun.*

*My vision flew from the past to mere days ago.*

*Again, I stood in the cellar of Donwell Abbey, which glowed a pretty blue.*

*Again, I saw the flicker of blue under the plants on Berry Hill. Not just blue: the saturated sapphire purity that had surrounded the wyfe of song.*

*But in all directions, as near as a mile, as far as hundreds, blight spawned, a spreading rot, a fruiting pestilence ripe for release...*

"Is it the right one?" Harriet repeated. She peered into my eyes. "Emma?"

"It is. We have it." My mind was overfilled with images; my eyes brimmed with tears. I blinked both away. "At Pemberley, we saw a vision of ancient wyves attempting to heal the song. I just saw it again, but I understand more. A great wyfe must *bind* Fènnù. That is the purpose of the great items, how they can heal her mind and heal the song. That is why, when the great wyves attempted the ritual, they were not all bound. It was not an error or a weakness. It was necessary."

The wyfe of war had been unbound. But the wyfe of song... I had thought her bound before, but the sapphire glow did not reach outward, it only surrounded her...

Harriet was excited. "Is that why *you* did not bind?"

The idea of binding Fènnù, that insane colossus of destruction, made my skin prickle. "I hope not. I know only that Fènnù must be bound, and soon. The blight is seeded across England like a plague, and every rotting cancer is tied to the corruption of the song."

"Georgiana has been saying that for ages," Harriet noted matter-of-factly. "We should go. The way out is on the middle floor."

I put the amulet in my reticule. We replaced Harriet's emptied box on the shelf and closed the doors before hurrying down the stairs. But the Overseer was on the middle landing, fuming. He ignored our protests and herded us down to the first floor, then pointed toward the teaching room. "Get along."

Harriet gave me a tense shrug. We would have to brazen it out.

The teaching room had tea-colored walls and undersized windows. There was no sign of Mrs. Goddard, but it was filled with a score of her older students and boarders, all standing and whispering. One exclaimed "Harriet!" when we entered, and heads spun. Harriet signaled for caution. Swiftly, everyone turned away. Too swiftly. It was as if they knew we were in danger.

Harriet and I had just found the farthest, most gloomy corner when a man's voice reached us from the hallway. "Skillful is the hand that reforms England!"

That was the voice I had recognized—Mr. Elton. I could not imagine a more detestable person to encounter again, as much for his maltreatment of his wyfe as his violence toward me.

While I bristled, Harriet snatched two of the school's riding hoods from pegs on the wall. She thrust one at me. Of course; Mr. Elton would recognize us at a glance. I pulled mine on and followed her example by tugging the hood forward to hide my face. Mrs. Goddard's practical philosophy helped. She had added beds for paid boarders, not luxuries like modern windows or good lamps.

Men strode in: Mr. Elton, looking intense and self-important, and two Overseers, the one we had just met and another, haughty with a bushy beard, his dark gray coat made of leather.

Mr. Elton adopted what I thought of as his greeting smile, the beatific stretching of his lips he assumed while his congregation filed in for services. I had witnessed that in worse circumstances while trapped in his coach, and it made my skin crawl.

"*Such* an assembly of young ladies," he said. "You do your mistress proud." His gaze roamed over the women and stopped on Harriet and me, draped as if for a long walk.

"Where is Mrs. Goddard?" a girl asked bravely. "We have not seen her for days."

His gaze moved to her. "Mrs. Goddard. Exactly so. She is preparing a celebration, a testament to your education and piety. We shall join her, humbly, to serve the great, restored True Church, and I have not a doubt of our success."

He gestured toward the door, and I saw my brother-in-law, John, watching from the threshold. He seemed unwilling to enter. His pompous confidence had shattered. His face was sweaty, his chin and jowls loose.

Mr. Elton called to him solicitously, "Have you a report from Mrs. Goddard?" John seemed confused; his features contorted, and he did not answer. Impatiently, Mr. Elton snapped, "Have you prepared the *house*?"

John dithered, eyed the Overseers, then abruptly he stumbled back and left. I heard his hurrying feet, then the school's door open and slam.

Mr. Elton scowled but recovered. He spread his arms rapturously to encompass us all. "The True Church ascends, and through His divine foresight, Highbury shall be the temple of His triumph. Two hundred years past, a witch made her home here—the Witch of *Woodhouse*." He crouched theatrically, as if expecting childish *oohs*, but the audience was quiet as death. Irritated, he resumed, spitting his words, "Her vile influence has dogged our families for generations, spurring disrespect from wyves, inducing rebellion against fathers and brothers, even... even against *husbands*, those selfless men who enforce the strictest virtues while battling... while *betrayed* by their... by female..." He stopped, shoulders heaving, then forced a measured tone. "Rejoice, for from the witch's ancient sin comes salvation. The Witch of Woodhouse unearthed a foulness in Highbury, and the Emperor himself comes to purge it. We shall bear witness as that blasphemous seraphim is cleansed!"

That grand finish was met with echoing silence. Mr. Elton's lips worked wetly, then he stamped away, leading the Overseers out of the room.

A pair of soldiers drove us after them. Soldiers blocked the other paths—the stairs, a hallway to the rear of the house. In seconds we were all outside in the street.

Mr. Elton began a grotesque inventory, greeting each girl by name with an insipid smile and sending them to form a line.

"We have to run," Harriet said in a panicked whisper. Our disguises would never survive close inspection.

"They would catch us," I whispered. There were soldiers on every side. "Stand so that Mr. Elton cannot see me..."

I turned to the square where we had hidden with Mr. Knightley. *Please be watching.* Harriet, her robed back to Mr. Elton, set her shoulders wide and head high to block his view. Then I pulled my hood down and stared, still as a statue, at the concealing willow trees and ferns, willing that Mr. Knightley would see me exposed and understand...

"What are you doing?" Harriet hissed frantically.

"Requesting a distraction."

Orange flashed in the leaves, and a *crack* cut the air over our heads. The blast of a powerful rifle filled the street. The soldiers, French and Confederate both, scattered instantly leaving the students and Mr. Elton gaping in surprise. I grabbed Harriet's sleeve and ran the one direction the soldiers had not, yanking open the school's door and dashing up the stairs. "Where is the way out?"

"Here," Harriet said, taking the lead, and we ran down a hall into a small reading room at the rear of the house. She strained at the window. I grabbed it as well, and the sash flew up with a *bang*. Harriet swung a leg out. She grabbed my hands, "Steady me!" then got her other leg out and wiggled backward. Her hips caught in the narrow window, but she twisted and made it through.

"Come on!" she called softly from outside. She was crouched on a mildly sloped roof.

"I expected a door!" I said. She gave me a look, so I hitched up my skirt and repeated the ungainly process. Having no one inside to balance me, I teetered awkwardly, Harriet outside tugging my legs while I scrabbled for purchase on the floor and window frame until I wiggled out.

Harriet slid the window closed, frowning and rubbing her hip. "I was littler the last time I did that."

I looked over the roof's edge. The school had no grounds, so the rear faced another house's garden. Past that, it would be woods and farmland with a hundred places to hide. "Do we jump?" I asked. We were ten feet above the uncut grass, but I had never crawled through a window before. Jumping ten feet might be possible, too.

Harriet, though, shook her head and stepped carefully toward the edge. A graceful maple grew nearby, and a thick branch passed beside the roof. She hugged it, shimmied off the shingles, then dangled from her stretched arms and let go, falling the last few feet. I did the same. My grip slipped and I crashed down inelegantly but unhurt.

Muted by the tall house, we could hear the ruckus of shouts in the front street. A gun fired, and I was suddenly, painfully terrified for my husband.

Harriet caught my shoulders—I had turned to go back—and held me firmly. "Do not worry. Mr. Knightley sneaks around armies all the time. He is an adventurer. They never catch him."

I nodded, trying to imagine him grinning and regaling us with stories of troops running the wrong way.

"What was all that nonsense about blasphemous seraphim?" she asked.

That was likely to distract me, but the question was important. I had thought about it while Mr. Elton ranted.

"Queen Mary sent the amulet to the Witch of Woodhouse," I said. "You remember in the square it says '*the Witch of Woodhouse did scrye for the Queen Mary, and great magicks of draca were born*'."

"I thought the magic was the amulet."

I shook my head. "The amulet was given to her. I think my great—I am not sure how many 'greats'—grandmother, the 'Witch,' used the amulet to find something at Donwell Abbey. Something serpentine and winged and fiery. The sapphire dragon of song."

Harriet's jaw dropped. "Are you joking?"

"Not joking, but not sure, either. We must find out. I saw the glow when we were there, I just did not recognize it. But I saw it again in the vision. If there is a dragon of song, Georgiana and Mary must be told."

"So, what now? To the Abbey?"

"That comes last. First to the Westons, to meet Mr. Knightley, and then to Hartfield. Mr. Elton is taking the girls there. He will bind them to the crawlers that John bred." A reckless resolve filled me. I would not run and let him hurt more women. "We must save them."

# THE RESCUE

## MARY

"Mary!" a woman's musical voice insisted, again.

"Let me sleep," I muttered. This time, when I woke in Rebecca's room I would reach up and find my spectacles on the first try. The colonel would be well and waiting, and we would... no, we already went to the museum...

Cool, slim fingers stroked my forehead, my temples.

"Ow," I protested as pain lanced my ear.

Gentle arms slipped around me and hugged me. Disheveled hair scented of Georgiana flooded my cheeks and nostrils.

Painfully I got my arms around her and held tight. "Help me up." Strange sparks pinged across my vision. Pain flared in bruised joints and muscles.

A man's sturdy grip steadied my elbow, and Mr. Darcy said, "Is she well enough to stand?"

"Yes," I answered for myself, forcing sticky eyelids apart and getting my feet under me. Some residue of panic made me bat away the helping hands. The unseen touches were too like swarming crawlers.

Rebecca was sitting on the courtyard paving stones, hugging her bent legs and resting her forehead on her knees. I knelt by her to check her pulse and pupils, but when I asked her to count my fingers, she protested, "Enough, Mary. I feel better every minute. We are far more worried about you."

Her neck had been bandaged, a neat job with a pad of muslin secured by a torn strip of very fine white cloth. I touched it to check the tension, and the curator's long, lean form crouched down on the other side of Rebecca. "I took the liberty, Miss Bennet. There was no one else to help, at first. Is it satisfactory?"

"Very good. The French let you go?"

He sniffed. "Hardly. They never saw me. It is difficult enough to find cataloged items, and those stay in place. An animate object seeking obscurity is quite unrecoverable." His expression turned grave. "I am no doctor, but the soldier seemed past help."

I nodded; Colonel Fremantle had died instantly. His body was covered with a large swath of the same white cloth, probably something the museum used to wrap artifacts. I had an incongruous, sad flash of him telling the story of his lost Spanish beauty.

Song draca were scattered on the stones, their feathered wings ragged in death. Some looked crushed. Others lay in puddles of golden ichor, their scales ripped. There were not too many dead, not all who came, but it was a horrible toll.

Georgiana's fingers, cautiously, returned to my shoulder. Now her caress felt wonderful, an anchor. I rested my cheek on her fingers then stood, sorting too few facts into too long a gap. "How did you get here?" She was dressed oddly, a sturdy wool redingote thrown over her stunning but thin red silk *qípáo*.

"Yuánchi flew us," she said. "Lizzy is off with him, scouring the area. Miss Spoon told us of *la Demoiselle des Parfums*. Lizzy is... very angry." Her last words were raw with apprehension.

"Call her back," Mr. Darcy said to me. I peered at him through my crooked spectacles, and he added, "You can speak to Yuánchi. Call Elizabeth back. She needs to know you are well. I fear she will fall into darkness."

I had heard Yuánchi's voice before, but that had been his strength reaching to me, not something I initiated. Still, I surveyed the sky and the museum courtyard around us.

There were draca everywhere. Tough broccworms and lindworms guarded the entrances to the courtyard. A bronze-toned firedrake I had never seen before perched watchfully on the peak of the museum's roof. At least a dozen draca of smaller breeds were running about or stationed in a rough ring around us. More guards. I recognized this surfeit of creatures from an earlier London adventure. Lizzy had sent a mass summons.

Another firedrake, one of the cream ones that guided Yuánchi, was aloft and circling. I raised my arm and waved until she dipped her wings in recognition. "Lizzy has seen me." There was no further sign until, with the explosive suddenness of a hunting hawk, Yuánchi's scarlet wings burst over the museum. He pounded down in the courtyard with a ground-shaking thump. Lizzy ran over and swept me into an embrace before I could utter "Be gentle," so I gritted my teeth and ignored protesting bruises for a sisterly reunion.

"I cannot find the perfumer," Lizzy said immediately when she let go, her tone reminiscent of Lord Wellington's curt, military manner. "I have searched two miles in all directions. French troops are falling back southward, a vanguard that had advanced to here, but there is no woman with them. She may have hidden in a building—"

"You will not find her," I said. "She flew away on a giant, winged crawler." I squinted at Yuánchi's hulking mass. "Relatively giant. Large enough to saddle and ride."

"Where are they finding these massive crawlers?" Mr. Darcy asked.

I thought that was rhetorical, so I moved to more urgent topics. "The flute is destroyed. The museum had a remnant, the mouthpiece, all that survived. Even that was split and half burned."

"I know," Lizzy said, subdued.

Mr. Darcy, though, straightened. "You *saw* the flute?"

"What is left. I held the mouthpiece. The perfumer took it, but it was useless."

"Half burned, how?" he pressed.

This was the curator's field of expertise, and he enthusiastically claimed it. "The flute was recovered while excavating a funeral pyre in the Highlands. Black bamboo is dense and slow to burn, but I believe the mouthpiece was partially shielded from the heat, perhaps even by the fingers of the poor soul—"

"The great artifacts were fashioned from fang, scale, and claw," Mr. Darcy said. "The flute is claw, not bamboo. Dragon claw does not burn in mundane fire."

That was an excellent point, and it made me puzzle over another question. "The flute could never have been a claw. Dragon claw is harder than steel. It is one thing to mount a hilt on a tooth to create a dagger, but how could one fashion a tube? How could one drill the fingering holes?"

"As early as the sixth century," the curator noted eagerly, "Indian texts refer to the use of diamond dust to polish gems. Like can cut like. Another dragon claw, or perhaps a tooth, could shape it."

I was finding his pedantic tone annoying. "Fashioning a flute is not polishing a gem. The main body is over twenty inches, and draca claws curve. Imagine a drill—"

"If it was worthless, why did the perfumer take it?" Lizzy interrupted.

I closed my eyes and watched again as the perfumer pocketed it with a shrug. "A whim. She did not attribute value to it. She sought a gift to impress Napoleon, one that would ensure his victory in the war. When she saw the flute was destroyed, she chose a different gift—my death. Napoleon ordered that the great wyves must never unite. The death of a great wyfe ensures that."

"Bonaparte fears the united wyves," Mr. Darcy said softly.

Georgiana, stricken, took my hand. "I should not have let you leave Pemberley."

"I recall insisting," I reminded her. "It was bad luck that the perfumer had heard Londoners call me 'Great Wyfe.' She interpreted it literally."

That made me remember the sublime music which, briefly, I had seemed to comprehend. With my fingers laced with Georgiana's, I concentrated, seeking that perfection. Fragments of that tower of song returned, but it was again vast beyond perception, a celestial chorus cloaked from mortal eyes.

My thoughts had an effect, though. I had not whistled, but the loyal song draca winged into the courtyard and alighted on my shoulder. That softened an ache in my soul; I had been too afraid to check the fallen draca for his markings. I stroked him, reveling in the pebbled heat of his scaly head.

"Why are you alive?" Lizzy asked me suddenly.

Georgiana gave her a positively wrathful look, but it was a sensible question. "I told the perfumer I was not a great wyfe. I laughed at her."

Lizzy appeared skeptical. "She believed you because you laughed?"

I thought through our conversation. "I said a great wyfe would seek revenge. That my sister would burn her. Then, she believed."

Mr. Darcy crooked a smile. "The perfumer will seek out Elizabeth. How convenient. I will enjoy seeing justice done."

Lizzy, though, pushed him toward Yuánchi. "Rig the saddle for four. We are bringing Mary."

"Where are we going?" he called back.

"The French think I am dead. But there *is* a famous Bennet sister, the first wyfe in centuries to bind a golden wyvern..."

"Jane," I whispered.

## 32

# THE REFUGE

## LIZZY

The sheathed dagger weighed on my thigh as we flew to Netherfield, Jane and Charles's estate and their home with young Jemma. Yuánchi's strength flagged and the wind howled as we returned to Hertfordshire, where this all began. Here, Jane was stung, Lydia corrupted. Here, Jane, Mary and I had pored over the Loch bairn journal, that so-called family history which neatly excised an ancient Bennet betraying the great wyves.

Hundreds of yards below, a passing wheat field caught my eye. Half the field was the vibrant chartreuse of young grain. The rest was foul black, like it was smothered in crow feathers. Then a mile farther, a stand of majestic, old poplars appeared soaked in oily soot. It looked like the tainted gardens and forest at Pemberley, but Fènnù was behind us, following at the edge of my perception, not in front to spread her blight.

I spotted the town of Meryton. Beyond, a column of dirty smoke hung—but in the direction of Longbourn, not Netherfield. *There*, I thought, and Yuánchi swerved. The violence stewing in me, the fury that had saturated me when I saw Mary's bloodied body lying so still, boiled hotter.

Traveling the mile from Meryton to Longbourn took a few tens of seconds at this speed. *Be ready*, I thought to Yuánchi, and sun-like heat kindled in his breast. *Down*. He folded a wing and plunged sideways. Behind me, Georgiana gave an abbreviated shriek. This had been an unpleasant introduction to flight.

The cream firedrakes broke left and right, flying opposite directions around Longbourn. They circled it a hundred yards distant, their remarkable vision flicking through esoteric color schemes as they worked to peer through the smoky haze. The house was not burning, not seriously, not flames in the interior, but it was charred and damaged, fire licking from a hanging shutter, the front door wide open, a fence fallen in cinders, swathes of ground and garden smoldering.

Everything was deadly still. Fear and fury battled within me. What had happened?

The drakes tuned their vision to see lesser heat. That bloated the fires to featureless glares, but subtler details emerged. There were no living persons outside, nor any bodies—a body still shone warm an hour after death. But this perspective was a window to the past. The ground was painted in thirty-foot-long stripes of latent heat. Crisped, dead creatures filled them, some kind of crawler with glossy shells that reflected the heat. There were fires farther away, in a stand of trees and a meadow, all fueling the dingy pall.

We settled in front of the house. My feet hit the earth before Yuánchi had folded his wings. On Longbourn's front walk, I closed my eyes and reached out with my mind, reached *hard*, pressing my awareness to Netherfield and beyond, another mile, another five miles...

Nothing. "I cannot find Jane's wyvern."

I opened my eyes and saw Darcy running into the house, pistol in hand. Fool. I shouted at Georgiana and Mary, "Stay with Yuánchi," then summoned the drakes and ran after him.

Darcy had stopped inside the door, silent and listening. Not so foolish after all. I whispered, "I will check the top floor."

"How?" he whispered back.

Distantly, glass smashed. "One of the drakes," I said, my vision splitting as I saw through the drake's eyes. She had simply thrown herself through the window to Jane's and my old bedroom; glass was no threat to her scales. The floor was sprayed with transparent fragments and shattered frame.

Wordlessly, Darcy headed to the kitchen. I went the other way, checking the parlors and Papa's old library. I found Darcy again as he emerged from the pantry.

"Nobody," he said. "The kitchen door is standing open. The servants may have run that way."

His gaze settled on my hand, where Gramr's serrated blade gleamed. I did not remember drawing it, but Darcy held a cocked pistol, so he could hardly criticize.

"The house is empty," I agreed as the drake finished surveying the top floor. She floated down the stairway to us, the outer halves of her wings folded so tight to fit that their tips met under her claws.

Outside, Mary shouted, "Lizzy!" We sprinted out the front door. She pointed down the road where two riders galloped toward us. "I think that is Jane."

They were coming from town, not from Netherfield, but it was Jane. I had never seen her gallop a horse, but I recognized her riding form. Charles was with her, and he held up his arm to wave. Relief spilled into me, disarming the quivering violence in my muscles and nerves. Mary sighed softly and slumped, wincing, on Georgiana's arm. Darcy seemed the only one driven to action. He grabbed the well bucket and splashed water over the smoldering shutter.

Charles reached us a few horse lengths before Jane, and he reined his frothing mount to a skidding stop. "You have Jemma?" he shouted to Darcy as he leaped down.

Darcy froze, the bucket dripping in one hand. Charles spun to me, the question hot in his eyes as Jane arrived and dismounted, her face streaked with tears.

"Nobody is here," I told them both.

"Jemma is!" Jane screamed. "*She* is here!" I had never seen her like this, storming and desperate.

Everyone spoke at once, but some age-old ghost reached into my thoughts, cleaving my fear and leaving an edged focus.

"Who was with her?" I demanded.

Despite the shouting, Jane heard. Everyone quieted as she said, "Mamma is caring for her. We were in Meryton with Kitty, and we saw flying creatures. They came *here*..." She shuddered, and Charles wrapped an arm around her.

"Listen to me," I said. "We will find her. Where is your wyvern?" I did not know the perfumer's skills, but she might have sensed a wyvern...

Jane pressed her palms on her temples, forcing out words. "She always stays with Jemma." Perplexed, she looked around the ravaged garden. "Sometimes I can feel where she is..." She closed her eyes. A breath passed. Another. When her eyes opened, her cheeks were drained and white, her eyes hollow. She shook her head.

"A wyvern fought here," I said. I toed the earth at my feet, torn in three deep slices spread wider than I could stretch my hand.

"Fought *what*?" Jane asked pathetically.

"An evil woman," Mary answered. "She wields crawlers like Lizzy commands draca." Jane noticed Mary then, saw her bruised temple and bloody cut ear, her soiled and torn clothing, her hair in clotted tangles. She fumbled for Charles's hand.

"This way," I said. The firedrakes were overhead, and their vision revealed streaks of hot ground away from the house and toward the meadow. The signs were clear to human eyes as well: smoking earth, claw cuts. Even a stretch of exposed granite had ripped grooves—that could only be a wyvern. And everywhere, there were the scuttling stab marks left by crawler legs.

And killed crawlers. A hedge still burned over a half-dozen sizzling, ruptured insectile bodies, thrown there by the blast. The bodies had peculiar, charred stubs on their backs. I touched one, and Mary said, "Those were wings. They fly." We hurried faster, following an old stone wall that led past our cherry tree.

Here, an eight-foot section of the wall was blown away, the foundation rocks hissing and shimmering with heat. A greater enemy had fallen. A corpulent crawler, as grossly heavy as a large pig, lay curled on its side, burned legs scrunched like a dead spider, charred wing stubs on its back, its inch-thick shell torn apart. A muddy reek rose from its clammy flesh, and the citric tang of crawler venom.

Cautiously, Mary leaned to look. "The internal structure is strange. The body contains vestigial shells, like compartments..."

Amid the char and soot, a leaf on a nearby bush shone in the summer sun. I touched it, and my finger came away coated with clear golden ichor. Draca blood.

"Why is a wyvern fighting on the ground?" Darcy asked.

"Her flame has all been thrown back, toward the house," I said. "She is defending a retreat. Defending someone on the ground."

"I know where they went!" Mary cried. She ran ahead, favoring one leg.

I caught up as she entered an old stone-fenced paddock. It had been a sea of overgrown hollyhocks. Those were obliterated, the ground coated in charred leaves and smoldering stems. Old stones were cracked from heat or smashed. Dead crawlers crunched underfoot, hundreds of the foot-long flying ones and another of those thick, heavy ones.

Mary was stock still, her face childish and pathetic with shock.

Mamma was curled against the last patch of intact stone wall, one corner of her skirts blackened, her smoke-stained face staring sightlessly at the sky. Beside her, Jane's golden wyvern lay unmoving, one wing broken and shredded, the ebony bones a ruined umbrella, the other wing tucked under her, the gleaming scales on her breast riven by a huge, paired sting.

We gathered, aghast. Some wept.

Jane did not cry. She whispered, "Quiet," then shouted, "Be quiet!" The grief choked into bewildered silence. Jane fell on her knees by her dead wyvern, pulling at her tucked wing. Charles was down an instant later, and they dragged the wing loose. From that crevice, the last defended point, baby Jemma blinked in the sudden light, her little face dirty and tear streaked, her thumb stuffed in her mouth.

Jane swept her up, curled herself against her fallen wyvern, and comforted Jemma while bawling at the same time. Charles shielded them in his arms, and his and Jane's heads touched in gratitude and sorrow.

Mary knelt, wincing, beside Mamma. She embraced her and then, with gentle fingers, closed her eyes. "She used to scold me when I hid here, but she remembered. She thought it would be safe..." Her voice strangled.

"It is not your fault," I said. My voice was perfectly clear, the words disciplined by past selves while they dissected the scene. A wyvern could not carry a baby; Mamma had done that. My selfless, scatterbrained, loving mother, who only ever wished to secure her treasured daughters' futures, had fled all this way while unthinkable ruin and destruction rained around her.

Part of me—witty Elizabeth Bennet, my mother's daughter—was helpless with loss. The rest, my older selves who had chosen vengeance, arrayed themselves in silent tribute.

Fènnù's mad whisper slipped into my thoughts. *I am waiting for you. You need not suffer. Grief is nothing to me. I savor it. Pass your burden to me, so you may fly.*

"My grief is my own," I whispered. Finally, heartbreak overcame my dispassionate ghosts, and molten tears filled my throat.

Georgiana was stroking Mary's bent form while wiping her own tears. Then her chin lifted, and she said angrily, "The blight is here, too!" A swath of meadow beyond the stone wall was a soggy charcoal gray.

Mary threw her tangled hair out of the way and shoved to her feet, kicking her skirts free of burned hollyhocks. "I do not understand why these things keep *happening!*" She yanked off her bent spectacles. She looked younger without them, as if we had slipped into some pleasant past, but her face was contorted. "I would have attacked the perfumer, Lizzy. I wanted to! But all I did was send her *here*. This is so... unfair!"

My internal dance of minds continued, and an ancient warrior used my lips. "The perfumer reports to this emperor? This... Napoleon?" When Mary looked confused, I snapped, "She spoke with you. *Think*."

"Reports?" Mary blinked, her posture crooked as she took her weight off her hurt leg. "I do not know. He gives her orders..." Georgiana slipped an arm around her waist, supporting her.

"She does, then," I said. "She is his swiftest, most lethal asset. He uses her for his most crucial tasks. She fought you, and won, and learned the flute is destroyed. She came here to kill Jane, and could not find her, but she thinks she fought and killed a great wyfe's wyvern. She will report back. He is a general. He has instilled obedience in her."

"Elizabeth," Darcy cautioned. His arm was half extended, just short of where Gramr's blade wove through the air between us, black serrations shining, my hand twisting it as if it had a mind of its own. Finally, he stepped lightly around the blade and touched my shoulder. "Put away the dagger. Grieve your mother."

"I can find Napoleon," I told him. "When we flew over London, I saw his forces. It was like a map, a window to his thoughts. A web where every strand reveals the spider. When I find him, I will find the perfumer."

Darcy shook his head. "He is protected by two countries' massed armies. You cannot reach him, and it is wrong to try. The perfumer has erred. She revealed our enemy's weakness. Bonaparte fears that the great wyves will unite. *That* is how we win. You must stay with Georgiana so, together, we can find Emma."

The conflict between my internal selves spiraled. Grief and fury ground together like millstones, flaking and splitting.

"Win?" Mary spat bitterly. She shrugged off Georgiana and waved her deformed spectacles furiously. Her eyes were reddened wrecks, her face tear-streaked and bloody. "I wanted to kill the perfumer. You would have, Lizzy, but I am pathetic. Now the colonel is dead, and Mamma is dead, even the *horses* are dead..."

Georgiana grabbed Mary's windmilling arms, holding her until she collapsed into a moaning embrace. Darcy began a speech about revenge and war and old prophecies, I was not even sure for whom.

*Give me your grief,* the mad voice whispered. *I taste it. I will remember it. You will be free.*

"My grief is my *own!*" I shouted it this time, brandishing the dagger, and a memory shifted my grip, pressing the pad of my thumb to the flat of the blade. The polished surface touched my skin—

It was cold, absurdly cold, impossibly cold, a chill that burrowed up the tendons of my hand and rode my veins to my heart. My grief and loss, those barbaric tortures, retreated to a remote place, crystallizing into an abstraction so alien it held only analytic interest.

*My wyfe of war,* Fènnù whispered in ecstasy, and a chorus of past wyves sighed in relief and despair.

In the field, Yuánchi shuddered. His head dragged up, turning blindly toward me, but I felt our binding flare in glorious brilliance. His voice was undiminished, and it thundered in my mind, *Elizabeth Darcy Bennet. Come back.*

The words barely touched me. An icy clarity sorted my thoughts. A revelation. Even Mary, who could argue for an hour why a mouse should not be punished for gnawing into a flour sack, had seen the truth. Victimhood was unjust. Grief was unfair, weak, and wrong. There was only vengeance.

*You are not a victim,* Fènnù's crazed voice said in my skull. *You are my wyfe of war.*

Yuánchi's voice roared again, *Help her!* This time, the others heard. Mary and Darcy winced, stopped their argument, and turned to me.

"Your hand," Darcy said, his face blanked by shock.

My thumb was cut. I had not felt it; the dagger's edge was that perfect. Blood wandered over and among my knuckles, insinuating its slippery presence between my palm and Gramr's leather-wrapped hilt. I held the dagger higher, admiring how the red reflected the light.

"Give me the dagger," Darcy said, his hand outstretched. I read the tension in the muscles of his palm, the wariness of his stance. He thought he was soliciting a madwoman. Behind him, Mary and Georgiana were wide-eyed.

"I am not mad," I reassured him. "This war is mad."

"What do you mean?" Darcy said cautiously, edging closer. Gramr flicked between us. I was adjusting the angle, watching how it made my blood run, though not yet along the blade...

"Mary is right," I said. "This war is unfair. This pain is unfair. It should end."

Georgiana lifted an appealing hand. "The war will end when we heal the song."

"*That* is mad," I pointed out. "The flute is lost. The song cannot be healed." I slashed the blade through the air to point out the infested field. It was not a threat—the tip passed at least an inch short of Darcy's cheekbone—but he ducked anyway, which made me smile. "We are too late. The blight spreads."

"Lizzy, I was not thinking when I spoke," Mary said. "Give Mr. Darcy the dagger."

"I cannot," I told her. "I need it to end the war. We thought we needed three great items, but we were wrong. The dagger is sufficient. We thought we needed three wyves. We do not. *I* am sufficient."

"The dagger is affecting you," Mary said. "Fooling your mind. Look!" She pointed to Yuánchi, dragging himself to us, his tremendous shoulders shivering, his blind head high as if he could see through the ragged, weeping black scales where his prismatic eyes had been. "You can do nothing alone. Yuánchi is too spent to fly, let alone battle an army."

I inverted the dagger. Blood trickled down the glossy blade. As it crossed each hidden symbol, smoke spit and hissed. Curious, I turned the blade horizontal. The symbols formed an uneven pattern—music, in some ancient form.

"That is not what I meant!" Mary cried, her voice speeding to a desperate staccato. She gestured frantically at Darcy. "Do not let her sing. She will summon Fènnù."

I laughed. Papa had loved my singing—I had a pleasant voice for a country lady—but these symbols were a cipher. She might as well tell me to sing by staring at a box of bolts.

"Shall I end the war?" I asked conversationally.

"Lizzy, this is not the way," Georgiana began.

Darcy, though, waved to quiet her. "How would you end it?" His eyes were intent. My husband trusted me.

"I have seen a thousand wars," I said. "Wars launched by idle cruelty. Wars over a misspelled word in a scripture, or skin that is too light or too dark, or food that is unfamiliar. I have seen wars that pander to imperial vanity. Wars that consume generations, fought by fathers and sons, then their sons, and then theirs. But I have also seen wars end."

Swift as a blade, the smoky daylight dimmed as Fènnù coasted over us, fifty yards high. Even with her wings still, her weight squeezed the air in my lungs. Her wake stained the sky to midnight. She settled in the field, not far from Yuánchi, and night settled around her. Yuánchi turned, hissing, his wings spread, but Fènnù ignored him. She watched me.

"There was no need to sing," I told Mary, who was floundering in the dark. "The dagger may summon the black dragon, but she seeks for her great wyfe unbidden."

I vaulted the collapsed stone wall and dashed into the meadow. Fènnù lowered herself and pressed the elbow of her wing to the earth. I ran up the leading bone, thick as a tree trunk. Her scales were rough, distorted by centuries of disease, and the uneven edges bit my boot soles. At her shoulder, I paused while she stood, colossal muscles sliding over one another, raising me more than twenty feet high.

"Elizabeth."

I turned. Darcy was behind me—he had chased me up Fènnù's wing.

"That was quick," I admitted.

"The dagger has your mind. Fènnù is filling you with anger. Resist her. Come back."

"My anger is my own." I could feel Fènnù's mind, dispassionate and superior, pruning my clumsy human logic. "Mary is angry. You are angry; it is in your eyes. But you are all afraid to act. Your grief and fear paralyze you. I have shed grief. I have shed doubt."

"At the end, my mother had visions," he whispered, "but I was too proud to listen. I ascribed them to weakness—to binding sickness, to madness. I see better now. My mother foresaw the blight and the return of the dragons. She knew she could not heal the song, so she chose to pass her strength to the next great wyfe of healing."

Irritation burrowed through my dispassionate mood. "Are you sure this is the correct speech? It seems to be for Emma."

"My mother passed a legacy to the next wyfe of healing. She charged me with another: to remember the great wyves and to defend them. To be faithful and bold to their cause. When I found you and loved you, I flattered myself that good fortune had aided my task. You were wise and strong, and I would always protect my wyfe. But here"—his hand chopped down toward Fènnù, under our feet—"you have chosen the wrong path. Fènnù has exploited your grief to take control. But you can resist her. Yuánchi told you that you are the strongest wyfe of war there has been. That is why he bound you. *You* can withstand Fènnù—"

Yuánchi's name jolted Fènnù's thoughts, splitting them into paranoid fragments. A past life replaced mine, the life that led to the breaking of the song. Darcy became a different man, a Roman general and a lover, then he was Imhotep, the Egyptian priest who betrayed me...

In the confusion, a spark lit my mind, Yuánchi pressing through our binding, trying to speak to me. But Darcy was right; I was strong. I stiffened my mind to block him. Sealed him away.

*Be still, my Fènnù*, I thought. *Be calm, my plague, my storm.* The wild fears eased and the past life retreated, leaving a trickle of cold sweat on the back of my neck.

"You fear that Fènnù controls me?" I said to Darcy. "She will do whatever I wish."

I pointed the dagger to the far side of the field, and Fènnù strode that way—one massive step, a second. *A little farther*, I thought, and she adjusted her stance to where I wanted.

Darcy, stubborn as usual, argued on. "You told me you might control her for a time, but that she will win. That you will lose yourself to her."

"You are confusing me. Am I strong or am I doomed?" He licked his lips, dismayed—Darcy hated to be caught in an error—so I took pity and reassured him. "Trust me, love." I flicked my blood off the dagger and slipped it into the sheath, then showed him my empty hands. I stepped closer, so close that the heat of his heaving chest warmed mine.

"If you leave," I promised softly, "I will tell you how wars end." I adjusted the set of my boots on the ragged scales of Fènnù's back.

Darcy's brow was furrowed, his dark eyes confused. We were close enough to kiss. I smiled willingly and rested my palm low on his chest, a handbreadth above his center of balance, then shoved. His arms wheeled, a foot skidded, and his stunned face fell out of sight. I leaned over and watched him land in the soupy pond below.

"Wars end when everyone dies," I called, but I was not sure he heard.

# 33

## HARTFIELD

### EMMA

Harriet and I ran on narrow footpaths and crossed fields until we reached Randalls Road. That felt safer, so we followed it at a fast walk, Harriet catching her breath while I rushed down every branching path, looking for Mr. Knightley. Finally, we reached the Westons. Anne saw us through a window and ushered us in.

"Is Mr. Knightley here?" I gasped as her maid locked the door and drew the curtain, but he was already running in from the parlor. My heart lurched from pounding fear to dancing relief as we embraced.

"Easy," he grunted. "I need to breathe, too."

Breath seemed irrelevant to me, and he held me just as tight. We inhaled drunkenly when we let go. I smoothed his collar. We were not at a properly decorous distance, but this was as far as I was willing to go.

Eventually, I made a little *hem* noise so Anne and Harriet knew to turn back from their examination of the hall clock.

Anne could not hide her smile. "Whatever happened to Miss Woodhouse, who told me since she was eight years old how she would never marry?"

"I suppose she had not yet met Mr. Knightley," I replied, giddy and secure at last.

We entered the parlor. Mr. Weston was sipping tea with Augusta in a quiet corner with a platter of sandwiches. A nanny was reading a story to the Westons' little daughter, who squirmed, more interested in the guests. It was a wonderfully normal scene, and frayed muscles eased in my tired legs.

"Did you get the amulet?" Mr. Knightley asked.

I drew it out by the chain. In the sunny parlor, it shone with radiant fire.

"You are brilliant," he pronounced.

"Harriet is brilliant," I corrected. "She did it." He bowed to her, and she looked down bashfully.

I considered the amulet. It was heavy—the gold chain of course, and the thick jade. Perhaps dragon scale was dense as well. I had not noticed the weight at the school, but one did not notice minor things when frightened. I had scraped my wrist going through the window and not noticed that, either.

I untied my feathered bonnet and passed it to Mr. Knightley, then slipped the chain over my head. It nestled inside my collar, dense and fluid. I tucked the amulet inside my clothes, hiding it completely. The cold jade on my breast drew a shiver, then it warmed. No mystical vision overcame my senses.

Mr. Knightley, with the eagerness of all gentlemen burdened with fluffy things, had passed my bonnet to the Westons' maid. Relieved, he said, "We have had remarkable success, but it means nothing if we do not escape. We should strike out for the coach. With luck, we can cross the French lines on foot and ride freely to Pemberley."

"As long as we take the Abbey trail," I said. "I must check for dragons." Mr. Knightley's eyebrows shot up, but I rushed on. "There is something more urgent. Mr. Elton is bringing Mrs. Goddard's students to Hartfield to bind them to crawlers. We must stop him."

I had forgotten Augusta was in the room. She jumped out of her chair at her husband's name, knocking the platter of sandwiches across the floor. Her hands pawed the air, fighting an unseen assailant. She looked disturbing and pathetic and fierce, her gown disheveled and torn where she had ripped off decorations, her gloved fingers furious claws.

I gathered her agitated hands between mine. Her eyes swam before settling.

"Your husband is not here," I said. "He will not hurt you again."

Her throat worked, and when she spoke, her shoulders jerked with every word. "I did it. *I* hurt them." She peered around the room and whispered, "We went into houses. I chose wyves to bring to Hartfield."

I had seen that when we were captive. Mr. Elton had used her and her crawler like a hunting dog, inspecting us to find wyves suitable to bind.

"You did not know," I said. "You were captive—"

She shook her head violently, launching tears. "I knew! I was afraid, but I *knew*."

I embraced her shaking frame and murmured soothing nonsense. Her hair against my cheek was clean and combed; someone, Harriet I suspected, had helped her wash while I celebrated my wedding night. But even with the grime of her abuse removed, my fingers sank between the ribs of her emaciated frame. How long had she been mistreated? Our cheeks brushed, and my deeper senses woke. I perceived again the burned, ash-like shadow from her connection to the crawler, although now it was etched in detail. I had broken that mockery of a binding, healed it in a fashion, but the scars were like fissures on her soul.

Moments ago, I had celebrated triumphs—clever escapes, recovering the amulet, my wedding. That felt unbearably selfish.

Augusta quieted to snuffling. Harriet took a turn, giving her a handkerchief and patting her shoulder, and I eased Mr. Knightley into the hall.

"Her husband put her through ungodly ordeals," I whispered. "We must bring her with us when we head north. I cannot imagine where else she would be safe. But I do not think we should take her to Hartfield."

"Is that our destination?" he asked. He was matter-of-fact about it, and I felt a whirl of affection and admiration.

"We cannot stop their army, but if there are no crawlers when Mr. Elton and the slavers arrive, the girls will be safe."

"A housecleaning," he said approvingly.

"Exactly. Hartfield is your home too, if you are not too attached to your Chelsea loft. It is a charming house when not infested with crawlers."

That drew a brief smile. "How would we remove them?"

"They had to drag Augusta's crawler toward me. It was terrified. It fought to stay away. And that was before I had this." I touched my dress where the amulet lay. Mr. Knightley's head tilted thoughtfully while I pressed on, "I cannot bear to have Mr. Elton do more terrible things. Please. We have succeeded so far. Trust to providence."

"Trust to peculiar events," he said wryly, "but yes, I agree. We had better hurry. The soldiers were scrambled by those shots, and herding frightened girls will slow them, but they will come."

I told the others our plan and forbade Harriet's offer to join us, but then Augusta stepped forward. Her cheeks were blotchy from crying, but her red-rimmed eyes had steadied and her expression was firm. "I will go with you. I know where the crawlers are."

"That is not necessary," I said. I was sure I could find them. Even before I had the amulet, I had seen their nascent black bindings flickering through the walls.

"I must do something," she said, and her voice cracked. "I *must*."

I heard in her what I had felt: urgency, duty. And perhaps atonement, or retribution, would heal her scars. So, I nodded.

The three of us set out, Mr. Knightley carrying the long, slim box with the Baker rifle. Outside the house, he swung past the Westons' wood pile and slung an ax over the other shoulder.

He patted the handle with a grim smile. "In case providence is busy elsewhere."

WE APPROACHED Hartfield from the rear along a wandering cow path. I would never have guessed my knowledge of odd routes would prove to be so useful for avoiding occupying armies.

Fifty yards short of the back gate, the groomed lawns of Hartfield's park opened, giving an angled view of the house's side and much of the front garden.

Mr. Knightley immediately drew me and Augusta into cover behind a dense sweet briar. There were soldiers in the front courtyard. Only three, though: the French captain we had met at Hartfield and two of his men.

"So much for providence," I whispered to Mr. Knightley.

His eyes were narrow, and his hand tensed around the rifle case. Then he shook his head. "They might flee without their commander, but I am no soldier. I cannot shoot a man because he wears the wrong uniform."

"I would not want you to," I assured him.

The soldiers appeared bored. They clearly had been there for some time. I remembered my last encounter with the captain, and an idea formed. My husband would object, but that was easily remedied...

"Wait here," I said and set out across the park toward the front door. There was one muffled protest behind me, then silence.

The guards were watching the carriage drive and lane, so I crossed the lawn and passed our espaliered pear tree before I was noticed. Then the French officer's head flew around. Belatedly, the other soldiers spun, their muskets ready.

"Capitaine Fournier," I said with a curtsy. "I thought your duty required you to be elsewhere?" When the slavers were preparing to bind us to crawlers, I had appealed to him for help. That had been his excuse as he left.

There was an awkward silence before he replied, "*Madame*. We were ordered back after you escaped." He studied me, perhaps wondering whether this one rather slight woman had wiped out the Confederate soldiers he left at the house. It was not a completely foolish thought. The deadliest people in this battle were women, the French perfumer and the slavers' captive wyves.

I realized I was wearing the very amulet the captain had sought at Hartfield. That was not so clever. But it was well concealed.

His soldiers had the baffled expression of people hearing an unintelligible language, so I gave them a disarming smile and proceeded. "In a few minutes, more slavers will arrive. They are bringing twenty women to bind to the crawlers inside my home. Once they perform that brutality, they will force those women into battle. They will threaten them, drug them, and beat them." The captain's jaw clenched. I had no way to interpret that, so I trusted to instinct and continued, "Some of those women are only girls. You said you have a daughter. Imagine watching her marched into that house."

"Why tell me this?" he said stiffly.

"I would like you to move your men away. A few minutes will be sufficient. I shall visit my house, and when the slavers arrive, there will be no crawlers to bind."

While I spoke, he straightened with military pride, his chin high. In his beautiful uniform, he looked quite picturesque. In a friendlier time, he might have been a European visitor posing for a portrait—*French Captain at English Manor*.

Just as I began to doubt, he bowed, a courtly motion different from an English bow, then strode away, issuing orders in French. His soldiers shouldered their muskets and followed, including another I had not seen by the far corner of the house.

I watched them reach the lane and walk south, away from the village. When they were out of sight, I waved at the shrub, and Mr. Knightley and Augusta ran over. I thought they might congratulate me—I had been somewhat daring —but they were too uneasy, watching Hartfield's front door as if monsters lurked. As they did.

Augusta was pale, lip pinched in her teeth, hands clenched.

"Are you sure you wish to come in?" I asked her. She nodded. Mr. Knightley looked extremely solemn as well, so I asked him, "Are *you* sure?"

He relaxed his shoulders and chuckled, sliding the ax to a jaunty angle. "I am eager. I hear it is a charming house."

The door opened easily, and for a moment I was simply returned to my life. We kept a wall of mementos and keepsakes by the door, and the sight brought a flood of fond memories. Guests often added tokens—a dried flower, a place card from dinner with a little note. Perhaps Mr. Knightley would leave his ax.

But even in the entry, there were signs of disruption. The French troops had ransacked the hall wardrobe, throwing coats and boots in a messy pile. Panic squeezed my lungs; Hartfield had to be perfect...

I waited for the miasma, that specter of Papa's unrelenting slide into illness. It did not come. Nor was there any sign of the questing, black ropes, the crawler's bindings.

The house was very quiet. Silent. Nobody met us; the servants had vanished. Ever since Papa's death, Hartfield had felt painfully empty, particularly when I sat with a good fire beside his favorite chair, but this stillness was disconcerting.

Augusta, kneading her wrists, retreated into a corner. Mr. Knightley, quiet and efficient, checked Papa's study and the parlor.

"I wish you had met my Papa," I said to him to have some sound. "Imagine if he were here, and we arrived to surprise him, already married."

Mr. Knightley returned, satisfied with his inspection. "Would he be cross?"

"He would act very formidable and demand to know your living, and scowl when you said you were a musician, but he would scowl no matter what you answered. Secretly, he would be thrilled. He was a great romantic before his health failed. My mother and he were a love match. He always hoped I would marry for love."

The memories caught my heartstrings. Romantic as he was, Papa had also hoped my fortune would attract a lucrative marriage and secure Hartfield's future. Well, my fortune was stolen, and my marriage would not pay many bills, but even so he would have clasped our hands and beamed.

Gently, Mr. Knightley touched my elbow. "We cannot linger."

"Of course not." I dabbed my eyes and turned to Augusta. "You can still leave." She shook her head and turned in the direction of the kitchen.

Together, we went through the house to the kitchen door. Cautiously, I tried the knob. It turned, but the door was immovable, blocked somehow. The bitter scent I had caught last time made my nostrils twitch.

"The garden door is even more sturdy," I said, "and John has blocked all the windows. I think we should try here. Can we force it?"

Augusta spoke, her first words since we left the Westons. "It opens like this." She went to the corner and pulled a string concealed by a little table we used for curios. There was a sound of heavy wood sliding aside.

Mr. Knightley took the lead. He kept the ax, leaned the rifle case against the wall, then turned the knob, pushing with his shoulder when the door resisted. The bottom grated unevenly across the flooring, catching on clods of dirt. It jammed half open, wide enough to enter. A heavy wood bar was visible to the side, pulled away by the string. That was new and certainly unnecessary for a kitchen. The bitter scent flooded out, biting the flesh of my throat and depositing a scummy-sweet aftertaste.

The room was dark. Every window was covered. Worse, I sensed something stir. A twining black rope skittered through my vision, illusory but profoundly wrong. It swept completely through Mr. Knightley—I jumped at the sight—and stretched within inches of me, then pulled back as if burned and vanished.

"What is it?" Mr. Knightley asked. He had not seen it. He was peering into the dark.

"There is something within." The odor made my voice hoarse. "Can you fetch a light?"

"Perhaps you should." He had raised the ax two-handed, watching the dark opening.

I went to the parlor, found a flint and lit a lamp, and returned, adjusting the wick until it stopped smoking.

"Ready?" he asked.

I nodded, and he eased through the door, his motion falling into the supple forms of the morning exercises he practiced. I followed, then Augusta. In the lamplight, she looked as white as a sheet, but she did not hesitate.

The scent strengthened, but the kitchen appeared almost normal. Stove and fireplace, cold. Cupboards and drawers, neatly closed. Shelves with crocks and jars for flour and sugar and butter. There was our ancient, massive cooking table of dark oak and a small pastry table surfaced with marble.

But the windows were crudely boarded up from inside. The planks were studded with poorly driven iron nails, many of them bent. The floor was caked with dried mud and clay.

Mr. Knightley shifted the ax to one hand and lifted a wooden bucket from the floor. He sniffed it. "Pitch. They use it to waterproof ships."

Augusta began a soft, desperate noise, *uh uh uh*. I followed her frightened gaze to some dim objects on the cooking table. "What are those?"

Mr. Knightley took the lamp and held it close. Two hinged iron loops were fastened to thick chains. The ends of the chains were bolted to the table.

"Shackles," he said with profound disgust. "Like those on slave ships. Brutal tools. We have aided escaped slaves that lost a hand to infection or rot."

"They hold the wyves for the binding," Augusta whispered. She edged to the table, trembling. She laid her thin wrist beside one of the open, hinged circles as if measuring a bracelet at a jeweler. "Mr. Elton put them on me. Then he told me to pray. I could hardly bring my hands together."

"How can that man claim to be God's servant!" Mr. Knightley exclaimed in disbelief.

"He was always a monster," I said. "Just one with a clever disguise."

Mr. Knightley found another lamp on a shelf. He lit it and left it on the cooking table. The shackles cast long, wavering shadows. "Where are the crawlers?"

I had expected to follow the illusory tendrils, like greasy, living rope, but there was no sign of them. I turned slowly. "I am not sure," I admitted. Tucked under my petticoat, the amulet pulsed, a second heart. Had it frightened them away?

Augusta pointed to the trapdoor, flush with the floor and across from the cooking table.

"Tell me that is not a cellar," Mr. Knightley said.

"That is the cellar," I said.

He undid the latch, then rubbed his fingers and sniffed them. "Pitch." He pulled the trapdoor up and over, laid it flat, then held the lamp through, revealing steep, descending steps.

Augusta whimpered and edged away. "I cannot go down there."

"You do not need to," I reassured her. "I feel them now." Light or sound had woken them. More than one black binding flicked past my eyes, and beyond that, I sensed... suffering. Pain. There was an answering surge of warmth on my breast, but it did not fill me with some grand sense of power. Instead, I felt pity.

"I hear... something," Mr. Knightley said. "Emma, I am no longer sure we should attempt this."

"When Mr. Elton brought that crawler, it would not approach me. They fear a great wyfe. Let me go first. I will only look. And, I have *this*."

I drew the amulet from behind my clothes and rested it openly on my chest. It felt dense and vital, part of my being, not a passive decoration. Yuánchi's scale shone now, visibly rippling with carmine and gold waves of strange fire.

I took the lamp from Mr. Knightley and descended the steps into the cellar.

It was not a deep cellar, dug down only five feet. The ceiling was the kitchen floor, built a little above ground. Together that gave enough space that one could stand upright, only ducking for the beams.

I stood that way, astonished, until Mr. Knightley arrived beside me.

Hartfield's cellar had been a snug fit in the past, full of sacks of turnips and potatoes and grain, a few racks for wines, and wheels of cheese.

Now, it was a vast cave. The floor by my feet still had its fitted brick tiles, but a few steps farther, that fractured into churned earth. Ragged pits sank even deeper. The raw soil sucked up the lamplight, turning every shadow inky black.

The usual foodstuffs were gone. Instead, there were oak casks like those used for Madeiras and brandies, dozens of them, the wooden exteriors streaked with glistening crystals as if they had leaked and dried. The smaller ones, those a strong man might lift alone, were stacked in upright pairs. Others were large, as tall as my waist. Those lay on their sides, some resting on curved wooden braces so they would not roll, others half buried. The large ones had oval wooden lids on the top side, curved to fit the barrel. Two of the half-buried barrels were massive, longer than baths, almost boat hulls. The lids on those would admit a cow.

Pungent, sweet-sick odors of rot hung in the air, stinging my eyes. The flame of the lamp sparked and fluttered, casting fleeting halos of green and blue.

"What is in the air?" I asked. The bitter odor persisted, but something new hung, a choking blanket so thick I fancied it blurred my sight.

"Alcohol," Mr. Knightley muttered, "and some noxious ether. Also, fumes from the pitch." He pointed to the lid on a nearby barrel. It was sealed with sloppy smears of an oily, black substance. "One does not use pitch on barrels of brandy. It would make the spirits inedible."

"I do not think these contain spirits," I said softly.

"Nor do I." He shifted his grip on the ax and used the head to sift through a pile of wood from a smashed barrel. He hooked something and lifted a carapace from a large crawler. It was empty, like a discarded shell, and as long as my arm.

"Now what?" he asked.

The beating heat at my breast quickened. The fiery gleams on Yuánchi's scale were brighter. They rippled faster.

"Do you see these lights?" I asked, touching the setting.

Mr. Knightley, after a moment, said doubtfully, "I see the amulet."

So it was illusion, or rather my other sense, the one that saw bindings. But bindings were real. This was, too.

Most of the rotted, black bindings had retreated when I entered the cellar, but a thick one flickered reluctantly in and out of view. It came from one of the boat-sized barrels.

Carefully, I approached it, holding the lamp high, Mr. Knightley at my side with the ax. As we drew near, there was a dull slosh. The wooden frame shifted.

"If this is one of those monsters the slavers use in battle, we should not open it," Mr. Knightley whispered. "They have only been killed by trapping them and having troops of men shoot. Or cannons."

My senses were filling with awareness of life inside that wood, like how I sensed draca's bindings at a distance but... this was diseased and hurt and helpless. "We will be safe. It is not... ready."

"Not *ready*?"

"I cannot explain, but I am certain. The barrel is not well sealed anyway." When it sloshed, a brackish liquid had spilled from under the wooden lid. It was puddling slowly on the earth below. "If it could get out, it would."

"Although I am enjoying my tour of Hartfield," Mr. Knightley noted politely, "I am not sure the cellar casts it in the best light."

"I show guests my framed embroideries. You are not a guest."

Gingerly, he tapped the blunt side of the ax against the long, oval lid. Nothing moved. He bumped it harder, and the lid shifted slightly, stretching the sealing pitch. He gave a resigned sigh, stepped back, and swung. The hatch broke loose and fell off the far side, revealing a roughly sawn hole two feet across and longer than I was tall.

Inside, viscous liquid rolled in glutinous ripples around a humped, unnatural shape. I moved the lamp to see better.

It was unmistakably a huge crawler. There were the jointed, sharp legs and the heavy, lobster-like rings of shell. But crawlers had their own insectile grace, lethal and swift and flexible. This body was bloated, much thicker than any crawler I had seen, and distorted, composed of many thick lumps or masses, all wrapped inside a single translucent, organic sheath.

"Look," I said, "It is more than one. They have put many crawlers together. They are... merging, somehow."

"Is it how they make those giants?" Mr. Knightley asked, revolted.

"This is unnatural, even for crawlers. There is cord tying them together. The shells have been cracked so their flesh meets. It is some gruesome experiment."

"Perhaps they are dying," Mr. Knightley said hopefully.

I removed my gloves and crammed them into my dress pocket, took a bracing breath, then, ignoring Mr. Knightley's warning, dipped my fingers into the liquid to touch the translucent sheath.

Agonizing pain. Fear. Primal, pounding life in transformation.

I wiped my damp fingers on my dress. "It is a metamorphosis. A miracle of natural life that has been wickedly distorted."

"You cannot be sorry for these vermin."

"I am," I said simply. "They have been brutalized. They are not dying, though. They are full of life. They will emerge as something new."

Quietly, Mr. Knightley said, "We must kill them."

I did not answer.

"Emma, those girls will be brought here. Shackled and—"

"I know you are right. I am just sad to be among such suffering. These creatures are victims too, in their own way. But we must save the girls."

"Should I just..." Mr. Knightley mimed chopping with the ax.

"Step away!" a man's voice ordered behind us. I turned.

Mr. Elton stood on the cellar stairs, his pistol pointing at us, Augusta trapped under his other arm with his hand over her mouth. His eyes were fevered, his hair mussed. Fresh fingernail scratches bled on his cheek.

"Emma!" he exclaimed delightedly. "How considerate of you to return. The French have soured on Woodhouse witches, but I kept faith you would prove useful. Even though you cast spells with your... pert lips and bright eyes..."

"Angry eyes," I corrected. "You are in *my* house without my permission. And I would rather be a witch than a hypocrite and false clergyman and traitor."

Mr. Knightley had turned with me. He was dangerously still, the ax clenched in both hands.

Mr. Elton adjusted his aim to the center of Mr. Knightley's vest.

"I would not fire that," Mr. Knightley said, "if I were you." Mr. Elton grinned dismissively. Mr. Knightley carefully removed a hand from the ax and pointed to the lamp I held. "See how the flame spreads inside the glass? Like firedamp. Whatever foul mixture you poured into these vats has rendered the air combustible. It needs only an open spark."

Was that true? I had read about a catastrophic explosion in Felling that killed ninety miners. Or was this a bluff?

Mr. Elton seemed concerned. He backed up the cellar steps, pulling Augusta. He reached the top, bending to keep us in view, and waved the pistol threateningly at Mr. Knightley.

"Come out, then. You first. Or I will shoot you from here, and we shall see what happens."

I was suddenly, profoundly unwilling to cower while Mr. Elton threatened my husband, so I walked to the exit and climbed the stairs. Mr. Elton scrabbled back to the cooking table. He seized a handful of Augusta's hair, and she yelped as he shoved her into a seat. He moved the lamp to one side, then pressed her wrist into an iron shackle. It locked with a *clack*.

All that time the pistol pointed at me, lowered to the floor, rose back, wobbled aside, came back...

I placed my lamp on a shelf beside the sugar. Better to have my hands free. Then I watched him with distaste. "Do you really need a pistol to control a woman?" Perhaps he would set it down.

"It does not hurt," he said, after a moment.

The pistol swung to Mr. Knightley as he came up from the cellar. The aim became far steadier.

Mr. Knightley still carried the ax.

Mr. Elton said, "Throw it in the cellar."

"You have one shot," Mr. Knightley replied. He did not put down the ax.

"What of it? You think Miss Woodhouse will overpower me while you lie dying?"

"She is Mrs. Knightley."

Mr. Elton's lips twisted through shock, then disbelief, then fury. "Proud Emma Woodhouse is rutting with some bastard born on a slave?" He barked a laugh. "She once accused me of having fond thoughts of a Negress. *I* had the good sense to be offended."

"Perhaps you could shoot *me*?" I suggested. "That would be less painful than your nonsense."

Mr. Knightley waved a do-not-be-brave signal at me, but I was not being brave. Mr. Elton would never shoot me. That would leave him facing Mr. Knightley with an ax.

"Where are the slavers?" I asked.

"The soldiers will be here soon enough," Mr. Elton answered. "I am to open casks for the celebration. I fear it will put quite a dent in Hartfield's cellar. Your brother-in-law was to meet me—it is *his* stock, really—but it seems he has run away." He sighted the pistol carefully at Mr. Knightley. "I will not ask again."

This time, it was I who signaled desperately at Mr. Knightley. His face hardened, but he tossed the ax down the cellar stairs.

"Better," Mr. Elton said. Augusta began moaning. One handed, he grabbed her neck and pressed down, shoving her cheek against the table. His gaze continued to flicker between Mr. Knightley and me, back and forth, then settled on me. "I begin to understand. What choice had you? A ruined woman..."

"I was never ruined," I said. "I was never even *affected*. You are a petty, pathetic man who will rot in hell."

Mr. Elton, though, switched to addressing Mr. Knightley. "Did you know? Could you *tell*? Or are you not sophisticated enough to judge?"

I realized, suddenly, what was being revealed to my husband.

Mr. Knightley crouched, his body tense, his arms ready at his sides. I had seen this pose before when he unleashed lethal violence against the slaver who held Harriet hostage. Even then, he had not looked as vicious as he did now. His face was granite, his eyes lit with fury. But he had a room to cross and a pistol aimed at his heart. He might reach Mr. Elton, but he would die doing it.

"Do not let him goad you," I said desperately. "He is beneath you—"

There was an unexpected, metallic *clack*.

Mr. Elton looked down in surprise. Augusta, her face jammed against the table, had managed to fasten the remaining shackle around his wrist.

He hissed angrily. His free hand kept the pistol aimed at Mr. Knightley while he twisted, working his shackled fingers into his coat pocket and dragging out a brass key. Augusta grabbed for it, and they wrestled, a bruising battle as the shackle chains jerked and banged. The key flew free, bounced off the table, and clinked into a dark corner.

There was a moment of silence. Then Mr. Elton jabbed the pistol toward me and snarled, "Fetch it, will you?"

I did not move. Shooting me would trap him.

"Shall I convince you?" he whispered and aimed the pistol back at Mr. Knightley. "Or shall we wait for the Overseer?"

Augusta stood, knocking her chair away. Her shackled arm yanked painfully as she dodged her husband's grab. "No!" she screamed. "I will not let you hurt more women."

With her free hand, she took the lamp off the cooking table and threw it. It soared across the room, sweeping shadows through arcs as it flew, and crashed on the cellar stairs. Flaming oil sprayed, framing the trapdoor in flickering orange.

There was no explosion; that must have been a bluff. Or, not quite a bluff. The flames puffed up in a green-tinged cloud, nothing like normal fire, sucked back into the cellar, then roared out, orange and angry. The wooden frame began to burn.

While Mr. Elton stared, transfixed, Mr. Knightley moved in a rush. The men collided with a meaty thud. The pistol fired harmlessly into the ceiling, loud in the enclosed room, then Mr. Elton was thrown to the ground, his tethered wrist half suspending him beside the oak table.

Mr. Knightley towered over him, legs apart, fists raised. Ready to do murder.

"No," I cried. "Free Augusta! We must get out." The fire had started smokeless, but the wood around the cellar door was catching and spilling fumes. Noxious black smoke billowed, filling the top of the room and shrouding the remaining lamp.

I fell on my knees in the corner where the key flew. There was dirt and splintered wood and dried clay. The light dimmed as the smoke swelled. The floorboard seams under me began to glow, parallel lines of fierce yellow that blew scalding air and haze. I held my breath and searched by feel, thankful my gloves were off. But there was nothing. The key could have bounced anywhere.

Mr. Knightley was trying to free the chain attached to Augusta's wrist. He vaulted onto the table itself, heaving on the chain two-handed, trying to rip the bolt from the table. The table did not even wobble. It was a massive thing of old-fashioned split logs that dated to the house's construction.

That view vanished in a cloud of smoke. My next breath was ashy grit. The floorboards under my fingers were too hot to touch.

Coughing, I ran in the direction Augusta had been. Instead, Mr. Elton's head emerged. He was trying to stand, blood streaming from a gash in his nose. Two-handed, I pushed his chest; he reeled and vanished. The smoke was so heavy, I could barely see my outstretched arms. I ducked low, grabbing a breath where it was fresher.

A deep-throated *wump* shook the ground under my feet. Heat blasted from the cellar door; tips of my hair sparked. Fire erupted outside the half-open kitchen door, illuminating what had been our exit, now a furnace. The fire had broken through the floor.

I felt the pleats of a woman's gown, then made out Augusta's profile. "We will get you out," I told her. Mr. Knightley reappeared. Somehow, he had found a heavy metal ladle. He jammed the handle into the shackle chain where it joined the bolt, cranked it around and strained with two hands, but the handle snapped.

"Go," Augusta told me. "I am where I should be." Mr. Elton's soot-stained face reappeared like a disembodied wraith, gibbering with fear. Augusta's shackled hand grasped his, and she smiled at her husband.

I recoiled as a sheaf of live flame curled past like a python, then I heard nails wrench and wood splinter. A rectangle of gray sunlight penetrated the smoke-saturated air. Something large flew past my shoulder, then hands seized my waist, and I was thrown after it. My ankles smacked the window sill; I flipped and landed hard in our cucumber patch. The impact knocked away what little breath I had. For a few seconds my body bucked and struggled to breathe, then air, sweet air, filled my lungs.

Above me, the smoke pouring through the missing kitchen window was so dense it looked solid. A chair lay in the garden, thrown before me to break the glass.

I scrambled up, trying to see inside, but it was a hellscape of soot and smoke and fire. Then a strong hand grasped the window sill. I grabbed Mr. Knightley's other arm and helped drag him through.

We staggered back in each other's arms.

"I could not—" he began and fell into coughing and retching. He tried again, "I could not—"

"I know," I said, holding him, tears in my voice.

The smoke streaming through the window ignited with a *whoosh* and turned to a jet of pure flame. The heat was unbearable, so we stumbled back farther. A deep note rumbled, then thumped. The front parlor windows blew outward, spraying shards of windowpanes.

Finally, fifty steps away, we stopped. The remaining glass popped in a series of rapid pings. Every gap shot fire. The beautiful Caen stone on the exterior began to sheet off, the walls warping and charring behind it. A chunk of roof fell in—into Papa's study, I thought—then with a crackling roar, the rest fell in rapid sections.

Ash drifted down, only a few flakes at first. It thickened until it dusted the ground white, swirling like winter snow while I watched Hartfield burn.

# THE CORSICAN

## LIZZY

I flew blinded by a kaleidoscope of history, of cultures lost to time. Slowly, the extraneous memories fell away, and I was a single life: an Egyptian queen. Around me swirled images of a great sea battle, and then of a Roman general, a lover, who lay in my arms, his garment rent and blood soaked.

*Queen*, crooned Fènnù. *I honor your command. Together, we strike our enemy...*

Below us, on the shores of the river Tiber, vast Rome lay... *no.* My twisted reality straightened with a snap. That was the Thames; the city was London.

A memory of Darcy returned. We were in the British Museum, his eyes intense as he said in a concerned baritone, *Rome fell a thousand years ago.*

Darcy falling away from me, his mouth wide with surprise and betrayal.

I blinked in the pressing wind, and it was like a storybook spell fell from my eyes. I was straddling Fènnù's neck, wider even than Yuánchi's, the jet-black scales uneven and wickedly dangerous with no saddle.

I had pushed Darcy away.

*Strike. Unleash your vengeance. End them...* Fènnù's thoughts skidded through mine, trailing ecstasy and fury. Her grip tightened around my mind like a noose. Pain stabbed my temples.

"I am not a queen," I said to the sky, squinting. "I am Elizabeth Darcy."

We banked over south London, Fènnù's body heeling hard. The speed pressed me into the hollow of her neck, defying the recklessly tilted horizon. I could see straight down over her shoulder.

The troops, English and French, were conspicuous from the air. The brilliant modern dyes of their uniforms made even a handful of men catch the eye. The Confederate colors were subtler, but my other senses picked them out—each group had an enslaved wyfe simmering with the tainted, oily strength of crawler venom.

As the landscape revolved, the battle assembled in my mind, an overlay on the city and countryside like a cartographer's tracing page. The smoke from musket fire and cannons marked conflict, tight and dense in active fighting, diffuse from past skirmishes. That revealed motion: here a front advanced, there one retreated.

From that and a thousand past battles, the strategy emerged, a window into the mind of the great French commander. The spider who spun the web in which we danced.

With comprehension came surprise: The assault on London was tactical. Already, those troops withdrew. The bulk of the French army, many thousands, was securing a different objective...

"South and east," I whispered. Fènnù heard my thought, and we turned that way, her great wings sweeping with tireless efficiency.

The regimented city roofs thinned to scattered villages and farmland, but the French troop deployments strengthened, a massing so extreme it weakened other critical flanks. What objective could be so crucial? We were overflying a rural part of England, no ports, no military significance, just... Surrey.

That name tugged memories from before I went into the lake. Surrey was home to Emma, the great wyfe who should have bound Yuánchi. Conflicted feelings pricked; I liked her, I had sympathized with a lady thrust into this morass, but possessiveness and jealousy made me reach out through the brilliant thread of my binding.

*Yuánchi*, I called.

Fènnù bellowed in protest, her chest heaving. Her will, irresistible as iron, clamped my mind, hiding the spark of my binding.

*Strike!* Fènnù screamed in my mind.

Grief drowned me, my own stolen pain multiplied a hundredfold and then slammed back—Mamma lying in ash, her eyes staring sightlessly, Mary bloody and still, both victims of the French, of their perfumer. I screamed into the rushing wind. Fènnù's breath primed. Freezing blackness streamed from the trailing bones of her wings, from the ridges along her back, and we hurled down on a column of marching soldiers—

AWARENESS RETURNED IN A CONFUSED HALF-STATE, as if drowsing and dreaming, but raw physical discomfort broke the trance. Rough scales chafed my thighs. Melting ice clung to my soaked dress. I shuddered convulsively, my hair rattling in the wind, every lock a melting icicle.

*Hold close*, Fènnù crooned. *Warm yourself.*

Automatically, I embraced Fènnù's neck, heedless of crooked scales cutting my skin, reveling in her violent, over-heated pulse.

We were circling. The earth below had been farms, the modest holdings that worked the acreage between the villages dotting London's perimeter. And there had been troops... Now it was a seething, blackened waste, submerged in an inky flood broken by severed tree trunks and a few buildings blasted to icy shells.

"What happened?" I asked, stupidly.

*My wyfe of war*, Fènnù sang. *My queen judges. She avenges.*

Fènnù's stolen image of Mamma's death hung in my mind, and the loss burned. That was why I had mounted the black dragon—to find her murderer. But the thought of vengeance raised vomit in my throat and blurred my eyes with tears. My ears rattled with hazy echoes of thunder and screaming men.

"I am not your wyfe of war," I whispered.

*You are mine, and I am yours. Until you die, you shall have only me, and forever I shall cherish you.*

Her skittering, crazed emotions caught mine and twisted, but the iron clamp had eased, and once again I saw my hidden thread, my binding to Yuánchi. This time, I did not speak—did not try to reach out to him. I cradled our connection in my private thoughts, I hid it, a north star in a storm, a lifeline to sanity.

Fènnù was surveying the land below with inhuman efficiency, the instincts of a supreme avian predator coupled with the military insight of a hundred wyves of war.

*There*, she concluded, telescopic gaze finding a small encampment a few miles beyond the frozen destruction. French troops ringed it, but at a distance. It required no massed guard because it had no exposed flanks, no weakness by which an army could approach. It was the center, the command. The nearby armies were all French—no Overseers with their corrupted wyves—but I sensed one wyfe, stronger, seething with foul power like I had not tasted since I confronted my mad sister Lydia a lifetime ago.

Fènnù coasted down, air shuddering under her cupped wings as she slowed our descent. And while her attention was fixed below, I saw farther south something unexpected...

Fènnù reared, colossal wings sweeping, and we settled to the earth. After the ceaseless rush of flight, the scattered shouts and cries around us seemed soft.

*Down*, I thought, and she pressed her body flat. I trod a few steps along her angled wing until the drop was safe, then jumped, damp skirts flapping.

Traces of Fènnù's black breath surrounded us, remnants from her exhalations and sharp, pungent spurts from the diseased drops falling from her wings. It formed a thin, waist-high fog that looked like swirling coal dust and pooled in the deep wheel ruts from cannon carts.

A large, plain tent was erected ahead of us, clearly the general headquarters. Several officers stood outside in extravagant uniforms with plumed hats and gilded coats. They watched Fènnù with expressions ranging from disciplined unease to raw horror.

In front of them, commanding and calm, a man in his mid-forties stood in a plain green infantry uniform and rumpled, unbuttoned gray redingote. He wore a black felt bicorn hat, famously turned *en bataille*, the points aligned with his shoulders instead of front-to-back.

I walked to the emperor Napoleon, the black fog parting around my skirts and merging behind me in a rising wake, a mimicry of the sky-blotting destruction that darkened the horizon behind us.

He gave a courteous nod. In a heavy French accent, he said, "Mrs. Elizabeth Darcy."

He seemed quite certain of that, given I was supposed to be dead.

"Have we met?" I said.

"*Non.* I have had not the pleasure. But I suspected *la dame de guerre*, the wyfe of war, she must be you. *Ah.*" He smiled, belatedly understanding my question, and fished in his coat pocket. "I have this..."

He unfolded a sheet of notepaper, a charcoal drawing of myself. I did not recognize the hand. It was not Darcy's or Mary's, and certainly not Georgiana's; her likenesses were astonishing. It was a romantic rendering, my eyes bold, my cheekbones excessively sharp. It did not show the blemish from Fènnù's frozen breath, the one scar not erased by my slumber in the lake.

"Drawn by Mr. Wickham," the emperor explained. "Your sister's husband, but a great admirer of you."

My last sight of Wickham had been his severed boot after he encountered Yuánchi's claws. "An admiration that was not returned."

The emperor made a *comme ci, comme ça* noise. "An unimportant man. I meant no insult. The fault is my English. I have studied your language only two years, since I understood that England's *monopole sur les draca* would decide this war."

Fènnù, impatient, shifted her wings. The wind stirred my hair and flapped the walls of the tent. The officers steadied their plumed hats and retreated a step.

"*Elle est magnifique*," Napoleon said, admiring Fènnù's towering mass with no sign of unease. "*La dragonne noire de l'apocalypse. La porteuse du désespoir. The poisoned winter that has killed a dozen kingdoms. Et voilà.*" He nudged his boot into one of the ruts in the ground. It was filled with dense, black fog. A tiny crawler scurried out.

"Are you not afraid I will kill you?" I asked.

He scoffed, a swift exhalation through pursed lips. "The wyfe of war does not assassinate generals and kings. Least of all, emperors. She destroys armies. Cities. Countries." He considered me, and, unwillingly, I felt the intensity of his persona. There was a candid aspect to him—confidence of course, which was commonplace in powerful men whether justified or not, but also a transparency, a sincerity that was rare.

"You remind me of Lord Wellington," I said, and remembered what I had glimpsed from the air before landing.

Napoleon nodded, "A good general," but he seemed distracted. His gaze surveyed my clothes and lingered on the dagger at my thigh before his eyes met mine again.

Fènnù's impatience was building, a steepening slope toward violence. Privately, I cradled my binding to Yuánchi, a lodestone for my inner self.

Yuánchi's binding was in motion. Flying. Then, through that link:

*Lizzy. Where—*

I heard it in my mind, like a draca's speech, but the words were English, not the abstract comprehension that flowed from a draca's thoughts.

"What?" I said. The voice had a woman's timbre but was exceedingly faint, fading too soon for me to identify.

The emperor cocked his head. He seemed relieved by my outburst. He tucked a hand in his pocket and asked, "Do you know why you will not kill me?"

I licked chapped lips. "I am all attention." Who had spoken?

"It would end this cycle too soon. The black dragon is sated for now, but her appetite for destruction will return. She needs it. You need it. She will spread the blight, and you will aid her." When I said nothing, his relief faded. His gaze returned to Gramr. "*Vous êtes trop calme.* You carry the dagger. You bound the black dragon. Where is your fury?"

It was difficult to focus on the conversation while resisting Fènnù's influence. For an instant, my control slipped, and anger swept through me, thudded into my pulse, but with it came memories—the insight of past wyves. *This man wants you to be angry*, they warned, then they were silenced, locked out by Fènnù.

Manipulations all around me. Fènnù pressed her vengeance and fury into my mind while hiding the counsel of my past selves. This emperor teased me toward some unspoken goal.

Deliberately, I opened myself to the past. *What does this man want from me?* A dozen past selves answered. *Slaughter. Annihilation.*

Napoleon was a master strategist. Even the most scathing English editorials acknowledged that. He was also deeply informed about draca and the great wyves; Lydia had stolen a wealth of knowledge for him. He knew draca lore and history even I did not.

He had tried to assassinate me. When that failed, he woke the black dragon and used Fènnù in war, but he knew Fènnù was ultimately uncontrollable, a force of unfettered destruction, not a military weapon.

"Why are you in England?" I asked. "Entering enemy territory is dangerous."

For a moment, his face closed. His honesty shuttered. That had been the right question.

"You were waiting when I came," I continued. "You expected the wyfe of war to find you. Why? Why meet me at all? You know the black dragon is mad. Why gamble I would not obliterate your camp, emperor and all?"

His features were stone.

"A skilled general does not take senseless risks," I finished. "You are here because the balance of victory lies *here*. In Surrey. And because you could still lose."

He called over his shoulder in French.

A severely beautiful young woman stepped out of the tent. She wore an exquisite emerald satin gown, although the bodice and collar were stained. Her impractically dramatic bonnet was suited for a promenade on a springtime boulevard. Unhesitating, she strode past the cowed officers and stood possessively beside the emperor.

Her eyes latched hungrily onto Fènnù then shifted haughtily to me. "*Devrais-je la tuer?*" she asked the emperor.

"Should she kill you?" Napoleon translated for me, politely.

The perfumer's wide bonnet flapped as her head twirled to him.

I had known she was near, sensed her foul power, and her callous embrace of violence encouraged the anger I was resisting. My desire for revenge. My fury.

"I understood her," I said through tight teeth.

"Are you not afraid she will kill you?" the emperor asked, copying my earlier question, but not for humor. He was quite serious.

"If I am harmed with the black dragon present, everyone will die." My arm shivered as I fought the urge to draw the dagger.

He nodded and angled his head reproachfully at the perfumer, like she was a child who gave a foolish answer in a lesson. Her attention flicked warily between him and me.

"She makes you angry," he noted.

Fènnù was drinking in my fury, tasting it, whispering, encouraging... I hugged my binding to Yuánchi, my lifeline to sanity, and it brightened, brilliant with the strength of the dragon of healing. And slowly, my fury matured into something difficult to bear but... more real. More true. The anger spurring my racing heart ripened into grief, then mourning for my dear mother.

And through my brightened binding, the woman's voice sounded again: *Lizzy, you must find us!*

Emma's voice.

What had Darcy said? The emperor feared the great wyves, united.

The silence was eroding the perfumer's confidence. She drew a small glass container from her pocket, dampened her finger, and raised it, trembling, to coat her lips. Her power seethed and grew as a dark citrus scent filled the air. Her oily blackness stretched out, probing.

"You are a wyfe of war," Napoleon snapped impatiently. "You hear them, *non? Cent deux,* one hundred and two wyves before you. You feel them"—he thumped his fist on his chest—"in your heart! They cry for revenge." When I did not answer, he said, "*La dragonne noire* has bound you. You must rise—"

The perfumer interrupted. "*La dragonne n'est pas engagée.*"

Finally, the emperor faltered. "The black dragon is not bound?"

"No," I said.

Understanding crept into his face. "This is why you are sane..."

"You have a clever plan," I said, "a daring plan. But it has failed." I switched my gaze to the perfumer's narrowed eyes. "He expected me to kill you. He knew you were outmatched by a great wyfe, but he sacrificed you, sent you to goad the bull to fury. You were bait—pretty to look at, useful at times, but disposable. A lure to drive me to madness, or if that failed, to draw me here so he could provoke me, break my mind with the thirst for vengeance."

I had spoken rapidly, and I could see she had not followed it all. She asked Napoleon a question; his answer sounded dismissive.

"*I* will take the black dragon," she said. The strength around her surged as she grabbed for the dagger on my thigh.

The perfumer, though, was no wyfe of war. She was an aristocrat who rose through the French court, ruthless surely, but fighting her battles with beauty, intrigue, and rumor.

Left-handed, I caught her grasping hand easily, pinioning her wrist. She gave a perplexed cry, tugging ineffectually, unsure how to respond to physical force, let alone pain. Then she rallied, summoning her crawlers—

"Mary sends her regards," I said and punched her with my right hand, a hooked blow that flattened the side of her ridiculous bonnet against her temple. It was not a hard blow, not the shoulder-spine-hip alignment that delivers lethal force, but it would have been enough to stun a strong man. The perfumer's delicate head rocked, and she collapsed in a limp heap of stained satin, laced petticoats, and sprawling jewels.

The watching officers bustled importantly, gripping the hilts of their swords, but they did not draw them. They waited for their emperor.

"Your resistance changes nothing," Napoleon said. "The black dragon has seeded the blight. England is doomed, only slower."

I drew the dagger, a whisper of razor-edged dragon tooth, and he became very still.

"You searched for the great artifacts," I said. "Your agents stole Gramr." I lifted the serrated edge between our gazes, a rippling midnight line that divided our faces, left and right, thesis and antithesis. "But you never held it. Touch it now. Touch the blade. That is the path to its power."

His eyes wondering, compelled, Napoleon rested a fingertip on the flat of the blade.

"Nothing," I told him. "You feel no strength. No connection to the wisdom of the past." I withdrew the dagger and pointed the hilt toward the fallen perfumer, mistress of poisonous crawlers, then to Fènnù behind me. "The power you covet is beyond your reach because you are not a wyfe."

Fènnù's relentless anger flared when I drew the dagger, a whirlpool around my mind. Now, she spoke: *Rise, my queen. Seek vengeance. Cast down our enemy.*

If grief is a wound, a laceration that pulses blood and makes us cry, then mourning is that first tender scar, our torn soul knitted clumsily together only to discover a hollow where something precious remains forever lost.

*Your queen is dead*, I thought. It was a simple thought, but Fènnù's churning anger snagged and, for a moment, lessened. *You grieve for her. I grieve for my mother. But grief should not be savored. Grief should heal.*

*You are my queen*, Fènnù insisted. *Our vengeance will reclaim your great empire.*

"Your queen is gone," I said aloud. "The empire you dream of will never come."

I had spoken to Fènnù, but Napoleon heard, and his face clouded.

Yuánchi's binding broke into my mind, melting the icy walls of Fènnù's strength.

*Lizzy!* Emma's voice was a dazzling sun. Yuánchi was much closer now, his binding brighter, but Emma had changed as well. Her voice was rich with loss and fortitude and certainty. *The wyves must gather. Find us. Find Yuánchi.*

I sheathed the dagger and left.

# 35

## HARBINGERS

### MARY

On shuddering wings, Yuánchi carried us past London.

With Lizzy gone, I rode in front. That choice was practical—I was able to converse with Yuánchi—but even while my heart grieved for Mamma, my pulse quickened when I took my place. We spend our lives plodding earthly paths of triviality and compromise. What could be a more transcendent remembrance than tears in the limitless sky?

But when we rose through the sheeting wind, I felt self-conscious. I distrusted eminence in others and detested it for myself, yet I was the black-clad figurehead on a scarlet-and-onyx dragon, a braggart Nike with flapping, lank hair.

My damaged spectacles were unsteady; I used one hand to hold them against the gusts. My lap belt was cinched tight, so my other hand rested lightly on the saddle's pommel for balance. Georgiana sat behind me, riding double in the front saddle and strapped in with an auxiliary belt. Her arms hugged my waist, squeezing hard whenever we tipped. Mr. Darcy rode in the back saddle, out of reach, out of hearing, and perhaps beyond caring. After Lizzy pushed him off Fènnù, he had limped back to us dripping and unwilling to speak.

One passenger had no qualms about the flight. The song draca had protested when I coaxed him into my dress pocket, but he was delighted now, his sapphire-beaded head poking out to admire the view.

308

Georgiana pressed her chin to my neck and shouted, "Has Emma said anything more?"

I shook my head. Yuánchi had told me the wyfe of healing called us—that was why we attempted this flight—but nothing more.

Yuánchi's launch had been ragged, and we flew low. London's packed roofs whipped barely beneath his tucked claws. But even a struggling dragon is swift, and the landscape soon greened to woods and farmland. Then in a blink, the greenery vanished, and we were crossing a funereal expanse of ice-ravaged, black-misted earth. I had seen this destruction before—Fènnù's breath had struck parts of London during her rampage—but this was a mile wide. Were those splayed branches a flattened forest? That level stretch, a road? Those still lumps, the bodies of soldiers?

*Mary Bennet*, Yuánchi thought, the words vibrating my brain like a clanged bell. This time, I managed not to wince.

"Yes?" I answered. It was hard to break the habit of speaking aloud. The wind whipped the sound from my lips and left a sour flavor of black rot and frost.

*Fènnù*, Yuánchi thought, but when conveyed through his mind, that mundane word, the Chinese for wrath or fury, was a simplistic title for an unthinkably ornate composition, one befouled by a grating discord.

One of the cream firedrakes veered, drawing a sight line to the left. I let go of the saddle and pointed so the others would see the black dragon rising, her wings spinning sable squalls from the frozen landscape.

I could just make out a woman's form on her back. Lizzy.

With three huge strokes, Fènnù climbed over us. My neck craned as she soared higher. When birds fought, they attacked from above. Were we about to be blasted out of the air by my possessed sister?

*The wyfe of healing says stay true*, Yuánchi thought. *The wyfe of war hears her. She will follow.*

"Very well," I said. What else does a figurehead say to a ship? The drakes resumed their heading toward Surrey, and Yuánchi followed, his great muscles trembling.

The devastated region ended, but the green hills and fields of Surrey were soiled with dark patches. They looked like spilled ink. Georgiana shouted, "The blight," against the wind.

Yuánchi began to descend. I spotted people ahead and leaned to look, then Yuánchi's next wingbeat hitched—an aerial stumble. We rocked wildly. I braced myself against his muscular neck, my palm jammed into a patch of rough, blackened scales, and beneath his thudding pulse, I sensed the same discord I had heard in Fènnù's name. In the scarlet dragon it was a poison, a spreading corruption of the broken song.

Yuánchi's right wing spasmed and folded. The horizon tilted sideways, the lap belt yanking my hips while treetops rushed toward our right side. Yuánchi writhed like a dropped cat, the sky whipped through a dizzying circle, and somehow we were upright by the time the trees struck, branches clattering and snapping harmlessly against Yuánchi's armored chest and belly. His wings fanned, scooping air to slow us—I plowed ignominiously into his neck—then we rammed the earth and skidded sideways across an expanse of grassy meadow.

Dazed, I clung while his stupendous lungs pumped breath through his body. My heart was rattling, my brow sheened with cold sweat. So much for the transcendence of flight. Something small squirmed from my pocket and flew away, the song draca deciding he preferred his own wings.

*Are you hurt?* Yuánchi thought.

*No*, I answered. We had landed in a meadow in a modest valley. There were scattered, untrimmed fruit trees and sprawling ruins from an ancient stone structure. *What happened to your wing?*

His neck and blind head settled painfully into the grass. *I am weak. I have grown weaker since I bound the wyfe of war. Now the black dragon is close, and the broken song presses deep.*

Mr. Darcy was already on the ground, and Georgiana was descending gingerly. I followed her, then ran alongside Yuánchi's neck to where his head rested, tilted to one side, his jaws cracked to ease his slow, heavy wheezes.

"Can I help you somehow?" I asked. He did not respond.

Emma was running toward us through the grass. Now Yuánchi stirred, lifting his muzzle to greet her. I had never seen him reach out to anyone other than Lizzy, and a needle of jealousy pricked my heart in defense of my sister.

Where was Lizzy? The sky was empty.

Mr. Darcy had run to the center of the meadow. He spun, a hand shading his eyes. I called, "Do you see her?" and he shook his head. Anger from the frightening flight and Yuánchi's illness filled me, and I yanked Emma's arm to pull her away from Lizzy's dragon. "You called us. You said Lizzy would follow! Where is she?"

"She answered through Yuánchi," Emma said helplessly. Her hazel eyes pinched with worry as she scanned the scattered clouds.

Her dismay undercut my frustration, and I noticed her state: ungloved, fingernails torn, her unfailingly pristine clothes wrecked with mud, her face soot-smeared. Flakes of ash were caught in the feathers of her gray bonnet and in her hair. The effect was unsettling. Her appearance had always been so perfect.

"What happened to you?" I asked as Georgiana joined us and gasped, "You found it!"

An amulet hung on Emma's breast. It was muddied too, but jade peeped through, and the scarlet was unmistakable.

Mr. Darcy, slump-shouldered, had rejoined us. He observed tiredly, "The amulet."

"It is how I spoke with Yuánchi." Emma lifted it slightly, a lady's demure display. "Through him, I heard Lizzy. I do not sense her now." She rubbed her eyes. "Yuánchi is terribly unwell. I did not know when I asked you to fly."

Emma's usually animated speech was flat with exhaustion. The soot on her cheeks was tracked by dried tears, and foreboding filled me.

"Where is Mr. Knightley?" I asked.

She smiled with some of her old confidence. "He is fetching Harriet. It is too dangerous for her to stay in Surrey. Papa gave *her* the amulet! It took us ages to sort that out. She has loaned it to me." To Mr. Darcy, she said, "Lizzy will come. She told me so, and I was right about the lake, was I not?"

He nodded, in acknowledgement or thanks, and adjusted his shoulders closer to his usual commanding posture.

"The blight is everywhere," Georgiana said.

Emma sighed at the splotched hills. "We had to run from crawlers bursting out of the Coles' turnip patch. We must heal the song quickly. The amulet showed me the vision again. The great wyves were better prepared than we thought. One was unbound because a wyfe must bind Fènnù to heal the song."

That left an uneasy silence. "*Who* must do that?" I asked finally.

"A great wyfe," Emma said. She adjusted the amulet and said firmly, "The artifacts are powerful. They will help."

Mr. Darcy was knocking dried mud off his coattails with precise whacks. His hand stopped midair. "You found the flute?"

Her confidence faltered. "I thought you would bring it."

A man's voice hailed us, and Mr. Knightley emerged with Harriet from a patch of birch trees. We ran to meet them. A babble of greetings rose, then halted when Mr. Knightley and Emma embraced with astonishing intimacy.

Harriet was bent, her hands on her knees and winded from running, but she waved dismissively. "Do not be foolish. They are *married*."

Even so, it was a bold display, but Mr. Darcy shook Mr. Knightley's hand ferociously while Georgiana happily congratulated Emma. I muttered something as well. Having watched Mr. Knightley dote over Emma for months, I supposed it was inevitable.

Mr. Knightley brushed away our attention, his gaze on Yuánchi. Even the most inexpert eye could tell the scarlet dragon was desperately ill. "I had hoped you flew here to rescue us. Or rescue the ladies, at least."

"I am done with flying," Georgiana said decidedly.

"Yuánchi will not be flying us anywhere," I said. He had not moved since his weak greeting for Emma. His breathing had slowed, but it was strained, not relaxed in healthy rest. How bad was he?

Mr. Darcy said bluntly, "The blight will consume England. We must heal the song. That is our sole rescue." With a touch of his old, dry humor, he added, "I expect that requires the ladies." Then his brow furrowed, and his gaze returned to hunting among the clouds.

"Is the enemy near?" Georgiana asked, and I realized we were exposed in a meadow with a very visible dragon.

Mr. Knightley answered. "The French are all through Surrey. The slavers are worse and closer, but Harriet and I met allies on our way. They will slow our pursuers." To Mr. Darcy, he added, "The 'widowed wyves' are here, a ladies' resistance. Your aunt, Lady Catherine, leads them with her wyvern."

Mr. Darcy gave a mirthless laugh, more long-suffering than surprised.

Harriet took Emma's arm. "Mr. Knightley told me about Augusta and Hartfield. I am so sorry."

"She was brave," Emma said. Her sad gaze traveled to the rest of us, and she explained, "Hartfield is lost. Burned."

"This has been a cruel day," I said, feeling Mamma's loss and pity for beautiful, perfect Emma, her fortune lost, her home gone. Of course, she had somehow also managed to marry Mr. Knightley.

Harriet had her arm around Emma's waist. She scowled. "I have not one ounce of sympathy for hideous Mr. Elton!"

Whoever that was, it made Mr. Knightley sweep Emma into his arms for a fresh embrace. When finally they let go, Emma dabbed her eyes and declared bravely, "Well, I am quite looking forward to a little loft in Chelsea. No more nonsense with cooks and maids and gardeners."

I snuck a look at Georgiana, wondering if she was following this better than me. Loft?

"And I forgot to tell you," Emma continued. "The third dragon is somewhere nearby, though I am not sure where."

That launched eager conversation. By the end, Mr. Darcy was tromping in rapid circles. "It is no coincidence that we gathered here," he declared. "Queen Mary chose to send the amulet here. We can bind the dragon of song!"

"Do we not need the flute for that?" Emma asked.

"We are missing more than the flute," I said. "Where is the *dragon*? There is no lake. No big river like the Thames."

"We have only ponds," Emma admitted. "But I see the glow everywhere." Her eyes roamed the stone ruins and the meadow's ruffled heath. "The Abbey. The hills. It is the glow of the wyfe of song in the vision." To Georgiana, she said, "It is the glow that connects you and Mary. You must sense it. Or do you hear it as music?"

Georgiana did not answer. She had not spoken since Emma announced the third dragon.

Mr. Darcy, back to searching the sky, said, "When I spoke with Elizabeth, she..." He stopped and spun to Georgiana. "We must be prepared when she arrives. We need the third dragon. Georgiana, reach out—"

"I am considering *how*," Georgiana snapped at her brother. "I do not sense what Emma described. And Lizzy is already bound, so how is this supposed to work? Are you saying Emma will bind Fènnù? Or shall we draw straws?"

Her tone perplexed me. Georgiana had a temper when provoked, but she was never petulant.

I tried filling the silence. "Perhaps you need to do something to sense the dragon. When Lizzy needed to bind Yuánchi, she projected her mind to where he slept." Every face turned to me. I squinted through my crooked glasses and realized they were surprised. "Did none of you ask how she bound him? I was very curious. She told Yuánchi she would share her life with him. Share her experiences."

Georgiana was very still and watching me. I tried to unravel her expression. Uncertain? Frightened? But frightened of what? She was fearless with draca. I could understand her being frightened of Fènnù, but this was a dragon of song...

"I do not 'project my mind,'" she said at last.

"No," I agreed. "You sing."

She closed her eyes and drew a deep breath. The others might have thought that was resignation or disapproval, but I had seen her shoulders relax to her singer's posture.

Her lips parted, and she began a song rooted in old pentatonic forms but filled with modern, restless accidentals. This was her music, the music of the wyfe of song, music that reached and called...

Power unfolded around her. I had expected it, but the intensity staggered me. The hours of the day, the seasons of the year bent in time. The valley became an amphitheater. And her call grew stronger, shivering the very fabric of the draca realm, crying for an answer...

Her last note faded. Nothing happened. There was no response.

Georgiana's eyes were fixed on mine. She licked her lips, and I thought she would speak, but she did not.

The loyal song draca flew up with a showy flick of his wings and settled on my shoulder.

"Could the little one be the third dragon?" Mr. Knightley suggested hopefully.

"No." Emma and Georgiana answered together, and Georgiana smiled at that. But when she continued, her tone was edged. "If a dragon slumbers here, it is beyond my reach."

Another song draca swooped up, then a third. The new arrivals settled side-by-side on a ruined wall.

"You can wake it," Mr. Darcy said abruptly. "You must. You are a great wyfe."

"Fitz, I *cannot*."

This time, I had concentrated on her voice, not her features, and I sensed an omission, something unsaid. Disturbed, I flipped my mind's eye backward, as if a pictorial history might somehow help. Unexpectedly, it did. "The song draca may not be dragons, but the perfumer thought they were important. She called them *les presages*. Harbingers."

Georgiana seized on that. "They could lead us to the dragon."

"No," Mr. Darcy pronounced. "We stay here. We stay together. Elizabeth may arrive at any moment."

"Fitz..." she said desperately.

"Do you not understand?" he burst out. "Elizabeth is astride the black dragon. If she is not mad already, it is a question of when. We must make every preparation to reclaim her. To... to overcome her, if necessary. You must *try*—"

I could not bear hearing them fight. "She *did* try! Her power filled these hills. Can you not trust your sister?"

He slammed around to face me, flushed, his brow furrowed. Mr. Darcy was not often interrupted.

Georgiana stepped beside me. "Mary and I will follow the song draca. We will stay close. I will know if Fènnù approaches, and we will return." Her brother scowled, but whatever had unnerved Georgiana, it was not his anger. She stared back, equally intense and unmovable.

Finally, he conceded. His eyes drifted to the sky, and he said almost apologetically, "Go."

Without a word, Georgiana set out, choosing a thin rabbit trail toward the meadow's edge. I hurried behind her, the tall grass swishing my skirts. The song draca fluttered randomly around us, perching on ancient bricks, on bushes, on tree limbs. If they were guides, they were poor ones, and Georgiana ignored them. After fifty yards, she turned into the shade of a handful of birches and stopped, her back to me.

I had given up on guessing her thoughts. "What is wrong?"

She swept her hands outward, pushing away speech.

We had crossed a tiny wooden bridge before the birches, three aging boards over a stone-lined ditch. The ground was marshy with rushes and tufted, purple-topped moor grass. Feeling pathetically useless, I studied the trickling water. "These drainage works are everywhere, and very old. The stone is eroded. What if there was a lake in this valley, and they drained it to build the Abbey?"

"Then the dragon of song would be sitting in the meadow," Georgiana said tightly.

I brushed my finger along her wrist. "Are you angry with me?" When she shook her head, I said, "Then *tell* me what is wrong. You do not fear a hidden dragon, but you fear something."

She turned to me, tears in her eyes, and whispered, "I *sang*, but my song was wrong. I knew before I began." She intermeshed her fingers, squeezing until the knuckles blanched. "I have seen visions of the blight since my mother died. I thought they were a summons. A part I was destined to play. I even imagined that Mamma was helping me somehow, guiding me. But now, when the need is desperate, I am failing. What if that is because of what I am? Because of what *we* are to each other?"

I understood her, but I was too surprised to answer.

She rushed on. "You mean more to me than life. I regret no choice I made. I *had* no choice. But draca bind wyves who *marry*." She shoved her arm out, pointing at the meadow. "Emma married, and she senses a dragon. But when I sang—Mary, I *sang*. I held nothing back, and the answer was silence." She grasped my hands, her pianist's grip almost painful. "What if I cannot bind? What if what we have is... wrong, or inferior?"

"That is impossible." I lifted our joined hands, holding hers as tightly as she held mine. "Draca bind for our emotions. They seek out our passions. They have done so in hundreds of cultures for thousands of years. Human customs, our rulers, our religions... all that is ephemera to them. They certainly do not read marriage announcements in *The Times*."

Georgiana gave a crazed laugh at that.

I pulled us closer. "When I was young, my knowledge of binding was what society taught: A virginal lady of good family may bind, and only on her wedding night, and only by gifting extravagant wedding gold to the Church. We have seen all of those claims proven false. You know this. The Britons handfast any who love, even woman to woman. Do those wyves bind?"

"Yes," she admitted, and her desperate grip eased.

"Society's rules for binding are lies to protect the privileged. Ignore them. Draca exist outside of human prejudice and pride. What draca treasure is love."

Her shoulders rose roughly, then fell gracefully. "I know we have that." She rested her forehead on our linked hands, then brushed her lips to my fingers. "Very well. I am less panicked. But *something* is wrong."

"You just have not found the way yet. Be patient."

"You have relieved my mind on one thing. When handfasted wyves bind, they bind once as a couple. I was afraid Fitz was imagining you would bind Fènnù alone. But however these bindings are chosen, you and I will be together."

"Yes," I agreed with a helpless smile. "And, I have an idea about raising the dragon. Fènnù was summoned by the song on her dagger. There were markings on the flute's mouthpiece. I think they are musical notation."

"Could you read them?" she asked.

"No, but I memorized them. The dagger has markings, and the amulet may, too. If we compare them, we may decipher the notation. Then we would know the flute's song."

Her smile dazzled. "Brilliant. The perfect challenge for my great wyfe of song."

"Do not call me that," I protested. "When you sang, the power was—"

She stopped me with a fingertip on my lips. "A pipe organ with the stops pulled, or an orchestra *fortissimo*—those are power, but they are instruments. You *compose* music. How is that not a wyfe of song?" When I tried to answer, she pressed her finger firmly and continued, "And it is pointless to argue about who is or is not a great wyfe because when draca bind, they bind the couple. So, you decipher the song, I sing it, and we *both* bind. No, we should sing it together, of course..." She was supremely confident now and looked so lovely that I abandoned argument and kissed her finger. She smiled... then frowned. "Look at the song draca."

There were a half dozen fluttering, and they seemed to have found a direction at last, swirling excitedly ahead where the wooded patch curved around a rocky outcrop, the base of one of the hills bordering the valley.

"Perhaps they *are* harbingers," Georgiana said, amused. "I just wanted to escape Fitz." She started toward them.

One draca had not joined the cluster. The song draca on my shoulder sank his claws into my dress, flapping and pulling the opposite way. Then I saw the blight-blackened patch of heather beside the path.

I ran and caught Georgiana's arm. "Look." A foul crawler lolled in the rotted heather. It was normal sized, no monster, but very much alive.

A few feet away, a larger one, almost six inches, slunk into view around a small, carnivorous sundew plant. Larger yet and concealed on a birch branch, a winged crawler slowly spread its four wings like a huge dragonfly, studying us.

That variety I had seen only once before.

"We are in trouble," I whispered.

*La Demoiselle des Parfums* strode around the outcrop, trailing her fingers along the stone. We almost collided before she stopped in surprise.

A stale, musky scent surrounded her. Her stylish bonnet was gone, her hair messily fallen. A fresh bruise was purpling her left temple. Her clothes were stained where Rebecca had sprayed draca essence, but her kohl-lined eyes and red lip paint had been carefully reapplied.

The rest of the scene clicked into place as if I was solving a puzzle piece by piece. Her monstrous, saddled crawler waited in the shadows under a distant tree. There were flying crawlers everywhere, camouflaged in the grassy heath or among the birch leaves.

The perfumer blew an irritated sigh. This time, she offered no taunting greetings. She just shoved back her tumbled hair and declared, "I met your sister. The one you said would burn me." Mockingly, she spread her arms—see, I am alive.

"I am glad she did not," I said. "For both of you."

"She has the *dagger*." She threw the word like an accusation.

"Yes," I answered. There was no reason to deny it, but she seemed to be making some point...

"The Bennets have the *flute*." She grabbed my hands, pawing and flipping them as if I might be hiding a flute in my palm.

I shook her off, repulsed and mystified.

"I need the third dragon," she rasped. "Tell me how to wake it." Again, she shoved her unruly hair aside. Her other hand held her bottle of venomous drug. She slopped viscous liquid on her fingers and wiped them roughly across her mouth, leaving her lips and cheek smeared and glistening. The pungent scent burned a sour streak up my nose.

"I will not fight you," I said. A crystal of truth had been growing in me since our confrontation at the museum, since I had tried and failed to attack her, since I had watched Colonel Fremantle die and saved Rebecca, since I had heard Georgiana doubt the legitimacy of our love. "This is a war of men, of their egos and cruelty, not a war of wyves. Your Emperor gives you orders, but the gift you have, your strength, is *yours*. You do not need to serve him. Choose for yourself. You should do as you wish."

"What children Englishwomen are," she scoffed. "*Je fais toujours ce que je veux.*" I always do as I wish.

Her crawlers woke in the tufted grass, on the bending birch branches, their wings buzzing and humming.

Georgiana had watched all this with an air of extreme interest. Now she asked, "This is the one you met at the hospital?"

The perfumer's head pivoted, blinking as if she had not even noticed Georgiana.

"Yes," I answered.

"You did not say she was so pretty," Georgiana said reprovingly.

"I did not think it mattered."

Georgiana tapped her toe. Apparently, it mattered. She addressed the perfumer. "You hurt Mary. You killed her mother. All because you wish to kill a great wyfe."

The perfumer sneered. "*Qui êtes-vous?*" Who are you?

"*La grande dame de la chanson*," Georgiana answered in her superb French. The great wyfe of song.

The perfumer retreated one shocked step, then she lifted her hands. The buzz of her crawlers rose to a roar. Then, more swiftly, their wings folded and stilled. The only sound left was Georgiana's soft melody, a *sotto voce* hum brimming with martial readiness and threat.

Song draca gathered. Another ten. Fifty. They cycled in a menacing mass above the perfumer, a few darting down at her. She stared up into the swirl of sapphire.

"Please do not," I said to Georgiana. "Draca should not be weapons."

Georgiana's song did not falter, but, grudgingly, the violent edge softened.

The perfumer flung up her arms and screamed, "*Je suis aussi fort que—*"

Georgiana punched her on the chin. She fell in a heap.

"I did not know you could do that," I said, looking at the perfumer's unconscious form. She would have another bruise.

"The benefit of being raised by an elder brother," Georgiana said, ruefully examining her knuckles. "Should we tie her up?"

"Get rid of this, first." I took the vial of drug from the perfumer's limp fingers and emptied it into the dirt. I searched her pockets, found another vial and dumped it, but nothing else. "I gave her the flute, what was left of it, but it is gone."

"I thought you memorized the markings?"

"I did, but the amulet and dagger have their own power. The flute may as well."

"I trust in the music," Georgiana said. She gave one of the birch trunks an experimental shove. "We could tie her to a tree..."

"Would she be safe? There are so many crawlers."

Georgiana shrugged with an impressive lack of concern, then brightened. "We can drag her back! One arm each."

I looked at the perfumer's unconscious form, and for all that a part of me wanted her punished, I was frightened by what would happen if Lizzy returned and found her.

"Tie her to a tree," I decided. "Lydia had the same affinity to crawlers. Even without drugs, they... respected her. They will not harm her."

Georgiana looked disappointed by that, but we dragged the perfumer to a tree. She groaned insensible French while I pulled her hands behind it and knotted her silk scarf tight around her wrists.

Georgiana went to examine the perfumer's monstrous, saddled creature. It hunkered down patiently, presumably watching us with its inscrutable, insectile eyes.

I sat on my heels, immersed in fading venomous scent and overcome by strangeness. The perfumer's emerald gown was tailored like court attire, the stitching so fine as to be invisible, the embroidery couched with goldwork. Her neck, lolling to one side, had the refined pallor of a lady who arduously avoided the sun. That must have been a challenge while flying around and killing people. Perhaps that explained her oversized bonnet.

"She murdered the colonel as well," I said. "He had dreams for a life after the war." Confused emotions chased through my head. "I am very tired of having to fight people who hate and hurt others."

Georgiana came to give me a hand up, then her face lifted with an air of listening. "Fènnù is coming." She shivered. "It may have to be us, you know. If Emma is the only one who can raise the dragon of song, we have to bind Fènnù." She rubbed her arms. "When Fènnù trapped my mind at Pemberley, I was terrified. I felt her crawling into my veins, spreading what you said. Hate and hurt."

"Her mind was broken by evil people. She is a victim."

Perhaps the perfumer was a victim too, or perhaps she had always wished to hurt others. Looking at her swelling bruises, then her wasted hips, a symptom of her drug, I felt pity, and guilt for offering her pity.

"We should go..." Georgiana began, then she asked, "Why are the draca so excited?"

The song draca were flashing along the rock outcrop, their wingtips all but grazing it. It was Bargate stone, common in this area, buttery yellow with reddish streaks of iron. The perfumer had been examining it when we met.

Bargate was a sandy stone, but here it gleamed as if polished.

Puzzled, I backed up a few steps, careful to avoid lingering crawlers. The glassy finish extended as far as I could see, the reddish streaks rolling and coiling until they vanished below the weeds and soil.

"I know where the dragon of song is," I said.

## 36

# BREAK OR BIND

## EMMA

Iknelt in the grass, holding the amulet in one hand and resting my other on Yuánchi's muzzle.

The scarlet dragon lay still as death, his fire-bright scales mottled even more with midnight darkness. His sprawled form reminded me of an illustration of a beached whale I was shown as a child. I had cried when that was explained to me, that magnificent creature powerless and doomed outside of its natural domain. Now, I felt the same despair. I could sense the broken song eroding whatever lifeblood gave draca their miraculous vitality.

I squeezed the amulet again, closed my eyes, and thought, *Heal*. Nothing happened. I may as well have thought, *Turn the moon to cheese*. After all this time, even clutching an artifact held by my own ancestor, my gift of healing was merely a window to suffering. I felt a harsh envy for Lady Anne Darcy, so skilled a healer that she had gifted her ability to me through her long-dead wyvern, even if that benefit had been short-lived.

But if my gift was a cruel window, it was a spectacular one. Yuánchi's binding was a scarlet tether surrounded by a huge aura. It stretched into the distance like a dazzling beam of sunset. And that was different from before. When I first met the Darcys, I had been unable to touch Lizzy; their binding was too bright. Now, immersed in that power, I felt wonder.

Wonder, and curiosity. I saw draca bindings as the color of their draca. Yuánchi's true binding was pure scarlet; what I had seen as black streaks were foreign strands wrapped around it like a choking vine.

But even the scarlet core was... flawed...

Yuánchi's blind head stirred weakly. *The wyfe of war comes. The broken song surrounds her.*

"Lizzy is coming," I called to Mr. Darcy, not sure whether to convey the rest. He nodded and rolled his shoulders like a man preparing for battle. Perhaps the rest was assumed.

Nervous, I stood. I knew Lizzy had heard my message, but she and Fènnù should have arrived long ago, and I worried about the delay. I ran my fingers over the burrs and dirt on my clothes. Strange that those imperfections no longer mattered. They seemed proper, a sign of life, of taking risks and caring. But in the back of my mind, a new unease lurked. My obsession with the imagined miasma had been replaced with something real: the spreading blight.

Harriet and Mr. Knightley came to stand with me. The three of us linked arms and watched the sky.

"There have been dreadful moments today," Harriet said, "but wonderful ones, too. I am thankful we returned. You saved all those girls, and I know every one of them."

"That would not have happened without you," I said. "We would not even have the amulet."

"There," Harriet said and pointed.

Fènnù had cleared the horizon, distant enough to appear bird-sized if her wings had not swept with such slow, brutal power. Even that weak illusion faded as she came closer. Half a mile away, she was simply huge. She turned and began a circle around us—a jerky path with swoops and bucks, her head swinging.

"The steed fights the rider," Mr. Darcy said. He crossed his arms, his fingernails white where they squeezed his tensed biceps.

"Perhaps that is a good sign," I said. "Lizzy is seeking control."

Fènnù ended her circle and turned toward us. Blackness began billowing in her wake, the sign of her deadly breath priming.

"Or not good," Mr. Knightley said. "Should we run?"

"If you wish," Mr. Darcy said. "I shall stay." He had described the devastation they crossed while flying here, an area larger than this entire valley. A few yards hardly mattered, and even less to Mr. Darcy. If his wyfe chose to attack, I doubted he cared to escape.

I touched the amulet.

Yuánchi's awareness filled me as if I had embraced his body, the wasting poison of the broken song but also his binding to Lizzy, pulling taut and glowing brighter and brighter.

"Lizzy is drawing on her binding," I said. She was also hastening Yuánchi's descent into whatever fate awaited a dragon mis-bound, but that die was cast when Yuánchi bound her to end his despair after Lady Anne's death. Perhaps he had sensed the decay of the song and knew time was running out.

Fènnù reached the edge of the Abbey meadow and reared stallion-like in midair, black poison spilling from her wings and splattering among the trees. She bellowed; Harriet covered her ears. Then the black dragon smashed down fifty yards from us, each massive claw crushing a wagon load of earth, the crook of a wing pulverizing one of the Abbey's six-hundred-year-old walls.

Lizzy was on the ground; I did not even see how she managed so fast, only that she had run between us and Fènnù. She faced the black dragon, her arms raised wide. Fènnù bellowed an ear-ripping roar, and Lizzy shouted, "No!" The strength of the wyfe of war's command hit me, magnified by her binding to Yuánchi—strength enough, barely, to turn the black dragon from her prey. Fènnù hooted a peculiar, piqued snort, then her wings unfolded to span the meadow. A gale blasted, flinging branches and clods of uprooted grass. Mr. Knightley pulled Harriet and me to him, sheltering us with his back to the storm until the torrent quieted.

"Good God," he said when speech was possible again. "We cannot seriously intend to bind that monster."

Fènnù was airborne and vanishing over the hills. Lizzy stood a few steps from Mr. Darcy, her face pale, the rose-colored mark on her cheek livid. After the unthinkable power she wielded in the world of draca, the woman looked small and vulnerable.

"I am myself again," she told her husband, "for a while."

Mr. Darcy had crouched facing the gale rather than turning away. He was flecked with stems and leaves, his chin grazed by some flying rock. His back was still streaked with drying mud from being pushed off the back of a dragon. Silently, he rose and offered his hand. Lizzy took it and leaned into his chest.

An itch of wrongness, a tug like the old miasma, dragged my vision to the trees sprayed by Fènnù's poison. The black was consuming the bright spring foliage.

Lizzy broke away and ran to where we stood with Yuánchi, pulling her husband with her. She threw her arms around the dragon, her forehead pressed to his cheek. "I can barely sense his mind. This is killing him."

"The broken song is within him," I said. "I see it, like I see the blight spreading in the hills, but I can do nothing to stop it."

She pressed tears from her eyes. "His binding is all that saved me. Fènnù would have taken my mind otherwise."

Mary and Georgiana were rushing across the meadow. They arrived panting, and Mary gasped, "I feared Fènnù was attacking."

"Almost," Lizzy said wearily. "I flew her over the battlefields. England is mustering more troops."

I gathered Mr. Knightley's hand for a hopeful squeeze. "Will we win?"

Lizzy shook her head. "Not against Overseers and their crawlers. They are too lethal. And Napoleon only needs to hold us off. He never planned to conquer England. His goal is more brutal: use Fènnù and the blight to destroy us so he can rule Europe unopposed." She bent to stroke Yuánchi. "That is also his weakness, the reason he is here. He must ensure the great wyves do not heal the song."

"Then the song *can* be healed," Mr. Darcy said. "There is hope."

"The emperor thinks so. And he thinks the key is in Surrey." Lizzy peered at me. "You found the amulet!"

"I do not know what it achieves without the flute," I said, "but it is potent. It showed me the vision again, the three wyves trying to heal the song. To succeed, we need to bind Fènnù."

Lizzy drew back. "*Bind* her?"

There was a babble of discussion, but I was watching Lizzy stroke Yuánchi. Her touch made their binding blaze...

"Give me your hand," I said to her, holding out mine.

She hesitated—I had shied away from touch in the past—but she took it, and their binding flared into exacting detail, a living thing with shifting layers of thread-like filaments. It reached from Yuánchi to Lizzy and then, in a softer, weaker form, touched her husband.

Where it met Lizzy, there was... not a gap exactly, but blemishes. A thread here that would be better there, another that was loose, two that were tangled...

"You are not matched," I said. "Not perfectly. Yuánchi chose to bind you, but a wyfe of war is not his intended partner."

"I know," she said.

"That left flaws." Now that I had seen them, I could not look away. My chuckle hurt; I had practiced so hard to overcome this. "Imperfections I obsess upon." A reckless idea built. "My affinity is manipulating bindings. What if I can break your binding?"

Her eyebrows climbed. "What?"

"Bindings cannot be broken," Mr. Darcy said. "They are until death."

"I broke one," I said. "Not a draca binding, but something like it. I broke the binding between one of those large crawlers and a captive wyfe."

"Those are drug-fueled perversions," he said, "not true bindings."

Mary spoke up. "Draca and crawlers are related, perhaps even the same species." Mr. Darcy scoffed, and Mary bristled. "I performed an experiment—"

"Mary, please wait a minute," Lizzy said. She watched her husband. "Your mother was a wyfe of healing. You told me she released her wyvern."

"Released," Mr. Darcy agreed. "She did not break a binding."

"What is the difference?" Lizzy stood. "This could save Yuánchi, and the wyves could bind correctly. Emma with him, then..." She left the rest unsaid, but her finger rubbed the blemish on her cheek from Fènnù's breath.

"I dislike it," Mr. Darcy said.

"*I* dislike it," Mr. Knightley agreed. "Emma, I was there when you broke the binding. Your mind was gravely affected. I had to *carry* Augusta. And that was only a crawler. This is a dragon."

"I have the amulet now," I pointed out.

"It is still dangerous," he insisted.

"May I speak yet?" Mary asked.

"In a moment," Lizzy said. "Let me ask Yuánchi." Her eyes became distant, then she swallowed. "I can barely feel his mind... Yes. Do it. Yuánchi is failing."

"Just like that?" Mr. Darcy exclaimed. "Without... debate?"

Firmly, Mary said, "That is what I usually say, so it is my turn. First, the debate is short. I saw the great song, or whatever glimpse of it a human mind can perceive. The song is complex and perfect, and it is built on three foundations—the three dragons' songs. It will be impossible to heal the great song if they are mis-bound." Mr. Darcy opened his mouth, and Mary said, "*Second*, Georgiana and I located the third dragon. So, this is not insanity. We can try to bind the dragons."

There was an explosion of questions.

Lizzy ignored them and asked me, "How do we break Yuánchi's binding?"

"Give me your hands." I reached out to her and Mr. Darcy.

"Not yet," Mr. Darcy said to his wyfe. "I agree we should break the binding. But if you are not bound to Fènnù, and she returns, you will be defenseless. We must get everything ready first."

"What else?" Lizzy asked.

I answered. "We must raise the dragon of song."

# 37

## FIRE AND SONG

### MARY

Georgiana was answering the flood of questions. "Mary solved it when she saw the valley walls."

I pointed down. "The dragon is in the stone below us."

Every head dropped to examine the dirt. Mr. Darcy shifted the toe of one boot. "How do you know?"

"I never understood how Fènnù could sleep in the Thames without being found. The river has been sounded countless times. But when Yuánchi and Fènnù rose, the earth shook, and then I remembered the Loch bairn journal, '*her wæs eac eorðstyrung on lak manegum stowum*'—an earthquake at a lake. When draca return to the water, they swim in a fish-like form, but when dragons sleep, they dig into the bottom, into stone itself, then burn it to seal it. The shaking is when they break free." I pointed to the hillside we had seen. "The stone here has been melted and cooled."

"How do we wake a buried dragon?" Mr. Knightley asked.

"Fènnù was raised with her song," Georgiana said. "We need the third dragon's song."

Mr. Darcy shook his head. "Fènnù was raised with her song *and* with the dagger."

"We do not have the flute," I admitted, "but we may have its song. The piece of the flute I held had markings. I think they are musical notation. May I see the amulet?"

Emma lifted it over her head and passed it to me. I rubbed off the dirt, revealing the layered iridescence of Yuánchi's scale. The jade whorls of the setting were intricate but too uniform to conceal information, so I flipped the amulet over.

The backside had irregular, fine radial grooves. Their lengths and spacing varied. I rotated it, mentally piecing them into a horizontal sequence like a musical score.

"The markings on the flute are like these," I said with a surge of excitement. "Musical scores have a... feeling. A structure one sees at a glance. This is notation."

"Can you sing the flute's song?" Georgiana asked.

I was spinning memorized images of the flute in my head and matching the symbols. They were the same, but... "I have not *heard* either song. This is like memorizing an alphabet without hearing the letters." I passed the amulet back to Emma, thinking. "We need Fènnù's song as well. That is the reverse situation: I have sung it, but I have not read the dagger's markings."

Harriet wrapped her arms around herself. "The dagger is dangerous. It summons the black dragon." I had forgotten she was forced to use it while drugged by the slavers.

"Read the markings," Mr. Darcy advised, "but do not sing them. Before we call Fènnù, we must raise the dragon of song, and Emma must break Yuánchi's binding and bind Yuánchi... and Georgiana must bind the dragon of song..." His cheek twitched. It was a daunting list, even if his logic was sound.

Lizzy drew the dagger and shook back the sleeve on her other arm, but I stopped her. "Let me do it. You will make a mess." She hesitated but passed me the dagger.

I used the point to prick the tip of my left, littlest finger, then pressed the flesh with my thumb until drops welled. I painted that down the flat of the blade, away from the serrations. The notation, presumably, was on the smooth part.

Patches of blood began to hiss and smoke, stinking like burned hair. Symbols emerged, metallic-bright in the carbonized ash. I turned the knife horizontal, realized it was upside down, and reversed it. "It uses the same notation."

Eyes smarting from the smoke, I picked out the symbols. More examples helped; rules clicked into place. The markings were more abstract than a musical staff, which literally conveyed pitch. This was like a composer's short-hand for chordal structure. That was a breakthrough, and the symbols fixed in my memory. Structure was easier to recall than randomness.

"Can you sing it?" Mr. Darcy asked, his voice tight. "We do not have much longer."

"Do not rush her," Georgiana warned.

"I am still working on the notation," I muttered, rereading the dagger. Reading was easy now, and this time I imagined Fènnù's song in my mind while I read. I knew the song; I had even transcribed it to paper. "The marks are not a melody. The same symbol can indicate any of several notes. What we humans sing, what we call the song, is one melodic line of many."

Mr. Darcy checked the sky. "We do not need the theory—"

"Be quiet," Georgiana said. "It matters." Mr. Knightley added a cautioning look at Mr. Darcy, who nodded rigidly.

"The notation is like a *cantus firmus* in counterpoint," I mused. "It defines what the song permits. It is rules for how to choose the notes, not the notes themselves..."

"You are marvelous at counterpoint," Georgiana said supportively.

I reread again, hearing Fènnù's song in my mind and sinking deeper into this alien form, music that was not only unfamiliar but inhuman, the harmonic system of another species. As my eyes skipped from symbol to symbol, a whispered voice echoed the tune...

I yanked my eyes away and frowned at the watching faces. "Do not sing."

Heads swiveled. Georgiana said, "Nobody sang."

The whispered voice crooned on in my mind, an inhuman rendition filled with fury.

"Fènnù heard," I realized. "She heard my *thoughts*." I bunched a handful of my skirt and pulled the blade through, stripping whatever power it drew from the blood of a wyfe. The cloth fell in two, sliced by the passing edge, and the blade emerged pristine, the obsidian finish reflecting the sky, but the whisper continued. I slipped the blade through the leather loop for my reticule and let go, spreading my arms wide so my hands were far from it.

"I still hear her," I said.

"Is she coming?" Mr. Darcy asked.

Lizzy turned to the south. A breath later, Emma and Georgiana turned the same way. Through the music, I heard triumph and pursuit...

"Yes," Lizzy said.

"Blast," Mr. Darcy said.

"What do we do?" Emma asked.

"Raise the third dragon," Georgiana said. "Mary, we need the song of the flute."

"I have not even *started* that!" I closed my eyes to shutter distractions and summoned the symbols etched on the flute's joint. Now that I understood them, they were upside down. Drat. Twice in a row. I flipped it, which was harder than reversing the dagger in my hand. I had to read the symbols right-to-left, turning each one mentally and reassembling them...

The notation on the flute emerged from the charred wood then finished cleanly. "I memorized the end of the song. The beginning was burned away."

"Sing the end," Mr. Darcy said. I had never heard his voice so tense.

"I cannot! Each note depends on what came before. They must be derived in order, start to finish. The notation tells *how* to choose what follows each note."

"Music does not work like that," Mr. Darcy exclaimed.

I opened my eyes to explain that, yes, music works exactly like that.

Mr. Darcy was not even watching me; his face was raised to the southern sky. The horizon had been swallowed by a rising wall of black, an inverted thunderstorm boiling up from the earth.

Georgiana took my hands. "Ignore him. I understand. Could we guess the beginning?"

I started a mental list. "Hundreds of beginnings would match... no, hundreds of *thousands*."

"Some variations will sound better," Mr. Knightley said. "Counterpoint can sound pleasant or terrible. Or it may not matter. Try any melody that fits the notation."

"I do not *have* the opening notation! It was lost when the flute burned..."

Except... the French did not think that. They had lore we did not, stolen history of draca and of the Bennet family, and all along, they had insisted that a Bennet had the flute. Even today, after I had handed the perfumer the burned remains, she accused me of having it. She had grabbed my hands.

Lizzy was pacing. "I no longer sense Yuánchi's mind at all. Emma, it is time. Break my binding."

Mr. Darcy tore himself away from the nearing storm. "Fènnù is coming. You will be defenseless."

"That was always the plan. It is just happening sooner than we thought."

Emma gathered Lizzy's and Mr. Darcy's hands, then bowed her head, eyes closed. Mr. Knightley took firm hold of her arm.

"Prepare yourself," he said to Lizzy. "This will be unpleasant."

Georgiana's touch, feather-light, guided my attention back to her. She smiled. "What else can we try?"

I attempted to focus on the flute's music, but my memory refused. It had fixed on a different, irresistible path. Scenes clicked backward through time. A puzzle was solving, but a different puzzle than I had thought...

An image: the museum door labeled *1750–1766*. Then the interior of that crowded storeroom: the curator placing the burned flute in my hand. That was not the key, but it was a clue, one of the discrepancies tugging my attention.

"The notation on the flute was marked on the joint," I said. "That is an odd place to mark something. Assembling the flute would wear away the symbols."

Georgiana's supportive smile did not waver, but her "Good point" sounded forced.

My trail of memories was obliterated by a tremendous power in the draca world, a tension like a celestial bowstring being drawn. Emma's body hunched. In my mind's eye, the amulet blazed up like a sun.

Yuánchi's huge body convulsed, his mass landing hard enough to vibrate my shoes. Lizzy gave an abbreviated, pained cry. The tension wound tighter, as if the world around us was being wrung, a hawser stretched by an elysian windlass...

"What is important about the joint?" Georgiana gasped raggedly. I blinked, forcing my attention away from the world of draca, away from the black storm in the south, and the trail of memory snapped to the instant I sought, the curator's description of how the flute was assembled.

I quoted him aloud: "'A mouthpiece and body joined by an annulet.'"

Georgiana's supportive smile finally failed. "What?"

"An annulet is a circle," I explained. "It would be the diameter of the flute." I let go of her hand and held my thumb and forefinger an inch apart. "*That* is a simple object. That is a shape one could carve from a dragon's claw. It would survive a funeral pyre. It would never melt, not even in a smith's forge, not even submerged in molten metal." I was certain now. "The third wyfe in the vision *did* have the flute."

"We saw her," Georgiana protested. "She had nothing."

I had memorized that scene, three ancient wyves in foreign clothes amid strange plants. Unsure what mattered, I had committed every scrap to memory: shoes, hair bindings, hands...

"She wore a black ring on her thumb," I said. "The color of dragon claw."

The incredible tension in the world of draca skidded then caught, tore then steadied, screeched to an unimaginable peak, and then something beautiful ripped asunder. Lizzy screamed the raw cry of a woman in agony—a mother losing a child, or a mother birthing one. The world froze as scarlet brilliance saturated my brain. That faded, leaving me reeling.

Georgiana fell against me, dazed. Lizzy's screams softened into wailing loss, muffled as she thrashed in her husband's embrace.

Emma dangled lifelessly in Mr. Knightley's arms. He eased her to the ground, called her name, and shook her. Desperately, he shouted, "Mary!"

I helped Georgiana to kneel, then staggered to them and half-fell by Emma's side, the aftershock of Lizzy's broken binding muddling my balance.

Mr. Knightley chafed Emma's whitened face. He put his ear to her lips, then shook her harder. "She is not breathing!"

Training from the clinic returned, in its own way as automatic as memorized music. I pushed him aside. "Let me see." I felt her wrist for a pulse, then the carotid artery... nothing. Her heart had stopped. But it had been only a few seconds... I moved the amulet out of the way, held my fist two measured handbreadths above her, and thumped the precordial region of her chest. I pressed my ear down and heard the frantic pound of a racing heart.

"That worked," I marveled. "I must tell Dr. Davenport. I only saw him try it once, and it did not."

Mr. Knightley, wisely, was ignoring me and comforting Emma while she gasped for air. I tried to order my scrambled brain. What were we supposed to be doing?

"Bind Yuánchi," I told them.

I could hear Lizzy moaning; I remembered the flute and ran to her. Her flailing had stopped. She hung exhausted in Mr. Darcy's arms, her cheeks wet.

Be literal. Be accurate. I dragged my gaze from her pain and spoke to Mr. Darcy. "When you married, Lizzy gave you Papa's wedding ring. I need it."

He raised his head; he was weeping for his wyfe. He stared at me in astonishment. Georgiana staggered to us then and grabbed my shoulder for balance. "Fitz! Give it to her."

Uncomprehending but obedient, he pulled Papa's golden ring off his finger and passed it to me. It felt unexceptional, a man's ring, but it was a

Bennet heirloom—our only real heirloom other than the journal. It had passed through generations, a posy ring inscribed on the inside with verse, but the verse was a family joke because it was worn to illegibility and forgotten.

I held the ring at an angle, peering at the markings inside. The soft gold was worn and scratched, but that was not why it was unintelligible. The symbols were not letters. They never had been. They rose and fell in patterns, musical notation blurred by a layer of gold.

"The Bennets had the flute all along," I said. A thousand years ago, our Scottish ancestor, the son of a great wyfe, had claimed the annulet from the ashes of his shamed mother's pyre. Then he carried it and his Bennet name south to found the Loch bairn estate and start anew.

The dagger still hung from my reticule loop. I pulled it out and slipped the point through the ring, then stabbed it into the ground, staking the ring in place. I summoned the little song draca—it was easy now, I did not even think of music, just thought of him—and he fluttered to the ground at my feet.

I tapped the ring, spinning it around the dagger. His little head pivoted, curious, and I imagined fire.

Not much bigger than a sparrow, he blew a hissing, transparent blue flame from his muzzle, narrow as a pencil but hotter than a bellows-driven forge. The grass and earth around the ring flashed into spitting fire. I blew and waved away the smoke.

Resting in a tiny splash of molten gold, a black circle gleamed.

The blade of the dragon-tooth dagger shimmered with heat, but the hilt was cool. I flipped the ring onto fresh grass, then stomped on it, driving it into the moist spring earth. Steam puffed under my shoe, warming the sole.

I fell on my knees. Georgiana did the same across from me.

The ring was embedded in steaming soil, a shining, perfect black circle unmarred other than a few wayward specs of gold.

"What are you waiting for?" Georgiana asked.

Gingerly, I touched it—

*I SAW three great wyves crowned in shining auras of gold. Rhythmic thunder hastened the surf. Blackness shrouded the sun.*

*The wyfe of healing reached up, drawing forth from the black dragon a black binding, but the binding was fouled with corruption, and blackness drowned them all...*

"MARY!" Georgiana insisted.

"I am..." My fingers shook, feeling that icy death. "Yes, this is it."

I pried the ring out of the steaming earth and held it on my palm between us—the invulnerable annulet that had joined the halves of the flute. Stripped of gold, it was obviously dragon claw, an iridescent shade less black than their teeth, closer to stained, aged pewter.

And scratched inside the circle was notation.

"It is so small," Georgiana said, squinting. "Can you make it out?"

I settled my damaged spectacles, thankful I had not lost them in the flying and crashing and running. "Yes." This was the part I had seen on the burned flute. I rotated it a half turn. "I see the start of the song." I ticked through the symbols, the mysterious notation now as legible as browsing a printed score at Hatchards.

The last symbol locked into memory. "I have it." I held the ring out to Georgiana.

She did not take it.

I moved it closer. "It is powerful. Wear it. You will need it to wake the dragon."

Carefully, she picked it up from my palm. She turned it wonderingly, then took my left hand in hers. "I was foolish to doubt us." She slipped the ring onto my fourth finger. "Mary Bennet, great wyfe of song, the ring is yours. It wedded your sister to my brother, your father to your mother, and wedded all the Bennets before them. Now it weds us, wyfe to wyfe." Then she laughed because the ring hung very loosely on my finger. "But it will be safer to wear it like this." She slipped it on my thumb instead.

Rhythmic thunder quickened to a gale, rippling our hair over our faces, and blackness shrouded the sun.

# 38

# HARMONY

## MARY

Fènnù hung above us, a mountain suspended, rising and falling with the strokes of her wings. Dark cloud boiled outward, and black spray struck the earth.

Lizzy cried out as Fènnù's triumphant thoughts hammered us: *My queen is free.*

Georgiana stared up at the huge shape shadowing us. "I hear her music, but it is wrong..."

Mr. Darcy yelled at me, "Sing, dammit! Raise the third dragon." He turned to Lizzy. "Do not let her bind you. She will carry you away. You are the strongest wyfe of war. *Fight.* Resist her."

Lizzy, eyes raw from losing Yuánchi, took a step toward the black dragon. She lifted a hand, and I braced for the crush of her command, but instead she called to the dragon, "Your great queen is dead." Fènnù bellowed in the air, and Lizzy shouted, "Remember her. I grieve with you. But I am not your queen."

Fènnù's black wings slammed down a freezing blast that tore mist from my breath, then she settled fifty yards away with a savage grace that belied her size. The wind died into stagnant, bitter cold. Grass stalks bent under prickling hoarfrost. The sky stayed inky black, and dusky smoke clung to poisoned patches of moss and turf.

Fènnù's huge head peered forward, her faceted eyes studying Lizzy.

"Hurry," Lizzy advised quietly.

Mr. Knightley had helped Emma to her feet. He half-carried her to Yuánchi, and she collapsed against his huge shoulder. I saw her lips move, then Mr. Knightley shouted, "We must wake Yuánchi. The draca must choose to bind."

"She needs the amulet's song," Georgiana said.

We ran to them, and I sang the first note of Yuánchi's song. I had never heard it, but the first symbol had a single interpretation: the opening note. After that it was an exercise in composition, using the notation's rules to choose notes for our oversimplified human rendition while, in my mind, an elaborate polyphonic song grew, the complexity rising, the constraints on harmonic choice tightening with every measure.

Georgiana listened, her eyes narrow with concentration but unintimidated. Melody was her domain, and draca as well; I felt her power wake. After two measures, she joined, her brilliant soprano singing a harmonic line perfectly fitted to the framework I was building. A bar later, Mr. Knightley joined by doubling my melody, his face jubilant as the song surrounded us. This was more than the mysterious influence of draca; it was musicians improvising in perfect rapport. He smiled and sang to his wyfe, drawing her in, and Emma joined him with a light, untutored, naturally gifted soprano.

As I solved the notation in my mind, I saw that Yuánchi's song did not stand alone. The three songs were linked: a single composition. One great song. I blinked and concentrated harder; that meant all three were necessary to choose the right notes. Mentally, I stacked the notation from the flute, dagger, and amulet, reading them in parallel like a conductor's score.

The song woke the world of draca. Power swirled and grew. Then Yuánchi's scarlet-and-black wings rustled. He dragged them from their crooked rumple and folded them smoothly. His oak-tree legs twitched like a dog dreaming, and a healing warmth seemed to shine from him, a summer sun emerging from cloud.

But the complexity of the song was wild now, and the rules for progressing were unwieldy. It was harder to find a note that satisfied the tripled notation. Despite the freezing air, sweat beaded my forehead. I sang a wrong note and skidded to the correct one. The close call tensed my throat, bad vocal technique which thinned my voice. Georgiana watched me, her tone flawless but her eyes worried.

The song jammed in my mind. I stopped, silenced, unable to find the next note. Georgiana stopped at the same instant. Mr. Knightley and Emma fell silent.

"It is too complicated," I gasped through trembling lips.

"Not complicated," Georgiana said. Her lips moved silently as she remembered what we had sung. "Blighted..."

My mental notation was stuck at the moment we failed. I searched the harmonies, the form of this music, but there was *no* note that satisfied the rules. I backed up a bar, thinking I had picked the wrong path and steered us to a dead end... No. The constraints were so exact, the form so precise, there was only one path, one inevitable result that traced all the way back to how we began.

Latent power still swirled around us, and Yuánchi snorted. Shivering, he yawned cavernously, displaying gleaming black teeth and a viciously scaled tongue. Emma gave a joyful cry and pressed herself against him.

Yuánchi's waking mind spoke, blurry like a person fresh from sleep. *Emma Knightley Woodhouse, wyfe of healing, I choose—*

"No!" I screamed. "Do not bind." I yanked Emma away from him. "The songs are connected—*together* they are the great song. If you bind, Yuánchi's song will be locked in place, and then we cannot change the rest."

Fènnù, inscrutable and looming, had watched our performance. Now, she stirred. Her head tilted. Her jeweled eyes fixed on me, and her icy intelligence pressed suspiciously into my thoughts.

Lizzy was a dozen yards from me, facing Fènnù with Mr. Darcy at her side. "Mary, what are you doing?" she hissed. "She will not wait..."

"This is why the great wyves failed before! Yuánchi was bound before they began, bound with his old song. That doomed them. It was impossible to alter the great song—impossible to heal Fènnù's song."

Fènnù's muzzle approached and sank until her prismatic eyes were level with mine. Her jaw grazed the ground, and the meadow grass, already freezing, shattered to black dust in her shadow. Her breathing changed to a whirring, endless inhalation, the continuous through-breath unique to flying draca, and black exhalation spewed from the ridges along her back.

Her insane croon filled my mind. *My queen is dead. My song is her vengeance. It is unalterable. It is the last. There is nothing to heal. You meddle, wyfe of song.*

Lizzy dashed between me and the black dragon. "My sister is not harming you." Fènnù's attention centered on Lizzy, and the black exhalation stopped.

Then Lizzy shuddered, and I felt a tremendous pressure, a claiming and a grinding conflict... the black dragon had chosen to bind, but Lizzy was resisting.

Lizzy gasped over her shoulder, "Do something!"

"What?" I asked her.

It was Georgiana who answered. "Heal Fènnù's song."

Incredulous, I turned to her. "Did you not *hear*? Fènnù's song is poisoned, but we cannot alter it without breaking the others. The great song itself is *poisoned*."

"I heard," Georgiana said simply. "We need a new great song. So write it."

I laughed in raucous disbelief. "The song is beyond human comprehension. It is so complex—"

"Not beyond yours. You *see* in musical form. You understand it in ways I do not." She took my hand. "Why do you think two wyves of song, melody and form, were born together? You were needed. You are destined for this."

The meadow darkened. Soft clacks and buzzes rose like night creatures awakening. A swarm of flying crawlers erupted from one of the wild fruit trees, spreading and settling in a dozen others. Through the grass and gorse, unpleasant dark shapes scuttled. On a hillside, a stream of blight spread like a dark river.

By our feet, one of the blackened patches of moss split. Crawlers stretched sluggishly in the cold, flexing poisonous stingers then skittering in different directions.

"Mary," she whispered, "just *sing*."

I sang the first phrase that came to mind, the summoning song I used with the little song draca. It was an excerpt from the first fantasia I wrote, a simple piece but one that touched my deepest feelings. It was the first of my music that Georgiana had played.

It was a foolish choice. I should have picked the intellectual rigor of a Bach fugue, or the stupendous breadth of a Beethoven symphony. Those were nearer to the towering complexity of the music of draca.

But Georgiana sang with me, as sure as if our minds were one, and the little song draca flew to me, singing in his clear, bell-like tones. The song changed and grew. My simple fantasia was not lost; it had been a composition of longing, my imagining of a better world, and that remained like the charcoal sketch underlying an oil painting. But Georgiana's voice soared atop the musical foundation I created, an improvisatory descant of pure joy, and her song erased that old pain.

338

Mr. Knightley joined in his powerful tenor—he was nearly as gifted a singer as a violinist. He drew Emma to his side, singing to her, and Emma beckoned Harriet as well. Together, the three of them led one melodic line of the immense construction rising in my mind's eye. Theirs was a melody of care and healing, the scarlet dragon's new song as the lead.

Yuánchi clambered to his feet, wings furled but firm, and he sang a rumbling basso profundo. Emma looked at me, teary-eyed but ready, and I nodded. She wrapped her fingers around the amulet and reached out with her other hand, offering her life and passions to Yuánchi.

*Woodhouse, wyfe and healer,* he answered, *I choose you.*

Their binding took hold, a flawless rose and scarlet sunrise, and warmth swept through the frozen meadow.

Lizzy was still defying the black dragon, withstanding the crushing pressure to bind. Mr. Darcy supported her, his strong arm around her, his stubborn courage aiding her resistance.

The black dragon writhed in frustration and stalked them, the muscles of her hulking chest flexing, her neck curling to whip her carriage-sized head. Ice spread beneath her, and in my mind's eye I saw her old song beside the tower I was building, Fènnù's broken and poisoned song, seething black within a diseased binding that stretched closer and closer to Lizzy's breast...

A scarlet glow surrounded it and pressed it back. Emma's hand was outstretched, the amulet gleaming. The wyfe of healing had bound at last, and Yuánchi's brilliance filled her like the sun.

The black dragon whirled to attack her, rough scales screeching across each other, jaws spreading to strike. But Emma pronounced, "You bind without consent," and the black dragon drew back, shamed, a puppy the size of a warship caught chewing a shoe.

Georgiana and Mr. Knightley were still singing, and I joined them, guiding us to the next theme, the next voice. We gathered around Lizzy and Mr. Darcy. Lizzy lifted her exhausted head, but she sang with me like we had sung together at Longbourn as a family. I wove in the next theme, rich with acceptance, the freezing chill of grief thawing into mourning and then blossoming in the transcendence of hope.

Fènnù snorted and bucked her head, then her immense voice shook my lungs as she joined the verse while Lizzy sang, "Forgive." Their binding took hold, powerful but not frozen and black—it shone with a rich brass glow, tough and resilient.

Georgiana and I sang on, her right hand in my left, the dragon claw ring, last remnant of the flute, touching both our thumbs. In my mind's eye, the rewritten notation of the first two songs receded to harmony, their foundation complete, and the third song filled the colossal fairyland tower, the lead voice in a chorus of healing, justice, and harmony. The last measure was unimaginably complex, finally more than I could comprehend, but I felt the ring warm, and its power invoke. A flock of little song draca swooped around us in celebratory circles, piping harmony in their high voices, and in my mind's eye, the last peaks of the great song resolved in unison.

The ground trembled, swaying the meadow's grass and blooms, then it jolted hard to one side. Blinding light blazed. I closed my eyes, balancing effortlessly while the world wrenched and changed.

An alto voice filled my mind. *Great Wyfe. Mary Wollstonecraft Bennet. I am called Hé Shēng.*

The syllables of the name were foreign, but I knew their meaning better than any feeble human words: the purest harmony, the restful conclusion of a moving melody, the perfect chord whispered by melted drops falling in a snowy glen.

*See me.*

I opened my eyes.

The false night Fènnù erected over the meadow had become a sapphire dawn.

The dragon of song's scales were a mosaic that swirled from sea-blue azurite to grassy emerald. Their shoulders stood as huge as Yuánchi, but it was hard to judge exactly; their wings were half open, tremendous and patterned and iridescent, and my vision was dazzled. I craned my neck as their majestic head rose, silhouetted by nine shining abalone-and-sapphire rays. Invisible warmth radiated; my chilled body drank it, and the blackened patches remaining from Fènnù's breath steamed.

The facets of their eyes flickered through rainbows as they looked over my rumpled, black clothes, then their head lowered to peer beside me and cocked to a bemused angle. Georgiana had fallen to her knees, her head bowed, an arm hiding her eyes.

I whispered, "Get up," and tugged her arm until, eyes still hidden, she stood. I drew her close and said, "You can look." Georgiana lowered her arm and gave a child's amazed gasp.

Hé Shēng's wings rippled, a gesture that should have defied my comprehension, but I sensed welcome and benefaction while wind gusted and the shining rays around their head reflected on azure scales.

*My wyves of song*, Hé Shēng sang affectionately.

Their bright gaze turned to where Yuánchi stood beyond Emma. The scarlet dragon, even blinded and scarred by the blight, was strong and welcoming.

Emma, too, was on her knees with her husband and sister, but Emma's face was lifted and joyful.

*Emma Knightley Woodhouse*, Hé Shēng sang out. *Go forth. Heal the blight. Heal my brother.* Happily, Emma nodded.

Hé Shēng's head and neck turned to Fènnù. The black dragon was a coiling mass, her roughened scales clattering over each other. She was fearsome and proud, and I heard her new song ring out, free of discord.

*Elizabeth Darcy Bennet*, Hé Shēng sang, *help my sister forgive. She tends to rant and storm. Can you teach her a little less prejudice?*

Lizzy and Mr. Darcy were kneeling, heads bowed, their hands clasped with each other, but when Lizzy spoke, she was amused. "If I can achieve that by teasing and quarrelling, I will succeed."

Hé Shēng took a step nearer to Georgiana and me, and the ground trembled in reverent awe. Vast wings washed the sky with patterned whorls, and I saw in them ethereal music as yet unheard.

Sparkling sapphire threads materialized around Georgiana and me, the five mundane lines of a human musical staff but overlaid with the exotic symbols of the draca's music. They settled gently around our shoulders, and with a slight, fond tug, sank through our skin, through muscle and bone until the third song joined our hearts.

The dragon of song sang one last time, rustling my skirts and blanketing me in scents of blooming spring:

*Bound lovers, my brave wyves of song. Go forth and make music.*

# 39

# THREE CODAS

Lady Catherine de Bourgh lay on a quiet Surrey hillside amid birdsong and fresh sun. One side of her gown was dark with blood. A few feet away, a patch of blight slowly spread. By her other side, her bronze wyvern lay curled as if sleeping, her scaled chest rising and falling, the motions strangely slow.

Hesitantly—she had never dared before—Lady Catherine touched her fingers to the wyvern's shoulder. The scales were perfectly fitted, as smooth as porcelain, and as hard as diamond. Warmer than a person, but no warmer than a cat.

The wyvern's muscled, battered, mud- and blood-stained form did not respond. She lay as if dead other than those slow, soft breaths.

The carnage of battle covered the slope. This patch of Surrey, on the fringe of the Donwell Abbey grounds, was a very easy distance from Hartfield. For hundreds of years, it had led an uneventful existence. Now, the dead littered the ground. The victims were foul crawlers and the men who wielded them, the Overseers in their dark gray coats.

The slavers' captive wyves had been spared while their masters died. Drugged and confused, the wyves had wandered away.

One crawler, the length of Lady Catherine's arm, survived as well. It was exploring the dead a dozen yards away from her. Dissatisfied, it reared the first third of its body above the ground, pointed legs weaving, the tongue-like organs between its pincers hunting for scents. It flopped down facing her.

Lady Catherine pried another rock from the ground—a sturdy, apricot-sized rock. She threw it. The rock missed, but the crawler retreated a few feet. Lady Catherine was, however, running out of rocks.

"You don't have to kill them no more," a young boy's voice told her.

Wincing, Lady Catherine twisted her head.

The boy was about ten years old. His bottom lip poked out as he considered the lady's blood-drenched gown and the charred, bedraggled ostrich feather in her turban.

"What else does one do to a crawler, child?" Lady Catherine demanded.

"You just got to make music. Any music. Watch…" He pursed his lips and whistled the tune of "Frère Jacques." Lady Catherine scowled at the choice, but perhaps a mother or an aunt had sung it to him to teach him a few words of French.

The crawler was unaffected. It rattled closer. The boy finished his recitation and watched it fearlessly.

A small, iridescent, sapphire bird swooped overhead, splaying its forked, swallow-like tail. It landed neatly a few feet from Lady Catherine and inspected the motionless wyvern with curious, flicking attention. Instead of a beak, it had a muzzle covered with shining, pebble-like scales.

The song draca hopped around to face the nearing crawler, then it sang—not birdsong with its pleasant, short recitations, but music incandescent with emotion, romance, and longing. The crawler reared, its pincers clicking as it listened.

The song finished in transcendent joy. The crawler relaxed to the ground and writhed into a curling mass, twining, shell segments clicking. It looked like a skein of wool winding itself. The two stingers began extruding a cloudy blue silk, and swiftly it wove a cocoon, arching and rolling its body to cover every part until it was wrapped in fleecy blue, a woolly oval the size of a loaf of bread.

"See?" the boy said proudly.

"I do," Lady Catherine said. "What happens to it now?"

He shrugged. "Don't know." Then his mouth formed a guilty O, and he waved both arms high, shouting in his young, piercing voice, "Found her! Over here!" He whispered to Lady Catherine, "I forgot I was supposed to yell. You won't tell, will you?"

"Certainly not," she agreed.

Mr. Knightley ran up the hill. "Lady Catherine. We were concerned..." He slowed when he saw the dead and fell silent when he saw her condition.

"There were rather more of those fools than I expected," Lady Catherine explained. She sounded tired, and her voice shook a little.

Mrs. Knightley arrived after her husband, puffing from running up the slope in her long skirts.

"You are in a state, woman," Lady Catherine observed disapprovingly.

Mrs. Knightley's gown was thoroughly ruined, and she was both ungloved and her head uncovered. She seemed unconcerned about her clothes though, and knelt by Lady Catherine, looking with great worry at the blood. Mr. Knightley stood gravely while his wyfe took Lady Catherine's hand in both of hers.

"I gather you succeeded," Lady Catherine said. "You and my nephew and... the great wyves."

"Yes," Mrs. Knightley said.

"I saw..." Lady Catherine's strong blue eyes turned to the azure sky, awed, and she did not say what she had seen.

Urgently, Knightley asked his wyfe, "How bad is she?"

"My ability to sense that has passed," Mrs. Knightley answered. As if reminded, she lifted one hand from Lady Catherine's and, unassumingly but with an irrepressible hint of style, swept her fingers through the encroaching, blighted patch. The oily, sticky blackness shed where she touched, running like rainwater and vanishing into the earth.

Lady Catherine's gaze had returned to her bronze wyvern. For the first time, her wrinkled eyes admitted concern. "She was brave and loyal," she said. "More than I deserve. What is wrong with her?"

Mrs. Knightley gave her a comforting smile. "The world has changed. The draca are sleeping to find their place in the new song. Each must choose how they wish to proceed, and to choose their new name as well. She will wake soon."

Mrs. Knightley then looked more carefully at the sleeping wyvern, and at Lady Catherine. She smiled and whispered in the old lady's ear, and a sparkling tear of joy ran from Lady Catherine's eye.

"Where is the nearest doctor?" Mr. Knightley asked his wyfe.

"Whyever do you keep interrupting?" Lady Catherine demanded crossly before Mrs. Knightley could reply. "Are you ill?"

Mr. Knightley, awkwardly, indicated Lady Catherine's blood-drenched gown.

"Heaven and earth! That is not *my* blood." Lady Catherine frowned, very much offended. "I have twisted my ankle. Be useful and give me a hand up."

LORD WELLINGTON STOOD atop a low rise, surveying the victory that would cement his fame.

For this conflict, with the survival of England at stake, he had relied not on battle-hardened troops but the militia, the least renowned of Britain's soldiers. The militia trained for a few weeks a year. They were scorned as grubby farmers and posturing gentlemen by the cavalry and infantry who fought England's wars overseas. But those regular troops were trapped in Spain or shattered by the Confederates' lethal crawlers, so Lord Wellington had sent stealthy agents behind enemy lines to muster the militia in towns and villages. He committed that ragtag force to a last strike, an unimaginable attack from within the conquered south, a blow intended to penetrate the heart of the enemy by capturing or killing the emperor Napoleon himself.

It would have been a bold plan had it a chance of success. Lord Wellington, a consummate strategist and pragmatist, considered it a fool's gamble. But it was better to gamble than present the keys of London to the invaders, so Lord Wellington grit his teeth and sent orders to twenty-two near-amateur regiments in occupied territory. Then he dispatched his most trusted aide north to Pemberley to seek a miracle.

The outcome should have been defeat, a brutal and bloody last stand in eternally dull Surrey. Instead, he beheld the career-capping achievement that would ultimately launch him to Prime Minister in a remade Britain.

In most ways, the spent battlefield looked like any other. Confusion, suffering, exhaustion, and celebration. The surrendered French and Confederate soldiers had been herded into demoralized groups. Carts were carrying wounded to surgeons in tents outside the worst of the muck.

The difference from prior battles was the occasional glimpse of women in filthy, tattered skirts, the captives of the slavers.

His expert gaze stopped on three distant, red-coated militia soldiers clustered oddly, their muskets leveled. Lord Wellington mounted his borrowed gelding, rode several hundred yards, and called, "What have you?"

"If you please, m'lord," one said, and they parted to show a girl dressed in what might charitably be called the worn remnants of a fine white dress. She looked fourteen years old, a child. "She got one of those *monsters*," the soldier pointed out. He spat nervously and aimed his musket at the huge crawler by her feet. It was a foot thick and as long as the girl was tall, one of the heavy-shelled creatures that had torn through English lines.

When the soldier pointed his musket, the girl took a quick step to stay between the barrel and the creature.

Lord Wellington dismounted. The girl's eyes were the muddy brown of the battlefield, the whites bloodshot, the pupils massive, but her gaze met his steadily enough, an achievement not every general could manage.

Beyond her, several Confederate soldiers and an Overseer lay dead, limbs swollen and contorted. The Overseer had a bloody twinned sting on his neck and a pistol in his hand.

"Victory belongs to England," Lord Wellington told the girl. "You are free and safe. Where are you from?"

She had to think a long time before answering, "Brighton."

A soldier guffawed. "Nobody's *from* Brighton." He shrank under Lord Wellington's glance.

"That creature is dangerous," Lord Wellington said to the girl. "Stand aside so we may dispose of it."

She shook her head, and her thin hands clenched to fists. The crawler hissed and clacked sword-long pincers.

"I would be dead without it," she said with a young lady's diction. "At the end the slavers, they... were shooting the girls." She swallowed, and her gaze counted the dead men. "I had to do something."

"The slavers were ungentlemanly criminals and cowards," Lord Wellington noted. "They deserved a foul end. You did nothing wrong."

"What of the others, though?" she whispered. "I remember them, too. I know I will remember them all."

Lord Wellington had spoken with freed wyves. He granted pardon, explaining they had been drugged, tortured, and unaware. But facing this girl, different words emerged.

"We have been soldiers, you and I," he said. "We have done terrible things, but when the battle is done, we return to our lives. The evil memories are left here." He cast his hand at the muddy battlefield, discarding something unworthy.

The girl eyed him distrustfully, which showed her intelligence. He had lied. The memories always followed.

"Gor Blimey," a soldier swore, and the others spun, heads tilting skyward.

The black dragon circled the battlefield once, then settled far enough away that the wind merely rustled their clothing. Lord Wellington lifted his nose to check the air. The wind held no killing cold.

A woman and man dismounted and walked toward them, the man tall, the woman short and swift-paced. Soon, they arrived. Their clothes were as muddied and torn as any soldier after a hard fight, but the man's had been shaken out, the seams pulled straight, his neckcloth retied. The lady's appearance had been recently repaired as well. Lord Wellington, unhappily married and familiar with the intimate habits of a shocking number of women, recognized hair and clothes neatened as much as one could without one's own bedroom and maid.

"Wellington," Mr. Darcy said.

"Darcy," Lord Wellington returned. He bowed to the woman. "Mrs. Darcy."

Mrs. Darcy did not speak.

Lord Wellington's gaze traversed the field of battle. "Fortune favored us today. The slaver's control of their crawlers collapsed as we attacked. Without them, our enemies were swiftly reminded that they were overextended and outnumbered in hostile territory." His gaze finished at the black dragon, colossal, patient, and still. "I assume I should attribute this good fortune to you?"

Mr. Darcy waited for his wyfe to answer, but she either did not hear or did not care to speak, so he replied, "The world of draca has changed. The creatures we call foul crawlers are changing, too."

Lord Wellington nodded once. "I sent a man to Pemberley. Lieutenant Colonel Fremantle. He has not returned."

Mr. Darcy's posture, already excellent, became exact. "He delivered his message and aided Miss Bennet on a crucial and dangerous task. He was a hero. Unfortunately, he did not survive."

After a difficult pause, Lord Wellington asked, "Miss Bennet is well?"

"Yes." Mr. Darcy seemed to have more to say on that topic, but unusually, he struggled to express it. He looked over his shoulder to the south. A wave of tiny birds were approaching, swooping to explore every corner of the battlefield, and watching them, he said, "Quite well." He turned back and asked, "What of Bonaparte?"

Lord Wellington addressed his answer to Mrs. Darcy. "Captured. He is being brought here to formalize terms. He requested, respectfully, to surrender his sword to *la dame de guerre*."

Mrs. Darcy spoke at last. "No."

She walked around Lord Wellington to reach the girl, who was tall for her age, so they were of a height. To her, she said, "The dead are gone. The vengeance they seek, the guilt they would bestow, goes with them into the night. You are forgiven. But keep your memories. Memory is all they have left."

The girl nodded. Mrs. Darcy walked away toward the black dragon.

Lord Wellington, who had watched many soldiers on many battlefields, said to Mr. Darcy, "Care for your wyfe. Take her away from this. She has seen too much."

"I know," said her husband. "I will."

The wave of song draca passed over their heads, and one landed by the girl, singing.

MARY BENNET, dramatic in dark black, puzzled her way through a maze of shattered Bargate stone. An entire side of the hill and thirty yards of the meadow below had been blown apart. The depth of the hole at the center was impossible to judge—it was choked with debris, the bottom already obscured by steaming water.

Freshly fractured gravel slid under her boots as she tried another path. Carefully, she skirted a boulder taller than her which radiated piercing heat. She stopped to examine another, adjusting her crooked spectacles to see the clawed grooves cut into the rock, spanning wider than she could stretch her arms.

This path succeeded, and Mary exited the worst of the debris. She walked beside a rocky outcrop and reached *la Demoiselle des Parfums* who was sitting tiredly, tied with her back to a tree.

"*Mademoiselle Bennet*," the perfumer said hoarsely. Her clothes and face were dusted with crushed stone, and she licked parched lips.

Mary walked to the perfumer's flying steed. It was now a fluffy cocoon of cloudy-blue silk large enough to conceal a pair of oxen. Gingerly, she pressed the side, feeling the stiff chrysalis-like wall beneath and, under that, the churning vigor of metamorphosis.

Cocoons were all around them: secured in trees, tucked in sheltered spots beside rocks. The smallest were fastened under delicate glovewort blossoms.

Mary returned and sat facing the perfumer so their eyes were level. "You have no allies. The slavers are stripped of their perverted servants. Your Emperor is captured. The French soldiers are surrendering, and the English soldiers are searching for you. They despise you. They may shoot you on sight."

*La Demoiselle des Parfums* did not deign to answer, just adjusted her shoulders to a more comfortable position. She eyed the ring on Mary's left thumb.

Mary's hand clenched the lustrous, black band. "Why did you kill my mother?"

"She wielded the golden wyvern. I thought she was *une grande dame*, a great wyfe." The perfumer shrugged. "*Et c'était enfumé.*" And it was smoky. She worked her lips, clearing the dust. "But you are the great wyfe."

Mary burst to her feet, her black-clad arms splayed. A storm of song draca erupted from all sides, filling the air, beating time with their wings, and above them the sky itself folded and turned sapphire. Then the tiny draca settled on branches and bushes, some peering curiously at the silky cocoons, and the great wings withdrew. The clearing quieted.

Mary's shoulders rose and fell. From her reticule, she took a small knife used to lance wounds. She knelt behind the tree and sawed through the tightly knotted silk holding the perfumer's hands.

The perfumer brought her arms forward, grunting and rubbing them.

Mary removed her black spencer and dropped it on the perfumer's satin-clad lap. "Do not flee south. The occupied territories have risen up. A French accent will not serve you well. London is twenty miles north and east. Lose yourself there, if you can."

The perfumer, stiffly, got to her feet. "Why do you free me?"

"It is a time of rebirth."

# 40

## APSLEY HOUSE

### MARY

Georgiana and I rode down Piccadilly, our heavy town coach swaying as we stopped and started in the crowd. It was March, ten months since what they now called the Battle of Highbury. The afternoon sky was blue and the air crisp. The pleasant weather had packed the road, and horses and people cut between the stalled carriages.

"I think I shall walk the rest of the way," I decided. "Meet me at Chathford House for dinner?"

"Wonderful," Georgiana said. She wore, if not the latest fashion, the latest fashion she considered tasteful, a coat cut like a militia officer's uniform, double-breasted and scarlet with prominent angled lapels and shining brass buttons. Some ladies even paired the coat with white pantaloons, but Georgiana had chosen a white wool skirt and a sapphire knitted bonnet that matched her eyes.

"Do hurry," she added. "I missed you during your trip."

"You could have come with me."

"I have had enough of *that*, thank you very much." She examined me with her critical artist's eye. "You look beautiful. Every bit the Bar—"

"Do *not*," I warned. She sealed her lips innocently.

I rapped on the coach's ceiling. We stopped, and the footman let down the step. Georgiana came for a farewell embrace. I buried my nose in her hair, her wool bonnet scratching my temple, and we held each other rather long for a public street. So long, a passing pair of working men, strolling openly hand-in-hand, tipped their hats with a wink.

When the song blossomed, more than draca had changed. London's prejudices were fading in the brilliant spring.

The carriage rolled off, and I picked my way through the Piccadilly crowd, Green Park on my left, mansions on my right. The crowd was abustle with good cheer and normalcy. I attracted few looks; my black gown and scarlet petticoats were no longer noteworthy. Young ladies who wished to shock had moved to a fashion borrowed from Paris fifteen years ago. Then, it was called *croisures à la victime*—victim crosses, red ribbons crisscrossed on a dress to mimic the bloody guillotined executions of the Terror. The English revival, illogically, was also named in French: *cicatrices à la dame*, or wyfe scars. The dresses were black as blight, the back low-cut to expose the shoulder blades, and horizontal red ribbons were strung to mimic the scars of wyves whipped by slavers.

I thought it purposeless, a pursuit of shock, not a call to action. The war was past, and those wounds were healed. Newer causes called.

A pair of young ladies *à la dame* glanced at me as we passed, looked again, then gasped and curtsied. I hurried faster.

Apsley House was one of the larger manses, another notch in the tally of wealth stretching west as London prospered. The front door was standing open and the house under noisy renovation, so I ignored the bell and went in, dodging a spray of dust from workers messily banging bricks out of a wall. I tried my usual path but had to detour around an obstructed door and then a floor torn to bits.

A maid spotted me just before I reached my destination. She rushed to the door before me and announced, "Your Grace, the Baroness Bennet." I must have scowled, as she departed even more swiftly.

The Duke of Wellington rose from his comfortable chair and rubbed his hands happily. "What a ring that has! A duke and a baroness meeting for luncheon."

"At least you sought your title," I muttered. "A peerage is a nuisance. People look at me." There was a freshly opened wooden crate on one side of the study. I brushed aside the straw and found a pair of andirons shaped like dragons. I dragged one out to check the sculpting, straining as it was heavy. "Did you ask for these to be *gilded*?"

"No. That must have been Wyatt. He claims to be an architect, but really he designs furnaces that burn money. I am grateful for your help in reining him in."

"If I am to visit, I need to defend myself from his taste." I frowned at the golden dragon. Why put gilt on something that would be covered with soot? At least this time they had the right number of limbs. The first shipment had been four-legged.

The duke watched with a hint of smile. "I appreciate your help. You are a good friend, Mary." I was considering how to answer when he continued, "If you detest your peerage, why not refuse?"

"Refusal was... discouraged." This led to a topic on my list. "And it presented an opportunity."

The duke, though, was not done with his prior topic. "In the world's eye, Mary Bennet is the sole great wyfe. How amusing that only your identity became public knowledge."

"Amusing," I agreed sourly.

"Cheer up, Mary. You must embrace the politics of the thing. The Prince had to reward someone. And he had to secure your loyalty, or appear to. You bound a dragon."

I settled my spectacles. "I have never commented on that."

"Your pardon." The duke bowed. "It is *rumored* that the Baroness Bennet of Derbyshire is bound to a dragon."

"Dragons—and wyves—do not seem very valued. He rewarded you more handsomely." That sounded petulant, and I regretted saying it.

The duke smiled, not the slightest bit abashed. "Shall we proceed?" He led me around stacked tools and paints into the longest room of the house. The sides had tall scaffolds for installing gilt filigree on the roof and walls. "I think I shall call this room the Gallery. That wall can be paintings depicting the battle. And then down the center, we will put a long table where, once a year, friends, soldiers of every rank, gather to reminisce. We shall toast the future and remember the absent."

His voice roughened at the end. We had our political disagreements, but I respected his love for his men.

We sat at a plain workman's table in the center of the room. The duke noted, "I see you still wear black and scarlet," as a pair of footmen brought platters with silver covers.

"I am mourning the unjust death—"

"—of our fellow sentient animals," he finished with me. The footmen removed the covers, revealing pork chops and pâté. He hastened to explain, "There is no meat. Mushroom pâté, and the pork chops are made from some sort of Chinese bean pudding. If I must eat vegetables when you visit, they may as well *look* like food."

I fiddled with a silver spoon. "I sometimes imagine telling Mamma about being a baroness. She had quite given up on me being *anything*. Her feet would have floated for a day. She adored titles."

"She was your mother. She knew you would achieve great things." The Duke of Wellington lifted his glass. "To Mrs. Bennet, who raised a remarkable cadre of daughters." I had to fumble my spectacles aside to dab my eyes while the footman served the food.

The duke continued, "I did not see you last week."

"I traveled. To America."

The duke gave me a sidelong glance. "An eight-week trip, according to the shipping schedule. Be careful, or you will confirm certain rumors. But why America?"

"I have always been curious about it. It was peculiar to see. Huge plains that are tremendously flat, and only now thawing from winter. I had several meetings attempting to comprehend the politics. The slave states of the Southern Confederate Alliance poured immense funds into the French alliance to conquer England. Defeat weakened them, but also embittered them. They will secede, and civil war is imminent, south against north, earlier than it would have been otherwise. But I think that haste will shorten the conflict. Slavery is more reviled than ever. The abduction of English wyves proved the lie in the slavers' claims of racial entitlement. And the south spent much of their political capital fanning the war with England and Canada, to the cost of everyone."

In my mind's eye, I returned to a street corner in Manhattan. Two American ladies were handing out abolitionist pamphlets. They wore red-ribboned dresses, copying the fashion in London, but in America the style was called *cicatrices à l'esclave*, scars of the slave.

The duke spread mushroom pâté on a slice of rye bread. "If only the government analyzed foreign policy as succinctly as you. I have long held that women are more observant and practical in these matters."

I cut a bite of faux pork chop. "Then you will be pleased tomorrow. I am taking a seat in the House of Lords."

He put down his knife. "You cannot be serious."

"A life peerage entitles one to a seat," I observed mildly.

"Not for women! How do you dream up such modern nonsense?"

"The law does not stipulate gender. And the concept is hardly modern. In the thirteenth and fourteenth centuries, countesses and abbesses served."

We argued about that until the duke was frustrated by the facts and fell into a moody silence.

I, on the other hand, felt invigorated. "There will be objections when I arrive. Will you support me?"

"A woman in the House of Lords..." He stabbed his pork chop with his fork.

"Think of it as a great wyfe rumored to have bound a dragon. The Prince supports me, but privately. He cannot say so publicly."

"The *Prince*?" The Duke of Wellington's brow beetled.

"He chose to 'embrace the politics of the thing.' Is that how you put it?" Mentally, I reviewed the list of lords I had spoken with. "I have support from liberal members, but a word from you would make a difference. The Hero of Highbury would sway die-hard conservatives."

He glared at his plate. "You are more stubborn than your sister. I shall think on it." He took a bite of the faux pork chop and made a face. "This is like jelly. Between this and politics I have lost my appetite."

I was unconvinced by the Chinese bean pudding myself, but I took a hearty bite.

The duke pushed his plate away, folded his arms, and settled irritably in his chair. Finally, he said, "How are your sisters?"

"Kitty wishes *she* were a baroness," I said, picturing her flabbergasted expression. "Jane's new twins are wonderfully healthy, and Jane is back to her sunny self. The binding sickness after her wyvern's death frightened me, but Emma's skills cured it. It was a near thing, though. Emma had to invoke... remarkable power." My skin prickled at the recollection. "I suspect it was worse because Jane had been afflicted before."

The duke nodded, sipping his wine.

I knew which sister actually interested him, but we had arrived at another topic on my list, so he would have to be patient. I tested possible phrasings, then proceeded. "Jane had a difficult few weeks after the twins were born, a type of sadness not uncommon with mothers, so Jemma came to live with Georgiana and me. Jane is past that now, but Charles and Jane have suggested we make that a regular event. Jemma will foster at Pemberley for a few months each year, then longer when she is older. Georgiana and I intend to establish her as heir."

The duke burst out in laughter. "Mary Bennet! You have secured your succession. How aristocratic. Find a spare while you are at it."

"It is not a succession," I said, annoyed. "The peerage is only for life, or I would certainly have refused. Hereditary privilege is a crime."

"Do announce that in the House of Lords. I shall enjoy the show." He considered me, rather like he was appraising a battlefield. "What do you intend to achieve with this new political influence?"

"Voting reform for parliamentary elections, to start."

"To *start*?"

"And an end to the laws that persecute those who love unconventionally."

The duke looked less surprised by that, and more concerned. "You would have better odds in the courts. Have you even observed the House of Lords? I would not have much hope."

"Hope is not something that you have. Hope is something that you create." I pulled out a folded sheet of cheaply printed newspaper, a galley proof before publication. "The editor of *The Morning Herald* sent this to me. He demanded five hundred pounds not to print it."

I handed it across the table, and the duke unfolded it. The title was visible: "The Unnatural Intimacy of Two Famous Ladies."

He read it silently, every word, flattening the creases with businesslike efficiency. When finished, he tossed the page to me. "Tell them to publish and be damned."

After discussing the renovation—we decided to add sculpted dragons to the already elaborate Gallery doorcases—the duke escorted me to the front door. A burst cocoon had been mounted inside the doorpost, the empty puff of silk neatly sliced open from within. It was a common decoration. Many cocoons had opened on a warm day last month, and London, briefly, had been resplendent with glorious creatures. Londoners called it the Day of Song as everyone had heard the music. Only a lucky few perceived the true wonder, a palace etched beyond the tallest steeples, a symphony composed of the emotions that make life precious—and a shining ideal that guided us to greater things than pettiness and strife.

"And Mrs. Darcy?" the duke asked at the door.

It must have required tremendous self-control to wait so long before asking. The best I could answer was, "Lizzy intends to proceed with her plan."

# DONWELL ABBEY

## EMMA

M
r. Knightley and I crossed the dewy lawn of Highbury square. It was morning, not yet ten o'clock. A few locals were about on errands, but most were still at home, busy with the chores that keep a farm or a home pleasant and productive. Soon, they would set out to call on friends or visit the shops, and we would be recognized.

"Take a look at this," Mr. Knightley called. He was bent over the large boulder at the rear of the park, his white-gloved hands clasped behind his back, the elegant topper on his head at a rakish angle.

I walked over. On one face of the boulder, there was a fresh engraving:

*On May 9, 1813, the Battle of Highbury raged in these hills. Commanded by Lord Wellington, the Militia mounted an onslaught of unparalleled valor, and Britain's enemies were put to rout.*

"No mention of great wyves," Mr. Knightley noted.

"That pleases me. Anonymity is welcome."

Mr. Knightley brushed a wayward blonde curl off my forehead. "I fear we are not *that* anonymous." We shared a whimsical smile.

The boulder's little pool was fresh and sparkling, the spring that fed it a happy trickle, but one side of the hillock was blighted, the plants black and stunted. We had traveled through the worst afflicted regions, and compared to those wastelands, this was a little stain, not a threat to a desperately needed crop or a revered stand of stately trees.

Mr. Knightley studied it with a professional air informed by much practice. "It no longer spreads. It has begun to heal itself." He ran his gloved hand along the fresh green sprouting from a patch of blighted stems.

"The blight has passed its worst," I agreed.

I removed a glove and rested my fingertips on the stained earth. The vigor of nature filled me, earthworms and grubs and the even smaller living things that pervaded healthy soil, so tiny I could not make them out with my eyes. Still, it was unpleasant that a pretty hillock looked so sad. I cast a quick glance over my shoulder to ensure we were alone, then the black ran down the stems and vanished into the earth. The healing spread, outward and upward along the slope, until the foliage was green, if a little the worse for wear.

"Where shall we visit next?" Mr. Knightley asked. When I hesitated, he offered quietly, "Hartfield?" and I nodded.

We strolled up Broadway, passing Mrs. Goddard's school. After the invaders surrendered, Mrs. Goddard was discovered locked in her pantry and very furious. She immediately gathered her frightened students and resumed daily instruction in posture, polite conversation, and such accomplishments of literature and music as were suited for country ladies, assuming quite correctly that this was a path to healing.

Two older students, about sixteen years old, emerged as we passed, and they recognized me. "Miss Woodhouse!" one cried, and the other corrected her, "Mrs. *Knightley*."

"It is me, yes," I said cheerfully. I pretended to struggle to recognize such stylish ladies—they were very grownup since we last met—then we shared news of the village. They nudged each other while we conversed, and there was a great deal of concealed, feminine examination of my husband.

One finally blurted, "You are both in a book."

"I know," I said. "Have you read it?"

They nodded. One said superiorly, "It is inaccurate."

"It is not supposed to be accurate," the other protested. "It is social satire."

We bade our farewells and left them debating the matter.

My steps slowed as we approached Hartfield, and Mr. Knightley tightened his hold on my arm. The grounds came into view. The gardens far from the house were overgrown, in some spots wild, in others blighted to bare earth. Of

Hartfield itself there were only low ruins: a perimeter of loose Caen stone from the cladding and collapsed chimneys shorter than my shoulders, each surrounded by sprays of bricks. Not a stem had sprouted within the boundaries of the house proper; even fallen leaves that drifted there had been consumed by blight and the residue of the slavers' poisons.

My brother-in-law's scheme to steal Hartfield ended when he fled. He had made enemies of Britain, France, and the Southern Confederacy. The latest rumor was that he was shivering in a log cabin in Missouri Territory.

"We could rebuild it," Mr. Knightley said.

"And miss enjoying your little loft?" I said.

This had become our game. I had watched Mary and Georgiana exchange knowing glances whenever Chelsea was mentioned, and I had seen the ease with which Mr. Knightley hired coaches, tailors, and accommodations during our long tour of England. There was more to my husband's fortune than the uncertain income of a performing musician. The details, however, he kept to himself other than a few teasing smiles.

"In fact, I have decided to gift Hartfield to Harriet," I said. "That and the amulet. Papa did intend it for her." This seemed like the right time to end our game; it would not be fair to let it impact my sister, so I asked, "Could we rebuild it for her? It does not have to be as grand as it was before, but empty dirt and overgrown gardens are not much of a gift."

Mr. Knightley nodded, accepting the adjustment to our rules. "I think that very suitable. Although Harriet seems happy in London." As headmistress, she had reopened the Martin school, and she was extraordinarily busy the last time we met.

"She is happy, but I think she will miss the countryside eventually, and Mrs. Goddard cannot run the local school forever. Or Harriet could offer Hartfield to let. A lady benefits from diverse income. Either way, I will need a project after this." I touched the breast of my gown; the amulet was tucked within. "Harriet can tell me what she wishes for her house, and I will hire craftsmen and pester them until they send me on pretend errands to have some peace."

Mr. Knightley smiled at me and ran a gloved fingertip along the amulet's chain, exposed above my collar; a pleasant shiver climbed my spine.

"You think it is time to part with it?" he asked.

I drew the amulet out, cradling the jade and the familiar roughness of Yuánchi's scale. The vital energy of the dragon of healing filled me, and in the woods, a few lingering, hidden cocoons stirred and opened. Shining creatures met in dancing flight above Hartfield's grounds. In the last months, the cocooned crawlers had erupted in a dizzying variety of forms. These had humming, dragonfly-like wings with patterns as colorful as butterflies. They lit on the ruins here and there, and the black blight receded. Hartfield was transformed, no longer stained but filled with potential.

They finished and flew into the woods, and I tucked the amulet away. "I will need it once more."

DONWELL ABBEY WAS FULLY SUBMERGED NOW. The valley's flood began slowly but inexorably, fed by subterranean springs released when Hé Shēng rose. After that, the pace quickened as the ancient drainage works failed. Some had been damaged by the earthquake. Others, mysteriously, became plugged with rocks and wood debris, often on moonless nights when the deepening lake shivered with swift ripples and strange splashes.

I missed the scattered fruit trees, seeded wild from the orchards, but the lake brought its own beauty. The young shoreline was a mess of submerged brush and the odd rotting tree, but ducks nested and dove with industry, fish jumped, and a few swans drifted elegantly.

Yuánchi's spread wings became visible in the west. He had been far in that direction for weeks, somewhere he called "the sunset rock." I thought that was likely Ireland, although I could not be sure. Draca did not share humans' obsession with names and borders.

He circled the lake, the pair of ivory firedrakes scouting ahead, then landed in a flat, grassy patch. We walked to him, enjoying the warming morning while he half-spread his wings in the sun.

*Emma Knightley Woodhouse*, he greeted me, then added, *Musician*, to Mr. Knightley. That was high recognition from a being who was old when the Vikings rowed their ships to our shores, old when Christ was born, old even when the first druid chanted a song to nature's wonder.

His scales were almost fully scarlet now, the discolored ones gradually shed and replaced. The new ones emerged brighter red and slightly flexible, then hardened to a rich, deep color and diamond edge. His beautiful eyes, though, were beyond simple healing. They remained weeping pits of ragged scales. A more profound slumber was needed for that.

He moved his huge muzzle close, and I scratched hard under his chin, a trick I learned from Lizzy. One had to scratch the right direction though, or the scales cut. He rumbled affectionately, a purr that made my skirt hems tremble.

"There was a wyfe of healing before me," I said to him. "Lady Anne." To help with the name, I imagined her sculpture at Pemberley, young and strong, her wyvern at her side.

Yuánchi's head tilted while he thought, a mannerism shared by humans and draca. *I felt her while I slept.*

"She made a sacrifice so the song could be healed. You remember your bound wyves. I wish she could be in your next song."

Yuánchi snorted. *We did not bind. I do not know her.*

"The wyverns hold the lore," I reminded him. With the amulet in hand, I reached out to those sparks of wisdom scattered across Britain. Collected memories returned, a portrait of a great wyfe, of a caring healer, of a woman who foresaw the blight. Of a Darcy, faithful and bold.

Yuánchi studied the memories, curious like all his kind. He would not be swayed by maudlin sympathy, so I was in suspense until he concluded, *Moral right. Sacrifice. Loyalty. I shall weave her into my song.*

He sighed, or it seemed like a sigh. It almost knocked off my bonnet.

*I must go into the deep*, he thought.

"Do you wish to say farewell to Lizzy?"

*I have.*

Awkwardly, for he was very large, I hugged him for a full minute. Then Mr. Knightley handed me the plaited red lanyard, and I tied it around one of Yuánchi's claws. It would not hold for long—the claw was too sharp—but it completed a path, one healer's wisdom aiding another. And it was a token of two weddings as well.

Mr. Knightley and I backed away, and dabbing tears, I watched the scarlet dragon fly high and descend into the water, frightening the ducks.

Mr. Knightley put his arm around my shoulders, and we watched the world. A hundred years might pass before the scarlet dragon rose, or a thousand, but when he did, he would be freshly named, and the great song would advance, an ever-changing chorus. For life is change.

"Where next?" Mr. Knightley said at last.

"Pemberley."

## 4 2

# FAREWELLS

## LIZZY

I stood in Darcy's and my bedroom. Pemberley truly felt like home now, and I was leaving.

"I will finish packing," Lucy assured me, "and do it better than you. You forget the little things." As illustration, she held up the silver comb she preferred when doing up my hair.

I thanked her, not mentioning that I had tucked a simpler shell comb in a side pocket, then gave her an impetuous hug. Lucy was a young lady now, refined of speech and certain of opinion, and she was often off sharing a meal with the Digweeds or walking with young Thomas. I had a strong suspicion where that was headed, and I would not be surprised if my arms held a future headwoman of the Britons.

I walked the halls of Pemberley, moving slowly to cherish it, but past lives whispered when I was alone, so I picked up my feet. I spotted activity in the library and stuck my head in to see.

"Lizzy," Mary noted, her spectacles catching the light as she looked up. Pemberley's restored Venetian glass chandelier hung behind her, the fixtures reshaped to celebrate the myriad forms of new-hatched draca. Even unlit, it was beautiful in the morning light.

Mary had an array of hoary old books spread on one of the library tables, the bindings battered and frayed.

"Are you sorting?" I asked. Mary was an inveterate sorter. That thought, like so many, plucked absurd emotional strings, which made me laugh at myself. Sorting was not a profound thing.

Mary considered my laugh with mild frustration, unsure why I was amused, then she explained, "Returning books, not sorting." She swept her hand above them, and I saw the titles were references on draca and histories of Pemberley and the Darcys. The most ancient, in French and Latin, were three ragged volumes on *L'Enfant du Lac*, the Child of the Lake.

"These are the books Lydia and Wickham stole," I exclaimed. "How did you retrieve them?"

"I have a covert acquaintance in the Paris court."

"Really, Mary, you are becoming positively frightening."

She blinked at me, unconventional with her straight hair and elegantly fitted but inky-black gown, and she looked like a fierce-minded northern baroness in one of Georgiana's moody, romantic paintings.

"I am making my way to the garden," I said, as a gentle reminder.

"I know it is time. I was just not yet... able." She settled her spectacles. "I have some books from Longbourn. I thought you might wish to take these?" From a stack on another shelf, she offered me three slim volumes titled *Visions of a Fair Society* by James Bennet.

"The books Papa wrote," I said, looking them over.

"You intended to read them," Mary noted, "and they are not very big."

"Are they good?" I did not need to ask if she had read them.

Mary seemed mystified. Finally, she emphasized, "They are by *Papa*."

"You do not need them?"

"I remember them," she said. "And I have this."

She showed me a different book from that stack, opening it to the title page: *A Vindication of the Rights of Woman* by Mary Wollstonecraft. It was signed by her in June 1793, two months before Mary was born.

Below that, Papa had added a later dedication:

*"Dear Mary. Play all the Beethoven you like. With great love, your foolish father."*

She said, "He gave it to me because of the ball..." then her voice failed.

"How lovely."

She removed her spectacles to wipe her eyes. "I shall miss you, Lizzy."

"And I, you."

FAMILY AND FRIENDS were assembling in the north garden. Kitty ran to me while an unfamiliar Navy officer followed in her wake looking hopelessly smitten.

"Goodness, Lizzy!" she said to me. "You are dressed like a man!"

"Flying gear," I explained. "It is cold and windy up high. Damp, too, in the clouds." I showed her my goggles, which I would not put on until the last moment. She pursed her lips, unconvinced by my fashion choices.

The Duke of Wellington was waiting with a characteristically quirked smile. His bow was casual. "Mrs. Darcy. I have not gotten a straight answer from your husband on where you two will go."

"We have not fully decided," I said. "Darcy has arranged meetings in Egypt, so we shall start there. That is where the song was broken. But the history of draca and binding are farther east, and much more ancient."

"What do you expect to learn?"

I lowered my voice. Some here would understand; some would not. "It is not about learning. I am... overfilled with the passions and vengeance of past wyves. I hope to set them to rest, one-by-one, or at least to understand them better. It will be a long enterprise."

The duke's gray-blue eyes were compassionate. "May they, and you, find rest."

Mary and Georgiana arrived then with Darcy. He took his place at my side, looking very technological wrapped in leather flying gear with several unnecessary attachments, compasses and sextants and the like.

The duke nodded a greeting to Mary and said to us both, "Tinsdale sends his regards."

"He would not dare," Mary scoffed.

"He certainly *would* dare," I said. "That man has always fantasized he had influence and respect beyond his merits."

"I think his merits fit very comfortably in his small prison cell," the duke replied.

"What of Bonaparte?" Darcy asked him.

"He is on St. Helena, a remote island, in exile. Another prison, but more comfortable."

"You saved his life," I said. There had been bloodthirsty calls for Napoleon's execution after his defeat. It would have happened if the Hero of Highbury had not insisted otherwise.

"I also seek to put aside vengeance," the duke answered, his gaze serious.

The Knightleys watched from beyond the bustle. They made a striking couple, his hair and coat black, her dress and bonnet canary yellow. Emma tilted her head toward the wild northern edge of the garden, and Darcy and I slipped behind a holly hedge to join them in the ivory alcove with its carved stone table and mysterious old statues.

Darcy took Mr. Knightley's hand for a long, wordless time—an emotional spectacle for him. Then he clapped him on the shoulder. "I read your and Herr Beethoven's interview in *The Times*."

Mr. Knightley laughed dismissively, but Emma was having none of that. "They are partnering to promote his music in Britain. We had luncheon together to celebrate, although I did not understand all the German chatter."

"Our meeting—our reconciliation—would never have happened without your encouragement," her husband told her, and they smiled.

"It was a coup for Knightley Press," Darcy noted. "At this rate, you will be the preeminent music publisher in Britain." He always admired a well-run business.

Darcy turned to Emma next. She offered her gloved hand, and he bowed over it. They watched each other for a breath before he said, "Mrs. Knightley," and she returned, "Mr. Darcy."

I sometimes wondered what had transpired between them during my months in the lake. I did not feel jealous—that was impossible when I was so securely wrapped in Darcy's love—but they had a rare intimacy for a gentleman and lady.

"So, the great wyves part," Emma said to me.

"Do not blame me," I protested. "You two traipsed around England for a year."

"Your trip will be longer," she said with the mystic certainty she occasionally produced since her marriage and binding.

The four of us rejoined the gathering, and I issued a silent call.

Georgiana found us and gave her brother an unashamed, adoring hug. Then she presented him with a novel. "Something to read on your travels."

Darcy frowned. "Fiction," he pronounced disapprovingly.

Georgiana smiled innocently. "You may be surprised. She has a sharp eye for character."

I stifled a snort. After Lord Wellington introduced me to the author, I had spent several afternoons recounting events. The published version of *Pride and Prejudice* had turned out quite differently and was very much fiction, but the portrayal of Darcy had a certain... accuracy.

Fènnù's great form winged into view over the north hill. Even after all this time, her sheer heft was shocking. She settled in a cleared area that overlooked the lake. She was sleekly clothed in bronze scales, and when her voice sounded in my mind, it was still haughty as a queen but no longer ranging with mad cadences.

*Wyfe of war.*

*Lizzy*, I thought back firmly, and we stared at each other in what had become a familiar impasse, her eyes faceted, prismatic, and penetrating, mine... brown, I supposed.

Mrs. Reynolds scolded the wavering footmen until they carried the trunks over and began strapping them in. Then she approached and curtsied gravely. "Mr. Darcy."

"Mrs. Reynolds," he replied, and bowed.

She curtsied to me next. "May you have a fair flight, madam."

I knew she had no more patience for gratuitous display than Darcy, so I answered simply, "Thank you. You have always made me very welcome. Do take care of Georgiana and Mary."

"They are the Mistresses of Pemberley," Mrs. Reynolds pronounced, and that said it all.

Darcy, though, turned back to Mary. "Have you checked on Helmsdale?"

"You asked me three days ago," she said dryly, "and it still proceeds well. The herring fishery is lucrative. That horrid factor fled telling tales of dragons, and the Staffords—they own the land—spent our meeting eyeing me and watching the sky. They have waived any tax, so the cannery benefits flow to the community." She smiled suddenly. "I *did* forget to tell you something. Kitty was a great help in securing the Navy contract."

"I know *all* the officers," Kitty said proudly.

"They really do have everything in hand," I said softly to Darcy.

"I know," he admitted stiffly. "It is just a very great change."

"Feeling regrets?"

He shook his head and smiled. "Never, Mrs. Darcy."

The harness maker, on loan from Harriet's school in London, was assisting Lucy and Nessy in explaining the luggage buckles to the footmen. When they finished, I waited while Darcy climbed the ladder-like stirrup to his seat. Then Fènnù swung the elbow of her wing to the ground. I hopped on and let her lift me until I could step nonchalantly onto the saddle. It was a showy way to mount, but the occasion called for panache.

To Fènnù, I thought, *We will fly far.*

Slabs of muscle shifted in her thighs, and we rocked upward. Fènnù took a huge step to the garden's edge and leaned expectantly, admiring the precipitous drop to the lake.

*Fly where?* she asked.

I pictured the Egyptian queen I first saw when I dipped my fingers into the frozen Thames, a vision from Fènnù's memory while she slept in the water below. Fènnù tensed, her bronze scales tightening into the defensive shield of draca, but she relaxed when I stroked her neck.

"We will learn of the past," I whispered, "and learn to forgive. Then, we shall dance to the great song."

# EPILOGUE: PRESENT DAY

O livia rubs her strained eyes, rapid circles to purge fatigue. Her phone glows *Monday 9:14 AM*. She sits on a battered wooden rolling chair in the Apsley House research office. The office is not open to the public; it is a modern room concealed down a flight of stairs, half subterranean and renovated in the '80s. The high-set windows look authentic from outside but sport aluminum frames.

The double-paned glass is rose and orange with the onset of day, and it muffles the crowd milling in Hyde Park. A short walk away, the Thames rises and falls, tidal even in the center of London. Every month, the water laps higher.

Olivia is breathing fast. As confirmation, to test reality, she lowers her hands over the thick sheaf of paper, but her fingers flinch from touching—even after turning every page, years of conservation training scream: this is precious.

The final page is crammed with tidy, efficient cursive. The entire manuscript is the same. This is not a "fair copy" for publication—it is a working draft with inky crossings-out and corrections. The longer insertions are carefully sized rectangles of ladies' stationery pasted along a single edge so they can be folded aside.

After the story, a personal note is written:

*"The finished manuscript! It was difficult with the Darcys' whereabouts unknown, but I visited Pemberley to fill in the gaps. I have become good friends with young Jemma, who is only three but calls me Aunt Jane and loves stories of Fairyland.*

*I am very tired, though, so I chuse to leave this factual chronicle in your hands. If you can secure the assent of princes and find a publisher who tolerates an earnest female authoress, I shall be delighted to see it in print.*

*J.A., Apr. 23d, 1816"*

"Bloody hell," Olivia breathes and rushes her hands through her hair, hooking the strands behind her ears. She returns the pages to the nondescript cardboard box and cautiously carries it up the steps.

Apsley House is closed to the public on weekdays. She cuts through the empty Gallery, her gaze catching on a sculpted dragon, then through a short, modern exhibit, the exit for visitors after they tour the historically preserved parts of the house.

She pauses at a bell jar displaying a wickedly curved black claw the length of her longest finger. The card says:

*Firedrake claw, personal collection,*
*1st Duke of Wellington*

The wall behind holds a large poster featuring an artist's conception of a dragon in flight:

*Draca: Truth and Myth*

*Rare physical evidence, such as this claw, prove that draca were more than exotic birds and reptiles imported as pets. Indeed, the fewer than two dozen claws and scales in the UK are the object of intense scientific research. Their unique properties remind us of nature's ability to amaze.*

*More mysterious is the unexplained disappearance of draca. The last credible sighting was in Leatherhead, Surrey, 1823.*

*But did huge dragons fly in English skies? Naval logs from Nov 19, 1812 attribute England's disastrous losses to a dragon, and London newspapers from the time are filled with eyewitness accounts. However, skeptics claim exaggeration. The agricultural plague of 1813 and the horrors of the war, when French cannon-ades leveled whole neighborhoods of London, spawned hysteria—*

Olivia laughs wildly and runs, barging into the private wing of the house, then the administrative office.

The curator looks up from a book. "You're in early." His eyes narrow. "You look awful. Have you slept?"

"Hardly. I was here all weekend."

"Another repatriation?" he asks, resigned.

"What do you know about *Pride and Prejudice*?"

The curator chuckles. "Less than you, I'm sure." Olivia waits; the curator rolls his eyes and replies, "Austen's second published novel. Romantic fare that was popular during the 1812–13 war and the recovery. People were hungry for escapist fiction, and cleverly, she completely ignored the war. The book features Bennets"—he pauses, but Olivia says nothing, so he resumes—"and satirizes the reclusive and wealthy Darcy family, the subject of great social curiosity at the time. If I have any scholarship to offer, it's that I'm amazed the Darcys allowed publication. They had the resources to prevent it."

"Her first attempt to publish *was* blocked," Olivia says. "By the govern-ment. It was only after she rewrote it that she found a publisher."

"*That* is hearsay from her brother, and long after the fact. I can't conceive why the government would care. The Prince Regent was a fan of her books."

Wordlessly, Olivia slides the cardboard box in front of him. The last page is on top.

He fishes out his glasses and reads, frowning. "You can't seriously think you have discovered a note written by Jane Austen."

"Not a note. An entire lost manuscript. The *true* story."

He shakes his head despairingly. "Olivia..."

"Austen's invitation to Carlton House was always peculiar. Why invite an author to the royal residence? That's what '*assent of princes*' means—they were discussing whether to publish." She senses skepticism and hurries on. "It's her handwriting. Her signature. Why *not* her?"

He removes his reading glasses. "Because the Duke of Wellington would not *have* a lost Austen manuscript?"

"If you read back"—she leans across his desk, hunting through the pages —"he knew her. He introduced her to the Darcys. I think he wanted the truth recorded, even if it could not be published—"

The curator presses his spread hands outward, infringing Olivia's space until she retreats, wrapping her left hand in her right and thumping back into her seat.

"A historian's personal interests must not affect analysis," he says firmly. It is his turn to lean across the desk; he squints dramatically and reads her staff badge aloud. "Dr. Olivia *Bennet*. I understand your fascination. But your research grant is not to invent outlandish theories about nineteenth century novelists— or characters in their stories. Our narrow but valuable mission is cataloging the voluminous writings and miscellanea of the Dukes of Wellington."

Distant chants sound outside. Today is a day of protest, a march down Piccadilly to Leicester Square. Some of her friends are there. Her generation are cynics, impoverished while trillionaires burn the world.

Olivia is not a cynic. She knows how swiftly good can triumph. She is completing post-doctoral research on the Second Renaissance, the remarkable decade that blossomed after the Anglo-French-Confederate war.

"Read it," Olivia says simply. "Every word is true. I know."

The curator looks faintly disappointed. "How could you know that?"

She does not answer, only twists the ring on her left thumb, her family heirloom, lustrous and black with strange marks inside.

*The End*

THANK you for reading *Dragons of the Great Wyves*, the conclusion of the Jane Austen Fantasy trilogy. I began this as a whimsical homage to two literary loves: Jane Austen and fantasy (dragons, really), and the response and support has been wonderful.

If you join my mail list, I give you free ebooks! There are three "NOTES" editions now, one for each book in the series. They include a cozy novella *Emma in Highbury*, deleted scenes, alternate chapters, and interesting (I hope) thoughts on the writing and history of the series.

To get your free copies, sign up for news at mverant.com/join. You'll hear about my future book releases, and little else. I send very few emails, usually one or two a year.

Finally, I'd be grateful if you'd tell a friend about these books, or review or rate *Dragons of the Great Wyves*. Your recommendations and reviews are crucial for a book's success, and they help other readers find stories they enjoy. To quote Elizabeth Bennet: "My good qualities are under your protection, and you are to exaggerate them as much as possible."

Find out more about me and my books at mverant.com or follow me on Bluesky @mverant.com

May you be bound with love.

M. Verant

# SOLEMN SPECIOUS NONSENSE

## AN AFTERWORD

I began writing *Miss Bennet's Dragon* in late 2019. I'm writing this Afterword in the summer of 2025, five years later. A long time. For those who started reading when the first book released: Thank you for your encouragement. You have been wonderfully patient.

Writing *Dragons of the Great Wyves* was a little different from the prior books—this time, no new Austen novel was added. While working on book 2, I suspected the combined cast of *Emma* and *Pride and Prejudice* would be enough, and by the time I started book 3, I acknowledged the truth—there was already plenty going on! I had three big stories to finish: Mary, Emma, and Lizzy.

Mary's arc has been longest, from a determined but bookish middle sister to a great wyfe, and her story is bookended by her relationship with her father. She starts book 1 in conflict ("And did you eat no bacon this whole week?" asked Papa, astonished) and finishes holding the book he inscribed to her. I can easily imagine Austen's Mr. Bennet, younger but already sequestered in his library, reading incendiary Mary Wollstonecraft and deciding to name his third daughter after her—with all the crushing parental expectations that would entail.

I'm very fond of Mary... good thing, as she's been living rent free in my head for years. For me, she provides a moral bridge between Austen's nineteenth century society and our modern sensibilities (or mine, anyway). Still, I'm always surprised when I stumble across some 1812 political treatise and remember that Mary's progressive views were championed by Regency reformists.

Emma has had her share of darkness and danger, so I loved writing her and Knightley's slow-burn romance. I even adapted a famous Romance trope for their fake marriage—I think I wrote that on a dare. Emma may be the most changed character in these books, maturing emotionally while internalizing seismic jolts to her privileged identity. And here at last, we follow her into Highbury, meeting fabulous Miss Bates and sinister specters from Emma's past. I had not the slightest guilt about tossing Lady Catherine and the Collinses into the mix as well. Someone had to perform the wedding.

The story finishes with Elizabeth Darcy Bennet. Sparkling Lizzy will always be my favorite Austen character. She's very real to me; it was emotionally rough writing her illness in book 2, and then in book 3, shadowing her with violence from her past lives. From a writing perspective, she's also a fantastically potent character, which creates a challenge: What force can withstand the combined might of Lizzy's wit and a wyfe of war's power? The answer of course is Darcy in full Lancelot-style pursuit of love. I've written in his POV before (in the free extras), but here he grudgingly grants us a five-chapter visit to his disciplined world.

In my books, good triumphs, even if it takes a while. The trick for writing book 3 was to conquer evil without Lizzy hulk smashing all the enemies. (The perfumer is an exception, but she had it coming.) I hope I succeeded in telling a story of healing, not of conquest, and as the curtain falls, I see sparkling Lizzy restored and quirking a smile as she flies to her next adventure.

Some historical notes:

Both Mary's and Lizzy's friendships with Lord Wellington were inspired by a fascinating exhibit in Apsley House about his relationships with women. The duke was a famously conservative force in English politics, but he formed close friendships with intelligent women who challenged his opinions and beliefs. Mary's visit to Apsley House reflects the duke's friendship with Mrs. Harriet Arbuthnot, who advised and consoled him during his house renovations. (If you visit Apsley House, check the dragons in the décor. I'm pleased to say they are, correctly, two-legged.)

"Publish and be damned" is a Wellington quote, but from a different type of relationship. It was his answer to courtesan Harriette Wilson when she threatened to expose their romance in a tell-all memoir. One of Mary's lines in the Apsley chapter is also borrowed: after meeting climate activist Greta Thunberg, Alexandria Ocasio-Cortez said, "Hope is not something that you have. Hope is something that you create."

The account of Mr. Knightley's falling out with Beethoven depicts the real life of Afro-European violinist George Bridgetower, who inspired my Knightley character (I find Austen's Knightley, although admirable, rather unromantic). That history is so remarkable, I was tempted to add Beethoven as a character.

In the *Emma's Dragon* Afterword and extras, I listed historical reasons for the racial diversity and LGBT representation in Jane Austen Fantasy. The first chapter of *Dragons of the Great Wyves* provides another example, Dr. James Barry. Barry had a distinguished medical career, including serving at the Royal Military Hospital in Plymouth, but he is most famous because he was born a girl, Margaret Anne Bulkley. Today, we might describe him as transgender or gender non-conforming. His understated presence is a tribute to the brave trans people I know, who wish simply to live their lives with privacy and dignity.

Another real event in book 3 is the Highland Clearances. One joy of Austen's stories is escaping into her comforting and idealized country society, but—dragons aside—I try to portray a more realistic Regency. The clearance of the Kildonan strath spanned decades, but the harrowing events depicted here occurred in 1813, the same year that Austen set her novel *Emma*. Donald Macleod's account, republished decades later in Canada, provided details.

I'm a novelist, though, not a historian. Errors are either to serve the story or simply my mistakes.

Finally, this book ends with a present-day epilogue. This is a controversial finish; some like it, some don't. For me, though, this is my final bow to Jane Austen, a muse and a lifelong joy. In fact, my first draft had an even more escapist revision of Austen's life. You can find that in *NOTES of the Great Wyves*, one of the free ebooks I give to mail list subscribers. If you've not yet read them, please visit mverant.com/join.

Thank you for reading.

M. Verant

August 2025

# ACKNOWLEDGMENTS

I couldn't write these books without my wife, Jill. As well as being a wonderful person and a great story analyst, she has the gift of good taste, so she politely deflates my more cringeworthy ideas.

My writer critique groups have held steady for years. Every month, our small four-person CWC-derived group convenes. This is great practice because it's cross-genre: L. R. Shimer writes time travel romance, Dooley writes noir detective, and Chris Harget ranges from sci-fi to comic fantasy. I also participate in and help moderate the East Bay Science Fiction and Fantasy Writers, which hosted an excellent critique of this novel.

Thanks to all the beta readers who provided notes; many of you read all three novels! Adam, Carol, Donna, Jen H, Jennifer Snow, Jerry, Kate Pennington, Katherine Sturtevant, Leane, Mike Alvarez Cohen, Miriam Brookler, Philip Thorne, Rebecca Gomez Farrell, Stephanie Clay, Steve Brady, and Thomas White.

My plan for more on-the-ground research was thwarted by some dodgy stairs and a proximal humerus fracture (less funny than it sounds), but I did see *Operation Mincemeat* in London (that was funny), and I hope soon to visit Jane Austen's home and pay my heartfelt respects.

# ABOUT THE AUTHOR

M. Verant writes noblebright fantasy where good eventually triumphs and worthy people fall in love. His latest work is *Dragons of the Great Wyves,* which completes the award-winning Jane Austen Fantasy trilogy. Next project is likely *Tiger Seed,* a contemporary fantasy rooted in ancient Indus history. He's active in the writing community, moderating the East Bay Science Fiction and Fantasy Writers and serving on the SFWA Independent Authors Committee. In spare moments, he collects Jane Austen paraphernalia and two-legged dragons while dodging wild turkeys in the San Francisco Bay Area.

# BY M. VERANT

**Thrillers**

Power in the Age of Lies

**Jane Austen Fantasy**

Miss Bennet's Dragon

Emma's Dragon

Dragons of the Great Wyves